THE RUIN

Samantha Moran

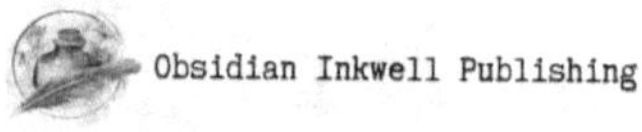

Published by Obsidian Inkwell Publishing, LLC
www.obsidianinkwell.com

Titles: The Ruin / Samantha Moran
Description: Paperback First Edition
Publication Date: May 16, 2023
Cover Design: Samantha Moran (Canva)
Formatting: Samantha Moran (Vellum)

Paperback ISBN-13: 978-1-959751-04-5
Also available in ebook, hardcover, and special editions.

TABLE OF CONTENTS

BONUS CONTENT: DEALINGS IN THE DARK

DEDICATION

This book is dedicated to my husband, John. Thank you for always encouraging me to pursue my dreams, even when I didn't believe in myself. If it weren't for you and our amazing date in South Haven, Michigan way back in 2017, this story wouldn't exist. I'm thankful for every chapter you've read, re-read, and re-read again, as well as your incredibly valuable input. You are my hero and my guide.

This book is also dedicated to my friend, Marissa. I'm so glad I found you through that strange twist of fate in 2019. I believe the universe brought us together for a reason. Finding our friendship made all of the challenges that followed worth while. Thank you for being my number one hype-girl, for your unwavering support, for our late night text messages, and for your unfailing belief in me. Know that I have the same for you.

AUTHOR'S NOTE

The Ruin is a work of urban fantasy that discusses difficult real-world issues such as cancer, poverty, drug addiction, childhood abandonment, self-harm, disease, and death.

Concepts related to Norse mythology presented in this text are based on extensive research but have been adapted for a fictional reimagining. Please be advised that not all details will remain true to historical evidence or actual practice.

THE RUIN

We called to Her, and so She came.
On Solstice night, She heard our pain.
We asked for help, and She was kind.
We took Her gift. Our fates were twined.
Blood was spilled on sacred altar,
Yet with Her magick, we did falter.
Our contract broken left Her enraged.
The gift was spoiled and blood curse engaged.
What was rebirth turned fast to death,
Our people shunned, and so we wept.
She waits for us to redeem our clan
Or bring destruction upon the land.

— ANCESTRAL PROPHECY

CENTENNIAL BANK OF BALTIMORE

Established 1883

Ms. Kara Edwards:

Centennial Bank of Baltimore thanks you for your personal debt consolidation loan application. After reviewing the provided materials and your credit report, we regret to inform you that the Centennial Bank of Baltimore cannot offer you a debt consolidation loan. Several credit-related factors impacted this decision; these factors are listed below. Although we cannot assist you at this time, we hope you will continue to use Centennial Bank of Baltimore for all of your future banking needs.

Negative Factors Impacting Decision
    IV: Balance to Credit Ratio Too High
    VIII: Average Length of Established Credit Too Low
    XII: Late Payments Reported
    XVI: Insufficient Monthly Income
    XX: Medical Bills in Collections
    XXIV: Employment Status

How To Improve Your Credit

1. Pay down existing credit debt beginning with the cards with the lowest balance. The desirable ratio of debt to credit is 30%. Your current debt-to-credit ratio is 100% on all credit accounts.
2. Do not apply for more credit, including credit cards or personal loans, at this time. We recommend waiting five years from the time your last account was opened before applying for further credit.
3. Make payments of at least the minimum required amount on or before the scheduled due date for each credit account.
4. Pay off all outstanding medical bills as quickly as possible. Contact the party responsible for handling these outstanding medical bills to make arrangements.

Regards,

Elizabeth Aaron

Elizabeth Aaron
Senior Loan Officer
eaaron@centennialbaltimore.com

4582 East Lombard Street, Suite G
Baltimore, Maryland 21202

CHAPTER ONE

T he thin white envelope shakes as I slide my finger beneath the seal. With each small tear, a foolish surge of hope washes over me. I take a deep breath and blow it out slowly, trying to steady my hands.

This time will be different, I tell myself. Centennial Bank will help me. They have to.

The response is a neatly folded letter, a single page. Before I even unfold it, I know this answer will be exactly like the rest. The reply is too short.

My tired eyes scan the simple response before I lean back in my creaky desk chair, letting my hands fall into my lap. It's yet another rejection. My misguided hope immediately abandons me, replaced by emptiness and despair.

Dejected, I sigh and crumple up the letter, dropping it into the small garbage can with the seven other rejections I've already received from banks and lending agencies throughout Baltimore. Their heartless responses contain an undeniable truth – I desperately need help, the kind of help only banks can give, and I'm not going to get it anytime soon.

It's absurd to think they would care about anything other than their bottom line. I know this. All that matters to these big banks is that I have nothing to offer them in return. So, why does every rejection letter cut so deep?

To these banks, I'm just another college dropout. On paper, they're right. I have a dead-end job, a boatload of bills I can't afford to pay, and no collateral to speak of. They have no reason to help me, no sense of humanity. And yet, what else can I do but try?

On my desk, the candle's tiny flame pulses vigorously, letting the late-night shadows creep closer. The wick slowly drowns in the puddle of wax, sputtering and fighting to stay alive.

This is my last one, and without electricity, it's my only source of light. It will burn out soon, I know, leaving me to stumble through my studio apartment in the dark as I have done so many nights before.

I can't help but resonate with the irony of the flame's struggle. I'm burning out, too.

The weight of the day's exhaustion sets in, blurring my vision. With a sigh, I rub my tired eyes. Finding them dry beneath my fingers, a hollow laugh escapes me. Was it the second or third letter that depleted my tears? Honestly, I'm not sure anymore.

It doesn't matter. What's done is done.

I tear my eyes away from the reminders of my failure, reluctantly accepting there's nothing more to do about my finances tonight.

It takes a monumental effort to force myself to stand. My aching muscles rebel and throb with my movements, but I ignore them and carry the flickering candle over to the tiny bathroom, allowing my mind to wander through the events of the day.

I've spent entirely too much time on my feet between this morning's long shift and my trip to the hospital to visit Mom. The hours that passed sitting by her side were anything but peaceful. I argued with three different doctors about how to treat her cancer, walking in and out of the surgical recovery room so many times I now know precisely how many steps it takes to get from the uncomfortable chair to the hall and back again.

Of course, each one of them, despite barely knowing her, had been absolutely certain their chosen course of treatment, or lack-there-of, was the only correct option. Their cool confidence was annoying, but I listened to them ramble on anyway, one after another, nodding my head at the appropriate times and telling them I would take their suggestions into consideration.

I know the truth. Ultimately, none of them care what happens to her. Valerie Edwards is a name on a chart, a means to collect their ridiculously expensive fees before moving on to the next patient.

As Mom slept deeply in the hospital bed, blissfully ignorant and sedated, I spent more than an hour of frustration on the phone with the gas and electric company trying to work out a payment plan. Despite my protests that the winter temperatures have been far too low to cut off someone's heat, they refused to accept anything less than a fifty-percent payment of the past-due balance. Their willingness to meet me halfway aside, I won't have the money until my next paycheck clears, and even that's questionable.

There simply isn't enough money to go around. The pantry in our tiny kitchen is almost bare. The apartment is a mess, and I have no time or energy to clean it. The laundry is dirty, and I ran out of quarters last week. My entire existence is a hopeless black void.

I drag my thin sweater over my head, tug off my jeans, toss them into the hamper, and slip into a pair of ragged sweatpants and a t-shirt before the chilly air can raise goosebumps along my arms. My pajamas are old and not much to look at, but they're warm and comfortable, and tonight, that's what I need.

When I finish changing, I pop a rubber plug into the sink and pour a splash of water from a nearly empty gallon jug into the basin.

How long have I been without water now? Two weeks? Three?

I dip my toothbrush into the bowl and dab a small pearl of toothpaste onto it. As I brush my teeth, I watch myself in the mirror.

My face has changed significantly over the last year. Tired green eyes stare back at me, sunken into dark black circles and streaked with thin red lines. My skin is pale, much paler than it should be, and the angles of my cheekbones are sharp. I've lost quite a bit of weight. My shoulder-length brown hair is in desperate need of a trim and a good brushing. In essence, I reflect every bit of the stressed and depressed young woman I've become.

I used to care so much more about my appearance. I don't anymore. Time has brought different priorities, and vanity has been set aside.

Looking away from the ghost of myself, I spit my toothpaste into the toilet, dip a paper cup into the sink and rinse my mouth, then wash my hands with an old bar of unscented soap. Finished, I pull the plug and stare as the rest of the water drains away.

Tomorrow, I'll have to try to stop over and visit Connor so I can take a shower at his place. I feel gross for going so long without one and terrible for using my best friend, but I'm also thankful he's kind enough to help me while I struggle with all of these bills. He's the only one who does these days. Connor and his younger sister Ally don't have much either, but their apartment is warm and their water is running. Compared to my run-down studio, their place is a luxury hotel.

For a moment, I imagine Connor sitting in his salvaged lawn chair and playing Call of Duty while Ally sprawls out on the thick window sill and scrolls through TikTok. I wish I could be there with them now. My apartment is too quiet with Mom in the hospital. It leaves far too much time to think about all of the stressful things dragging me down, and that's the last thing I want to do.

I walk back into the living room and blow out the candle. Only a sliver of wick remains. It won't relight again after tonight, so I toss the stub into the garbage. Careful not to trip, I pad over to my lumpy futon and lay down, tucking myself snugly under the old quilt. It's full of holes after all these years, and it's not very warm anymore, but at least the quilt still smells faintly of Mom's perfume.

A brief smile flits across my face as I remember the days she spent stitching the patchwork together in her recliner. That fall, she gathered up my old school t-shirts and a set of used curtains from the thrift store, cut them into squares, and sewed the pieces together. We still had our little row house on Fleet Street back then. Mom spent hours working on the quilt every night, and I, about thirteen at the time, regaled her with tales of whatever I deemed important that day.

One time, I prattled on and on about the bucket drummer I'd seen playing for tips in the Inner Harbor on my class trip to the National Aquarium. I remember telling her that someday, I wanted to be a musician, too. We both knew I was extremely tone-deaf and I couldn't hold a rhythm if my life depended on it, though. Mom laughed without saying a word, and I joined in with her, then she pulled me into a tight hug and told me to always remember to follow my dreams.

I rarely allow myself to dream anymore.

The row house was one of the first things to disappear when she was diagnosed with cancer. After her treatments, Mom couldn't climb the stairs to her bedroom anymore, and the rent was too expensive with all of the added medical bills, anyway. So, we gave up the lease and moved into this tiny studio together. This hole-in-the-wall is all the way up on the seventh floor, but the rent is cheap and there's an elevator, so the two of us have managed to make do.

Still, there isn't a day I don't miss the way things were before.

I pull the quilt tightly up to my chin as the wind whistles through the crack in the window frame above my head. It's going to be another cold night. The forecast calls for a low of 35 degrees, and the heat has been out for almost a week.

CHAPTER TWO

The night is still a deep shade of purple when the shrill ring of my phone rips me from the grip of a horrendous nightmare. With a start, I bolt upright and clutch the quilt tightly to my chest. Reality settles in slowly, separating the terrifying images from the cool, dark room around me. As the fog of sleep fades away, I focus on my ragged breathing to calm my racing heart and bring sensation back to my frozen limbs.

It takes a few moments to regain my composure. Flashes of the dream continue to seep through: staggering blindly through inky darkness over abandoned wheelchairs, IV poles, and hospital beds; the biting scent of bleach and disinfectant, grotesque creatures with transparent skin and vibrant blue veins cornering me up against an immovable steel door.

But, that hadn't been the worst of it. The worst had been finding Mom's putrefied corpse in the center of the crisp, white room, unbreathing, with tubes dangling from her sides. I tried desperately to rush to her aid, only to wind up bound by restraints that bit into my wrists and ankles, holding me back.

The creatures finally caught up to me, thrusting my body against the glass of the window pane on the far wall until it shattered and gave way. My broken and bruised body crashed to the pavement. The blood that poured out of my lacerated flesh ran across the hard surface beneath me, forming a sharply-angled symbol. It called to me, commanding me to keep my eyes on the shining maroon wetness. I resisted the pull, knowing I had to put myself together, to get up off the ground and back to Mom's room.

I managed to drag my eyes away, but when I cast them back to the window, there was Mom. Her frail frame cast a long shadow onto the ground below.

Mom's features were twisted. Her once beautiful smile had morphed into a perverse grin. Her sharp teeth glinted under the light of the moon, and thick, scarlet blood dripped down to land on my cheek.

She had become one of the creatures.

I sniff and wipe away the tears that have fallen in my sleep. My throat's raw as though I've been screaming, and maybe I was. After a dream like that, it wouldn't surprise me one bit. It'd been so real, and even though I know it was only a dream, goosebumps still prickle my skin.

Unconsciously, I rub my wrists where the imaginary restraints had dug in. There are no cuts or bruises, but the pressure remains all the same.

I'd been helpless in my dream, completely unable to save Mom. My single greatest fear had been realized.

The quiet chime of a voicemail breaks the tense silence of the room, drawing my gaze to my desk where my phone rests, blinking. Reluctantly, I reach down to toss the quilt aside. My fingers skim across the cold, soggy fabric. For a moment, I'm confused. Then, a deafening boom and flash of light answer my unspoken question. A thunderstorm rages outside.

I lift my gaze to the broken window above the bed.

Rivulets of water run down the wall until they pool on my pillow and soak into the mattress and blanket below. It must've been raining for a while because the entire futon is drenched. It makes a suctiony, sloshing sound as I push myself up to stand.

The bright white numbers on the lock screen of my phone read 3:30 am. It's been a handful of hours since I tucked myself into bed and succumbed to the weight of sleep. Next to the clock, the little voicemail symbol flashes red, and beneath the symbol is a number I don't want to see: "Doctor Nicholas Mitchell, St. John's Hospital."

I hesitate. No one should be calling at this time of night, and after the dream I had, seeing a call from the hospital fills my veins with icy fear.

What if something's wrong? What if… What if Mom's gone?

Calls from Doctor Mitchell at 3:30 in the morning do not bode well. The last time something like this happened, Mom had been rushed into surgery. Her lung had collapsed. If something like that's happening again, what are the chances she might survive?

Whatever is in this voicemail, I'm certain it won't be good news.

I reach for the phone with shaking hands and fumble to unlock the screen. Taking a deep breath, I will myself to be strong and bring my phone up to my ear.

Doctor Mitchell's tired voice crackles through the speaker.

"Ms. Edwards, this is Doctor Mitchell calling from St. John's Hospital, Baltimore. I need to speak with you as soon as possible regarding your mother's recent surgery. Please come as soon as you get this message. There are important forms for you to sign, and this matter cannot wait. I won't discuss it over the phone."

Click. Silence.

Without hesitation, I grab my keys, throw on my shoes, and lock the apartment door behind me as I run out into the night.

CHAPTER THREE

Although it takes fifteen minutes to make the drive from the apartment to St. John's, my anxiety stretches the trip into hours. The abysmal weather does nothing to help. Freezing rain has left the roads as slick as glass, and my car, in dire need of new tires, struggles to find the slightest hint of traction as it skids around tight corners. Luckily, there isn't much traffic at this time of night, even in a big city like Baltimore. Silently, I thank the universe for clearing the way and press harder on the gas.

When my car skates around the last bend, the white concrete of St. John's Hospital slides into view. The enormous structure hulks over the much smaller historical buildings of the surrounding neighborhood. With a light tap on the brakes, I slow to a reasonable pace to pass an ambulance as it unloads its human cargo in the loop and turn into the connected parking garage, a structure of four wide floors, that stretches out from the side.

The bottom levels are completely packed, so I loop around until I find my way to the top. It's remarkably empty, probably because no one wanted to deal with the snow or worry about climbing stairs coated with ice. If I wasn't so worried, I might have laughed at the realization that the hospital could easily drum up more business by skimping on salt. I'm sure any number of people have fallen on their ascent and wound up being wheeled inside on a stretcher.

A vacant spot beneath the hospital's overhanging roof catches my eye. It's conveniently close to the stairs and free of wintery debris, having been shielded from the worst of the storm. I slip my car into the compact space and throw it into park before slowly peeling my fingers away from the steering wheel. My hands shake, white-knuckled and stiff from the tension of the drive. A combination of fear and cold has left them numb.

The clock on the dash blinks 3:52 am.

Looking up, I catch sight of myself in the rearview mirror. The wild eyes and matted hair of the woman staring back at me remind me of something feral. I can't walk into the hospital looking like this. My entire life may be a mess, but the doctors don't need to see that. Personal experience has taught me that young people like me are dismissed far too easily. At twenty-one, any sign of weakness might make them think I can't be trusted to care for Mom. Worst case scenario, they could stop pursuing her treatments altogether. After all, what harm could a twenty-one-year-old do to a hospital like St. John's if they "accidentally" let my mother die?

I hadn't bothered to stop and change before rushing out the door, and that might already be a huge mistake. My ratty pajamas project an image far from the capable daughter I want them to see. There's no hairbrush in the car, either. There are, however, a handful of velvety scrunchies wrapped around the shifter's base. I snatch one of these and use my nails to drag my hair out of my face and up into a messy bun. At most, it's a feeble attempt to make myself look put together, but given current circumstances, it's the best I'm going to do.

I'll have to put on my toughest face and pretend I know exactly what I'm doing, hide my panic and reassure the world everything will be fine. I've been doing it for two years. I should be able to get it together and push through one more night.

"You can do this," I whisper to my reflection. "Never let them see you cry."

Putting on a mask is far from a new concept for me. I've been doing it since I was a child, and in these years since Mom's diagnosis, there have been times I've come close to forgetting I'm not the cold young woman I've been pretending to be.

There isn't anyone else to step up and help me take care of Mom. She and I are effectively alone. Richard, my father, left when I was only six. One night he was there, and the next morning he was gone. As far as I know, he's never contacted Mom again. Clearly, he's not breaking down the door to help anyone, and I don't have the time to track him down. I'd only be disappointed if I tried.

When it comes to him, all I have to cling to are broken memories. The last time I remember seeing my father was in our little row house. It was night, and my parents were in the kitchen arguing in hushed tones. I was supposed to be asleep, but I had gotten out of bed to ask for a glass of water, as children often do. Something about the way they spoke to each other made me pause and watch from the hall. Richard looked defeated and Mom was livid. I remember trying to make out what they were saying to each other, but no matter how hard I listened, I couldn't catch on.

Mom was never one to mince words. I would hazard a guess she probably used some harsh language and told Richard to stick something somewhere the sun doesn't shine. She and I are very alike in that way. Many times when I was growing up, the two of us bickered so intensely that we couldn't stand each other. Now, I long for those days when Mom was healthy and strong.

The next day when I woke up and rolled out of bed, things felt strange, but I couldn't figure out why. I went downstairs to make myself a bowl of cereal. To do that, I had to climb up on my special step stool to get the box, and when I happened to look out our little kitchen window, I saw Richard's car was gone. Its absence wasn't unusual since he sometimes worked early shifts on the weekends, but what was odd was that he hadn't mentioned it to me the day before. Richard always told me when he had to work on the weekends and what time he would be home because I was a daddy's girl through and through. I worried about him every time he was away. Obviously, a lot has changed since then.

I remember going to wake Mom up to ask where he was, but when I walked into her room, she was already awake. She looked like she hadn't slept at all. She was leaning against the headboard, knees propping up her elbows, and staring at the open closet door. Her face had been so blank, and her cheeks were streaked with tears.

I followed her gaze across the room. Half of the closet was empty. The drawers in the dresser next to it had been thrown open and clothes were left hanging off of them. Richard's watch wasn't in the jewelry bowl. In fact, I couldn't see anything left in the room that belonged to him.

Even at six years old, I knew better than to ask what had happened. My friends had divorced parents. The signs were there. Richard was gone, and he wasn't coming back.

At first, Mom didn't acknowledge my presence. She was too lost in her thoughts and misery. I didn't know what I could do to help, so I went back down to the kitchen and poured two bowls of cereal, then took them both upstairs. Silently, I deposited her bowl on the nightstand. I sat beside her for a while, but when she didn't talk to me, I leaned over and planted a kiss on her shoulder, then took my bowl back to my room. My sister was still sound asleep in the adjacent bed.

Later that day, I carried my empty bowl back to my parents' room, intending to take Mom's down to the sink alongside my own, but when I went to pick it up, I found she hadn't eaten any of it. Carefully, I collected the soggy cereal from the table and dumped it out in the kitchen sink before finally sitting down in the middle of the floor and crying, all alone.

It took a few days for her to snap back to reality.

Though I'm certain Mom knows what happened, and though I have asked for answers repeatedly over the last fifteen years, her lips remain tightly sealed. The only answer she's given is that sometimes, things "get in the way" and that someday, I would "come to understand."

In high school, I decided she must've meant Richard left because he met another woman. It seemed like the only logical explanation, given her reluctance to tell me anything about that night. Then again, Richard and Valerie married when she was only twenty years old. After that, she never imagined her life without him. She told me so herself many times. Maybe the situation was simply too painful to discuss. I can imagine it would be like pouring salt into a fresh wound each time. Regardless, I stopped searching for answers and hoping the door would magically open to reveal him on the other side.

The devastation Mom so clearly felt because of his absence was terrible to witness, especially as a child. Hot tears burn my eyes as I recall how she used to sit and stare at her wedding ring, the one I now wear on my right hand. For a long time after he left, she kept it tucked away in her jewelry box and only took it out when she thought she was alone.

I shake my head to clear my thoughts and dry my eyes. There's no use dwelling on such painful memories.

Who else could have taken care of Mom? Her mother, Marianne, had a heart attack when I was fourteen. Her father, Harry, succumbed to cirrhosis not long after Grandma Marianne passed. The man used to go through a twenty-four pack of beer a day, but I never thought that was what killed him. More likely, it was the hole left behind when my grandmother died.

Of course, there's my sister Jennifer, but last I knew, she was too busy running around with losers and far more interested in getting high.

I roll my eyes at the thought of her having anything to do with our mother's medical care. What a mess that would be. Besides, she won't come around for anything. I've already tried.

Jennifer's useless. Even though she's four years older than me, she's always been far more immature. She bounces from one job to the next, and none of them have amounted to anything. She works for a few weeks, finds the prospect of real responsibility too daunting, and never shows up again - no notice or anything. She's just gone. In that regard, she must take after our father. Maybe it's a family trait to leave people high and dry.

A few years ago, Jennifer found herself in some trouble with the Baltimore PD over her idiot boyfriend, Marcus. He was busted chopping up stolen cars and selling parts in his father's garage, and Jennifer was the one luring the owners away from their vehicles before the heists.

Unlike me, Jennifer has what many consider "classic good looks," with long, bottle-blonde hair and a slender frame. I suppose she figured she was putting them to good use by helping Marcus. It wouldn't be the first time. Back in high school, she was incredibly popular with the boys. No matter how she treated them, they loved her, even when she used them and cast them aside. She's no stranger to flashing a charming smile and walking away with her prize.

I, on the other hand, was the smart one. I wasn't as popular, but I had a few decent friends. My nose was usually tucked safely inside a book, and I did my best to stay away from the petty drama as much as I could, even though Jennifer had a way of bringing it home. Also unlike my sister, I had been curvier before Mom fell ill. That was one thing I always loved about myself. Now, as I stare at my reflection in the rearview mirror, I realize many of my curves are gone. I miss my full cheeks and the dimples that used to pop up when I smiled. An unhealthy diet and constant stress have left me looking more like Jennifer than I ever have before.

I asked my sister to help when Mom was diagnosed. Her response was as expected: taking care of Mom would be "too stressful," and it "wasn't her responsibility." She claimed she didn't have the money or the space to take our mother in, even though every time Jennifer found herself in trouble, Mom always had a warm bed and a hot meal waiting. She even told me to put Mom into a hospice facility to live out the rest of her days instead of seeking treatments, but Mom is only forty-four years old. Needless to say, Jennifer and I don't associate with each other much these days.

Occasionally, Mom asks about her oldest daughter, but I quickly change the subject whenever I can. I'm sure she knows why, but she gracefully abandons the topic. As much as I try to protect her feelings, it isn't like Jennifer comes to visit, and Valerie Edwards can be called many things, but one word you'll never find on that list is unintelligent.

The numbers on the clock flash: 4:00 am.

Unlike Jennifer, I dropped everything to help when Mom was diagnosed. I was halfway through my first semester when she got the news. She didn't ask for my help, but I knew I was needed, so I put my freshman year at NYU on hold to come back home and oversee her cancer treatments.

I went apartment hunting with her when Mom decided the row house was too expensive. I moved us into the studio apartment to help her pay the rent. I held her hair as she vomited from the poison coursing through her veins, and I brought her headscarves when there was no more hair to hold back. In between all of these things, I picked up a job at a local cafe. I even opened up seven credit cards to help take care of Mom's needs. She doesn't know about these. Now, they're maxed out from groceries, chemo, homecare nurses, and hospital stays.

Jennifer didn't do any of that. She sat on her ass in Marcus's apartment in Reisterstown.

It doesn't matter. No one else matters.

4:04 am.

I don't want to go inside…

I twiddle Mom's wedding band and summon up my courage. I rushed to get here, but it takes a lot more strength to actually follow through. I can't wait any longer, though. This isn't about me. I have to set my fears aside.

I reach into the back seat, grab my jacket, and slip it on. Before climbing out, I check my wallet to ensure all the essentials are there: my license, Mom's license, an insurance card, and a long-term parking pass. There's no cash, of course, but at least I have everything the doctors might ask for today.

I allow myself one more moment to prepare, then place the parking pass on the dash. As I step out of the car, I force myself to leave behind my biggest secret, that lonely little girl who cried in the middle of the kitchen floor. My mother needs me, and I'll be damned if my apprehension leaves her alone for one more night.

CHAPTER FOUR

The greeter informs me Mom has been moved to room 354, so I power walk to the elevators and step inside. When the doors open out into the intensive care unit, a shiver having nothing to do with the cold temperature crawls its way up my spine.

I had hoped she would still be in recovery, but I knew it had been a long shot. Too many people need the beds, so I should have expected they would move her in the middle of the night. But, to intensive care? The last time she was here, Mom nearly died. Her oxygen saturation dropped too low and several of her organs had shown signs of shutting down. Her doctors couldn't tell me if we had years or a matter of minutes left together. I had never been so afraid in my life.

I don't know if either of us could survive if it were to happen again. That kind of experience gnaws at you. It takes a toll you never bounce back from.

I'm lost in my thoughts as I follow the signs toward 354.

The calm of the unit in the stillness of night contrasts with the frenzied panic coursing through me. During the day, this place would be bustling under bright, fluorescent lights. I'd be dodging nurses with carefully tended smiles and stumbling past carts laden with medical supplies. Patients' families would be keeping vigil at their bedsides.

Not now. Things are too still. The overhead lights have been dimmed to help the patients rest. Every other fixture is nothing but a translucent rectangle trapped among the checker-patterned drop tiles. It has the effect of casting the ICU into shades of blue and gray, making it seem as if the ward has become a mere shadow of itself, something in between. Considering so many of its occupants hover between life and death, maybe that's what it's always been.

Of course, the diligent nurses continue their poking and prodding throughout the night, though fewer of them wander the unit. Occasionally, they pass me and offer a silent nod, but the night staff doesn't try to chat. Weariness tugs at their shoulders.

There are no private rooms in the ICU. Unlike the rest of the hospital, this section is a long hallway with curtain-veiled cubbies running along each side. Nurse's stations have been strategically placed roughly thirty feet apart with double desks that face out in opposite directions to make it easier to monitor their charges. The cubbies are small and sparse, hardly large enough for two people and the occupant's bed to fit inside.

When a patient is stable, their heavy canvas curtain is drawn, but when there is imminent danger, it's cast to the side. As I pass these spaces, not much has changed since Mom was here last. The hospital beds are still centered against the outer wall and the monitoring equipment remains stacked off to the left. A modest nightstand with a phone, a vinyl guest seat, and a small cabinet on wheels are pressed to the wall to the right. An additional hard plastic chair sits outside each cubby for waiting family members who can't fit into the room.

Since these rooms are meant to be transitory, they don't offer much in the way of comfort or personalization. The only indications of who currently resides inside are the whiteboards the staff use to track the patients' statuses. These hang outside of the cubby above the spare chairs. Thick black stickers in the upper left corner designate the room number. Below that, the nurses have written the patients' names. Various magnets indicate specific risks to the occupants. Different colors correspond to different conditions. During the years Mom has spent in and out of this place, several have adorned her boards, but one always remains: black for cancer. There are several of these black magnets on the many whiteboards along the way.

Some of the rooms are empty. A grim thought settles over me as I pass. I hope they're waiting for new patients and are not the solemn places of mourning where the previous occupants left their friends and family behind.

As I slow to a stop outside of Mom's room, a breath of relief escapes me. Her curtain is closed. No anxious nurses keep vigil from the station a few feet away. They must think she's safe enough to be left alone or it would be open like the rest.

Mom is okay. Mom is okay. Mom is okay, I silently repeat until my frayed nerves are somewhat soothed.

Before settling down in the chair, I leave a message with the nurses, asking them to page Doctor Mitchell. Assured they will, I wander back to the curtain and let my eyes rove over the board.

Someone has hastily written Mom's name in all capital letters on the line that reads "Patient" with Doctor Mitchell scrawled in the "Attending" space underneath. On the line for "Nurse" is the name Jasmine.

"Great, Jasmine," I whisper. I can't stand her, and Mom doesn't like her, either.

When Mom first came to St. John's, her oncologist decided her chemotherapy sessions would be best given during an in-patient stay. Since it was just the two of us at home, he had been concerned about comfort and aftercare. I'm glad we took his advice because the first course had been incredibly harsh. For days, she ached and vomited. No matter how many blankets I piled on, she shivered and groaned. It was an awful sight to see. I'm not sure we could have endured it without the help of the hospital staff.

Unfortunately, though many of the nurses had been kind and attentive to Mom's needs, Jasmine wasn't one of them. During one of the worst times of the stay, she left Mom completely unattended for over an hour. For a little while, Mom's stomach had been calm, so she thought it would be a good idea to eat. We took advantage of this brief period of relief and ordered her something light.

Mom slowly picked at the meal, but not long after, her nausea returned. A green tinge crept over her skin as she clutched her stomach and repeatedly pressed the button for the nurse. No matter how many times we tried, Jasmine never came.

Mom vomited all over herself. Her gown, her bedclothes, and her hair were covered in sick. I had to chase down the charge nurse to help me clean up the mess. It was awful. We both told Mom over and over again it wasn't her fault, that these kinds of things happen with treatments like hers, but I'll never forget her look of shame. I'll never forgive Jasmine for abandoning Mom when she needed her. Never.

When Jasmine finally returned, the charge nurse gave her a stern reprimand. The woman's voice carried down the hall, and several visitors stuck their heads out of the rooms to listen to the scene.

Jasmine turned toward Mom's room and saw me staring. She flashed me a look of heated contempt before disappearing again. I don't know what the consequences had been, but they must have been severe because for several hours, Jasmine conveniently "forgot" to check on Mom, and to add insult to injury, she reeked of smoke when she eventually came into the room to change the saline bag.

"What kind of nurse smokes while taking care of a lung cancer patient?" I asked her, furious.

She didn't answer, which only made me angrier. I wanted to punch Jasmine then, but I knew if I did, I wouldn't be allowed in the hospital. So instead, I filed a formal complaint. The board issued Mom a written apology and discounted the stay. I had hoped they would put a note in Mom's file about the situation with Jasmine, too.

They probably didn't. They likely did the bare minimum because they didn't want to be sued.

Another magnet on the bottom of the board pulls me from my thoughts. In bold, bright red letters, it reads: "Patient Restricted."

The magnet is another riddle, one more thing getting in the way. I'm not allowed to see Mom, but I have no idea why.

Anger surges through me, as it so often does these days. A tiny rectangular magnet, one I could easily rip off and hurl across the hall, serves as an impenetrable lock separating me from her. I know it won't change the situation, but for a moment, I contemplate doing exactly that. It would feel so good to have an outlet, to be destructive. I want to pick up this stupid plastic chair and smash it to bits on the floor. I want to pound it into the ground until it snaps and bends. I want to make something submit to my will, unlike the cancer that has beaten my mother down, beaten me down. I want to have control over something, to not be in the dark, and worried, and exhausted, and lonely, and broken, and...

But, I can't do that. I can't lose my cool. I have to keep it together for her, even if she has no idea I'm here. Frustrated, I grind the palms of my hands into my eyes and let them fall softly to my sides.

Behind the curtain, the room is quiet. The muted

rhythmic beep of the monitor indicates Mom's heart rate is stable. I watch the secondhand on the clock and count for thirty seconds, then do the mental math. It's a little low, 52 beats per minute, but if she's sleeping or still sedated, that's fine.

I strain to listen for anything else.

A rhythmic sucking and whooshing comes from some-where close by. It sounds like a ventilator, but it doesn't seem to be coming from inside. That's good, too. She's breathing on her own.

Quickly, I glance back to see if anyone's watching. A second nurse has joined the first at the station, but both are engrossed in their tasks, so I bend the rules and peer around the edge of the curtain.

Slowly, I peel it away from the wall. It's too dark inside to make out much, but the bright green numbers on the monitor confirm my estimations. Blood Pressure: 115/65, Pulse: 54, Oxygen Saturation: 93. I search for the source of the whooshing sound and come up empty-handed. There's no ventilator in sight.

I don't have the chance to see anything else before a heavy hand grabs my shoulder and startles me, causing me to jump back and drop the curtain closed. I've been caught in the act, and dread settles over me like a student who's about to be sent to the principal's office.

The logical part of my brain recognizes I haven't techni-cally broken any rules. I didn't go inside. Plus, it's perfectly reasonable to want to know how she's doing. So, I slip my mask back on and turn to face whoever stands behind me.

Of course, it's Doctor Mitchell in his immaculate white lab coat. Tonight, he's layered this over a clean navy dress shirt and a pair of expensive khakis. His brown leather shoes shine, peeking out from beneath his neatly hemmed pants.

Fine lines spread out from the corners of his eyes, and his mouth turns slightly down into a frown.

For the first time, I notice he's fairly young for a doctor, maybe thirty-five? He hasn't been Mom's attending for long, having started working for St. John's about three months ago. The only conversations we've had have been about treatments, so I never thought to ask his age. I was always too busy to care.

"Ms. Edwards," he says, voice low. "I'm glad you came so quickly. I didn't know if you would get my call tonight or in the morning. I'm sorry if I startled you."

I blink up at him. "Of course you did. Who calls at 3:30 in the morning if it's not an emergency?"

"A doctor who is very short on time," he answers. "You really shouldn't peek behind the curtains, you know," he whispers. His voice holds an attempt at humor.

"Yeah, well," I say, unamused.

Doctor Mitchell clears his throat, noticing his joke hadn't landed well.

"Would you mind coming down to my office so we can have this discussion in private?" he asks, running his fingers through his sandy-blonde hair.

His request is a statement, not a question. He keeps his left hand firmly attached to his belt loop as he waits for me to respond. The gesture projects authority. It makes him look larger than he is.

"Of course."

Doctor Mitchell nods, then turns and walks away in the self-assured manner of someone who's used to getting what he wants. He knows he's important, and he knows he's in charge. I, on the other hand, know that to him, I'm neither of those things. I'm just the one who makes sure he gets paid... sometimes.

I cast another glance at Mom's curtain before turning to follow him down the hall. I trail behind until we reach the elevators and follow him in. He pushes the button for the fourth floor, and we ride up in silence. Nervous, I distract myself by counting the small tiles on the floor and listening to the misplaced cheery music floating down from the speakers.

I've never been to his office before. Mom might be alright, but I dread what comes next. It must be something awful if it has to be said away from prying ears.

Please, don't let my mother die.

CHAPTER FIVE

"I've spoken with your mother's surgeons, and I'm afraid Valerie's operation was not as successful as we had hoped it would be." Doctor Mitchell watches me, unblinking, as he delivers these words from his plush leather chair behind his oversized cherry desk. His face is blank, making his intentions hard to read.

I shift uncomfortably in my plain wooden seat as I wait for him to continue.

He doesn't. He simply stares. It's unnerving.

"I don't understand…"

Hands tucked into the pockets of my jacket, I fidget with Mom's wedding ring, spinning it around and around in an attempt to stay calm. Worried my voice will crack, I clear my throat before speaking again.

"When I left the hospital a few hours ago, you assured me the tumor had been removed and Mom was recovering well. That's the only reason I went home."

A veil of concerned professionalism drops over his face as he clicks and unclicks the pen in his hand, carefully choosing his next words.

"True, I did say that. However, it has become apparent I was," he stops to think, "misinformed. While you were gone, we ran some routine procedures to monitor for internal bleeding. Now that some of the swelling has subsided and we have been able to get Valerie in for an X-Ray and a CT scan, we have a much clearer picture to work with."

Doctor Mitchell reaches for a pile of manilla folders arranged in a neat stack on the corner of his desk. I grimace when he tugs the thickest one free. The name "Edwards, Valerie" appears in slanted blue letters on the tab. He plops the folder down in front of him and opens it, revealing a translucent image of a scarred set of lungs. This he turns over in his hands before swiveling around to place it in the large clip of the backlit board behind him. He flicks a switch, sending light through the scan and illuminating the damage.

The room is silent as we study the image. The problem is Doctor Mitchell knows what he's looking at, but I don't. All I know is healthy lungs definitely aren't supposed to look like these. They should be a matching set, extending down on each side, but Mom's aren't. One's much shorter than the other, and neither is uniform in color. I wish I could interpret what he sees.

"Explain," I demand, sounding much more confident than I am.

He clicks his pen again and sighs.

"Although we did our best to excise the entirety of the tumor without compromising Valerie's lung function, her scans show a portion of the growth, roughly the size of a dime, remains." Doctor Mitchell reaches up to a veiny cluster at the bottom of the shorter lung and circles it with his finger, then looks back to me. I think he's waiting for me to say something, but I don't, so he proceeds.

"I was concerned with what I saw on the scans, so I spoke with one of Valerie's surgeons, Doctor Fuentes. He informed me that the remaining portion of the tumor hadn't been visible during the surgery. In any case, after reviewing the scans himself, Doctor Fuentes has assured me this portion of the tumor is too far enmeshed into the lung's vascular network to retrieve."

"Okay," I answer as I try to make sense of his meaning.

"Had this portion been visible and had we attempted to remove it, it's likely Valerie would have either bled out on the table or suffered a total lung collapse. The consequences of an incident of this nature would have left her with dangerous dead tissue and inadequate blood flow which would have certainly dropped her oxygen saturation to unsustainable levels. Doctor Fuentes and I have agreed it would be unwise for us to attempt to extract it again at this time."

Once more, Doctor Mitchell waits for me to respond, but I'm at a loss for words. I heard what he said, yet my brain refuses to connect the pieces. Slowly, I turn the explanation over in my mind. The truth dawns on me as he clicks his pen again, then drops it to the desk and steeples his hands beneath his chin.

Some of the tumor is still there, and they aren't going to cut it out. I can't believe what I'm hearing. It doesn't make sense. When we talked about Mom's options before, Doctor Mitchell made it very clear that for the surgery to be successful, the entirety of the cancerous tissue had to be removed. If it wasn't, there would be no further treatments. None of them would be effective because if even a small section of the tissue remained, the tumor would grow back.

This surgery was all we had left. What are we going to do now?

"Ms. Edwards, you may recall going into this surgery, we gave an optimistic estimate of a thirty-percent chance of full tumor removal. All involved were aware there was a statistical probability we would be unsuccessful. Unfortunately, that is exactly where we stand."

"Wh... What does this mean for my mom?" I ask, tripping over my words. I struggle to rein in my emotions and straighten my spine. A thin sheen of sweat beads on my forehead. Doctor Mitchell's office is warm, but inside, I'm as cold as ice. The overwhelming panic has returned.

Keep it together, I scold myself. I walked into this office knowing I had to be strong, yet my strength is slipping away with each passing heartbeat. I've endured this conversation a hundred times in my mind, but all of those imagined scenarios pale in comparison to the real thing.

I force myself to summon up my courage. I think back to my childhood, to all of the parent-teacher conferences Mom went to alone, to all of the times she had been asked about my father in front of others, to her stoic face as she bailed Jennifer out of jail.

What would Mom do? I ask myself. *Well, she certainly wouldn't break down and cry.*

Briefly, I close my eyes. I take a deep breath and blow it out slowly. I hadn't noticed my hands were shaking until I suddenly find them calm at my sides. I concentrate on the way my worn shoes feel on my feet, the way the chair digs into my back, the sound the heater makes as it kicks on and blows arid warmth against the back of my neck...

When I open my eyes again, I've done my best to shove my fears away. I find a cool sense of detachment and arrange my face into a blank expression. I lock on to Doctor Mitchell's gaze.

"As you know, we've exhausted our *traditional* treatment options for your mother," Doctor Mitchell explains, emphasizing the word traditional a little too much. "Chemotherapy has not proven successful in reducing the size of her tumors, nor in slowing their spread throughout her body. Valerie has nodules in her lungs, several lymph nodes, and both of her kidneys. Her disease is advanced. I believe it is safe to say this surgery was our last chance," he pauses, "at *conventional* treatment."

As I watch, he retrieves the scan of Mom's lungs and

tucks it back into her file. For the first time in our conversation, Doctor Mitchell is nervous. His eyes refuse to meet mine. The hard edge of suspicion creeps in as I stumble over his implications.

"What are you trying to say?"

He reaches up and adjusts the collar of his shirt, leaning back in his chair and putting distance between the two of us. My suspicion is replaced by the simmering heat of anger as he avoids my question.

I don't have time for this.

"It's 4:30 in the morning. You've just told me my mother is dying, and I'm not here to play guessing games with you. What's going on? Can you help my mother, or are you telling me you're going to do nothing and let her die?"

Doctor Mitchell studies me. His gaze roves over my unkempt hair, my jacket, and my pajamas. Some sort of debate wages in his thoughts, but he's keeping me in the dark. With each passing second, my anger rises.

It's the same feeling I've had for months, a complete lack of control. I flex my fingers and fight back the need to destroy his office, much as I had curbed my impulses in the ICU. This time, the urge is stronger. I want to grab onto Doctor Mitchell by his expensive dress shirt and shake him. I want to flip his fancy desk. I want to stomp on the anatomical models displayed around the room and hear them crunch beneath my feet. I want to make him feel like I do, scared, angry, and alone. I know it isn't his fault my mother has cancer, but right now, as he sits there in his position of power and dangles critical information just out of my reach, he might as well be cancer in the flesh.

"What the hell is going to happen to my mother?" I demand. "Tell me *right now.*"

To his credit, Doctor Mitchell remains calm and professional. He doesn't chastise me for my aggression. Instead, he unlaces his fingers and opens the top drawer of his desk. Silently, he withdraws a new folder, one with a geometric design and bold, black letters stamped across the top, then slides this across to me.

"Ms. Edwards, a few days ago, I would have told you there was no chance for your mother's survival. I still have to tell you the likelihood is *extremely* low. In her condition, with her track record, I would say she optimistically has three months to live and is almost certainly not going to see the new year. The outlook is grim. However, she may have a *slight* chance. That depends on what you decide to do next."

"I'm listening," I answer, still trying to rein in my destructive tendencies. Deep within my pockets, my fingernails dig into my palms. Blood wells beneath the surface. The stinging keeps me focused on Doctor Mitchell's words.

Better me than him, I tell myself. *He holds my mother's life in the palm of his hand, and I can't afford to antagonize him. I can't push him away.*

"Should you decide to continue to seek treatment, I can offer your mother a new drug called Novemion. Keep in mind, use of this drug is unconventional, and there are absolutely no guarantees."

"How unconventional?"

"In essence, Novemion is an IV infusion that boosts the immune system to unnaturally high levels and encourages healthy cell growth. In theory, it helps enhance the body's ability to fight off dangerous cells by encouraging healthy cells to overpower the cancerous ones. The hope is that it will serve as a guidance system for the existing immune system, teaching it which cells to suppress and which cells to produce. It's administered over the course of several months for a total of up to thirty treatments."

He takes a sip of water from the bottle on his desk, then resumes.

"In animal trials, Novemion showed promising results. There are, however, some very serious complications that have arisen. Some of the larger animals experienced permanent blindness, infertility, and internal bleeding. Some developed a different, more aggressive form of cancer after treatment. Proceeding with Novemion would pose a huge risk to Valerie as, at this phase, it has not yet been tested on humans. It's a highly experimental treatment."

"But, how can you offer Mom a treatment if it hasn't gone through human trials? Doesn't the FDA have strict regulations about stuff like this?"

Doctor Mitchell's forehead furrows. He brings one hand up and pinches the bridge of his nose, then rubs his eyes. When he looks back at me, there's a wariness in them that wasn't there before.

"They do, and therein lie the secondary risks. Should the FDA or any additional hospital staff learn what we're doing, they will certainly halt the treatment. I will lose my medical license, and most likely, both of us will be sent to prison. Coarser Industries will not take the fall. This is not a decision to be made lightly."

My heart nearly stops as I take in his warnings.

"Why? Why would you even bother then?" I ask, incredulous. "Why take such a huge risk for someone you barely know?"

"Because, Ms. Edwards, I believe in the oath I took to do no harm and save lives. You and I both know the medical system is inherently flawed. I can't fix insurance laws, but when given an opportunity to save someone's life, no matter the risks to myself, I have to try."

Silently, I stare at the lamp sitting atop Doctor Mitchell's file cabinet. Its faint glow illuminates a small vase of white flowers sitting beneath the shade. Phrases like "immune boosting," "internal bleeding," and "more aggressive cancer" echo through my thoughts.

This is dangerous. If I choose to do this, it will be the riskiest thing I've ever done. It would no longer be Mom's life on the line, but my life and Doctor Mitchell's life, too. Can I take the chance the treatment may fail and leave Mom in worse condition than before? There's no proof it would work, not without human trials. Can I risk being sent to jail when she has so little time left? I don't want to leave her alone. Could I let Doctor Mitchell risk everything he's worked for? And, if we're caught, could I let him take the fall? More importantly, can I walk out of this door and make the decision to let my mother die knowing there was something I could have done? Could I live with myself?

Numbness overcomes me once more.

"Before you make a decision, there's one more thing you should know."

"There always is, isn't there?"

"Unfortunately, it seems to be that way."

"What is it?"

"Getting my hands on this treatment won't be easy. I have connections to the right people, and if I had the time to bargain, I might be able to procure it for a reasonable price. In fact, knowing certain people in the pharmaceutical industry is how I got this job. It helps to have friends in high places."

"What does that have to do with me?"

"Considering Valerie's condition, I'm afraid we don't have the time we need to negotiate properly. I've already reached out to my contact in the company, and they've given me a very specific price. They know they have the upper hand here, and they're not willing to compromise."

My jaw drops to the floor. "A price?"

"Everything has a cost, especially deals made under the table. As you are probably aware, your insurance provider will not pay for experimental treatments. We couldn't hope to approach them with this matter due to the risks I shared moments ago. This would mean your mother would have to participate in the treatment "out-of-pocket," as a paying customer so to speak."

I tense as every nerve in my body comes to life, the numbness and shock instantly fading. My skin burns hot like fire, and it takes everything I have not to reach across Doctor Mitchell's desk and do something incredibly stupid.

Through gritted teeth, I grind out, "This is extortion. You're going to sit there and demand money from me while my mother's in the other room, dying? What's wrong with you? I thought this was about saving a life?"

My volume rises with each word I fling at him. Rage washes off of me in waves. By the time I'm finished, I'm on my feet and practically screaming. My hands grip the edge of his desk so hard it hurts. Doctor Mitchell stares at me, eyes wide and mouth hanging open.

"You're sick, you know that? What kind of doctor – "

Doctor Mitchell's on his feet, too. He holds his hands out before him as though trying to calm a savage beast and gestures his head toward the door.

"Ms. Edwards, you've got it wrong. I don't want your money. It wouldn't go to me. The payments would be processed as donations to the manufacturer of Novemion. Now please, lower your voice. Others will hear you, and if they do, I won't be able to help you anymore."

"You'd better be telling me the truth," I threaten. "If I find out you've extorted other families, I'll – "

"I swear to you, Kara," Doctor Mitchell replies, abandoning the formalities and calling me by my name. "I swear to you on everything I have, I would never use your situation to cause further harm. I swear."

He cautiously picks up the Novemion folder and offers it to me.

"Here, see for yourself. I promise, Kara. Everything I've told you is true. I need you to trust me. I would never do that to you or Valerie."

Slowly, I lower myself back into my seat. Doctor Mitchell follows suit. Some of the nervousness fades from his expression as I snatch the folder. Before looking at the contents, I flash him one more menacing look.

He nods, so I take out the packet tucked inside.

I scour the papers in search of anything helpful. The packet details the way the drug is expected to work, the side effects of Novemion, information gathered through the animal testing process, and the plan to seek FDA approval later this year. There are even details about a plan for expedited human testing and columns and columns of data I could never understand. In bold red letters on the last page are the words, "Novemion has not yet been tested on humans for the treatment of cancer. This treatment may be deemed ineffective or dangerous after human testing has concluded and does not yet have FDA approval."

Doctor Mitchell isn't lying.

I blink and will myself to calm down. It takes several moments to reduce my rage from boiling to a low simmer.

"You mean to tell me this company is asking me to put an exact value on my mother's life with no guarantee of her survival?".

"Yes."

"And if I do consent to use this treatment, I'd be breaking the law?"

"Yes."

"So would you."

"That's correct."

I prepare myself for my next question. Dread settles into

the pit of my stomach, but I have to know. "How much money do they want?"

Sympathy fills Doctor Mitchell's voice this time. "A substantial amount."

"How much?" I demand.

"Five thousand dollars," he says, "per treatment. Cash only and at regularly scheduled times."

Despair grips me in its gnarled fist. I can barely breathe, barely think.

"Five thousand dollars," I repeat. "How many treatments?"

"I don't know."

"In cash?"

"It has to be untraceable."

"Oh my god…"

"Ms. Edwards," Doctor Mitchell starts, returning to the formalities now that I've settled down. "I know this is a lot to take in. A treatment like this, aside from all the risks, could run you upwards of a hundred thousand dollars. I won't judge you should you choose not to pursue it. I simply couldn't let the opportunity slip by without giving you a choice. Your mother would understand…"

He trails off. I stare blankly at the papers in my hands. The room falls silent once more.

There's no way I can afford this treatment. My cards are maxed out and my credit is trashed. I can't ask for any more loans. There's no family money to speak of. Minimum wage at the cafe can't even pay the bills we already have.

"What do you want to do, Ms. Edwards?" Doctor Mitchell asks. "The ball is in your court."

I can't do this. I don't have the money. This would not end well…

But, my mouth moves independently of my brain as I say, "I'll do whatever it takes to keep my mother alive."

CHAPTER SIX

After an hour of discussing the next steps involved with the Novemion treatment, I stumble out of the hospital into the bleary light of early morning. The air is still chilly, but the temperature has risen enough that I can no longer see my breath. Ice melts beneath my feet as I trudge my way back up the parking garage stairs. The sounds of morning traffic fill my ears. The world is waking up, but all I want to do is go to sleep and forget this night ever happened.

Due to the nature of the surgery, Mom has to be kept under heavy sedation for at least forty-eight hours. While this isn't standard protocol, Doctor Mitchell deemed it necessary because of the remaining drainage tubes. He claims Mom would be safer kept unaware of her current condition since the discomfort from the operation and the open wounds might lead her to remove them herself. She's done it before, and neither of us feels comfortable assuming she won't do it again.

When I insisted I could still stay by her side while she's sedated, he made the valid, and extremely annoying, point that the exposed tubing and open wounds also increase the risk of infection, especially when coupled with the chemo-therapy and radiation treatments Mom has already received.

I wanted to argue, but I couldn't. My job at the cafe means I interact with too many people each day to ensure I don't bring anything back to the hospital with me, and though I want nothing more than to be there when she wakes, it would be selfish of me to take that chance.

Anticipating my resistance, Doctor Mitchell assured me Mom isn't on a ventilator, she's receiving supplemental oxygen as an added precaution, and her blood pressure, heart rate, and oxygen saturation have been relatively stable. He also agreed to text or call me with status updates at least once a day as he ushered me out the door.

Too many emotions bombard me as I slam the driver's side door and buckle myself in, casting me into a state of detachment. The drive home is longer than the trip to the hospital. With heavy eyes, I navigate the crowding streets downtown as I wend through the harbor and turn back toward our apartment. I'm so tired that I roll the window down because I'm afraid of falling asleep at the wheel. The cool air caresses my face, keeping me alert and in my lane.

For a few minutes, I allow myself to be distracted by the colors of the progressing sunrise. Stressed though I may be, the way the light glints off of the choppy bay is stunning. Shades of pink, blue, and gold reflect onto the surrounding buildings and spark off of the surface. If I stare hard enough, I can almost convince myself the water is on fire.

The view helps. It's one of my favorite things about living in Baltimore.

I pull into the parking lot of my apartment complex and wait for a space near the door. In this part of town, it's not a good idea to park far from the building. There are too many thefts and assaults. However, since most of the residents haven't left for work yet, the process takes a while. The lot will be half-empty by nine, but at six am, it's full. It takes two trips around for someone up front to leave before I snag a decent space, roll up my window, and head inside.

Normally, I'd be rushing to get ready for my shift at the cafe by now, but it's Friday. For the first time in weeks, I have the day off. It hadn't been easy to get it. In the end, I had to trade shifts with "Despicable Jason," the misogynistic and handsy guy everyone at work avoids. Of course, now I owe him a favor. I can only hope he doesn't ask for anything creepy. I'd probably throttle him, and I don't want to get fired.

This Monday, I worked a double shift from six am to eleven pm so he would take my shift today. I had intended to spend a few hours at the hospital with Mom, then use the rest of the day to take care of myself for once. I was going to clean up our place, borrow Connor's shower, and maybe mooch a few hours in front of his tv. I need a break now more than ever, but unfortunately, after meeting with Doctor Mitchell, my plans have changed.

I check my phone to make sure he hasn't called on the drive back, but my screen is blank. With leaden feet, I climb the crooked steps to the seventh floor. I could have chosen to take the elevator, but I don't have the patience for its ridiculously slow pace. It's faster to climb up myself, and I just want to be home, so I avoid the creaky stair between two and three and dodge the exposed nail on the fifth-floor landing. I'm out of breath by the time I reach the apartment.

The familiar stale smell washes over me as I twist the key and shove the door open. It sticks when it's damp, so I lean my full weight against it to ensure it closes before kicking off my shoes and locking it behind me. I don't bother to hang the keys on the hook. Instead, I rip the scrunchie from my hair and toss the key ring and scrunchie onto the desk. I stop by the bathroom and open the small window to let in some fresh air.

The futon is still damp, so I peel off the pillowcase and sheets, then half-collapse onto it, ready for some much-needed rest. Not for the first time, I wish I had electricity and heat because even stripped down to its bones, the mattress is remarkably cold. Shivering, I shut my eyes.

Before I allow myself to drift off, my thoughts turn to the days ahead. I can't believe I'm about to do this. Still, I would never abandon Mom. That's not who I am. I'll fight with everything I have to keep her alive and by my side.

"It's dangerous, it's illegal, and I'm going to make it happen," I mumble. "Let them come after me for saving my mother's life. I have to try."

In what feels like an instant, I'm sound asleep. This time, there are no nightmares. I don't have the energy to dream.

CHAPTER SEVEN

It seems the few hours of sleep I managed to get have served me well because I woke up this morning with a plan.

I fought the idea at first. I argued with the little nagging voice in my head that asserted I was better than this. I delayed following through by cleaning up some of the smaller messes around the apartment and paying the few bills I could with my measly paycheck. But, as I leaned up against the counter and forced down a disgusting bowl of stale cereal, reality set in.

There will be times in my life when I can afford to hold myself to a higher moral code. In those moments, I'll behave as my conscience expects me to. I'll open doors for strangers. I'll share my change with the musicians in the harbor. I'll be kind, and smile, and give compliments to the mother and her kids playing at the park.

This is *not* one of those days. I don't have the luxury of following the rules when my mother's life is on the line.

I gathered the few remaining things of value we possessed and stuffed them into my purse. It wasn't much: my class ring, a bracelet my father gave me for my fifth birthday, two sets of Mom's old earrings, and an iPod Nano given to me years ago by a friend. Then, I carried the hamper full of dirty clothes and two large bags of trash downstairs, tossed the hamper in the trunk and the trash in the dumpster, climbed into my car, and left the apartment behind.

It didn't take long for me to end up parked in front of Marcus's apartment complex. I barely remember the drive. Once I pulled onto the Beltway, my brain went into autopilot, giving me time to think about what I need to say when I knock on his door and see my sister for the first time in over a year.

No part of me wants to have this meeting, but I don't have a choice. I'm fully aware I can't pay for Mom's treatments on my own, and it's time Jennifer steps up to the plate.

I have several compelling arguments mapped out. I plan to get her alone and sit with her on the steps outside to calmly see things through. Hopefully, without Marcus breathing down her neck, she'll come to her senses. I want to do things the easy way, to work together toward a common cause. As much as I can't stand who Jennifer has become, I do love my sister. If we can handle things like adults, everything will be fine.

However, I *highly* doubt that will be the case. Thus far, each time we've talked about her helping Mom has resulted in a massive disagreement which ends with me being thrown out on my ass. So, I also have a backup plan.

I've managed to build up a rather extensive list of things her beloved Marcus has done over the years, many of which are still going on. Should she behave as I expect, I will be forced to put this knowledge to good use. One phone call to the local police should suffice.

While blackmail is not my preferred method of negotiation, I'm sure they would love to hear about Marcus's newest side job helping his uncle run Fentanyl through his grocery store down the road. I've got the station on speed dial and won't hesitate. If she refuses to help me through the goodness of her heart, maybe my leverage will give Jennifer an open mind.

Reluctantly, I drag myself up the steps and knock on their apartment door.

No one answers.

I knock again, and when there's still no response, I peer over the railing to search for Marcus's silver truck. It's parked in the last row next to Jennifer's car, a little red Camry. They're definitely home, so I press my ear to the door and listen.

It's silent.

Slightly irritated, I reach into my purse and pull out my phone. Jennifer's number is at the bottom of my list of "Favorites," so I tap it and wait. Through the door, I hear the muffled sounds of her phone ringing, like someone has covered the speaker with their hands. I wait to hear voices or footsteps, but they don't come.

Knowing my sister would never leave her phone at home, I turn the doorknob to see if the apartment is unlocked. The knob twists easily in my hand. The door opens up slowly, sending out a repulsive mixture of cat piss and old garbage. I choke on the smell, but when I look into the room, disgust stops me in my tracks.

Marcus's apartment is a complete disaster. I can barely see the floor underneath piles of dirty laundry and trash. Old, half-full takeout boxes have been haphazardly tossed to the side. Thick crusts of mold creep over the edges of the styrofoam containers filled with rot. Empty beer cans and whisky bottles cover most of the surfaces. In the far corner, a well-used litter box overflows with feces. Jennifer's cat, Sir Meowverick, bolts for the door.

I scoop him up and scratch behind his ears as he purrs. The poor thing is skin and bones. His collar jingles and nearly falls off his neck when I set him down. Quickly, I shoo him away from the threshold and shut the door behind me to keep him from escaping down the stairs. He rubs against my jeans and makes figure eights between my feet. I make a mental note to find him a better home. No animal should have to live like this.

Jennifer and Marcus are lying on the couch. As far as I can tell from the doorway, both are sound asleep, completely oblivious to my presence in their home. My sister's face is turned toward me, and her long blonde hair, thinner and duller than I've ever seen, hangs down to the floor. Marcus is drenched in sweat. His strained face and occasional jerks are enough to confirm he's having a terrible dream.

It doesn't take long for me to figure out why. The coffee table, or what's left of it, is littered with open pill bottles and used needles. This isn't the scene I had expected to find.

I inch closer to Jennifer, careful not to trip and fall into the mess. It's difficult to pick my way across the room without making excessive noise. Though the two seem to be sleeping off quite the high, I don't want to startle them. Marcus has been known to attack first and ask questions later, and if I frighten him, I'm afraid of what he'll do.

Kneeling by Jennifer's side, I'm struck by the unwelcome idea that I may have just discovered my sister dead in the arms of her favorite dealer. The figure before me is incredibly thin, and her skin is so much paler and waxier than it used to be. Track marks run up her arms, and there's a tourniquet tied loosely beneath her elbow. Her eyes have sunken deep into her face, and her lips are dry and cracked. She looks nothing like the sister I know.

I'm appalled. She's been in trouble over drugs before, but I've never seen Jennifer in a state like this.

Logic takes over as I lean in closer. I focus on her chest, waiting to see the rhythmic rise and fall of her breathing, but it's too hidden beneath Marcus's arm. I consider reaching out to grab her wrist and take her pulse, but I hesitate. I don't want to find her body stiff and cold in my grasp.

My eyes search the room for something of use before landing on a powder-covered mirror beneath an empty bottle of Jack. Soundlessly, I drag it out from beneath the liquor and wipe it on the arm of the couch to clear the white dust away. With nervous hands, I hold it beneath Jennifer's nose. Two small puffs of steam spread across the surface.

I let out a breath I didn't know I was holding. *My sister is alive.*

"What the fuck, Jennifer?" I whisper, shaking my head in disbelief. "How could you do this to yourself?"

It's then I notice the large diamond ring sparkling on her finger.

Chop-shop Marcus must have proposed, and my idiot sister, who never thinks of the consequences of her actions, had accepted.

"Great," I add. "That's just what you need."

I shift my disgusted gaze over to him. Up close, he appears healthier than Jennifer, but even his once handsome face shows signs of wear and tear. His short-cropped hair is thinning around his temples and deep lines extend from his eyes and cut across his forehead.

I stand and take several steps back until I'm sure I'm out of punching range, clear my throat, and call out my sister's name.

"Jennifer Edwards, what the hell is wrong with you?"

She doesn't stir, so I try Marcus instead.

"Hey, Marcus! Wake up! The house is on fire!"

Nothing. Not even a snore.

"You've got to be kidding me," I complain and toss the mirror to the floor.

What am I supposed to do now?

I can't speak to Jennifer when she's like this. Even if I do manage to wake her and drag her ass outside, she won't remember a thing. Once again, she's found a way to screw everything up.

I pull out my phone and start to dial.

My fingers have pressed 9 and 1 before I pause. A new plan forms in the back of my mind.

There are a number of nice, expensive things buried beneath the piles of filth. I turn slowly on the spot, surveying the place. A large flatscreen television is bolted to the outer wall. Cables run down to an Xbox and a PS5. A shining gold watch has been draped over the neck of a half-empty bottle of gin. Who knows what I might find if I were to put in a little effort and dig through the junk? It could very well be worth my while.

The same guilt I felt over blackmailing my sister tries to weasel its way into my conscience, but I ignore it. I cast a glance back to Jennifer and her fiancé. A thin line of drool dribbles down Marcus's chin, solidifying my decision.

Neither of them needs these things. Clearly, they aren't making smart decisions with the money they have. As far gone as they are, I could tear this place apart beneath them and they'd never even know. So, I steady my nerves, cross over to the closet, and pull out several of Jennifer's designer bags.

"You're going to help Mom whether you want to or not," I announce as I open one and set the Xbox inside. "Both of you."

Neither of them makes a peep as I squirrel away everything valuable I can find, including a thick stack of bills from Marcus's nightstand. It takes several trips down to the car to load up the haul. I pass one of Marcus's neighbors on the way out and offer up a charming smile.

Once I have what I need, I scoop up Sir Meowverick and

put him in the passenger seat. I run the seatbelt through his collar and buckle him in, just in case, before heading back upstairs for the last time.

"I'm not sorry," I say as I bend down and twist the engagement ring off of Jennifer's finger, tucking it into my pocket for safekeeping. "You've brought this on yourself. I can't save you from yourself this time. I have to help Mom."

With one more look at her sleeping form, I roll my eyes and lock the two inside.

In the car, I finish my call to 9-1-1. The operator is patient and kind when I tell them two people in Apartment 3A may have overdosed on unknown substances. At the end of the call, she asks me to stay on the line, but I hang up without leaving my name.

The ambulance flies by heading in the direction of Marcus's apartment complex as I pull onto the entrance ramp, merge into traffic, and disappear down 695.

CHAPTER EIGHT

Convincing the owner of the pawnshop to accept the collection of obviously stolen goods was easier than I expected. There was a hint of hesitation at first as he eyed the game systems and designer bags, but once I dropped Jennifer's engagement ring into his hands, the deal was sealed. It took only half an hour to haggle over the price and reassurance that no one would go looking for these things for me to leave Garrett's Pawn Emporium with $5,600 more than I had when I walked through the door.

That had been the easy part. Any guilt I felt over stealing from my sister faded when Garrett placed the stack of cash into my hand. $5,600 was enough for a single Novemion treatment. If I hadn't forced Jennifer to contribute, I'd be exactly where I was this morning - wondering what the going rate for a kidney is on the black market. At least for now, I can keep my organs.

This part will be much harder, but as so many things in life do, Mom's treatments require me to make a sacrifice. I have to give up something I love to save someone I love more.

So, I fire off a text to Connor and wait patiently for him to respond.

> Pick me up @ the lot on Prentice in an hour?

It doesn't take long before three blinking dots appear. I stare at the screen and wait. Sir Meowverick purrs and nuzzles against my thumb as I absently stroke his furry belly.

Sure, what r u doing out there?

> Fill u in when u get here.

Sounds good. Need a lift 2 the hospital?

> Ur place ok?

Anytime. B there soon.

Warmth fills my chest. I don't know what I've done to deserve a friend like him, but I wouldn't trade him for the world.

I must have found an itchy spot because Sir Meowverick kicks and scratches at my hand. As I look down at him, I realize I have to ask for one more thing.

> Can we stop @ the pet store?

It takes Connor a bit longer to respond this time. I'm sure he can't figure out why I would need to stop by a pet store since I don't have the time to care for an animal or the money to feed one. I can almost see his confused face, brows drawn into a slight frown, little wrinkles creasing the center of his forehead, as he types his answer.

What 4?

> I have an errand 2 run.

@ a pet store?

That's an odd request.

Yes. Trust me?

Of course. U never have 2 ask.

Relieved, I slip the phone into my pocket and lean over the center console to grab what's left of my things from the back.

With my jacket on and my purse stretched across my chest, I unclip Jennifer's cat. He licks my cheek affectionately when I lift him into my arms. The trail his velcro tongue leaves behind stings, but he's so incredibly sweet that I don't care. My lip wobbles as I stare down into his bright, mismatched eyes, one a pale blue and the other a vibrant green. I've always loved his eyes.

He was only a kitten when Jennifer moved out. I begged her to leave him behind, but she wouldn't. I wish she had. He would've been great company during the sleepless, freezing nights.

I snuggle Sir Meowverick close to my chest. He seems to enjoy the attention, and I can't help but wonder when he last felt loved? Given the state of the apartment, I'd wager he hasn't been properly cared for in months. What an awful thought. I'll get him squared away for the night, then find someone I trust to take care of him. He deserves that much.

I open my purse and settle him inside, careful not to bend his tail too harshly or snag his little toes. He can't be allowed to run around freely yet, so the safety of my bag will have to suffice. He doesn't fight as I zip it most of the way closed, leaving his head poking out from the corner. It's adorable to see him tucked away. He eyes me curiously as I grab the papers off my dash and step out of the car.

My fingers trace along the roof and my hand pats gently on the hood as I take a moment to appreciate my beat-up, yellow Beetle. It isn't much, but it's the only thing I own that has always been mine.

Mom bought it for me for my sixteenth birthday. It was already used at the time, but I didn't care. I picked it out myself and worked all summer at the ice cream shop to save up a thousand dollars of my own for the down payment. She covered the rest. I don't know how Mom managed to do it, but it was the best surprise I've ever received.

I've driven this car every day for the last five years. It's been to college and back and down just about every road in Baltimore. It pains me that after all of our adventures together, it's time to say goodbye. I wouldn't have this car without Mom, and it's fitting I return the favor to save her life.

"Good luck, Sunshine," I mumble as I walk away. "Keep it together, okay?"

It feels silly talking to an inanimate object, but Sunshine is chock full of memories: my senior skip day with Connor, driving to the National Harbor to watch movies on the Potomac, moving into my dorm at NYU, and so many more. I'm letting go of a friend, not just a vehicle.

I don't look back, afraid I'll change my mind, as I cut across the lot and head inside.

"ALRIGHT, MS. EDWARDS," THE SALESWOMAN SAYS as she hits the last few buttons on her keyboard. "It looks like we're done here. I'll just need the car keys and a few signatures, then I can get you on your way." Her thick black glasses flash when she turns her eyes back toward me.

I fish the keyring out from underneath Sir Meowverick and remove my keychain, placing the ring gingerly down on the saleswoman's desk. She gives me a sympathetic smile when she drops the keys into her drawer. In exchange, she hands me a laminated bus pass.

"To ease the transition. Just in case," she offers, shaking my hand.

I nod, not sure what to say. It's a nice gesture, and I'll probably need the bus pass for work, but I would so much rather have Sunshine.

She disappears for a few minutes before returning with a thick stack of papers, still warm to the touch, presumably straight off the printer.

I sign my name on every dotted line, date every page as directed, and leave the dealership with a hand cramp and an oversized envelope containing $2,100.

I'm fairly certain the saleswoman cut me a better deal than she should have. Sunshine is in decent shape, but the value of cars depreciates over time. I'm not about to point that out, though. Instead, I add the money from the pawn-shop and Marcus's apartment to the envelope, tuck it under Sir Meowverick, and head out to the lot.

As much as I regret selling Sunshine, with this last task done, I'm that much closer to affording Mom's second treatment. Where the rest will come from is uncertain, but I'll find it somehow.

A car is just a car, I tell myself as I scan the parking lot looking for Connor.

I'm not surprised to find him parked next to what used to be my Beetle with his feet on the dash, kicked back in the driver's seat. He has a habit of showing up to places earlier than he needs to, but he never seems to mind. He typically tunes out the world for a while and listens to his music while he waits. Last week, it was the soundtrack to *Rent*. Who knows what he's listening to this time?

Connor doesn't see me at first. He's completely absorbed

in his music, tapping out the rhythm of the bass on his knees. My eyes travel over his relaxed frame. Naturally tan, his black hair has recently been trimmed. It brushes the tips of his ears. A pair of gold sunglasses rests atop his head. His brown eyes are closed as he nods to the beat.

I rap my knuckles on the driver's side window to let him know I'm here. He looks up with a grin and unlocks the doors as I make my way to the passenger side and slide into the seat, careful not to crush Sir Meowverick beneath me. He tosses my bag of dirty clothes into the back and notices the cat as I place my purse gently on the floor.

"Hey, Kay," he greets me, using the nickname he gave me when we were kids.

His tone is cheerful, and I'm genuinely happy to see him, but I have so many emotions running through me that I can't bring myself to smile. Connor quickly notices and adjusts his demeanor, bringing it down a few notches. He watches me closely as I buckle myself in.

The silence in the car isn't awkward. That's how it's always been with him. He never expects me to share before I'm ready. But after a while, the quiet drags on for too long, so he elbows my arm lightly.

"Why am I picking you up? Something wrong with Sunshine?"

I lean my head onto his shoulder and cry.

"I sold her. I don't have a car anymore." I sniffle and wipe my eyes on the sleeve of my jacket.

"Oh, no. Kay, I'm sorry. You love that car."

I nod, and he pulls me into a tight embrace. Falling apart over a car might seem stupid to anyone else, but Connor understands. My tears soak into his shoulder. Still, he doesn't budge. After all, we've known each other since Kindergarten. He threw a handful of sand into my face, I shoved his head into the sandbox, the teacher called home, and suddenly we were best friends. So, why should he care if I spill my emotions on him from time to time?

It never matters what the problem is. We're always there for each other. It's been that way for as long as I can remember.

When Connor's mom told him he was going to have a little sister, he'd been set on running away. I helped him pack a bag full of Fruit Roll-Ups and granola bars because childhood logic said they would make well-balanced rations to get him through the trip. I even convinced him to pack a notebook and a pen so he could write me letters while he was gone. We made it as far as the monkey bars at the elementary school playground before he changed his mind. I didn't give him a hard time or make fun of him. I just walked him back home and never said a word.

When Richard left, he sat beside me on the swingset in his backyard and listened to me cry. I used to make up wild stories about where my father might be, and Connor never shot them down. He helped me come up with little details to fill in the blank spaces to make me feel better and pass the time.

I was there when Connor's first girlfriend cheated on him. He was there for me when Jennifer and I fought.

That's the way our friendship works. We don't hide things from each other.

He strokes my hair and holds me until the tears fade.

When I'm settled, I pull down the visor and put my face back together as best as I can. My skin is red and blotchy, and my eyes are swollen, but it feels good to let it out.

Panic! At The Disco quietly serenades us for a time.

"So, where to?" Connor asks, trying to lighten the mood. He must've reached his limit for being quiet. It never lasts long. It's one of the things I enjoy about him.

"Wherever I can get a cheap litter box, litter, and cat food. I'm responsible for Sir Meowverick right now."

"I noticed. How'd that happen?"

"Not yet," I answer. "Later."

"Okay."

"Then back to your place? I could use a shower and a washing machine."

"You've got it."

"You don't mind?"

"Hell no. If it puts you in a better mood, I'm all for it."

I'm so glad. Lately, I'm never sure if Connor will want company at his place because of Ally and her new boyfriend, Rob. They can't seem to keep their hands off each other. More often than not, he busts them doing "unspeakable things," as he calls them, in common areas of the apartment. She's eighteen now, and she can do what she likes, but he still sees her as the little annoyance who constantly trailed behind him while we were growing up. And, Rob? Well, in Connor's mind, he's not good enough for Ally. I doubt anyone will ever be.

"Will Ally and Rob be there?" I pry.

"No. Rob invited her over to his parent's place for some family thing. She'll be gone for the rest of the night. The coast is clear."

"Cool."

"We won't have to walk in on them doing the *naked tango* again if that's what you're worried about," he mumbles, disgust tinting his words.

I can't help but laugh. It's nice to be here with Connor after a rough day. At least I have my friend.

"You mean, we won't get to see them do that thing where Ally..." I tease, smacking him on the knee.

"La, la, la, la, la!" Connor shouts. "My sister is an innocent little angel! Shut up, Kay! I'll kick your ass out of my car and leave you on the curb!"

"No, you won't."

"I might."

"You never have before."

"There's a first time for everything," he retorts, laughing.

"Indeed, there is. But, you'd never strand this little guy." I pout and lift Sir Meowverick out of the bag. "I mean, look at his face…"

He glances over at the cat and smiles.

"Fine, but only because he's nicer than you."

"Oh, absolutely," I counter, enjoying our banter.

Connor shifts his car into drive and pulls out into the busy traffic. "Well then, our next stop is Le Chat Boutique, then Hôtel Winters, mon ami. Its amenities include poorly insulated walls, hot water full of bay gook, and whatever scraps you can find in the disgusting refrigerator."

"Sounds lovely!" I answer with a laugh.

It's good to know some things never change.

CHAPTER NINE

As much as I love Ally, I'm glad Connor was right. She's already off somewhere with Rob, so we have the apartment to ourselves and space to let Sir Meowverick settle in. Connor agreed to let him stay here for a while until I can find a better place. I'm thankful. Between him and Ally, I know Sir Meowverick will be safe.

Ally's absence also allows me to dodge the usual interrogation about Mom, work, and whether I've been on any dates recently. She's always trying to hook me up with someone she met at school, but I'm not interested. I don't have time to fit a new person into my life. It wouldn't be fair to me or them. I know she means well, but the questions and hints would be too much. It's been a long day and my patience is shot.

I clear out a space in the bottom of the entry closet for the cat's litter box since it will be out of the way and accessible there. It doesn't take long for him to find it and break it in. After Sir Meowverick seems comfortable, I find a place for his food and water in the corner of the living room, away from the door in case he tries to run out again.

Connor tosses my dirty clothes into the washing machine and starts it for me while I handle the cat. It'll be nice not to smell like hospital or coffee grounds until my next shift.

His shower is tricky, so he turns it on for me, too. The knob broke off shortly after he moved in, so an old vice grip suffices in its stead.

"How hot do you want it?" he asks.

"Burn my skin off, please."

"Girls," he answers with a shake of his head. "You're all the same. Doesn't that sting?"

"No, not anymore." I laugh when he shoots me a look of disapproval.

"Whatever, I suppose. How's this?"

I step into the room and run my hand beneath the hot liquid spewing from the faucet. It's perfect, and I can't wait to jump in.

"Great, thanks. Towel?"

"Hall closet." He points as he shakes off his hands. "Washed them yesterday. I had a feeling you'd stop by to run up my water bill soon."

He means it as a joke, but I shoot him a look that says, 'Sorry...'

"I'm just kidding. Don't worry about it. Besides, Ally's gone half the time these days. You're using the water she isn't."

I smile politely when he pats me on the shoulder and squeezes by, leaving me behind to enjoy the heat and steam. Within seconds, I lock the door and peel off my clothes, hopping in.

The sensation is exquisite. I scrub off the dirt and grime of the last few days, then stand perfectly still, letting it work the knots of tension from my shoulders and back. Ally has excellent taste in shampoo, so I massage it into my roots and allow myself to feel like a human being.

I never understood how important these small moments were until they became so rare. I won't take them for granted again.

After nearly thirty minutes, I force myself to step out of the shower onto the cold bathroom tile. The water continues to rain down behind me. Connor will turn it off once I'm dressed, so I hurry to dry myself and grab the pile of clothes I left on the toilet, slipping into them one piece at a time. Moving to stand in front of the condensation-covered mirror, I swipe a section clean and take in the tangled mess that is my hair. Starting from the bottom, I use Ally's hairbrush to tame the wild mass, then retrieve my deodorant, toothbrush, and toothpaste from my purse to take care of the rest.

My reflection stares back at me with pink-tinted cheeks, giving off the impression of vitality. Soaking wet, my hair is longer, dark and thick. It cascades in waves down past the center of my back. My shoulders sit appropriately, relaxed at the base of my neck. I haven't seen this side of myself in a while. This is what I'm supposed to be. It's who I remember being before Mom's diagnosis. It's such a stark contrast to who I am these days.

Traces of Mom's features linger below the surface of my own, especially in my hooded eyes and full lips. I bring my hand up to gently touch them. At a different point in my life, knowing I look like my mother would have made me smile. Now, it breaks my heart into a million pieces.

What if the Novemion treatments don't work? What if Mom dies? Every time I look in the mirror, I'll see those bits of her staring back at me. How could I bear that for the rest of my life?

Mom isn't gone, but I miss her so much already. As the treatments have progressed, she's lost much of her goofy personality, the headstrong energy that defined who she was. I miss how she used to host game nights with our friends. I miss thrift shopping before school started. I miss watching her sew and paint and listening to her sing. I miss the way her eyes used to crinkle when she smiled. She doesn't smile often enough anymore, and when she does, it's never as authentic. It doesn't reach her eyes.

How can the burden of loss be so heavy when it hasn't happened yet? How can we both have lost so much and still be together?

Haunting thoughts fill my head as the depression and anger settle back in. Mom's face from the morning after Richard left flashes in the mirror. It morphs into the look of heartbreak when we handed over the keys to the row house. One after another, sad memories consume me. Mom, sick and weak after chemo. Holding her hair out of the toilet and rubbing her back as she sobbed. Her surgical-capped head, smile full of resignation, as they wheeled her down the hall.

Doctor Mitchell's words overlap with the images. Percentages. Chances of survival. Tumor mass. No more treatments. Novemion. Out of pocket. Experimental.

Images of Jennifer, oblivious to the world wrapped in Marcus's arms. Mom asking when Jennifer will come to visit. Blowing out the candle and tossing it into the trash. Empty refrigerator. Barren pantry. Broken windows and sodden futons. Rejection letter. Rejection letter. Rejection letter.

My thoughts grow more insistent, sending me spiraling into a pit of despair. I struggle to use the coping skills from my childhood therapy sessions. I focus on my breathing and count backward from ten, but the sorrow, and the anger, and the fear keep coming.

My sister's words lance through me. *"I don't have the time or money to care. Put her in a home, Kara. It is what it is."* The creatures from the nightmare chase me. Bill collectors knock on my door. Doctor Mitchell talks about money. I drop the empty water jug into the trash. I pull Jennifer's engagement ring from her finger like a monster and abandon her. The hospital machines are beeping… beeping… beeping… The horrible blare of the flatline stabs at my heart.

"Enough!" I scream at the top of my lungs. I let go of the

sink and swing my fist at the mirror with every ounce of strength I possess. The impact is jarring, but I barely register the pain as I punch it again, and again, and again, unable to control my rage. The glass creaks, then it cracks and shatters around me. I look down to see my hands coated with hot, sticky blood. I sob and slide to the floor.

Connor bangs on the bathroom door. He begs me to unlock it and asks me what's wrong over and over. I can't move from this spot. Instead, I drop my face into my bloody hands. My body shakes uncontrollably. Ringing fills my ears.

I want it to go away. I need it to go away. The whole world and everything in it.

I can't breathe.

Mom's dying. There's nothing I can do. I'm helpless to save her. There isn't enough money in the world to keep her alive. I'm trying so hard. Working so hard. Fighting so hard. Ruining my life. I've turned to stealing and starving, and for what? It's going to be for nothing. Nothing can save her. I'm failing.

I'm so dizzy I can barely hold myself up. My chest tightens, threatening to collapse in on itself.

I let myself fall and curl into a ball on the tile. Shards of glass dig into my side, but I couldn't care less. I've completely shut down, lost in my panic and grief.

I'm only vaguely aware of Connor bursting through the bathroom door and shouting at me. His eyes are wide with fear as he asks me if I'm okay.

"Kay, oh god! Hang in there. Hold on. I'll be right back."

I watch with detachment as he rushes to the hall closet and returns with towels. He wraps them around my arms and holds them too tight. The pressure stings, but I don't pull away.

Connor scoops me from the floor and pulls me into his lap. My limp frame sags against his chest as he cradles me in his arms. I've never seen him like this before. Concern for his well-being, not my own, drags me out of the depths. I want to help him, to calm him, but I'm so bone-achingly tired.

As he instructs me to take deep, even breaths, my lungs remember how to cooperate. I drag the moist air in and out, coughing deeply from the burning sensation. It's so damn hard. Breathing shouldn't be this hard. I do it every day. Still, his guidance helps. My heart slows to an acceptable pace and my limbs steadily regain feeling.

"I'm sorry," I whisper when I can breathe again. "Your bathroom…"

"Kay, I don't give a shit about the mirror. I only care about you. Are you okay?"

Words are too hard, so I bury my face in his chest.

Time moves slowly for a while. I don't know how long we sit there together, but he rocks me in his embrace and runs his fingers through my snarled, wet hair.

Look what I've done. I've ruined everything again. This is all my fault.

I'm so defeated. I just want to sleep.

Eventually, Connor determines I'm no longer in significant danger. He slides me from his lap and lifts me into the tub where the shower water is still spraying. It's cold now, and it seeps into the fabric of my clothes, but I don't care. Bit by bit, the blood washes away.

He turns to the vanity and withdraws a medical kit from the bottom drawer, putting his pre-med skills to good use. Before opening the kit, he washes his hands and lets them air dry. Then, he retrieves handled tweezers and gets to work removing the bits of glass in my skin.

Connor talks to me as he works, trying to keep me calm as he cleans the wounds and wraps them with gauze, but I'm too fascinated with the blood swirling down the drain to care.

When everything is neatly wrapped and sterilized, he turns off the water and lifts me out of the tub. For a moment, he eyes me warily before instructing me to stay still and promises he'll be right back. The sounds of water dripping off of me ensnare my attention. A puddle forms on the floor beneath me.

Connor returns with a broom and sweeps away the broken glass, then dries the puddle with my towel. He tosses the contaminated medical supplies into the trash and leads me out of the room and into his own. I let him.

Once inside, he helps me peel off my wet clothes and pull on a dry pair of his sweats and a hoodie. They're warm and they smell like him. It's more than I deserve.

A small piece of myself returns. He eases me down onto the edge of the bed and sits with me, giving me space, but still holding my hand.

"I... Kara? What's going on?" Connor whispers.

I take a deep, shuddering breath. I haven't lost it like this in a long time. I never meant to do this here. I never meant to scare Connor. I never meant to destroy his things.

"I'm sorry..." is all I can say. "Connor, I'm so sorry." I try to look away, but he turns my face back to him.

Connor motions to the room. "Kara, I couldn't give two shits about this place. Break anything you want. It's replaceable. You aren't. I'm worried about you. What's happening? Whatever it is, it's serious, and I don't know what to do. Tell me. It has to be more than selling the car. I want to know right now." His words come out in a rush and his voice is stern, more so than it's ever been.

"I'm sorry..." I whisper again. I move my arms to hold my head, but a sharp pain shoots through them, so I drop them back into my lap. "Connor, I thought I was okay. I didn't mean to do this. I was fine in the shower. I don't know what happened."

"Yes, you do," he says, sounding assured, "and you're going to tell me."

There's silence, and for the first time in our entire friend-ship, there's palpable tension in the room. Connor's angry, visibly shaken by what happened. He's not angry with me, but he is angry *for* me. His protective instincts have kicked in.

"I didn't want to dump this on you."

"You better," he replies.

"It's a lot…"

"Funny, I figured that much out already."

Shame wells up in my stomach. "I need a minute."

He looks at me with disbelief. "You want me to leave you alone?"

"Just for a minute so I can find the right words," I offer. "Like I said, there's a lot to this."

He studies me. I can see his thoughts as he works through the options. Years of friendship win out over the doubts. He lifts himself up and moves to leave, scooping my discarded clothes off the floor.

"If you aren't in the living room in five minutes, I'm calling 9-1-1. And, I'm not closing this door. You better not either."

"Fair enough," I answer, staring at my feet. "Connor, I'll pay for all of this. I swear."

"If you so much as hand me a penny, I'm kicking your ass. I'll tell Ally that, too."

He leaves the bedroom door cracked when he steps into the hall. His hand lingers on the knob as he casts one last glance back at me, then disappears.

I'm embarrassed and disgusted with myself. I can't even bring myself to consider the damage I may have done to our friendship tonight. The cuts and bruises throb through my knuckles and forearms.

I steel myself for a conversation I didn't want to have. After all of this, Connor deserves to know the truth, though how much of the truth is the question.

I can tell him about what happened with Jennifer and the dealership, but is it safe to share the truth about Novemion? What will he think of me?

But, we don't keep secrets. Not telling him is a betrayal, and after the incident in the bathroom, what do I have to lose?

CHAPTER TEN

I'm so ashamed of losing control that for a while, I can't bring myself to be near Connor. It's not because he's done anything wrong, but because I can't believe I let myself spiral so far that I became destructive, to myself and to his home. So, instead of taking the other haggardly lawn chair he offers me, I perch on the wide window ledge, knees drawn up to my chest, arms wrapped tightly around them, and stare down at the goings on in the city below.

It's cold in Connor's apartment, but warmer than it would be in my own. The mingled scents of his cologne and musty old carpet permeate the large room. This building is old, but it's been tended to more frequently than mine. The sparse furniture in the shared spaces of the apartment gives off an aura of emptiness. A battered army trunk has been turned into a television stand, and a 32-inch flatscreen and Xbox claim the space on top. There's a standing lamp in the corner and a stack of textbooks piled precariously by the base. It's the epitome of college living.

I remember when Connor salvaged the two lawn chairs out of the dumpster last summer. Someone threw them away when they moved out. He was so proud that he had a place to sit in the living room after he brought them upstairs, though they had seen better days before he claimed them for himself. Ally, only seventeen at the time, complained that they were gross and threatened to throw them out the window, but somehow after she moved in with him that fall, he managed to keep them. It's not as though Ally spends much time in the living room. She prefers to be in her own space or out and about with Rob.

I know he's watching me. I can feel his gaze boring holes into my back, but I don't know what to say. Words won't repair broken glass or undo the fear he felt as he held me and rocked me on the wet floor, the fear I caused.

Connor knows Mom's situation is dire. He's aware I'm working my ass off to get her proper care and that in general, my life has fallen apart, but I don't think he realized it was this bad.

There's no hiding it anymore.

It's possible after seeing me in that state, he understands my situation better than I do now. Or, maybe I understand my situation perfectly well and don't want to admit the truth to myself. My stubborn nature has always been my fatal flaw. If something's worth fighting for, I'll run myself into the ground for the cause.

Mom used to blame it on my sun sign. She loves horoscopes. Since I was born in May, that makes me a Taurus, an opinionated and bull-headed yet loyal person who regularly sees the world in black and white. I don't do well with gray areas, and I don't give up, even when I should.

In the face of Mom's cancer, everything is gray. There are no certainties, one way or the other. It's beyond my control, and it tears me apart and sets my brain on fire.

Am I doing it again? Am I fighting against a reality that can't be avoided? Will I lose my mom regardless of the choices I make? Does it matter?

If ever there was a cause worth fighting for, it's this one. I couldn't back down if I wanted to. It would kill me.

I chance a look in Connor's direction, only to find he's turned his eyes toward the window as well. His expression is vacant, one of someone lost in thought. He leans forward, propping his elbows on his thighs.

No matter what the outcome is, I don't want to be alone in the end. At the rate I'm going, that's exactly what will happen. Lately, my touch seems to poison the few relationships I have. There are days when I feel cursed to bring destruction down on everyone I meet. I can't afford to let my walls slip. I have to rein it in. If not, I'll lose everyone I've ever cared about, even Connor, and I can't fathom a life without my best friend.

"We need food," Connor announces, interrupting my pity party. "Good food has never failed to make a shitty situation better. I'm thinking Dragon Dynasty. Is that okay with you?"

"Sure," I rasp. I haven't spoken in so long that the words stick in my throat. Clearing it, I add, "Split a meal like we used to?"

"No, I don't want your weird beef and broccoli order. You get your own."

"I can't really…" I start to explain I don't have the money to spare, but he waves my words away.

"I didn't ask for your money. It's already covered."

"Connor?"

"Don't start with me, Kay."

I sigh and lean back against the wooden window frame. I won't win this argument. There's no use trying.

By the time dinner arrives, the sun is setting over the city. Connor spreads an old blanket over the floor, then distributes the food onto paper plates. He adds a pot sticker and a piece of crab rangoon on top of my pile of beef, veggies, and rice before doing the same to his plate of General Tsao. I open my mouth to protest, but he gives me a look that says, "Argue and I'll hold you down and feed it to you myself," so I pick up the steaming appetizer and take a bite.

The food is delicious, salty, creamy, crunchy, and far fresher than anything I've had in a long time, which is saying something since the majority of it is fried. It warms my insides and tempers my mood. I'm sure my hunger hasn't helped with emotional regulation, or lack thereof, but I'm hungry so often I barely notice most of the time.

When the plates are nearly empty and I can't eat another bite, Connor clears the food and deposits the containers into the kitchen trash. Sir Meowverick wanders onto my lap and settles down, purring as I absently scratch along his back. Taking a seat on the floor once more, Connor scoots closer this time, placing his hand on my knee and looking straight into my eyes.

"Alright, Kay," he demands. "Tell me what's going on."

I run my fingers through my hair nervously as I arrange my thoughts into some semblance of meaning. As the words begin to flow, I fight the tears that threaten to spill like waterfalls from my eyes.

"It's Mom," I tell him. "It's so much worse than we thought."

"What happened with the surgery?"

"It didn't work." I sniffle.

He frowns and squeezes my leg supportively. "Why?"

I launch into the explanation Doctor Mitchell gave about the remaining piece of tumor and the decision not to try surgery again. My voice wavers and my face heats when I tell him there won't be more chemo or radiation.

"There's a treatment we can try, but it's all out-of-pocket, and it's going to cost over a hundred thousand dollars. Jennifer's still useless. I went to her place this morning to ask for help. I was prepared to blackmail her with some things I learned about Marcus, but when I got there, she was so high I couldn't wake her up. She and her idiot *fiancé*," I put emphasis on the word. Connor's eyes widen. "were passed out on the couch. She still had the tourniquet on her arm."

"Oh, man. That's… intense."

"I was angry, and I still needed money so I stole a ton of their stuff. I sold it all to Garrett, and I have enough for the first treatment now, but one treatment isn't going to help. That's why I sold my car."

I stare at the floor, willing myself not to look at Connor's face, afraid of what I'll see there. Off the top of my head, shock and disgust come to mind.

"Where does that leave you?" His words are calm.

"It's still not enough. It's *never* going to be enough."

He's quiet as I pick at a loose strand of carpet.

"You know the bills are all behind. I paid a few this morning so I can have heat and water again for a while and not have to be such a burden over here."

"You're not a burden."

"That's what you say, but you don't have to rely on the kindness of others for a shower and a hot meal. It feels gross, like I'm using you."

"But, you're not. I'm offering it to you freely."

"I know. Somehow, that makes it worse."

Connor tugs me into his side as I carry on.

"I don't want to think about going back to that hole-in-the-wall apartment alone while Mom's hooked up to every tube the hospital has."

"So, don't."

"Connor, I have no more credit available. All of my cards are maxed out. I've tried every bank and lending agency I can think of, and no one will help me. I can't make enough money at work, but I'm working every shift I can. I work so much I barely have enough time to see Mom these days, and when I do, I have to show up late or leave early."

"You know Valerie understands. You can't be there every second of every day."

"I'm afraid I'm going to lose my job," I tell him. "I'm having nightmares again. After the surgery, Mom's doctors won't let me in to see her. I feel so useless, like I'm letting her die."

Connor takes a moment, thinking over everything I've said. When he finally speaks, his tone is cautious and full of concern.

"I love Valerie," he whispers. "She's been like a mom to me since the first day we met. She's strong, patient, and feisty. If anyone could beat cancer, it's her..." His voice trails off.

Connor's words bring a small smile to my lips. Mom *is* feisty. He's got that right. That's where I get it from. It's one of the ways we're most alike.

"I've seen you fight for her, Kay. She's seen it, too. She knows you love her. She knows you'll do anything you can to save her, and you know she would do the same."

I nod and wipe the tears from my eyes.

"I can't imagine what this is like for you. I mean, how many kids would drop out of school to become their mother's full-time caretaker? I don't know of many. You're amazing."

He hesitates. When he continues, his tone is wary.

"I'm going to say something, Kay. I know you don't want to hear this, but I'm going to say it anyway, and you're going to listen."

"Connor," I interrupt, "you can't fix this for me."

"I'm not trying to fix it. I just need you to understand something." His expression turns hard, stern as if he's preparing himself for my wrath. "You have two options now. One, you can keep fighting like you have been to save Valerie. You can work yourself to death, stay out of school, and beg, borrow, and steal to make ends meet. I'll completely understand. But, *you* need to understand you could still end up losing her if you do all of those things."

"I know, but…"

"Or two, you can let her go. You can stop fighting, stop drowning yourself trying to save her. You can spend the time she has left by her side. You can make her comfortable, tell her you love her, and let her die in peace."

Tears well up in Connor's eyes.

My heart falls, hard. He's right, of course, and I'd been thinking the same thing for a long time, but this is my mom. I won't make that choice. Call me selfish, but I can't let her go, not if she has a chance.

Connor reaches for my shoulders and gently holds me at arm's length so he has a clear view of my face. It's like he's willing me to listen with everything he has.

"No one can make this choice for you. It's the hardest choice you'll ever have to make. Hell Kay, even I don't know what the right choice is, but it is a choice. I need you to know that it's not solely about whether Valerie lives or dies. It's about the kind of life she'll have if she survives. You have to think about that. What is she going to come home to? The apartment is a trash heap, anything that's worth anything is long gone by now, and you…" he says, sadness evident in his features.

"What about me?" I snap. Vulnerability raises my shields, making me defensive. I push Sir Meowverick off of my lap as I stand. He meows indignantly, but I ignore his complaints and back toward the hall. I'll apologize to the little guy later. Now is not the time.

"No, listen!" he urges, raising his voice, too. He stands and tries to approach me, but I take another step back. My withdrawal hurts him. He only wants to help, but I can't have him near. I don't know what it would do to my resolve.

"You have to listen to me. I'm not saying you aren't good enough. You *are* good enough. You've been amazing through all of this. I'm *so* proud of you for taking care of your mom, for sacrificing like you have to make sure she sees another birthday or another Christmas. I'm also worried about you all the time."

I shake my head. It's starting to throb, and I desperately wish he would stop talking.

"Look what this is doing to you. All of this. It's warped you somehow. This cancer is killing you, too. I mean, seriously, when was the last time you slept through the night? When was the last day you had off work?" I open my mouth to say today, but he keeps going. "When was the last time you stepped on the scale? I'm guessing you've lost almost thirty pounds in the last couple of years. If you keep this up, you don't just risk losing your mom. You could end up in the hospital right beside her."

"I'm fine. I - "

"You're NOT fine!" he yells, gesturing toward the bathroom. "You're in trouble, Kay. You're in trouble, and I want to help you, but I don't know how. You're having violent panic attacks in my bathroom! What am I supposed to do?"

"Back off, Connor," I warn.

"You say you're helpless, that you're letting your mom die... Well, damn it, Kara. I'm sitting here watching you die, and I feel the same way."

He drops back into the chair, too upset to keep talking. Hurt and fear consume him. His head hangs, and he grips his thighs so tightly I'm sure it will leave bruises.

"You're my best friend," he whispers. "I don't want to lose you."

I turn away from Connor and grip the corner, holding on for balance as I wade through his words. I hadn't expected this. I thought he might lecture me for stealing or chastise me for being reckless. I hadn't realized the depth of distress he was feeling. *Am I really so far gone? Is he truly afraid I might die?*

More importantly, why am I certain he's right?

This isn't the life I was meant to live. If Mom knew half of the things I've done to survive while she's been in the hospital, I'd never live it down.

It's not fair that I'm losing my mom. It's not fair that all of this is tearing me apart. It's not fair that it's hurting my best friend.

Life isn't fair. I learned that long ago.

I drag my hands across my face. They're like sponges that fail to scrub away the grime of cancer and the grit of death. Willing the confusion to disappear, I take a few steps toward him and sink to my knees by his chair, laying my head on his lap. He holds on to me protectively.

"You don't understand," I whisper. "I can't give up on my mom. You two are all I've ever had. I can't let her die, no matter the cost."

"I know."

"I get what you're trying to say..."

"No, you don't," he interrupts quietly. "*You're* losing Valerie, and *I'm* losing you. You won't let me help you. You're so stubborn."

"I can't let her die."

"You're so focused on Valerie that you don't see anything else."

"I have to be. Nothing else can matter."

"No, Kara!" he blurts, but he never finishes his thought. Instead, he lifts me up and brings his hands to my face. I still as Connor laces his fingers into my hair. He watches me and waits for me to push him away, but I don't. Then his lips crash into my own, gentle but insistent, as though he's willing his kiss to say the words he can't.

I'm breathless when he pulls away and presses his forehead to mine.

"You don't see *anything*," he whispers, his hands still wrapped in my hair.

Did Connor just kiss me? My Connor? A tingling, electric sensation makes its way through my body. Goosebumps rise on my skin. My cheeks flush.

Suddenly, everything has changed. One part of me wants to turn around and run out of the apartment, away from the chaos of my life, but a stronger part wants to pull him back to me and kiss him again.

I raise my fingertips to the place where his lips touched mine. Connor watches me, breathing quicker than usual, caught somewhere between panic and excitement.

Truthfully, I know this kiss would have happened sooner if Mom hadn't gotten sick. He is *my Connor*. He's the one I always call. He's the one who comes when I need him. He's the one whose stories never get old and whose jokes are always funny, even when they aren't. He's the one whose smell makes me feel safe and whose touch consistently feels right. He's saved me a million times, and I've saved him a million more.

I've thought about telling him I have feelings for him so many times, but it never seemed like the right moment. I had always been too concerned he wouldn't feel the same way. But, after that kiss, what do I do now? Do I risk kissing him back and shifting everything we have? Do I push him away and risk the same?

Blood rushes in my ears. Seconds turn into hours as I stare at him, and he stares back. We're both waiting for the other to say or do anything, but it has to be me. He won't push.

Cautiously, I lean in and brush my lips softly against his mouth.

"Connor," I whisper when I pull away, my face barely an inch from his. "Do you love me?" I ask.

His breath is hot on my skin.

"Yes," he whispers. There's a kind of desperate hope in his eyes I'm sure I share. "I've loved you for years."

"Okay," I say breathlessly, and press my lips back to his.

The kiss is soft at first, but that's not what I want. When he kisses me back, I wrap my hands around his neck, pulling him into me. He tumbles out of the chair and we land on the threadbare blanket, bodies crashing together in a tangle of arms and legs.

Like magnets, we cling to each other. His shirt slips over his head, and my borrowed hoodie disappears. His chest and stomach are warm as they collide with mine. Blood rises to the surface of my skin, flushing my cheeks. I lose awareness of our surroundings. I'm weightless, invincible for the first time in so long. His fingertips leave hot streaks as he trails them, feather-light, down my arms. Every touch is tantalizing. My hands glide to his waist. He grips my hips and pulls me closer, but I stop him, tugging off what remains of our clothes.

This is my Connor. This is real. This is happening. This is everything I want. There is nothing else.

"Don't leave me," I breathe as he moves to kiss my neck.

He stops and presses his forehead back to mine, holding my shoulders tightly in his hands.

"Never," he answers, voice full of certainty and longing, and he draws me into a kiss so deep the world fades.

CHAPTER ELEVEN

"Dan didn't see you come in, did he?" Christa asks as I sneak into the break room to deposit my jacket and purse. "I clocked you in a few minutes ago, just in case."

"Seriously? Thank you," I reply, out of breath from racing down the street to the cafe.

Connor and I spent too long in bed this morning, and by the time he dropped me off, there were no parking spots close to Renee's. He had to let me out by the aquarium, so I dodged tourists and fought with the crosswalks to get here. I still didn't make it on time. I'm only a couple of minutes late, but Dan's notorious for writing people up, and I can't afford another note in my file.

"No," I continue. "I don't think he saw me. He was inventorying the mugs and pre-packaged beans when I got here, so his back was to the door."

Christa's freshly painted pink nails glimmer on the tips of her golden-brown fingers as she picks apart her cinnamon roll and pops a glazed segment into her mouth. "Good. That man's nothing but a grouch. If he asks, you've been here the whole time."

"Got it. Busy today?"

"Eh, busy enough," she answers, taking a sip from her

mug. "The breakfast rush was slower than usual. We still have quiches left, if that tells you anything. But, I've been cleaning up after the night crew. One of these days, they'll figure out what it means to restock."

"No kidding." I roll my eyes as I tie the blue apron around my back, then grab the magnetic name tag from the bulletin board. "Sorry I'm late. I tried to get here on time."

"It's fine. I'm working a double." She looks up and eyes me with a grin, taking in everything from my bedhead to my worn shoes. "You look… different."

I frown as I tie my messy hair into a bun and drop my hat on top, securing the velcro underneath. "How so?"

Her grin transforms into a crooked smile. "I think you had a good night, that's all."

I blink at her, confused.

"Your lips are swollen. Your hair looks like two people slept in it, and there's a little glimmer in your eyes." She shakes her head at me. "Those cute boys will get you in trouble every time."

Blood rushes to my cheeks. My hand darts for my lips, and embarrassment settles into my stomach.

"Good for you, girl," she says, tearing off another bite. "It's about damn time you had something good happening in your life."

My answering smile is bashful, but honestly, she's right.

"Look busy," she tells me as she finishes off her mug, so I grab a bottle of French Vanilla syrup and head back to the front.

Dan eyes me suspiciously as I approach the counter, full bottle of syrup in hand. I twist off the screwtop and punch a pump through the foil, then replace the nearly empty bottle on the rack.

"Edwards, where've you been?" he asks. Something has him in a foul mood. I make a note to stay out of his path.

"Here," I say without turning around. The counter's clean enough, but I grab a fresh rag from the bucket anyway and proceed to wipe it down. "Why? I mean, I had to go to the bathroom, but I've been here the whole time."

Dan rolls his angry, wrinkled eyes. "Fine. You need a drawer. Go see Steve in the office before he leaves, and get back up here," he huffs.

"On it." I drop the rag into the dirty bin and spin to walk away.

"Go to the bathroom *before* your shift next time!" he calls.

It takes everything I have to ignore him as I make my way back to the office. Steve has the door propped open, so I stick my head in and knock.

"Hey, you have a drawer for me?" I ask.

He digs through the stack of papers spewed over the desk, then hands me a heavy plastic tray full of cash.

"What's up with Dan?"

Steve leans back in his computer chair and ponders the ceiling. With tired eyes, he rubs his close-cropped curly hair. He traces the edge of his line-up before rubbing his temples and letting out a groan. He and Dan don't get along, either. The two of them don't often work the same shifts, but they occasionally overlap, like today. "The usual? Supposedly, someone stole a bag of Dark Roast, so he's losing his mind."

"Nice. Over what, six dollars?" Steve nods. "Is that why he's doing inventory early?"

"Just keep your head down today." He leans forward again and straightens the papers into a neat pile. "I had to send Jenny home early because he made her cry."

"Noted. Thanks, Steve."

"You're welcome. I'm out of here in fifteen. Do you need anything?"

"A triple shot of espresso and a six-hour nap."

"Story of my life," he answers with a laugh.

I turn and march back up front, customer service ready.

After Steve vacates the space, Dan secludes himself in the office for quite a while, leaving me, Christa, and Eddie, a gangly, red-headed teenager, to handle the cafe operations. Honestly, I prefer it this way. We each choose our tasks and buckle down: Eddie handles bus duty, Christa runs the front counter, and I take the drive-thru window. Things run smoothly, and we end up with plenty of downtime.

My mind is left to its own devices, and after last night, steamy visions consume me. I daydream of this morning, waking up to find Connor fast asleep, his chest steadily rising and falling with restful breaths. His t-shirt was bunched up above his stomach, revealing the thin line of raven hair that trailed down to his sweatpants. Flashes of the way his muscles tightened last night as I trailed kisses down that path, and to so many other places, steal my breath. The phantom touch of his hands and lips exploring my skin sends goosebumps erupting down my neck and back. I try to hide these thoughts from my co-workers, but more than once, I catch Christa smirking at me as though she knows every dirty little secret.

During a particularly vivid memory, my hand slips as I pour freshly scalded milk into a paper cup. The frothy liquid runs down my arm, setting my nerves on fire from my wrist to the inside of my elbow. I cry out, dropping the drink to the floor.

Christa snatches the first aid kit from below the counter and abandons her register. She slides through the mess to race to my aid, coating the soles of her shoes with a sticky film. Thankfully, the searing pain is gone by the time she yanks my arm out and rolls up my sleeve. Only a pale pink patch mars my skin where the milk touched it. It should've been far worse.

Her eyes narrow as she takes in the thin cuts from last night. Many of them are almost healed.

"You're so lucky," she admonishes. "Pay attention, dreamer girl."

"I will," I promise, rubbing the place where my pale skin should be blistered.

By the time my lunch rolls around, I'm famished. Thank goodness for our employee meal. Christa rings me up as I pour myself a hazelnut coffee and grab a stale blueberry scone.

"You gonna tell me who it is?" she teases.

"Not on your life," I reply, winking at her and taking my food back to the break room to eat.

Alone, I settle in at the table and check my messages. There's a cute text from Connor.

> I'm glad u stayed over last night. Have a gr8 day @ work. I'll b there @ 8.

I smile, then listen to the voicemail Doctor Mitchell left, hoping for good news.

"Ms. Edwards, this is Doctor Mitchell calling from St. John's as planned. Valerie is doing as well as can be expected at this time. We will be lifting the visitation restrictions tomorrow morning, so you may stop by as early as nine am.

Regarding the other matter we discussed, I've made the necessary arrangements. I have the correct *forms*, so as soon as you are ready to *sign them*, we'll go ahead and get started. I'll be waiting for your response."

I press the little green button and return Doctor Mitchell's call.

"Hello, this is Doctor Mitchell," he answers. He must not have checked the number before he picked up.

"Doctor Mitchell, this is Kara Edwards. Do you have a moment to talk?"

"Ah, Ms. Edwards. Yes, hold on." His footsteps sound through the speaker as he presumably moves to a private location. "Are you calling about the *forms*?"

"I am," I reply. "I managed to find the correct *insurance card*, as you requested." Speaking in code like this feels ridiculous, but I understand the precaution. "When would be the best time to get it to you?"

"Are you available today?"

"Unfortunately, I'm at work until eight. But, if you get a chance to swing by for a cup of coffee, I can give you the card then."

He pauses, thinking over what I've offered. "Would I have to come inside?"

"We have a drive-thru, and I'm working the window today. It would be quick and painless if that's what you'd like to do."

Silence again. I wait impatiently until he returns to the line.

"Sounds delicious," he states. "Which cafe?"

"Renee's on the Harbor."

"I'll be there at 7:45. What should I order?"

Another codeword. Great.

I choose an unpopular drink. "A large iced coffee with two pumps of butterscotch syrup. And, a cookie."

"Have it ready when I arrive."

He hangs up the phone without properly ending the call.

I shake my head and pick apart my scone, not leaving any crumbs on the napkin. When it's finished, I take my purse to the bathroom, hoping Eddie and Christa won't bat an eye, and seclude myself in a stall to count out the cash. I leave five thousand dollars in the envelope, fold it up and stick it in my back pocket, then bury the rest back in the bottom of my bag.

A FEW MINUTES BEFORE DOCTOR MITCHELL'S slated to arrive, I check to see that no one is looking and sneak the envelope of cash inside of a small, white pastry bag. I toss in a wrapped chocolate chip cookie, then prep his drink and spray a swirl of whip on top, sealing the lid.

As his shiny silver Mercedes pulls into the drive-thru lane, a bitter taste settles onto my tongue. I adjust my headset and take my place behind the screen, waiting for him to approach the speaker.

For the first time today, I'm nervous. Before, we had only *spoken* about proceeding with the Novemion treatment, but once I hand off this money, a transaction has officially been made. I'll be in over my head with pharmaceutical companies and committed to something highly illegal. There will be no turning back from that.

What if Doctor Mitchell decides to extort me and change the cost of the first treatment? What if he keeps the money for himself? All of this is off the books. He could probably do whatever he wanted and get away with it. *Worse yet, what if someone notices I've made the order already and demands to look inside? What would they do if they caught me handing an envelope of cash to some man in the drive-thru?* They might ask questions, and the entire venture could go south as fast as it started, leaving Mom with no chance of survival.

The speaker crackles to life, and I clear my throat. Using my best customer service voice, I slip into barista mode.

"Welcome to Renee's, home of the Triple Threat Chocolate Mocha. How can I help you today?"

Doctor Mitchell sounds nervous as well. His usual professional facade slips as I watch him over the monitor. He loosens his tie and leans out of his window, then says, "Could I get a grande iced coffee with two pumps of butterscotch, please?"

I look down at the cup by my register. It's a venti, so that's a slight change of plan. I should have thought of that before.

"I'm sorry, sir," I respond. "We're out of grande cups at this time. Could I get you a venti instead?"

He blinks rapidly at the screen. "Yes, that will be fine."

"Alright, one venti iced coffee with two pumps of butterscotch. Can I get you anything else?"

"A cookie, if you have one?"

"Sure thing. Your total will come to $7.65. Please pull around to the window, and I'll have that right out."

Christa, busy shutting down the bakery, uses her headset to speak only to me as I go through the motions of packing a fake bag.

"We have plenty of grande cups," she says. It's more of a question than a statement.

I press the headset-to-headset button and reply, "True, but did you see the car this man is driving?" Christa glances up at the screen, then over to me with a confused look. "That's a Benz. He can afford it. What's Dan always saying?"

"Upsell, upsell, upsell," she mimics and rolls her eyes. She returns to the bakery with a chuckle. "Nice."

I blow out a sigh of relief as I realize I've gotten away with my lie.

Doctor Mitchell pulls around to the window. I lean against the circular lever, throwing the panes open.

"That's one venti iced coffee with two pumps of butterscotch and a cookie, correct?"

"Yes, that's right."

"$7.65, please."

He passes his bank card through the window and I run it through the machine. All the while, he fidgets nervously behind the wheel. When the receipt prints, I staple it to the bag and pass his order out to him.

"Don't open it now," I whisper. He nods and sets it down on the seat beside him. "There's five thousand in there. That's enough, right?"

"Yes, that's what we discussed."

"When will you start the treatment?"

"Tomorrow night."

Christa turns to look at us, so I speak a little louder. "Thanks so much for choosing Renee's. Have a wonderful night!"

"You too," Doctor Mitchell answers, then rolls up his window and takes off. I step away from the lever and lean up against the glass.

"Think he's the last one?" Christa asks, reaching for the mop.

"God, I hope so," I answer.

She makes a face that says, 'Me too,' then splashes the soapy water on the floor.

I spend the last few minutes of my shift tidying and restocking my station. Before I know it, it's eight o'clock, and I'm running to meet Connor outside.

CHAPTER TWELVE

With much of the afternoon traffic gone, Connor managed to find a half-decent space not far from Renee's. As I approach from the rear, I realize he's brought Ally along with him. She's leaning against the driver's side rear window. Her pixie-cut brown hair and round face are illuminated by the blue light of her phone. When I reach the front and tug on the handle, she looks up and greets me with an enthusiastic smile.

"Kara!" She practically yells as I take my seat. "God, I've missed you. Where have you been? It's been forever!"

I lean into the back and pull my friend into a tight embrace. "Around. I was over sometime last week and stayed last night, but Connor said you were out with Rob."

Ally pulls away and smacks her brother on the arm. Her wide-set, dark blue eyes crinkle with annoyance. "You didn't tell me Kara came over. I would have come home after dinner if I'd known!"

"See what you miss when you're out doing unspeakable things with your boyfriend?" he jests.

Ally frowns. "Yeah, because going to his parent's 30th-anniversary dinner is so atrocious. I should be burned at the stake."

Connor merges and follows the car in front of him around the bend.

"I'm sorry I haven't been around more often," I say, buckling myself into my seat. "Between work and Mom's treatments, I've been swamped."

Ally tucks her phone into her pocket and resumes her previous position. She leans her head against the glass and stretches her legs out across the seats. "It's okay. I know you're not ghosting us on purpose. How's Val?"

Connor reaches over and takes my hand in his. He flashes his sister a stern look through the rearview mirror. It's plainly a warning. They must have talked about some of the things that happened last night. Not that I hadn't expected them to. The shattered mirror would have been a pretty decent conversation starter. I'm sure she wanted to know how it happened. Hopefully, Connor left out most of the details. I don't want to share any stories tonight.

I hadn't known Ally would be coming with him to pick me up, but I don't mind. I've missed her, too. She's always so peppy, something I can't claim about myself. She rolls her eyes at her brother. They trail down to where our hands rest, joined together on the center console, imperceptibly widening.

"Oh, it seems like I may have missed *a lot*."

Connor squeezes my hand lightly before returning his to the wheel and taking the steep corner that leads up the hill.

We haven't talked about what last night means for the two of us going forward, so I quickly change the subject back to Mom. I figure we should work out the details before sharing them with the world. It seems Connor has a similar plan because he says nothing as he continues to drive. Ally obviously notices my avoidance, but she lets it slide.

"Things are rocky right now. The surgery didn't go as well as planned." I catch her up on most of the current situation, leaving the Novemion treatment out. She doesn't need to know. It would only put her in danger, too.

"Man, I'm sorry. What are you going to do now?"

"Another day, another treatment," I reply, keeping my eyes on the passing road. Imagine Dragons plays quietly in the background.

By the time Connor pulls into the parking lot of my apartment complex, Ally is relatively caught up on the Edwards family goings on. I shared a condensed version of what happened at Jennifer's and told her about selling my car. Those things earned me a series of shocked gasps from Ally and multiple declarations of disgust about my sister's current state.

Connor finds a space several rows back, throws his car into park, and we climb out into the dimly lit lot. I shove my key into the sticky building lock, jiggling it several times before the door swings free. The three of us climb up the stairs to my place, exchanging stories about each of our days, Connor in front and Ally trailing in the rear.

"I don't know how you do it," Ally muses. "How do you find enough time in the day to work and take care of Val? I can't believe Jennifer still won't help. So lame."

I can't tell her I spend most of my days so stressed and angry that I have massive panic attacks and take out my rage on unsuspecting furniture. It might scare her. Besides, it doesn't help much. I don't recommend that approach at all.

"I do it because I have to," I answer. "It doesn't leave much time for anything else, but that's alright. I get by. Most of the time. It's not really a choice."

"I couldn't do it," she replies. "If Jennifer was my sister, I probably would have strangled her by now."

"The thought has crossed my mind."

"Well, if I'm reading the room right, you might have a new sister, anyway." I turn to look at her, but she blinks up at me innocently from the stair below. "I'm much more suited to the role, and since it seems you and my brother have some explaining to do –"

"Ally!" Connor chastises. "Mind your business for once."

"Not a chance."

"Come on," he admonishes.

"You two have been in love with each other since what, the fifth grade? Earlier than that? Everybody knows."

I don't say anything, preferring to leave the siblings to bicker as we continue our ascent.

When the silence starts to feel awkward, I add, "Doctor Mitchell called. Mom's visitor restriction is being lifted in the morning, so I can go see her again tomorrow. Do you guys want to come?"

"Oh, please?" Ally pleads. "I love your mom."

"I'm sure she'd be happy to see you."

"I'd like to go, too," Connor adds. His expression is unreadable. I'm not sure why.

"Okay, it's settled then. We can be there as early as nine."

"It's a date," Ally pipes in. "Well, sort of." She laughs, and I can't help but smile.

I nearly run into him before I realize Connor has stopped dead in his tracks at the seventh-floor landing. His head is turned toward my apartment.

"What's going on?" Ally asks, stretching up on her toes to see around us.

The color drains from my face as I slowly approach my door. A bright pink notice has been taped to the frame, and a lock box covers the handle. My belongings are strewn through the hall in black garbage bags.

"Shit," Connor whispers. I'm frozen in place, so he grabs the notice and opens it up, reading.

Bayview Terrace Apartment Building
2311 N. Exeter Street, Baltimore, Maryland 21202
(410) 555-8246

Ms. Valerie Lynn Edwards and Ms. Kara Rose Edwards:

This notice is to inform you that as of today, you are hereby required to vacate the premises at **Apt 701 of the Bayview Terrace Apartment Building** at **2311 N. Exeter Street, Baltimore, Maryland**. In accordance with the rental agreement signed by both residential parties, this eviction notice follows multiple warnings of lease violations regarding the following matters:

- **Late payment of agreed-upon monthly rent of $927.45 for more than three consecutive months**

At the time of this notice, the tenants on this lease owe the following amount to the Smith-Phillips Property Corporation:

- **One complete month's rent of $927.45**
- **One partial month's rent of $273.67**
- **Three month's late fees of $75.00, totaling $225.00 in fees**

The total amount owed to the Smith-Phillips Property Corporation is $1,426.12

As pursuant to the rental agreement, the belongings of evicted tenants have been removed from the residence and placed in common areas of the apartment building. Evicted tenants have a term of **48 hours** to remove all personal property from the premises or it will be discarded at the evicted tenants' expense. Any rent or damage fees that have not been paid in full at the time of eviction will be sent to a collection agency for processing after a term of **30 days**.

If you have any further questions, call management at **410-555-8246** for assistance.

Justina Mendoza, Property Manager
Bayview Terrace Apartment Building

"NO," ALLY WHISPERS AS SHE READS OVER HER brother's shoulder. I don't even bother to take the paper and look at it myself. I know what it says. The evidence is right in front of me.

Connor shifts uncomfortably, looking back and forth from the door to me and Ally. "Kay…"

Filled with rage, I snatch the eviction notice from him, crumple it up, and drop it over the railing. It tumbles down several stairs as I watch, fuming.

Ally searches my face for something before following the letter and scooping it up, stuffing it into her coat pocket. "You might need this later." Her voice is timid. She's trying not to upset me. "For legal reasons…"

Connor places his hand on my back and attempts to pull me toward him, but I resist.

"It's fine…" I grind out. "Everything is fine. I'll take care of it. They said they'd work with us because of Mom's situation, so I can call – "

"No, stop," Connor interrupts, turning me to face him. "You're not in this alone. You don't need this place. That studio is a health hazard at best, and they're willing to turn you out onto the street and go back on their word. Don't give them a second of your time. Ally and I will help you. It'll be okay."

"How is this going to be okay!" I explode. I hadn't meant to yell at Connor. It's not his fault I have no place to live. He doesn't flinch, just listens. "It's bullshit! It's all bullshit!"

"I know," he starts, but this time, I cut him off.

"They said they'd work with me. They said they understood the rent would be late and I'd have to make partial payments from time to time because Mom's sick. They promised!"

"They're a big business, Kara," Ally says, reaching out for my arm. I pull it away, too angry to be restrained. "They make promises they never intend to keep. People can be evil when money's involved."

"Yeah! Tell me about it!" I yell.

I kick the wall by what used to be my apartment door, leaving a small hole behind.

"They charge you as much as they can for a tiny apartment that might as well be a prison cell, and then when you need their stupid apartment the most, they rip it away. Heartless!"

I kick the wall again, widening the hole.

"Monsters!" I kick the wall once more.

I sink to the ground, unable to hold myself up any longer.

Connor joins me on the floor. Angry tears stream down my face. He tips my head onto his shoulder. Ally sits to my right, and the three of us say nothing for a time.

Ally is the first to speak. With a determined look on her

face, she says, "You're just going to have to come stay with us for a while."

"I second that motion," Connor adds.

Ally nods. "Then, it's decided."

"No, I couldn't. You guys don't need to be dragged into my crazy life."

When I wipe the tears from my eyes and look up at my friend, Ally's face is stern. "We've got an apartment. There's plenty of space. You can take the living room, or you can share with me or Connor. It doesn't matter. It'll be better for all of us, really. Plus, I'm not around as often as I used to be. I spend a lot of time with Rob and his parents. I won't take no for an answer."

"Seriously?" I ask, letting myself feel an inkling of hope. "I don't want to make things hard for you guys, too."

"Seriously," Ally echoes.

"Yeah, stop arguing," Connor adds. "It's a done deal."

He stands, helps his sister to her feet, and reaches back down for me. Shakily, I grab his hands and allow him to pull me up, then dust off my pants.

When I'm on my feet, Connor grabs two of the garbage bags sitting on the landing, slinging one over each shoulder. Ally does the same. He turns to walk down the stairs, leaving me staring after him, Ally trailing behind.

Halfway down the first flight, he yells over his shoulder, "You better get a move on, Kay. We said you could move in, but we didn't say we would be your personal moving service! Let's get going!"

I shake my head in disbelief before turning to grab two more bags, tossing them over my shoulders, and following my best friends.

Once we're settled into Connor's car, I whisper, "Thank you." I'm so embarrassed and grateful at the same time.

"You don't have to thank us. You're family," Connor tells me.

"Absolutely," Ally answers.

"I love you guys."

"We love you, too," she says, hugging me from behind the seat.

"Don't tell Mom."

CHAPTER THIRTEEN

The maintenance workers who had thrown the meager collection of our things into industrial trash bags hadn't bothered to care about the condition they would be in when I returned for them. Luckily, there wasn't much to pack. They must have discarded what was left of our food and hygiene items, and management kept the furniture for themselves, but that doesn't break my heart. Most of it wasn't worth keeping.

Sitting in the middle of Connor's bedroom floor, I dig through the bags to assess the damage. The majority of them are stuffed with clothes, pillows, blankets, and sheets. These are easy enough to fold and stow away. The bedding finds a home beneath Connor's bed, and my folded clothes fit well enough into a few old milk crates. Once tidied, I return Mom's things to one of the thick bags and place it in the bottom of Ally's closet for safekeeping.

We don't have anything of value left since I've already pawned everything I could. There are only a few sentimental things I care about mixed in with the rest, items that can't be replaced. Thankfully, my quilt survived the shoddy packing, and so did my baby book, but one thing did not. When I pull it from the bottom of the bag, my heart sinks.

The old picture frame is broken in three places. Inside is

the only family photo we had ever taken. Mom is seated on a painted white stool, and Richard stands behind her, one hand resting on her shoulder. Jennifer stands in front of him with Richard's other hand on her shoulder, and I, no more than two years old, sit on my mother's lap.

The thick glass above the picture must have struck the corner of something because it's cracked. Sharp pieces of glass streak diagonally across the frame. The worst of the damage centers over Mom's face, and the effect is gruesome. The broken edges carve deep lines under her eyes and across her mouth, giving her a ghoulish expression. I had hoped the damage wouldn't run deeper than the frame, but those hopes are dashed when I shake the glass into the garbage. The picture has been destroyed. It will never be whole again, much like our family.

I turn the image over in my hands, numbness and disbelief setting in. On the back in Mom's neat handwriting are the words "Before the Ruin." Beside them is a rough sketch of the strange symbol from my nightmare. I run my finger lightly along the lines.

When I was younger, I had often taken the picture down from the shelf and imagined the family we might have had if Richard had stayed, but I had never taken the picture out of the frame, so Mom's caption catches me by surprise. *What an odd thing to write,* I muse. Then again, when Richard left, it had ruined our family, so I suppose it fits well enough.

I FELL ASLEEP IN THE COMFORT AND SAFETY OF Connor's arms, but the image of Mom's face, contorted and gashed, crept its way into my dreams. I found myself back in the deserted hospital, searching desperately for her at first, then discovering the monster she had become, and trying frantically to escape. She had nearly overtaken me when the soft chime of my phone ripped me from the haunting dream.

"Hello?" I answer without looking at the number on the screen.

"Ms. Edwards, this is Doctor Mitchell calling. I wanted to let you know Valerie's visitation restriction has officially been rescinded. You're free to visit her whenever you wish. We've also moved her to a private room since she's recovering well and needs less frequent monitoring. You'll find her in 602."

"Thanks. I'll be there this morning with a couple of family friends."

"That should be fine. Make sure you each follow proper handwashing procedures. Valerie is doing well, but until her incisions are fully healed, she's still more susceptible to infection."

"I understand. Thank you for the update," I answer with a yawn.

"Of course. The *forms* have also been managed. There was a slight delay. I'll *fax them over* tomorrow morning."

"You're sure?" I ask, suddenly alert at the mention of Novemion.

"I am. I've gathered all of the necessary *documentation*, and if the insurance company *approves further treatments*, I'll be in touch with more details. Plan on stopping by next week to look over our treatment plans."

Translation: If Mom tolerates the medication, he'll reach out to his contact and acquire more. Still, he wants the second payment by next week? I'll have to figure something out fast. This is moving quicker than I had planned.

"Of course. Thanks again."

We end the call with the usual pleasantries, then I flop back onto Connor's bed.

"Everything okay with Valerie?" he asks me, half-asleep.

I nod my head before realizing Connor's eyes are still closed. "I think so," I offer. "We're cleared to stop by this morning."

"Okay." He stretches and rolls to face me. "Do we have to get up right now?"

I check the clock on my phone. It's only 7:29. "Not yet."

"Then, I have other ideas..." he whispers, nuzzling into my neck.

I melt into his arms and let the lingering fear from my nightmare fade away.

CHAPTER FOURTEEN

What should have been a short drive takes nearly twenty-five minutes. As we cruise through the congested streets, Baltimore comes alive around us. The smell of breakfast foods fills the air as we pass restaurants. Men and women in classy business attire, many on their phones, walk down the sidewalks alongside tourists and joggers. Panhandlers accost those who are willing to stop and listen to their pleas. People file in and out of the Metro stations, and the musicians playing for change are busy with their lively tunes.

These are the sights and sounds of home. This city may not be perfect, but it's alive.

For most of the drive, Connor holds my hand in his. His thumb absently strokes the back as he nods along to the beat of today's music selection. Ally notices the intimate gesture and makes kissy faces at Connor and me from the backseat. He dutifully ignores his little sister, but I, ever the mature adult, thrust my middle finger in her direction. This elicits a smirk as we turn into the structure and Connor parks in a space at the base of the ramp leading up to the top floor.

"By the looks of things, it seems like you've got that covered," Ally retorts.

I can't help but laugh. The time I spent with Connor this morning has certainly lightened my mood.

As we step out of the car, a gust of icy wind slams into me. The frigid air whistles through the ramp, echoing off the concrete walls below. Last night's snow left drifts against the parked cars and barriers. I zip my jacket to fend off the chill and tug the hat I borrowed from Ally over my ears.

Though the three of us attempt to dodge the deeper piles as we climb the ramp, my worn shoes are no match for the wintry mess. My feet are quickly soaked. Instinctively, I loop my purse across my chest and tuck my hands into my pockets, sealing in whatever warmth I can.

With each step we take toward the hospital doors, my anxiety increases. I hate this place. For the last two years, it's brought Mom and me nothing but misery. My thumb reflexively reaches for my finger, ready to twist her wedding ring for comfort as I've done so many times before. I stop abruptly as it brushes up against bare skin.

Mom's ring isn't there.

"Oh, no!" I exclaim, flipping my pockets inside out. Connor and Ally turn to look at me, concern on their faces. "Mom's ring... I don't know where it is." I hold up my bare hand as proof of its absence.

"Did you have it in the car?" Ally asks, walking back to me.

"Yeah, I think so. Connor, was I wearing it?"

"Uh-huh. I felt it while I was driving."

"I thought I saw it when you flipped me off..."

"Shit, where did it go?" I kick the snow at my feet, hoping to find the ring nestled underneath.

"Did you put it in your purse or something?" Ally asks. She searches the fresh shoe prints along our path in case I dropped it along the way.

"I don't think so..."

"Check and see."

Quickly, I snatch the remaining cash out of my purse and stuff it into my coat pocket, then empty the contents onto the ramp. Panic seizes me as I dig through the odds and ends, coming up empty-handed. Tampons, receipts, cough drops, and chapstick litter the ground, but there's no sign of the ring.

First the picture, now this? Mom's wedding ring is the only thing of hers and Richard's I've managed to keep. I can't replace this. I have to find it.

"I don't see it," I announce as I stuff the soggy pile back into my purse and drop the money on top. Frustrated, I zip it closed, ensuring I won't lose anything else. "It has to be here somewhere."

"We'll find it." Connor helps me up and digs through his pocket. He pulls out his keys and tosses them to me. "Here, go back to the car and look. Maybe it slipped off of your hand and fell under the seat. We'll search the ramp."

I bolt back to the car and unlock it, throwing the door open. I drop to the snowy ground on my knees. Agitated, I swipe my hand under the passenger's side. I pull out everything I find: two empty water bottles, a handful of trash, and a crumpled fast food bag. It's not there, so I dig my finger into the creases of the seat. Nothing. I check the cup holders and door pockets, shake out the floor mats, and dig through the driver's side and back, too. No ring.

"Ugh!" I yell, abandoning Ally's hat and digging my hands into my hair. My fingers snag on a tangle, and I tug them out with more force than I intend to, ripping several strands free. "I can't believe this."

My eyes well up with tears as I dust the snow off of my saturated jeans.

I search the area around the car carefully, running my foot

across the top of the snow. My inspection turns up no sign of the gold band, so I hang my head in defeat.

"Excuse me, miss," a stranger's voice calls out from behind me. "Are you alright? You look pretty upset."

Caught off guard, I turn to find the tentative face of a young man, no more than thirty, considering me. Flakes of snow cling to his dark blonde hair, and his brown eyes are creased with uncertainty. A clean-shaven face accentuates his angular chin. The navy blue wool coat he wears is secured from his throat to his waist. Shining gold buttons gleam in the morning light, and a crisp white dress shirt peeks out from the top. He towers over me, a head taller than my five feet, five inches.

Doing my best to hide the traces of my approaching meltdown, I force a smile onto my face. "I'm fine. I've lost something important, and I'm trying to find it."

"I thought that might be the case. Your friends appear to be on a serious treasure hunt over there. Mind if I help you look?" His expression and his tone are kind.

A quick glimpse of Connor and Ally tells me the two have given up searching with their booted feet and are now on the ground, sifting through the snow with their hands. A mirthless laugh escapes me before I can stop it. "It couldn't hurt, I guess. I'm looking for a gold wedding ring, but with my luck..." I trail off.

"Consider me a professional," he says with a smile. "I lose things all the time. I've become quite skilled with the hunt."

I glance back up the ramp one more time. Connor and Ally have risen to their feet and are waiting for me. Their search must've been fruitless, too. Connor bounces up and down on his feet, rubbing his hands together and blowing on them. Ally, hands stuffed into her coat pockets, paces in circles as she continues to stare down at the ramp.

"I've checked everywhere around the car. Help me search on the way back to my friends?"

"Solid plan," the stranger answers. "I'll check the right side of the ramp. You check the left?"

"Yeah, thanks."

"Try using the flashlight on your phone. Since it's metal, maybe the light will reflect off of it," he suggests.

I nod, pulling my phone out of my back pocket. In the light of day, the flashlight is dim, but the rims of the car spark as I run the beam over them, so maybe there's a chance this will work. We pick our way slowly up the ramp, scouring the trodden mounds of snow. I toe aside chunks of ice and check the tire tracks where previous cars have driven.

Almost back to Connor and Ally, the kind stranger squats to poke around near the base of a car's rear tire. He passes the light from his phone over his hand and dusts snow off of something in his palm. Seconds later, he approaches me, face full of pride, and extends his hand. "Is this it, miss?"

My heart skips a beat at the sight of Mom's ring. I pluck it out of his open hand and slip it back on. The cold metal stings, but I don't care as long as the band is on my finger where it belongs. "No way! Thank you!"

"Of course. Glad I could be of assistance," he replies with a charming smile. "I couldn't help but notice the inscription inside the band: 'Val and Rich Edwards. Love is greater than destiny.' It's quite intriguing. Does that make you Val?" he asks, reaching out to shake my hand. His grip is firm.

"No, actually. Valerie is my mom. I'm Kara. Kara Edwards."

"Nice to meet you, Kara Edwards. I'm Matthew."

"Nice to meet you, too."

"By chance, and you can ignore this question if you'd prefer, is your mom *the* Valerie Edwards under Doctor

Mitchell's care? Forgive me. I'm being nosey, but I've heard her name before."

"She is," I reply, confused. "How do you know her?"

"I've worked with Doctor Mitchell from time to time. She was one of the patients we discussed. Let me back up. I'm Matthew Collins of Coarser Industries. I partner with Doctor Mitchell to promote pharmaceuticals for cancer patients."

Coarser Industries? Wait, don't they manufacture Novemion?

"Wow, small world," I say, hiding my surprise and tucking my hands back into my pockets. I take several steps toward my friends, and Matthew Collins follows, keeping pace with my strides.

"I wasn't aware Valerie had a daughter until now."

"Two, actually."

"Oh, Doctor Mitchell never said. I apologize." He appears genuine, but knowing his company is involved with Novemion still has me on edge. "Your mother, how is she doing? I'm afraid I couldn't be of any assistance when last I spoke with Doctor Mitchell. If I recall, her prognosis was… less than favorable."

"Well, she's still here, so…" I pause. "Her prognosis hasn't changed."

"I'm sorry to hear that." There's a hint of sadness in his words.

I don't like where this conversation is heading. If he works for Coarser Industries, he probably knows about Novemion, and if he knows about Novemion, I have to tread carefully. He seems kind enough, but I can't have him prying into my life.

"Aren't you a little young to be working for a big company like that? What are you, like 30?" I blurt, shifting the conversation onto him.

Matthew chuckles and gestures toward the building. "I'm young, but I've been working with Coarser Industries my whole life. My father, Elias Collins, is the CEO, and his father was the CEO before him. I guess you could say it's a family business. There's simply no escape from Coarser Industries."

"Ah, so you're a rich kid, huh?" I ask, jokingly. "I wish I had a few of your problems."

"My problems tend to be pretty… complicated. For example, I'm trying to convince the board of St. John's that our newest pain medication is worth the expense, and they don't seem to believe me."

I roll my eyes. "Is it though? Honestly?"

"I'd like to think so."

A bit of my pent-up irritation flares. "I'd like medicine to stop being so expensive. Guess we're at a standstill," I retort.

Matthew's taken aback. "Well, yes. I'd like that, too. Unfortunately, even though my father runs the company, I have very little say over financial matters."

"More than me."

He brushes this off. "My father is pushing me to get a contract with the new Chief of Medicine that would guarantee St. John's will purchase the majority of their medications from our company for the next three years, and I'm getting nowhere. I'm also trying to get a new treatment into human trials, and it keeps getting delayed. It's becoming very expensive. Novemion is so promising, but there are many hoops to jump through." He sighs. "As I said, my problems are a little complicated."

The color drains from my face at the mention of Novemion. This is bad. Not only does he know about the drug, but he's actively involved with it. I sway, suddenly dizzy, and Matthew steadies me.

Does he know about Doctor Mitchell's plans? Is that why he wants to talk about Mom?

"Are you okay?" he asks as I right myself.

"Sorry," I answer, recovering my balance. I scramble for an excuse to hide my shock. "Umm, there was ice. Be careful."

He glances at the ground and back to me, seemingly unconvinced, but his response is kind anyway. "Wow, I didn't see that. I'll let someone inside know they need to salt. Ramps and ice don't mix."

"Sure." I nod. "Are you supposed to tell me all of this? What if I worked for some kind of rival company and wanted to sink yours? Or, what if I wanted to steal your ideas? You're not a very secretive agent, Mr. Collins."

Matthew laughs. "You're probably right. If I told you any more, I'd have to kill you," he counters with a wink.

I laugh nervously and examine his smile before telling him, "I believe you."

As the two of us approach Ally and Connor, who are waiting under the overhang by the stairs, Connor eyes Matthew skeptically. "Did you find it?" he asks.

"Actually, yeah. Mr. Collins found it in the snow by one of the other cars. Weird." I show him the ring on my hand. "Oh, this is Mr. Collins. He works for a company called Coarser Industries. They manufacture medication."

Connor's eyes widen slightly when he hears which company Matthew works for. Luckily, Matthew doesn't seem to notice.

"Nice to meet you, Mr. Collins," Ally says as she reaches out a hand, oblivious.

Matthew graciously extends his own. "Likewise," he responds with a smile. "You can call me Matthew."

"Matthew then," Ally says. "It's lucky you were here to help!

"Yeah, lucky," Connor whispers under his breath. He reluctantly shakes Matthew's hand, too.

The four of us descend the stairs in awkward silence.

"Mr. Collins is the owner's son," I add as we reach the second-floor landing. "He knows about Mom, actually."

"Really, Matthew is fine," he insists. "Indeed. Valerie Edwards has become a bit of a famous case in this building, it seems." Matthew casts his eyes toward the building doors. Inside, an older man with graying hair waves impatiently to him. "Well, that's my cue. It was nice meeting you all."

"Thank you again, Mr. Collins," I reply.

"Call me Matthew," he yells over his shoulder. "Mr. Collins is my father. Hold on to that ring this time. I'm not sure we'd be able to find it again!"

I try to smile, but it doesn't reach my eyes. He seems not to notice as he steps through the door. For a moment, I think that's the end of things, but he turns back.

"Oh, Kara? Be careful with my secrets. You wouldn't want people to think you know too much," he says with a wink. "I'll let them know about the ice."

The door closes behind him with a swish, sending the familiar scent of disinfectant wafting toward us.

"Yeah, secrets," I whisper as the three of us follow Matthew inside.

CHAPTER FIFTEEN

Mom, much to my surprise, is upright and alert when the three of us enter the room. Her attention is on the television mounted in the corner, some real estate show. She spoons her least favorite flavor of Jello into her mouth and makes a face of disgust, then swallows it down. One of my favorite nurses, Trinity, busies herself typing Mom's vitals into her chart. Her waist-length box braids swish as she slides the rolling desk off to the side. Both of them look up at us and smile.

"Kara." Mom's expression fills with warmth as she reaches out for me. Her voice is airy, too light. The word comes out as a wheeze.

"Hey, Mommy. How are you feeling?" Careful not to disturb the wires running to the monitors, I sit beside her and hold her hand.

"Sore," she answers. "But I suppose that's normal after surgery. Other than that, I'm getting by just fine. Connor, Ally, how have you been? I haven't seen you in a while."

"Sorry, Valerie." Connor takes a seat in the maroon, hard plastic chair by the door. Ally settles onto the vinyl guest recliner. "I have midterms in a few weeks, so I've been spending a lot of time at the library."

"Good boy. What about you, hon? Settling into the new semester?"

Ally kicks her feet up and leans back. "Sure. Still trying to find my major."

"And, spending too much time with Rob," Connor tacks on.

Ally flashes him a deadly look. "There's nothing wrong with my boyfriend, Connor. Besides, like you've got room to talk. I —"

"Now, let's not argue," Mom interjects. Her gaze slides back to me. "Everything alright? You're pale. Have you been sleeping?" Ally softly chuckles, but Mom ignores her. "Eating?"

"As much as I can. Work has been hectic," I tell her. She gives me one of those concerned mom looks, brow furrowed and eyes slightly narrowed. "It's okay, though. Connor and Ally have been helping out."

I lean in and plant a kiss on her cheek. Beneath her bandana, what's left of her hair smells of fresh shampoo, honey and green apple. Trinity must have washed it this morning. It's the same shampoo Mom's used for years. The scent reminds me of safety during thunderstorms, softly covered eyes during the scary parts of movies, and rocking in the recliner before bed.

I pull away, willing myself not to cry.

"Good, good. Now, if you can convince Trinity to give me some real food, I'll be a very happy woman. I'm starving, and this Jello is practically rubber."

"Valerie Edwards," Trinity chides. "You know you can't have a big meal until later tonight. Doctor's orders. That Jello is perfectly fine. I swear you live to give me a hard time."

Mom's answering smile is as close to genuine as I've seen in months. "What else is there to live for?" she jokes.

"I'll take it as a sign of affection," Trinity answers. She

wraps the blood pressure cuff around Mom's arm and pumps the ball. The needle bounces as it drops. "Once we're sure the pain medication won't make you too nauseous, we'll get you a whole feast if you'd like." She removes the cuff and drops it into the wire basket at the bedside.

Mom waves her off. "After chemo and radiation, I have an iron stomach. A little oatmeal won't hurt."

"Doctor's orders," Trinity repeats.

"Fine."

Trinity shakes her head at Mom, then turns her attention to me. She gently squeezes my shoulder. "How are you, Kara? I missed seeing you around here the last few days."

"Doctor's orders," I repeat, dodging the question. Mom chuckles. "How've you been?"

"Oh, you know," she says, shutting her laptop and leaning on the cart. "Living the dream. I'm always good." She stands and wheels her computer to the door. "I'll give you guys some time. Valerie Edwards, you push that button if you need me. Understand?"

Mom nods and waves her away. "Yeah, yeah."

Trinity steps out into the hall and closes the door behind her.

"You're looking pretty good for a woman who just had surgery," Ally pipes up. "What's your secret?"

Mom chuckles again. "Stylish headscarves and medicated rest."

Ally playfully snaps her fingers. "I forgot to pick up some anesthesia at the pharmacy. I'll have to give it a try."

Mom shakes her head good-naturedly. I'm sure she's missed the banter. It must get lonely here when I'm not around. She squeezes my hand. "What's going on in the world outside?"

"Not much," I say, but Ally's words overlap mine.

"Big things!"

"Is that so?"

Connor shoots Ally a look, which she promptly ignores. A quizzical expression flashes across Mom's face.

"Don't mind her," Connor adds. "She's a fiend for gossip."

"Luckily, so am I." Mom watches him, one eyebrow raised.

I gently pull my hand away and reach into my pocket where I've stowed a little surprise.

"It's nothing," I tell her. "I brought you something." I pass the folded wad of fabric to her, and she opens it up. A pink and purple headscarf stretches between her hands. "Thought you might like a new one."

"Thank you, Kara." She blows me a kiss. "Can you put it on?"

"Sure, hold on."

I stand and reach for the bandana on her head, but Mom's eyes snag on my hands. The cuts have mostly healed by now, yet little pink ridges remain. I had hoped she wouldn't notice, but that was ridiculous. Mom has always been observant, especially when it comes to her kids.

"What happened here?"

"An accident." Guilt washes over me, bringing color to my cheeks.

"She lost a fight with a mirror a couple of days ago," Connor chimes in.

"Connor..." I warn.

"A mirror?"

"Really, I'm fine."

"Kara Rose Edwards, you tell me the truth, right now."

Her tone makes me feel like a small child. Reluctantly, I opt to share pieces of the truth, as I've done so often lately. "I was angry and I punched the mirror. It shattered. The glass cut my hands and arms, but Connor cleaned me up. It's fine now. I don't know why you worry so much."

"Because if I don't, who will? You don't take care of yourself."

"Please don't stress over me. You don't need that."

"You're my baby. I'll stress over you whenever I want," she replies.

"I'm looking out for her, Valerie. I promise," Connor reassures her. "Most of the cuts weren't that deep. I patched her up."

"How long ago?" Mom asks as she runs her finger over one of the marks.

"Two nights?" Connor says, thinking back.

"Two nights," Mom answers. An odd look settles on her face.

"I promise, Mrs. E. Connor is taking very, *very* good care of Kara. Isn't that right?" Ally emphasizes her words carefully. Insinuation drips from her tone.

Mom drops my arm, and I tie the new scarf around her head. Her eyes zip between Connor and me. "Is that so?"

"There's been a slight change in living arrangements," Connor says, trying to dodge the question. "I hope you don't mind, but Kara is moving in with Ally and me for a while so she can save up some money." He conveniently leaves out the eviction notice.

"And, everything is okay?" she asks, turning back to me.

"They're just helping me out. I have to let the apartment go for a while, but I can find us another one, a nicer one, later."

"Baby, I don't care about the apartment. I care about you. I've got a place to stay in here. It's not like they're going to let me go home anytime soon. They plan to keep me here until there's nothing left of me."

"Don't say that," I assert. "You're going to be fine."

Sadness floods into Mom's eyes.

Ally shifts and the vinyl chair squeaks beneath her. "So, who's gonna spill the rest of the beans?" she teases.

God, Ally is relentless. We're not getting out of this. I could smack her if she wasn't across the room.

"What else is going on?" Mom asks, turning her concerned stare back on Connor. "Kara keeps things from me because she's worried they'll upset *me*. It should be my job to protect her, but I'm trapped inside this rotten place, and she won't let me help her. You tell me *everything*, Connor. Don't make me get out of this bed."

She coughs, a heavy, wet sound emanating from her chest. The veins and tendons in her throat bulge. I pass her a tissue from the box on the bedside table, and Mom wipes her lips. When she hands me the tissue to drop into the trash, it's tinged with pink. Blood.

I cringe.

"Connor," she wheezes.

"I talked to Jennifer," I say. "She said she's gonna drop by soon."

"Uh huh," Mom says, eyeing me suspiciously. "And?"

"I'm taking care of Sir Meowverick for a while."

"Mmhmm, and?"

I blow out a breath. "I sold my car…"

"You did not! Kara…"

"It had to be done."

Mom drops her hands into her lap with a sigh.

Ever the tenacious one, Ally adds, "And?"

"Shut up!" I growl at her.

Mom stares at me, hard.

Connor looks to me for help, but I'm at a loss.

"You're such a brat," he snipes at his sister, then sighs. "Kara and I are seeing each other. I hope that's alright. That's what Ally wants you to know."

"Hey, you started it when you brought up Rob. Besides, if you didn't want Val to know you have a thing for her daughter, you probably should have stopped following Kara around like a puppy dog years ago!"

Mom smiles and gestures for Connor to come over. She pats him on the arm. "It's about time. I was hoping you two would figure each other out before..." Her voice drops off.

An awkward silence fills the room.

After a moment, I fill the void. "I talked with Doctor Mitchell, Mom," I announce, trying to sound confident. "He thinks the surgeons got most of the tumor. He wants to start you on another treatment. He's sure it will make a difference. I handled the paperwork the other day. You'll start tonight."

"Another treatment? I thought this surgery was the last one."

"Well, he found another."

"Kara..."

"He found another," I assert.

"Maybe it's time —"

"No!" This time I'm practically yelling. Mom studies me. "No. Don't say that. I'm not giving up on you. You know I won't."

She sighs and picks up her spoon, scooping the rest of the Jello into her mouth. I toss the plastic container into the trash.

No one says anything for a time. The sounds of the tv drone on, filling the void.

"Connor," Mom says, breaking the silence. "Can I speak with you, alone?"

I look at Mom, confused and hurt. She avoids my gaze.

Connor moves his eyes nervously between Mom and me. "Sure, Valerie. Whatever you need."

"Why don't you girls wait outside for a minute," Mom replies

Is she kicking me out? Unsure of what to do, I look to Ally who stands and moves toward the door. She gestures for me to follow.

It pains me to leave, but I do. I plant a quick kiss on the top of Mom's head, then step outside.

Connor throws me a look that says, "I'm sorry" through the rectangular window as the door clicks shut behind me.

CHAPTER SIXTEEN

"I can't believe she sent us out to the hall like children," I complain. "What could she possibly have to discuss with Connor that she can't talk about with me?"

Ally plops into one of the thinly padded chairs across from the door and pulls her feet up. "You don't talk to her about everything."

"Almost everything," I retort. "Do you tell your parents every detail of your life?"

"Hell no, but I also don't get mad when they keep secrets. That's their business."

My feet pound on the tile as I pace back and forth in front of the door. I'm angry, but not with Ally. I'm so sick of all of it, the secrets I have to keep, and apparently, the secrets being kept from me.

"How am I supposed to take care of her if she shuts me out?" I complain. "If I don't know what's going on, I can't make the right decisions, can I?"

"Maybe this has nothing to do with you taking care of her."

"What's that supposed to mean?"

"My guess is that she's worried about you."

"That's ridiculous." I stubbornly protest. "There's nothing to worry about."

"Uh, hello? Have you seen our bathroom?" Ally gestures widely at the open hall as though the room in question is right in front of us. "You KO'd the mirror because you couldn't deal. That's healthy?"

"That was an accident."

"Uh-huh. Have you seen your arms?"

My eyes drop to the raised pink ridges on my otherwise pale skin. "They're healing."

"Not the point," Ally says, rolling her eyes. "Kara, sit down, please? You're making me dizzy."

Glaring at her, I drop into the adjacent seat. My head bounces off of the thick plastic trim, sending a dull pain through my skull. I wince.

"Look, we all know things have been hard for you guys. She probably just wants to make sure you were being honest with her and give Connor the talk."

"The talk?"

"Yeah, the 'hurt-her-and-I'll-kill-you' conversation."

Now, it's my turn to roll my eyes. "As if Mom could hurt a fly. She's harmless."

"Still not the point…" she answers.

Frustrated, I throw my hands into the air. "Then, what is? What are you trying to say?"

Ally scoffs. "That she loves you and she wants you to be okay."

"Whatever." I lean my head back against the wall and shut my eyes.

Next to me, Ally flips through videos on TikTok. "Maybe she sent you out here because she knew if you stayed, you would act like a child. Exhibit A."

I hate that she's right. This behavior is absurd. It's nothing more than a temper tantrum. I need to rein it in.

No matter how hard I strain to listen, I can't make out their voices through the closed door. The sounds of the hospital, squeaky wheels on med carts, beeping machines, and the chatter of other people moving through the hall, drown them out.

I'm too agitated. My body won't stay still. My eyes fly open and I bounce my knees, which earns me an annoyed look from Ally. Before I realize it, I'm on my feet again.

The real problem isn't that she's talking to Connor without my being in the room. I realize that now. It's that I don't like the way Mom reacted when I mentioned the new treatment. Why wouldn't she want to try something new if the doctor recommended it? The alternative is to waste away on that bed until her cancer kills her. Obviously, I can't tell her what the new treatment is. If I could, maybe she would understand, be more enthusiastic. The look on her face screamed defeat. She can't give up now, not when I'm fighting so hard to see this through.

What about Connor? Why would she want to talk to him? Is Ally right? Is this some sort of motherly thing? I've never brought a boy home before, and I guess this is as close to home as Mom is going to be for a while. Is she really talking to him about being a decent boyfriend? That seems unlikely to me since we've both known Connor for so long.

So, what is it then? They've been talking for a long time. Or have they? I'm too frazzled. It's messing with my perception of time.

What if Mom is asking Connor to convince me to stop the treatments? No, she wouldn't do that. That's ridiculous. Right?

I keep pacing, leaving a trail of scuff marks on the otherwise pristine floor.

"Hon, what's wrong?" Trinity asks, stopping me in my tracks. I hadn't noticed when she emerged from the room next door, med cart at her heels. "Where did that cute little friend of yours get off to?"

"I've been banished to the hall. He's in there with Mom."

"Ah," she says. Trinity places a silver clipboard down on top of the cart and gives me a once-over. "Why is that a bad thing?"

"She's keeping secrets."

"People do that from time to time."

"Not Mom. Not from me."

Trinity smiles at me then, pity hidden just beneath the surface. "She's your parent, honey. I bet she has more secrets than you'll ever know."

Ally shoots me a look of 'I-told-you-so,' then returns to her phone. I do my best to ignore her sass.

"Are you and that boy together now?" Trinity asks. She takes a key from her flowered scrub pocket and opens the side of the cart. From the other pocket, she retrieves a bottle of pills and a pen. She scribbles a note onto the clipboard, then returns the bottle of pills to their place. Finished, she locks the cart back and stows away the key.

"Actually, I don't know what's going on. It's new," I tell her.

"They *so* are," Ally interjects. Her eyes are still glued to her phone, but her mischievous grin returns.

I scowl at her.

"Good. I like him. You're in here so much that it's like you're my own kid. I wondered if you'd find somebody. I'm glad you did."

My feet are tired, so I abandon my pacing and take my place once more in the chair. I wring my fingers and twist Mom's ring, then attack my unkempt nails.

Trinity watches me as I pick at my cuticles. "So, are you gonna tell me? What's got you tied up in knots?"

My hands drop to my lap. "She wasn't happy when I told her Doctor Mitchell wanted to start a new treatment."

Trinity sighs and leans up against the wall next to me. It seems like she wants to say something because she tucks one of her braids behind her ear. Her long locks spill onto one shoulder. The red-blonde ends cover her name tag. She toys with them for a moment before she speaks. "Look hon, I'm going to break the rules and tell you the truth. I know you don't want to hear this from me, but your mom has been in here for a long time. She's been through chemo, and radiation, and surgeries, and recoveries, and more tests than I can count."

"I know," I whisper.

"This isn't easy for her," she continues. "I know it hasn't been easy on you, either. So does your mom."

"Yeah, well. I never thought the word *'cancer'* would mean a vacation in the Bahamas." Sarcasm, my favorite defense mechanism, slips into my words. I reel it back. Trinity has been nothing but kind to Mom and me. I won't attack her. "I'm trying."

"We all know that. This kind of thing happens after patients go through so many rounds of treatment, especially if the results aren't what they need them to be. They start to weigh the costs and the benefits of what they're doing. They think about their quality of life, and the lives of their family and friends. Sometimes, they start making *plans*," She says the word 'plans' with a cautious emphasis.

"She's giving up."

"Maybe she is. This would be hard on anyone. It's not unreasonable of Valerie to want to spend what time she has left actually living her life instead of hooked up to machines and fighting the side effects of yet another treatment. You know that."

"She can't give up. I won't let her." Traitorous tears fall, darkening my jeans.

"You're young. You love your mother, and you want her to fight. That's not unreasonable of you, either. I see both sides."

Ally abandons her phone and wraps her arms around me.

"I need her to fight. She has to fight." It's like I'm begging the universe to understand. Not Trinity. Not Ally. Not Mom. My nails dig deep into my palms. Ally notices. She releases me from her hug and takes my hands into her own, loosening them.

"You know she'll fight for you if you ask her to. She already has. But, you should also know there will likely come a time when she doesn't want to fight anymore. When you both reach that point, when you both decide it's time to simply be together while you can, you'll need plans in place. Your mom probably wants to talk to your boy about that. She probably wants someone else she trusts to help you."

So many messy emotions swirl through me. Fury battles with grief and sorrow. I'm nothing but a helpless, lost little girl waiting for her mother to die.

"I'm not giving up, Trinity. I can't and I won't. She's my mother, and she can get through this." As the words fall from my lips, I can't tell if I'm trying to convince her or myself.

Trinity doesn't say a word. She stares down at me with her kind, sad eyes.

"You're wrong. This new treatment will work. I know it," I add.

"Maybe it will," she offers. "I hope to Goddess it does." Trinity reaches for a small copper charm dangling from her necklace. I've seen it before, but I never paid much attention to it. It's the same strange symbol from the back of the ruined picture and my nightmare, an angular 'M' with one side extending longer than the other. A small 'R' juts out from the top of the longer side. "Your Mom is a heck of a woman, Kara Edwards. If she passes, this world will not be the same. But, be prepared. Put something in place. It's the smart thing to do."

"It won't be necessary."

She shakes her head. "Alright."

Trinity pushes herself away from the wall and retreats to the med cart. As she's about to roll it away, a thought crosses my mind.

"Hey, Trinity?"

"Yeah?"

"Actually, I need help with something."

"Oh, what's that?"

I squash the wretched feelings and scrub my tears away with my sleeve. Regaining my composure, I sit up straight in the chair and plant my feet firmly on the floor. Ally lets go of my hands and returns to her phone.

"I need to make a different kind of plan and thought you might know a place to start. This is a little embarrassing, but I have to find a way to make money, fast. The new treatment I was talking about? The copay for it is pretty high."

"Insurance is the worst," Trinity groans. "Well, how much do you need?"

"Honestly?" I clasp my hands together. "I don't know. A lot. I'm still working, but you know how it goes."

"The money's always gone as soon as it comes in. I feel that."

"Absolutely. And, I've run out of things to pawn. I just sold my car. That was it."

"Well, I know of a place where you can make some money. It's not a get-rich-quick scheme by any means. Still, they pay pretty well. Have you ever considered donating plasma?"

"Like, the stuff in our blood?" Ally asks, suddenly curious. She drops her feet to the floor and leans forward, listening. "A couple of my friends do it for grocery money. A lot of college kids do, actually."

"Exactly. It's easy enough to do. There's a new place uptown that just opened, Plasmedics. The process is a little bit like donating blood, but they send the blood through a machine to separate it. They keep the plasma, and you get the rest back. It's called plasmapheresis."

"Why?" I ask, taken aback. "What do they use it for?"

"Oh, a lot of things. Plasma helps blood clot, so they give it to trauma victims. This company specializes in research and the development of new medications, though. They're at the forefront of the industry. Last I heard, they were looking for more donors and offering some decent incentives."

"How do you know about this place?" Ally asks.

"My community improvement group helped build it."

"Really?"

"Yeah. We volunteered on the weekends. One of our goals is to protect and restore the historic districts downtown, and the company plopped this modern structure right in the middle of one of the old neighborhoods. We helped out so the old buildings wouldn't be damaged by the construction."

"That's pretty cool," Ally chimes in.

Trinity smiles. "I think I might still have one of their business cards around here. Let me go look." She pushes the med cart to the closet, locks it up, and disappears down the hall.

"Some of these places pay good money. I don't know why I didn't think of it before," Ally states. "One of the frats has a rotating schedule for donations with a different center. They use it to raise money for their rent. It could be helpful. You gonna give it a try?"

I frown, looking down at my arms. "Do you think I should?"

"Why not? What've you got to lose?"

She's right again. *I thought annoying kid sisters were supposed to be naive. I guess Ally missed the memo.*

Trinity returns a few moments later with a glossy, white card. "Here you go. You know, if you donated plasma, you could help other people and help yourself."

I consider her words as I flip the business card over in my hands. I need the extra money. There's no way around it. And, I like the idea of helping other people. "How long does it take?"

"Longer the first time. Two hours maybe? It's shorter after that. There are screenings and intake questions for the first round."

"Do you know how much they pay?"

"One of the frat boys said he made $200 for his first donation," Ally offers.

"I think Plasmedics pays a little more. They're trying to draw people in since the company is so new."

"Two hours for $200?" I'm shocked. "That's more than I make in an entire eight-hour shift! How often can I go?"

"Usually, twice a week. You have to leave time for your blood to replenish before you siphon out more. Some go more often. It depends on what you can tolerate."

I glance through the rectangular window in the door. Mom holds Connor's hand in her own. His face is somber. She lets go, and he walks away, stepping out into the hall.

"What's this? Some super secret meeting?" he jests, testing my response.

"Thought you were busy having one of your own," I retort.

"*Okay*, sorry. Still mad."

"Apparently, we're all going to donate plasma so we can raise some money to help Val," Ally deflects, drawing the attention to herself. She plucks the business card out of my hand and flicks it at her brother.

Connor catches the card, though less than gracefully. "Plasmedics? Never heard of it."

"You don't have to go…" I start, but Ally cuts me off.

"We're all going, and we're all gonna put the money into a fund for Valerie's treatments." She shoots me a stern look. "You're gonna shut up and let us do it."

"No, seriously…" I try again, but this time I'm interrupted by Connor.

"Done. After I pick you up from work tonight, we'll swing by this place. No arguing. It's decided."

Ally flashes me a smug look. I turn to Trinity, but she holds her hands up in surrender.

"Hey, if I were you, I'd take all the help I could get. Sounds like you've got a good group here, hon."

Connor passes the card back to me. This is another fight I won't win.

"Fine, but if it sucks, you don't have to do it again. She's my mom, not yours, and you shouldn't have to pay for her medical stuff."

"She's basically my mom, too. I grew up with you," Ally says.

"Same," Connor adds.

"And besides, you're practically my sister, and you're my friend. What else do I have going on tonight, anyway? I can help. Maybe you'll stop sulking if we can raise a little cash."

"I'm not sulking!"

"You totally are."

"Ugh, you're the worst."

"I think you meant to say the *best*."

I want to be annoyed with Ally, but I can't. One look back at Connor washes away my frustration with him as well.

"Let me know how it goes," Trinity announces over her shoulder as she takes off down the hall. "Take care of our girl," she adds, pointing to Connor.

"Every chance I get," he replies.

He winks at me, and I blush, then he takes my hand. It's warm in mine, and his grip is steady. He pulls me into a tight embrace, and despite the stress and apprehension I feel, I dissolve into him.

"Come on," Connor says, gently peeling me away. "Let's go spend some time with Valerie. That's what we're here for, after all."

"Oh, so you two are done having secret conversations about me and my poor life choices?"

"Hey now, I'm one of those choices." He follows me inside.

"One of the best ones she's made," Mom says, smiling at the two of us. "I've been waiting for you two to get together for a long time."

CHAPTER SEVENTEEN

Connor's car smells of grease and salt as I shut the door behind me. I'm salivating before I can buckle my seatbelt. I didn't get a break during my shift, so lunch was a no-go. The music festival drew in more of a crowd than management expected. We were swamped and woefully understaffed. At one point, the line extended through the door and wrapped around the building. We had to shut down the drive-thru because there was no one to run it, so I've been on my feet, constantly moving since I clocked in. I haven't eaten since this morning before the hospital, and it's almost seven.

My stomach immediately growls, betraying how hungry I am. Ally laughs from the backseat and passes me an oil-spotted paper bag. I snatch it, a little too eagerly, and reach inside, ripping into the wrapped food. The tantalizing scent of pickles and onion teases me as I take an enormous bite.

"We brought you a burger and some fries," Connor states. A glint of humor flashes in his eyes. "Thought you might be hungry."

"Starving," I answer around my mouthful of burger. "Didn't have time to eat."

"One of the frat boys I told you about is in my class, the ones who donate plasma. I talked to him on my way out. He said you shouldn't go to the appointment hungry because you might pass out if you do. It's not the healthiest option, but a cheeseburger should work," Ally explains. "Protein and all that."

I nod and stuff a mouthful of fries into my face. It must be *glorious* watching me devour my food like a hungry bear, but I don't care. It's delicious. I lick the salt off my fingers and wipe them on my jeans.

"Slow down," Connor says with a chuckle. "I don't want you to choke. That kinda defeats the purpose, doesn't it?"

I narrow my eyes at him, but he leans over and plants a kiss on my cheek before he shifts the car into drive.

"Ugh, you two make me want to vomit hearts and rainbows," Ally complains, but I don't care. I'm too busy savoring the last few bites.

The roads are clear, so the drive to Plasmedics is smooth and uneventful. We pass Lexington Market and Edgar Allan Poe's grave, one of the places our school used to take us on trips. Connor turns deeper into a section of town crowded by apartment buildings that used to be factories during the Industrial Revolution. Some have been recently renovated and now house the well-endowed residents of this historic district. Some have seen better days. The centuries-old brick structures left untouched have crumbled in various places, and caution tape seals off the slim alleys that run between them.

Rounding the final bend, the modern structure of Plasmedics comes into view. Its sleek design of stainless steel, tinted glass, and white blocks is at odds with the space, a beacon of modernity amongst the remnants of Baltimore's history. Unlike some of the surrounding buildings, there are no bars over its lower windows or graffiti marring the pristine walls. Everything about it screams money and power.

Connor parks by the sidewalk as a set of automated

double doors open and close. A young black man exits the building and crosses the parking lot. Spotlights above the doors illuminate large red letters with thick black outlines that read "Plasmedics Biotechnology: Donation and Research Facility." A well-muscled security guard sitting on a stool in the atrium, newspaper spread out on his lap, watches as we climb out of the car. The light of the setting sun sparks off of the uppermost windows.

I hadn't been nervous before, but an unexpected sense of dread seizes me as soon as my feet touch the ground. It doesn't make any sense. I've donated blood before. Our school used to have an annual drive. It's not the prospect of the needle. That's never bothered me. So, why does Plasmedics give me such bad vibes?

Connor rounds the front of the car and takes my hand into his, interlacing our fingers and pressing his warm palm against mine. "Are you okay? You look a little pale."

"I'll be fine." My voice is airier than I'd like. "I must've stood up too quickly. I need a second," I lie. A glimpse of my reflection in the side mirror reveals the color has drained from my face. My legs threaten to give out beneath me. Though it's warmer today, I'm overtaken by a shiver.

I've had a long day at work. I must be tired, I tell myself. *That's it. I'm just tired.*

"Thanks for coming with me."

"We wouldn't let you go alone." He squeezes my hand. "You're not alone. Never. You know that, right?"

Ally steps up to join us. "Never," she echoes.

"Come on, let's go inside before I change my mind."

THE INTAKE PROCESS IS QUITE EFFICIENT. THE atrium guard checks our bags for illicit items, then sends us to the second room down the hall. An attendant seated behind a stainless steel desk with a black glass top swipes our IDs through a card scanner to generate a donor profile. Once that's finished, she directs us to a bank of computers on the far wall to complete our questionnaires.

The questions are pretty standard, much like those a doctor would ask before a visit: travel history, medications, sexual habits, recent tattoos, and drug use, among other things. I have nothing to hide, so I complete the survey in no time. As I press the button to submit my answers, the words "Approved For Donation" flash across the screen. Before I have time to stand, a nurse appears at my side and leads me back for a consult.

In the exam room, he asks me to confirm my birthday and allergies, takes my temperature and pulse, checks my blood pressure, and asks me a few basic questions about my health. Satisfied, the nurse retrieves a postcard-sized paper from his scrub pocket and affixes a label with my name and donor number at the top. He rattles off some information about blood samples for the donor file, so I let him prick my finger and squeeze a few drops into a circle on the page. I watch as it spreads to the edges and stops, bound by an invisible raised line. Then, the nurse escorts me back to the intake room where Connor and Ally are already seated amongst a row of white-padded chairs. He hands me a pen and a green clipboard with a stack of papers containing information on corporate policies and privacy notices and calls up the next donor. I take the empty spot next to Connor and wait.

I don't bother reading through the documents. It won't change anything, so I sign my name on the dotted line.

Another nurse calls Ally back first. She takes Ally's clipboard, looks through the documents, then passes them over to the desk attendant, who in turn stuffs the papers inside a beige file folder and adds them to a stack behind the desk. Connor is taken back next, leaving me alone in the intake room. I shuffle through a stack of magazines but find nothing of interest. It's not long before the same nurse who lead my consultation calls my name.

"Kara Edwards?"

"That's me." I drape my jacket over my arm and cross my purse over my chest before crossing the room. My hands tremble as I hand him the clipboard, dread returning.

"Okay. We're ready for you. Do you need to use the restroom before you go back?"

I shake my head.

"How about something to drink? Water? Juice?"

"No, thank you. I'm ready when you are," I respond, going through the motions.

The nurse flashes me a warm smile and checks my paperwork, then passes it to the attendant. He presses a hand to a large circular button that says "open," and leads me back.

"If you would please follow me, I'll take you to our lockers."

Without hesitation, he walks briskly down the hallway, passing several closed doors. I rush to follow him, tripping over my feet, but catch myself before he notices.

"You can leave whatever belongings you'd like in here," he instructs, leading me into an open space.

In the center of the large room, there are several more padded chairs and benches. Fifty or so half-sized lockers run along the length of the wall. Two large standing shelves of DVDs and Blu-rays are pressed up against the lockers on the left, while a large shelf of books stands against them on the right. A bin labeled "clean slippers" is perched next to the entrance. A bin labeled "used slippers" sits beside it.

"This locker area is secure, and you'll be able to take your key with you when you go back to your room. There's also a selection of movies and books you can choose from. Your donation station will be equipped with a portable player and reading light, so please feel free to borrow whatever catches your eye."

"Okay."

"We anticipate you'll be here for roughly ninety minutes throughout this donation process because today is your first time. In the future, you can expect the donations to take roughly an hour. We will also provide you with pillows and blankets as needed, so don't worry about leaving behind your outerwear. Do you have any questions?"

"No, not really…" I reply. "You were pretty thorough."

"You can choose whichever locker you like," the nurse begins again, "as long as there is a key in the lock. The lockers are free, so don't worry about needing change. These," he says, pointing toward the "clean slippers" bin, "are for your use. We prefer street shoes to be left in lockers for sanitary reasons. When you're finished with them at the end of your donation session today, you can simply leave them in the bin over there to be laundered."

"Got it."

"We ask that you leave all bags stowed away inside the lockers for security reasons. Cell phones are permitted, but please do not take any pictures inside the building. We need you to respect the confidentiality of our other donors, as I'm sure you would expect them to do for you." He has this speech perfectly memorized. Clearly, he's delivered it many times.

"Of course. I understand."

He smiles again. "I'm going to prepare your room. I will be right back, Ms. Edwards."

"You can call me Kara."

"Okay, Kara then. I'll be right back."

While the nurse is gone, I wander the length of the room in search of a locker. Several of them are missing keys, so there must be more donors here than I thought, though I hadn't seen many in the lobby.

After a moment, I settle on locker number 19, my favorite number, then fold up my coat and set it down inside. Tugging off my oversized hoodie, I wrap my purse in it. I shove these items all the way to the back. My shoes are a little wet, so I place them upside down on my coat. My thumb pushes through a weak spot in the fabric and leaves a tear. I'll need to buy a new pair soon.

Finished with my things, I close the locker and grab the key. It twists out easily enough, so I slip the little band around my wrist for safekeeping. I grab a pair of clean slippers from the bin and search the bookshelf for something to read. Just as I pick out a book, the nurse returns. The timing feels too perfect to be coincidental, so he must have been watching me. Logic dictates it's his job and it's perfectly normal, but regardless, it gives me the creeps.

"Are we all set, Kara?" the nurse asks.

"I think so," I answer, flashing him a nervous smile.

He misinterprets my reaction, assuming I'm worried about the donation, and seeks to reassure me as he leads me a few doors farther down the hall.

"Don't worry, it's not as bad as you probably think. It's a poke, a somewhat noisy machine, and some time to relax. You may feel some discomfort where the needle is inserted. Some patients experience dizziness or lightheadedness, but you'll be seated or lying down, so you shouldn't have to worry about a fall. There will likely be some bruising around the donation site. I'll check on you frequently, and you'll have a button to call for me, so please don't hesitate to reach out. Here we are..."

He stops in front of room 27 and taps his ID badge

against a card reader on the wall. The door unlocks with a heavy click as he pushes it open and steps inside. The lights turn on automatically, revealing a small room with a recliner, a thin hospital bed, and a cabinet pressed against the back wall. A white machine sits on top. He moves to the cabinet and retrieves a bundle of tubing, a sterile needle, and swabs.

"You can sit in the chair or lie down on the bed, whichever you'd like."

I choose the bed, climb up onto it, and stretch out on the starchy white sheet.

"Are you familiar with the donation process?" he asks as he begins to hook the tubing up to a machine.

"No, not really. A friend of mine suggested I make a donation here because I needed a little bit of money. How does it work?" I ask.

"Well, I'm going to insert a needle into your arm so we can retrieve some of your blood through your vein here." He points to the crook of my elbow. "The needle will be connected to this tubing," he says as he holds it up for me to examine, "and this tubing connects to this apheresis machine. This bag of fluid is an anticoagulant." He holds up a small pouch and attaches it to the machine. "It keeps your blood from clotting during the process. The machine will spin your blood around rapidly, separating the components. You'll be able to see them here." He points to several hanging bags. "This one will hold your plasma, and this one will catch platelets. Your red blood cells will be stored inside the machine. Once it's all separated, this machine will then mix some saline solution into your blood," he says, holding up another bag of clear liquid, "then reinsert the remaining particles back into your body. It may be a little cold, but it shouldn't be painful. Does that make sense?"

"I think so."

"Alright. Let's go ahead and get you started then."

THE WHIRRING SOUNDS OF THE APHERESIS machine lull me into an accidental sleep.

A memory from my childhood rises to the surface. Jennifer and I race through the crowded exhibits at the National Aquarium. Wondrous fish and oceanic creatures, some as big as me, peer back at me through the glass.

Richard scoops me up as I take a drink, tickling my sides. I laugh, accidentally shooting grape soda out of my nose. It burns and splashes Jennifer in the face. I think it's funny, but she decidedly does not.

Richard lifts me onto his shoulders so I can see over the crowd. A huge shark swims so close I can see its teeth, and I shriek.

Richard takes pictures of Jennifer and me next to a crab that's almost as large as I am.

Richard sings songs with us on the way home.

Richard's dresser is empty. His side of the closet is cleared out. His car is gone. I'm broken and alone.

The nurse comes back to check on me and accidentally startles me awake. Unwanted tears stream down my face, remnants of my dream. Before he notices, I hide my face beneath the blanket and use it to dry my cheeks.

Reality hurts. I count the minutes until this donation is over so I can go home.

CHAPTER EIGHTEEN

After my intense shift and our trip to Plasmedics last night, I passed out in Connor's arms as soon as we pulled the comforter over us. Every ounce of my energy had been drained out of me. I've slept so hard that I've barely moved an inch when my phone brings me back to consciousness with its piercing ring. Connor's soft snores mingle with the offending melody as I grope along the floor and find it, bringing it to my ear.

"Hello?" My voice is husky and my throat is dry.

"Hello! This is Nichole from Plasmedics Biotechnology. We thank you for your recent donation and would like to schedule you for another one as soon as possible. Do you have a moment to talk?" The woman's voice is annoyingly chipper for — I glance at the clock at the top of my screen — exactly eight am. Not one minute past.

"Sure, hold on."

Connor's arm is draped across my waist, so I carefully lift it off and settle it on the bed beside me. He grumbles in his sleep and slips his arm beneath the thick blue blanket, but doesn't open his eyes. Doing my best not to wake him, I pull the charging cord from my phone and tip-toe out of the room, heading for the bathroom. The overhead light is too bright, so I push open the window, letting the pink and yellow rays of the early morning sun illuminate the space. A chilly breeze follows the light. I hug my borrowed hoodie close, trapping whatever warmth remains. As quietly as possible, I take a seat on the closed toilet and speak again.

"Sorry about that. I needed a private place to talk."

"Oh, it's no problem at all," she practically sings. "We are very grateful for your generous plasma donation, and we're hoping you intend to see us again very soon. Just so you know, we have increased our rate for individuals with your blood type to $500 per donation. Does that sound like something that would interest you?"

The hand scrubbing the sleep out of my eyes drops to my lap. My mouth falls open in awe. I'm certain I must have misheard because there's no way that could be right. "Did you say $500? Per donation?"

"Yes, I absolutely did, Ms. Edwards. As I'm sure you're aware, healthy plasma, especially the kind we hope to study here, is in extremely short supply. So, we're more than happy to increase our payment for unique donors such as yourself."

"But, $500?" I blink rapidly, praying this isn't a dream.

"Yes, ma'am. That's correct. Would you be interested in pursuing another donation at this time?"

I'm speechless. $500 is twice the rate they paid me yesterday. It would take me almost a week to make that much at Renee's. A mixture of relief and gratitude overcomes me.

"Definitely," I answer, perhaps a bit too excitedly. "What do I need to do?"

"Well, let's go ahead and get you scheduled, okay? It's a simple process. We can do it right over the phone. For security purposes, could you repeat your name back to me?"

"Kara Edwards. K-a-r-a." I'm so used to others asking if my name starts with a 'C' or a 'K' that I don't wait to clarify.

"Thank you very much, Ms. Edwards. Can I also get your date of birth? Month and day will be just fine."

"May 16th."

"Perfect. I'm going to transfer you to Maria. She's our coordinator here. Maria left a note in your records that says she would like to speak with you personally. Is that okay?"

"Sure, that's fine."

"Alright, you have a wonderful morning, and thank you for donating with Plasmedics Biotechnology, where we strive to save the world through the kindness of others. Maria will be right on the line."

With a soft click, the woman's voice disappears, replaced by the smooth sounds of jazz. I yawn, fighting off the sleep that wants to draw me back in and lean back against the wall. It's not long before a new voice picks up the call.

"Ms. Edwards, are you still there?" Maria's voice is slightly lilted with a Spanish accent.

"Yes, I am." I lean forward again, fully alert.

"I hope you don't mind that I asked Nichole to transfer you over to me. I have a special interest in your case and was hoping to schedule several appointments with you instead of making one at a time. Would you be open to that?"

"I mean, if you think it would be best, I'm open to more donations." *How could I not be with pay like that on the line?*

"Excellent. You see, we require donors of your blood type at this time, and we want to make sure we're offering you opportunities to donate to our wonderful cause. Of course, we are also providing significant incentives for donations right now. Did Nichole share the increased rate for donors such as yourself?"

"She did. I believe she said it would be $500 per donation."

"Oh, heavens no. It's $500 to start. If you were to become a frequent supplier, there are additional incentives that will be added to your donation rate."

"What do you mean?" Unable to sit still, I rise and pace

back and forth through the small room. The tile is freezing against the soles of my bare feet. Though the overhead light is still too bright, I decide to go with the lesser of two evils and flip it on. When I pace back to the far wall, I shut the window, unable to handle the chill any longer.

"Let me pull up our incentive schedule for patients with type AB Negative." The clacking keys of Maria's keyboard punctuate the early morning silence. "Ah, yes. Here we go," she continues. She mumbles to herself for a moment, presumably scanning for the information she needs. "Our current offer is the standard rate for the first donation, which records indicate you made yesterday evening. That's already taken care of. Did you receive your pay?"

"Yes, before I left."

"Good. We are also offering an increased rate of $500 for the second donation, which you seem to already be aware of. It looks like there's an additional $200 bonus if you schedule two more donations within the next week."

My jaw hits the floor, and I stop in my tracks. My arm flings out to steady my balance, gripping the worn towel hanging from the wall. "$200 bonus?"

"Yes, ma'am. If you were to schedule two donations within the next seven days, you would receive $500 per donation and a $200 bonus on top of that for a total of $1,200. Is that something you would be interested in?"

I'm speechless. *$1,200 for a few drops of plasma and a couple hours of my time?* No matter how uncomfortable I had been when we walked into the Plasmedics building yesterday, there's no way I could turn this down. *But why so much? The rate seems insane...*

"Are you still there, Ms. Edwards?"

"I... I am, yes. Sorry. There must have been a problem with the connection. Why so much for my blood type? I'm not complaining, but that seems like a lot."

"Well, Ms. Edwards, AB negative is the rarest blood type in the world. Only one percent of the population can claim what you have. For patients who experience significant physical trauma, a donation of AB Negative plasma may mean the difference between life and death. There are also significant research opportunities associated with your blood type. So, it's important to our company to entice generous donors such as yourself to participate in our program. We find compensation is the most effective route."

"I understand," I tell her. *It's certainly an effective hook for me.* "Let's schedule the appointments and get started."

By the time I hang up the phone, my heart is beating out of my chest. I've scheduled two appointments for this week and two for the next. Pure excitement at the thought that I might actually be able to make enough money to afford Mom's treatments overcomes me. It pulses through my limbs as I stare down at the tiles in disbelief. An inkling of hope takes root again. I cling to it with dauntless conviction.

This time, things are going to be okay.

My phone dings in my hand.

Still riding the high from my conversation with Maria, I turn my cell over. Several notifications I hadn't noticed in my rush to answer the call from Plasmedics crowd the screen: eight missed calls and numerous texts.

Excitement gives way to confusion. I must have slept harder than I thought. I click through them and read.

The first text is from Doctor Mitchell.

> Ms. Edwards, I wanted to let you know insurance has authorized the first treatment, so I started Valerie on the infusion late last night. So far, she seems to be tolerating the new medication well. Should this continue to be the case, we will need to seek further authorization in one week. Please see me then to manage the necessary paperwork. I will keep you updated on your mother's condition.

One week? I'm thrilled to hear Mom is handling the treatment well. Still, some ignorant part of me was banking on having more time. I frown, doing the mental math.

I have $3,600 left after the first treatment and the plasma donation payouts that myself, Connor, and Ally chipped in last night. That, plus the $1,200 I'll make this week from my upcoming visits, will amount to $4,800. I'll still be $200 short for the next payment.

Where am I going to come up with the extra $200? I could ask Connor and Ally to donate, but is that fair to them? I pinch the bridge of my nose between my fingers and sigh. *My only option is to ask for an advance on my check… again.* I hope Steve answers the phone when I make the call. He's more likely to understand.

My head spins as I struggle to maintain my grip on the happiness that filled me so completely only a moment before.

Shoving my complicated thoughts aside, I send Doctor Mitchell a text to thank him for the update and assure him we will continue with the plan as long as he thinks it's safe.

The next text is from Plasmedics, thanking me for scheduling my upcoming appointments.

We at Plasmedics Biotechnology would like to thank you for sharing your plasma with those in need. If you need to reschedule or have any further questions, please give us a call at 410-555-7284 at your earliest convenience. We look forward to seeing you soon at Plasmedics Biotechnology, saving lives through the kindness of others.

With a swipe, I clear the message away.

Seeing the next notifications, I cringe. All the missed calls are from Jennifer, and so is the string of unanswered texts.

What the fuck? U were at my house? Seriously!

U called the cops? They took Marcus 2 jail!

I spent the night at the ER!

Ur such a worthless sister. Answer me!

Bitter fury has me moving my fingers across the screen before I stop to think.

So what if it was me? I probably saved ur life. What were u on, J?

I don't expect her to respond, but before I can lock the screen, three dots appear. Jennifer is typing away.

That's none of ur damn business. U stole from me!

If she wants to spout off angry messages, two can play this game. So, I answer her again.

Did I? I don't think so. I only stopped by 2 collect ur part of the payment for Mom's medical bills. U remember her, right? The mother u've left to die in the hospital? The 1 who has lung cancer?

I'll call the cops & turn u in!

4 what? What do u think I have?

What did u do?

Paid the bills

Screw u! I don't know what ur problem with me is, but I'm sick of it. We need 2 talk. Meet me @ the diner 2day @ 11. If u don't, I'm calling Mom & telling her what u did. I'm done with ur shit.

Aggressively, I push the button to lock my phone and cram it into the pocket of my sweatpants. After only one conversation with my sister, I want to hit something again.

Jennifer has the nerve to come after me? Yes, I broke into her apartment and stole pretty much anything of value I could get my hands on, but I don't care. I never claimed to be a good sister. Neither is she. Besides, it was the least she and her loser boyfriend could contribute to our dying mother.

I should have done more. I should have narced on her and her idiot boyfriend, sold them out to that dude that came to my apartment two months ago asking where they lived - some rival dealer. I should have shaken my sister awake and screamed in her face, or worse, punched her square in the jaw. But, I didn't. I called the paramedics and saved their asses.

I take a deep breath in and slowly let it out, bouncing up and down on my toes, working the outrage out of my system.

I shake my hands, trying not to punch the wall. I've done enough damage in this room. It takes a few moments, but I manage to calm down and pull myself together. I splash cold water on my face and neck, then dry my hands before leaving the room.

As I creep out of the bathroom and back into Connor's bed, he stirs, opening his eyes and flashing me a charming, sleepy grin. It doesn't last long when he notices my expression.

"What's going on, Kay?" he asks, worried.

I kiss him deeply, relaxing slightly at the touch of his soft yet firm lips. When I'm finished, I let my forehead relax onto his. He reaches up and plays with one of my long, brunette waves.

"It's Jennifer. I really need a ride."

CHAPTER NINETEEN

"Are you sure seeing Jennifer is a good idea?" Connor flicks his eyes to me and back to the road. When the light changes to green, he turns off the ramp and heads toward Reisterstown, passing the magnet school and several small businesses. His hands are tighter on the wheel than they need to be. Tension knots his shoulders.

"She didn't exactly give me a choice." My palms swipe across my jeans, dusting off the leftover powdered sugar from our gas station breakfast, a pack of stale donuts. "If I don't show up, she'll call Mom and tell her what happened. Mom doesn't need that. It would only upset her. I need her mind focused on healing, not on her delinquent daughters."

"I get that, but Jennifer pushes your buttons. She always has."

"She always will. What are sisters for?" The half-hearted sarcasm doesn't have the dismissive effect I intend it to.

"This is different, Kay." He drops his right hand to my knee and gently squeezes.

"I know. Honestly, I'll be fine. We'll talk, probably bicker, and I'll leave."

"What if she calls Valerie anyway?"

"Then she'll get what's coming to her."

"Kara…"

"I'm not perfect, Connor. I'm doing the best I can."

"No one is asking you to be perfect. That's impossible. I want you to be careful. Don't wind up involved in Jennifer's mess. This whole thing is so screwed up."

"I know what I did was wrong, but what's done is done. It was the best I could do at the time to get the money I needed to save Mom. If Jennifer wants to be petty and drag her into this, she'll see a different side of me. I'm not the meek little sister I used to be."

"But, is this what you need right now? You have so much going on with Valerie. Fighting with Jennifer — "

"What's happened has changed me. You know that. I will protect my mother and fight for her with everything I have, even if it means knocking my sister down a few pegs. I can handle her."

Connor falls silent as he turns into the lot and parks. I understand why he's worried. I do. Jennifer and I have never seen eye-to-eye, and it's gotten worse over the last couple of years.

"Look, I'll try to play nice, okay?" I say, leaning my head against his shoulder. He wraps an arm around me and drops his head on top of mine. "As long as she's civil, I'll be civil."

"Are you sure you don't want me to go in with you? I could mediate."

"No, I have to do this alone."

He kisses my hair and pulls away. As I move to unbuckle my seatbelt, he reaches out, stopping me.

"Hold on, I have something for you." Connor lifts himself off the seat and digs a small item out of his back pocket. It flashes in the morning light as he places it into my palm. The metal is warm from his body heat when he folds my fingers over it, a little silver key. "It's for the apartment. I thought this might make it official."

I smile at him before planting a firm kiss on his cheek.

"Roomies?" I ask, trying to diffuse his worries, but his face is serious.

"A reminder that you don't have to do everything alone." There's sadness beneath his words, curling around the edges. "I'm here. All you have to do is ask. I'll always be here."

My fingers press the red button, and with a click, my seat belt retracts. Leaning over the center console, I press my lips to his. The kiss is deep as I try to convey the words I don't have time to say: "I know. I love you. Thank you. Hero. Best friend." He kisses me back, sending secret messages of his own.

It takes tremendous willpower to break away. Tucking the key into my pocket, I climb out of the car. My fingers drag through my tangled waves and brush out the knots. I tug at the bottom of my jacket, straightening it.

"Don't be too long," he calls out. When I look behind me, he's cracked the window and is leaning across my seat. "I have to get you to Renee's before two."

I nod and cross the nearly empty lot, leaving Connor behind in the car.

The heavy gray door pulls open with a sucking "swoosh." Tiny bells nestled atop jingle as I step inside, announcing my arrival. The heady scents of scrambled eggs and burnt coffee greet me before the hostess does. She's busy wrapping silverware in napkins and sealing them with little green paper rings. She's no older than me, and her natural hair has been bleached at the ends, giving the impression of someone who has freshly arrived during a heavy snowstorm. It contrasts with her clear, dark complexion, large brown eyes, and the little golden clips she's added to hold back her hair where it's parted.

I wipe my feet on the welcome rug before approaching her to avoid making a mess. When she sees me, she flashes me her best customer service smile. I return the gesture with one of my own while she drops the new silverware into a basket beneath the podium.

"Welcome. My name's Maya. I'll be your hostess today. How many are we seating?" she asks buoyantly.

"Oh, uh... it's just me," I tell her. "I'm meeting my sister, Jennifer." I scan the large dining room and find her sitting in the far back corner. "She's over there."

"No worries, just go ahead and join her then," she replies. "Enjoy!"

"Thanks." I hesitate for a moment, watching Maya retrieve a dry-erase marker and update the specials board.

"Do you need anything else?" she asks, confused.

"No, sorry. I haven't been here in a long time. Just remembering."

Little about the diner has changed since I was here last. One of Richard's friends worked at Stevens University just up the road. We would come here for lunch and meet up with his buddy from time to time.

As I slowly cross the room to my sister, I slide my finger across the surface of one of the tables. In true diner fashion, they've always been sticky, no matter how often the staff cleaned them. They still are. There isn't a cleanser strong enough to combat years of children with free access to syrup and jelly packets. I should know.

Briefly, I remember my father ordering me a double-stack of sprinkle pancakes, cutting the shape of a heart out of the center, then handing me the syrup pitcher. He thought I would drizzle the sticky sap in lines like my sister always did, but instead, I decided to turn the pancakes into a sugary volcano, filling the hole all the way to the top. The syrup had oozed out of the sides until it dripped onto the table and formed a river that coursed all the way to the floor. I thought it was hilarious. The waitress did not. Richard tried to help her clean it up, but the patch of carpet where the syrup fell was a goner. It's still clumped together when I pass by.

Of course, Jennifer is seated as close to the corner as she can be. Her back is to the wall of clear glass blocks, there's a window to the right, and she's facing the door. She knows I'm here, but she doesn't look up when I slide into the green and maroon pleather booth. Instead, she pointedly studies one of the old paper placemats with a thousand advertisements on it and taps her foot on the floor.

As I pull off my coat, an older woman with a black waist apron strides over and sets down an identical placemat in front of me. She places a textured plastic cup full of ice water on the table, then reaches into her apron and retrieves a paper-wrapped straw. The metal tag on her shirt reads "Elena."

I take the straw from her and open it, then dutifully drop it into the cup.

"Hello there, darling. What can I get started for you today?" she asks as she pulls out a pad and a pen. The pen must be running low on ink. The skin around her eyes creases with frustration when she scribbles on the paper. "Anything to drink? Would you like to hear our specials?"

"Just a coffee, thanks," I answer. I feel guilty for not ordering anything else, but I don't have the cash to waste.

"What's the matter? Already burned through all of the money you stole from me?" Jennifer asks, finally looking up. Her pupils are dilated and streaks of red shoot across the sclera, nearly reaching her irises. She's high.

My foot connects with her shin beneath the table. This earns me a sharp yelp and a look of outrage.

The waitress, visibly uncomfortable, silently retreats to the kitchen.

Once we're alone, I address my sister. "What do you want, Jennifer?"

Her eyes narrow with fury. "What the fuck do you mean, what do I want? I want to know why you stole from me. Where's my shit, Kara?"

"I don't know what you're talking about."

"Yeah, okay." Her fingers drum impatiently against the seat. "It was a coincidence that for the first time in months, you called me, then someone snuck into my apartment and took thousands of dollars worth of stuff? You think I don't know you stole my engagement ring right off of my finger? How stupid do you think I am?"

"Pretty stupid," I reply, leaning forward. The promise of civility I made is rapidly slipping away. "You're engaged to Marcus, huh? Maybe one of his crew ripped you off. Did you ever think of that?"

"He runs his own business now, Kara. We're moving up in the world. No one would do that to us, except you. I saw you walk out on the security camera."

"What do you want me to say? Do you want me to admit I stole from you?" My voice drops to a whisper. "Fine, I did, and I would do it again today if I needed to because I'm trying to save our mother's life, you moron. But no, you can't be bothered to care about that, not when you have chop-shop Marcus drowning you in designer bags and coke, or whatever you were strung out on." Every word that passes my lips is coated with disdain.

Jennifer adjusts herself uncomfortably in her seat. She lowers her eyes to the placemat once more. "He doesn't work for the shop. He's got a new job. He's in... marketing."

"Mmm, marketing," I retort. "What exactly is he selling these days, might I ask?"

"That's none of your damn business!" Jennifer spits. She

slams her hand against the table, knocking my glass over and spilling freezing water into my lap. She smirks.

Suddenly, I'm thankful the waitress hasn't returned with my coffee. I glance over at the kitchen as I swat the water off of my legs. The older woman peeks out from behind the metal door but retreats back inside when my eyes meet hers.

Good. I want to keep her out of this. It's not her problem.

It takes everything I have to stay calm and level my voice. I place both of my palms flat on top of the table and push down, hard. The pressure helps. I really don't want to make a scene right now, but if Jennifer keeps this up, I might not be able to stop myself. I drag my eyes back to my sister's face.

"*You* made it my business when I asked you for money and help taking care of Mom, but *you* couldn't be bothered. *You* made it my business when *you* demanded I meet *you* here. *You* made it my business when *you* threatened to call Mom, and *you* knew I wouldn't let you do that. She doesn't need your shit, Jennifer. She needs our help. She needs money for treatments. She doesn't need you shacked up with some dipshit dealer, passed out on the couch soaked in god knows whose vomit and piss, closer to overdosing every day."

At this, Jennifer stands and slings out her hand, slapping me hard across my face. I barely register it at first. Then, a searing heat radiates from my left ear down to my jawline. I press my fingertips to my cheek. Marcus must have given her a new engagement ring because the diamond on her finger has left a long scratch. My hand comes away tinted with red.

"*You* stole from *me*, but you want to tell *me* that *I'm* trash? No fucking way, Kara!" she screams, not caring who's listening. The few people in the dining room fall silent and look up, blatantly staring.

Violence boils just below the surface of my skin. My hands bunch into tight fists as I stand as well. My mouth tightens and my nostrils flare. I lean toward my sister and drop my voice to an octave so low, I can barely hear it. "Don't ever fucking touch me again."

"You have no idea what you're doing," she threatens. "You're throwing everything away, and for what? Oh, Valerie is so perfect, isn't she? You're nothing but a mommy's girl. You have no idea what kinds of things she's done."

"What the hell are you talking about?" I ask. "What has Mom ever done to you?"

Jennifer laughs, a mirthless sound tainted with anger. "God, you're stupid. You want me to be the villain? Fine. I'll be the heartless daughter. I'll be the worthless sister. But, you have no idea what she stole from me. Valerie ruined my life. I won't give that woman a penny or a second of my time. And, look at you, turning out just like her - a thief and a liar. The apple doesn't fall far from the tree, does it?"

"You're nothing but an ungrateful brat!" I yell, gripping the edge of the table so hard I worry it might crack.

"Ask her, Kara! Ask her what she's done. You want to know why I am the way I am? Why I have to get high to shut out what my life has become? Go play the dutiful little daughter and *ask*."

Jennifer raises her hand to hit me again, but this time I snap. I shove the table out of the way and lunge for her, slamming her backward and pinning her against the glass block wall with my left forearm. She squeaks in protest, but that only makes me press harder. I bring my face close to hers and whisper into her ear.

"I tried to ask you nicely for help, but you'd rather let our mother die. I tried demanding your help, but you told me to fuck off - that it wasn't worth your goddamn time. So, yeah, I stole from you. And, you know what? I should have taken more. I should have taken your debit card, your credit cards, and your car. I should have gone through your fucking pockets. I should have scavenged for the drugs I know you have in your shithole apartment. Because you know what, Jennifer? You're dead to me. Don't ever call me or text me again. Don't ever call Mom again, either. If you do, I'll kill you myself. Do you understand?"

Jennifer's eyes widen with fear as she gasps for air. I can see my reflection in them, wild with rage. Behind me, silver bells jingle, and rapid footsteps approach me as Connor races into the room. He must have been watching me from the car. He wraps his hands around my shoulders and gently pulls me away.

"She's not worth it, Kay. She's not worth it," he urges. He squeezes a little harder, trying to convince me to back down.

I resist at first, staring straight into my sister's eyes, but I let Jennifer go. She drops with a thud to the floor.

Connor's right. She isn't worth it, and she never will be. Without breaking eye contact, I snatch my coat off of the seat. She rubs her throat in shock. The restaurant manager rushes out from the back as Connor wraps his arm around me and we turn to leave.

"Get out of here or I'm calling the police!" the manager commands, shaking.

"We're going. I'm sorry about this," Connor says apologetically, one hand in the air and the other ushering me out of the door.

"Don't come back!"

"Not fucking likely," I retort, stepping out into the cold. The door bumps my heel as I exit, like it's shoving me away, too.

Connor rushes me to his car and opens the passenger door, making sure I'm settled inside, then closes it behind me. He practically runs to the driver's side and slips in. Before he can throw the car into gear, Jennifer dashes out of the building and pounds on my window.

"Ask Valerie about my father!" she screams, beating her

hands against the glass. "Ask her what she's done. Don't be stupid, Kara!"

Connor slams his foot on the gas and backs away, leaving Jennifer staring after us in the middle of the parking lot.

"What happened to playing nice?"

CHAPTER TWENTY

"What the hell happened back there?" Connor's voice slices through the tense silence filling the car. It's been like this for the last fifteen minutes. "I've never seen you like that before."

Lunchtime traffic has us frequently starting and stopping on our way back to Baltimore. I keep my head pressed against the cool glass of the window and my mouth shut, listening to our tires grind along the asphalt and the occasional honking horn. The chill eases the burning from the scratch running down my cheek.

"Talk to me, please? I can't help you if you shut me out. I saw her hit you from the car, so I started to follow you inside, but by the time I got there, you had her pinned to the wall."

I turn to him, and the dull ache throbbing behind my forehead intensifies. Jennifer's slap had been harder than I realized. The same look of concern Connor had when he saw what I had done to the mirror is back on his face. His eyebrows are drawn, and his lips have turned down at the corners. I've scared him again.

I can only imagine what he saw when he burst through the diner door. Based on the glimpse I had of myself in Jennifer's eyes, I was a vision of feral fury. Is there anything I can say to soften what he must've seen? What he must've thought?

No, probably not.

Who knows what I would've done if he hadn't pulled me away from my sister. I wasn't in control of myself. I tried to fight back the urge to pummel her, yet she still ended up in my grasp.

What's wrong with me?

I'm tired of being treated like a child. I'm tired of fighting to find basic human decency in people. I'm tired of being angry, and confused, and lost.

Plus, what did she mean about Mom? None of it had made any sense, and I lost it.

My pulse is still racing nearly half an hour after leaving the diner when Connor exits the highway.

"Kay?"

He's supposed to turn right, but instead, he turns left, away from Renee's and back toward the apartment. But, that doesn't make sense. I have an afternoon shift today. I have to be there in a little over an hour...

The worried expression has faded away when I study his face once more. It's been replaced by an impassive one. His features may as well have been cut from stone.

"Where are you going? I have a shift at Renee's. You should've gone right..." I lift my head up and point.

"You are *so* not going to work today," Connor answers as he turns down the next side road.

"What do you mean?" I demand. "I have to go to work. I can't lose this job! You know how much I need the money!"

"You're sick today, Kara. When we get to the apartment, you need to call in. Tell them you've got a migraine or something. There's no way you can go there right now."

"They'll fire me, Connor!" I argue.

"If you go there and tear into a customer like you tore

into Jennifer, they'll fire you for sure. You need to go back home and calm down. Take it easy for the afternoon. Try to find some way to…"

"Don't tell me to relax, Connor."

"Okay, fine. But, you can't go to work today, Kay. You just can't. You know you'd lose it there."

"Now you're going to treat me like a child, too? Wonderful. *Marvelous!* Turn this car around. I'm a grown woman with responsibilities to handle. This is not up to you!"

My command echoes through the cabin loudly enough that it drowns out the man playing guitar on the street corner. A small crowd has gathered around him, tossing coins into his case.

"Jennifer always does this to you. She worms her way into your head and drives you insane. I've never seen you go ballistic on her before, though. That's not like you. And, what's worse, you won't tell me what's going on. So, I have to keep you safe. I have to keep everyone safe. I'm taking you home."

Rationally, I know Connor is right. It wouldn't take much to set me off, not after Jennifer provoked me. But even though I know he's trying to help, this is still a betrayal.

"You can't force me to go home with you, Connor. I want to go to work. Turn this car around right now. I mean it!"

"I'm not turning around, Kara. If you want to go to work today, you'll have to get out of this car yourself and walk."

He should have known better than to give me an ultimatum.

At Connor's challenge, I unclip my seatbelt and reach for the door. Just as I start to pull the handle, Connor slams the lock button down, securing me inside.

I fumble for the little knob on the top of the door, blinded by anger. Of course, it's gone. By the looks of things, it hasn't been there for a while.

I resort to manically tugging on the door handle. I use all of my strength, grunting and yanking, willing it to come loose and let me out. It doesn't budge.

Defeated, I turn to face him in disbelief. "What are you doing? Are you freaking kidnapping me?"

"Yeah, if I have to! I'm doing forty-five miles an hour, and you wanted to casually dip out like you could walk away from that? Jesus, Kara."

"If you don't let me out of this car right now, Connor. I swear…"

"What? What are you going to do? Are you going to lash out and hit me, too? I don't know what got into you back there, but you can't do that shit again. Seriously, that's not like you."

"She hit me first! You saw her do it. I know you did! I have a scratch on my face to prove it! You want to act like I'm the one who did something wrong?" I tug down the visor to examine the injury in the mirror, but it's already gone.

"No, Kay! No. I'm telling you this isn't like you. I'm telling you I'm worried about you. I'm telling you we need to go home, together, and calm down and process whatever the hell happened. Just listen to me, please. Let's go home."

"Whatever, Connor. Take Jennifer's side in all of this." Hatred, words of anger I don't mean to say, escape me. "Why don't you ghost me like she did, huh? I know you will eventually. And, where the hell is home? Your place? What, am I supposed to just crash in your bed forever like we're one big, happy family now? It's all a lie. I don't have a home! Let me out of this car right now. I'm so done."

Connor pulls into an empty space in the parking lot outside of his building. He turns off the car and the doors automatically unlock, freeing me.

Quickly, I jump out and start down the street away from him. He rushes after me, begging me to come back, but I ignore him. My breath steams and I shiver, but I don't turn around. I cross to the next street. Connor stops at the corner, staring and waiting.

When I don't stop, he shifts, looking behind himself and toward me once more. "Look, just come home soon, okay? I get that you're mad at me, Kay. I'm only trying to help. It's cold out here. Just take a walk and come home. Do you have your key?"

Mechanically, I reach into my pocket and hold it up without saying anything. I can feel Connor waiting there for a moment, staring at my back as I move farther and farther away, but when I look over my shoulder a few minutes later from a block up the road, he's gone.

I know he's right, even if I don't want to acknowledge it. I don't need to be at work around all of those people today. If someone comes through the drive-thru and pisses me off, I'll probably cuss them out or spit in their coffee. I'd lose my job and might even get sued. So, about ten minutes into my walk, I pause to call Renee's and let them know I won't be in tonight.

Steve answers the phone, thank goodness. I tell him I have a migraine, just as Connor suggested. He's not thrilled, but he cuts me some unexpected slack. It probably helps that I've basically picked up every extra shift I can find for the last few months.

While I'm on the phone, I press my luck a little further and ask if he might be able to cut my check a bit early this time. He argues with me for a few minutes, but when I remind him I've picked up several of his shifts too, he reluctantly agrees, saying I'm lucky I'm the best window worker he has and that Dan didn't answer the phone. We make arrangements for me to pick it up tomorrow with the assurance that he will never do it again. I thank him for everything, then tell him I'm going to lie down in a dark room for a while because of the migraine, and I hang up the phone.

It takes more than an hour of aimlessly wandering the neighborhood before I finally feel semi-calm. When I come down, suffocating guilt about how I've treated Connor takes the anger's place. I accused him of taking Jennifer's side! Never, in all of our years of friendship, had he so much as indicated he would take Jennifer's side in anything, let alone this. Worse yet, I told him his home wasn't my home and acted like his hospitality and the nights I'd spent in his arms had been nothing more than a joke!

I may as well have spit in his face. These past few days, I've felt so welcome and so loved there with him and Ally. I don't know if he will let me through the door now. *Did I just throw everything away?* It would serve me right if when I show up at the apartment, he's bagged up my things and left them in the hall, just like they had at my old studio.

What kind of a friend have I been? What kind of a girlfriend? Ugh, it's all so confusing. And, arguing about who hit who first? Seriously? Even to me, that sounded like some elementary school sibling squabble crap.

I reach into my coat pocket to feel for my wallet. It's not there. I must have left it on Connor's desk earlier. Luckily, I still have a crumpled five-dollar bill hidden away for emergencies in my inside pocket. This feels like as much of an emergency as a five-dollar bill might cover anyway, so on the way back, I stop at the corner liquor store. This place always has a surprising array of junk food, including boxes of candy. I pick up Connor's childhood favorite, Gobstoppers, hoping to apologize upon my return.

He used to sneak around with a box in the pocket of his cargo pants, especially when his mom went on her health food kicks every couple of months. They were his little rebellion.

I tuck the box under my arm and trudge my way back up the street to Connor's apartment. It's a lame peace offering, I'm aware, but it's all I have. Hopefully, he'll understand.

When I reach the door, I'm glad to see he hasn't thrown me out. I try to twist the handle, but it sticks. That doesn't surprise me at all. I always keep my doors locked, too. Connor's neighborhood is a lot nicer than my previous one had been, but the city is the city after all.

Struggling not to drop the box of candy, I reach into my pocket and retrieve the small silver key, but as I move to slip it into the lock, I hear voices just behind the door.

"It's bad," Connor says. "I don't know what to do. I need your help."

"I shouldn't even be here," a man's low voice replies. "Valerie shouldn't have called."

At the sound of my mother's name, my ears perk up.

"We're out of options. That's why I asked you to come."

"Just being here puts you all in danger. You couldn't possibly understand..."

I press my ear quietly to the door. *Who could be in there with Connor?* When I left him earlier, he'd been alone. As far as I know, Ally is still with Rob at his parents' house, wherever that is. So, it can't be Rob talking to him. *What does my mom have to do with this person?*

The conversation grows quieter and their voices sound muffled as though they're talking behind their hands. They've either moved away from the door or are intentionally being secretive. When I can no longer make out anything useful from outside the door, I tentatively slip my key into the lock and turn the knob, pushing the door gently open before me.

There, standing in the middle of Connor's kitchen, is the last person I ever expected to see - Richard Edwards, my father.

CHAPTER TWENTY-ONE

I left the winter chill outside when I entered Connor's building, but standing in front of his apartment and seeing Richard there in the kitchen is far worse. My body freezes to the spot, limbs becoming icicles, blood drained and numb. I want nothing more than to turn and run, but my mind can't force my legs to break away from the doorway. I'm breathless, and though I know my heart continues to beat, maybe harder than it ever has before, I find a hollow place in my chest where it should be.

At the sound of the door creaking open and bumping unchecked into the stopper on the wall, both Connor and Richard turn toward me. Richard's expression is unreadable, but whatever Connor sees etched on my face twists his own features into shock and concern. He sets his phone down on the kitchen counter next to him and takes three wary steps toward me, hands placatingly out like he's trying to talk down a wild animal poised to either strike or bolt.

At Connor's approach, more than a decade's worth of pain, abandonment, grief, and fury bubble up and course through me, thawing my icy limbs and replacing the bone-chilling paralysis with scalding heat. I clench my fists, trying not to shove Connor back into the kitchen or to scream loud enough for the entire apartment complex to hear. My eyes narrow and I take one step backward, a silent warning for Connor to stand down. Whatever is happening in this apartment, I need an explanation, and I need it now.

To his credit, Connor halts his approach.

"Kara, I know what this looks like – " he begins.

"Really, Connor?" I manage to breathe out between tight lips. "Tell me then. What does this look like?"

He hesitates, eyes turning toward the ceiling as if searching for the right words to say. This elicits a dry scoff from me because there aren't any words that could make this situation better. I bite down on the inside of my bottom lip so hard it makes my eyes water. The pain helps. My mouth fills with the taste of iron.

Connor sighs. "Listen, just come inside, okay? I promise if you sit down, I can explain what happened, and you can decide for yourself how you want to handle it. I'm not trying to hurt you. I swear."

My eyes flick toward my mute father, who appears not at all surprised by what he sees happening in front of him, then back to Connor.

Do I want to give him a chance to explain this? Should I turn around and walk away instead? What possible explanation could he have for Richard being here? How did he find him? How much had he told him before I opened the door?

My inner monologue spins so fast it makes me dizzy as I attempt to process the situation.

"Please, Kay. Come inside."

With considerable effort, I peel my fingers away from my palms and lay them flat against my thighs. The skin stings where my fingernails have dug in. Slick, hot blood pools against my legs. I wipe my hands absently on my jeans.

If I don't go inside, where the hell am I going to go? I don't have money to waste on a motel room. I can't sleep at the hospital with

Mom. Jennifer's place is definitely out of the question. I don't have an apartment or a car of my own anymore...

My brain works through these dead-end options like a math problem. I have nowhere else to go. It's inside the apartment to listen to Connor or out on the streets tonight. Begrudgingly, I step in and slam the door loudly behind me.

The air inside the apartment is thick with tension. I cut across the living room, intentionally choosing the lawn chair farthest away from the kitchen – farthest away from Richard – and sit wordlessly. There's no sound coming from the tv, but I stare at it anyway, avoiding Connor's guilty gaze.

Connor takes up the other lawn chair and sits with his elbows on his thighs and his face in his hands. Richard steps out into the hallway and softly shuts the door behind himself, giving us privacy.

Slowly, Connor lifts his head and addresses me.

"I didn't mean for this to happen this way."

"Yeah, I figured that part out," I parrot his previous phrase back to him with a sneer.

"When Valerie and I talked the other day, she gave me a slip of paper with his phone number and told me to only use it in case of emergencies. After everything that went down at the diner, this seemed like that kind of situation. I didn't know he would be here in town already and show up at my door. I figured he was somewhere far away. I didn't recognize the area code, 734-something. But then he was here, and then you were opening the door. I know it looks bad, Kay. Please, you have to believe me. I'm only trying to help, to do what your mom asked me to do."

I push my chair away and turn, increasing the distance between us.

"I didn't know what else to do! I was seriously concerned you were spiraling and about to go to jail for assault."

Turning back to him, I open my mouth to speak, but he continues.

"So, I made a call. You don't have to like it, but I think you need him here."

"I don't need him here!" I yell. "I haven't needed him here since he decided he didn't need *US* when I was in *FIRST GRADE*! All he knows how to do is make things worse! What the fuck is he going to do to help me, huh? He doesn't even know me, Connor! He left Mom! He left *me*!"

Connor's face is riddled with shame. His cheeks flush pink, and his eyes refuse to meet mine. Against my will, angry tears fall. Furiously, I swat them away.

When Connor speaks next, his voice is almost a whisper. "It was Valerie's idea, Kay."

"Why does that matter?"

He rubs his temples in slow circles as if he has a migraine coming on. "When she sent you and Ally out of the room, she asked me how you were doing. I tried to lie to her and tell her everything was fine, but she knows me better than that. She's been around me my whole life. So, I told her what happened with the mirror and how stressed you've been. I told her I was worried about you. She told me she was worried, too."

"Go on! How the hell did he end up in your living room, Connor?"

"Valerie said she knows she's dying."

"She most certainly is not!" I stubbornly interrupt.

"You have to listen, Kay. She knows she's dying, and she can't be there to help you through all of this, and she knows it's going to kill you when she's gone, and she couldn't let you go through all of it alone. I told her you didn't have to go through anything alone, that Ally and I would be there for you through all of it."

"And?" The simple question comes out as an accusation.

"And," Connor resumes, "she told me we wouldn't be enough. She told me you would need someone else, someone who was not a friend or a boyfriend to walk you through it all. She said there would come a time when you were faced with things you wouldn't understand and that even if I wanted to help you through all of this, Richard," he paused, fearing my reaction. When I don't immediately explode, he continues, "would be the only one who could help you. I swear, I didn't bring him up. I would never."

"What would make her think I needed him, huh?"

"I don't know! She kept babbling some nonsense about healing too fast and your scars. All she said was, 'The process has begun.' I don't know anything more. I swear."

I don't want to hear this. I can't stand the thought of Mom lying up there in a hospital room, contemplating her death and worrying more about me than herself. I hate the idea that Mom chose to talk to Connor about something like this, but not me. I'm completely confused as to why Mom thinks I need Richard to get through anything. It's not like he's ever been there for me before, not when it counted.

"Valerie told me that to find him, all I would need to do is call him or text him and leave a very specific message. She made me memorize what I had to say, made me repeat it back to her."

"What were you supposed to say?" I ask, more confused than before. *What words could possibly bring my absentee father back after all these years?*

"It didn't make a lot of sense to me. She told me to say 'The Ruin is approaching. Kara needs you. It's time.' That's it. That's the message I left. Well, I also told him what my address was so he could find me."

"I don't understand…"

"Before I came out to the hallway to get you guys, she said if I left that message for him, he would come. I thought he might call me first so I would have time to explain, but he didn't. He just showed up, and then we talked for a minute, and then you came home, and… God, I did not mean for all of this to happen this way. I was just trying to help."

"What does that even mean? What's the Ruin? What's approaching?"

"Your guess is as good as mine! It has to be a code phrase or something, right?" Connor throws up his hands, lost. "I just said what I was supposed to say. I promised her I would leave that message if it seemed like you were truly not okay. And, you haven't been okay. Today proved that. So, I left the message, and here we are."

"Yeah, here we are." I glower at him, fury rippling off of me in waves.

I'm pissed at Connor, sure. But, it's more than that. Had Mom known how to find Richard all of these years and never said a word? Why would she do that? I'd seen her suffer. I'd seen her cry for hours and hours at a time because my father was gone. I'd seen Mom work so hard to try to make ends meet. I'd watched her get sick and battle on, full of pride, until she couldn't take it anymore and ended up in the hospital.

She'd seen me suffer too, yet Mom hadn't summoned him home. But now, by some sort of magic or screwed-up arrangement, he's suddenly back? If she could bring him back home so easily, why didn't she do it before?

None of this makes sense. Even worse, I can't tell if the anger still burning inside of me is directed toward Richard for being here, Connor for calling, or my mother for keeping this secret for so long. Maybe it's all three? Then, there's the crippling guilt.

Do I have any right to be angry with Mom? She's laying alone in that hospital room right now. This is too much.

A few long moments pass and neither Connor nor I say a

word. The only sound is a slow drip from the kitchen sink, tap-tap-tapping on the stainless steel. It's as though the world has come to a temporary stop. I focus on my breathing. Part of me contemplates calling Mom but decides right now would not be the time because I might end up losing it on her, and that's the last thing she needs. I can't afford to make the situation any worse.

Eventually, Connor dares to speak again.

"Will you talk to him?" he asks, tentatively. His eyes search my face for some kind of confirmation.

"Connor, I..." I hesitate.

"If you talk to him, just this one time, maybe you'll figure out whatever it is Valerie thinks is important enough for him to be here after all these years. You don't have to bond, or whatever. Just listen? There must be a reason she wants him to come back. Figure out what that is?"

I look into Connor's eyes. Though I'm angry, all I see reflected back at me is hope and a kind of gentle sadness. He wasn't trying to hurt me when he left that message. I can't deny that.

I can't imagine Mom would try to hurt me, either. For some reason, she actually thinks I need to talk to Richard. If this is what Mom wants, maybe I can put aside all of that anger for a little while and find out why he's back. Besides, even though I want to send him away again as punishment for all of the years he wasn't around, I still have the tiniest childlike-longing to talk to my father, to find out why he left us.

"I'll talk to him. But Connor, if I don't like what he has to say, he has to leave. I have too much going on already to deal with whatever this is, and I'm not going to listen to him spew any bullshit. If he's not helpful, he's gone."

Connor's shoulders sag with relief as he says, "Fair

enough." He reaches over and gives my arm a gentle squeeze before standing and turning to walk away.

"Connor?" I call before he gets to the door.

"Yeah?" he replies.

"That's my *dad* in the hallway."

"I know."

I drag my feet up onto the rickety lawn chair and pull my knees in tight to my chest. Seeing this, he returns and squeezes my hand, then plants a kiss on top of my head, closing his eyes and holding me to his body.

"It's going to be okay. No matter what. I'm here."

"I know."

"Do you want me to stay with you? I could sit and listen, too. Or if you want, I could disappear for a little while. I could go find us some dinner and a cheesy movie for the night? It's up to you."

I want him to stay. I want desperately for him to hold my hand while I stare Richard in the eye and battle through this. But, if he stays, Richard and I might not be able to talk as openly. If I need to rage at my father, Connor might try to calm me down. If he upsets me too much, Connor might send him away. He's always been my protector, even when I don't want him to be.

No, as much as I want Connor here by my side, it would be better if he walked away for a little while.

"I think you should go," I force myself to say. "Find some dinner, please? Something we'll regret eating tomorrow?"

He lets out a breathy chuckle into my hair. "Okay, I'll try to be creative. Any requests?"

"Not spaghetti."

This time he pulls away to look at me and smiles. "Easy enough. Call me if you need me?"

"I will."

He brushes his finger against my cheek. I lean into it.

Pulling away, he retrieves his phone from the kitchen and moves to the door.

"Are you ready?"

"Not really," I answer honestly, "but you can send him in."

Connor nods. He grabs his coat off of a hook next to the door, sticks his car keys in his pocket, and steps outside. He says something to Richard, but I can't quite make out whatever it is. Then, it's quiet. A second later, the apartment door swings open and Richard steps inside. I straighten up in my chair, a calm resilience creeping over me, and prepare myself for a conversation I never expected to have.

It is time to talk to my father.

CHAPTER TWENTY-TWO

Seeing Richard standing in front of me is disorienting. This is the man who abandoned us, the man who packed up his things and walked out of the door without so much as a goodbye. On the other hand, this is my father. I never expected to see him again. My inner child longs to run into his arms. In his presence, I'm six years old once more. I want to stand on his toes and dance, to lift up my arms and be swung around, to have him plant a soft kiss on the top of my head and tell me everything is going to be okay. But, it will never be like it was.

Pain and loss course through me. In some ways, it's like my father has risen from the dead. I've grieved and resented his absence for fifteen years. I've spent so many nights wishing I could pick up the phone and hear his voice, only to realize it would never happen. Yet, here he is. It's almost too much to take.

Bewildered, I study the familiar stranger he's become. Though he still looks like my father, Richard has aged. His short hair, mostly chestnut brown, is streaked with lines of gray. Wrinkles surround his hazel eyes. Much like the ones on my face, purplish circles darken the space beneath them. His cheeks and chin are stubbled with several days of growth.

When I was younger, Richard didn't let his beard grow in.

He kept his face clean-shaven for Mom. She used to tell him she would never enjoy kissing a porcupine. When he did have a hint of stubble, he would rub it on my cheek and make me laugh until I couldn't breathe.

Those once pleasant memories hurt, so I force them down.

If his clothes are any indication, he's doing well enough for himself. A light gray, three-button blazer rests on Richard's shoulders, secured in the middle overtop of a forest green t-shirt. His jeans are dark and well-worn, faded in places. There's fraying on the bottom hems, but that could be the way they came. A tawny brown pair of soft leather dress shoes peek from beneath.

My eyes are drawn to his left hand where a simple golden band gleams on his ring finger. Out of all of his attire, this item looks to be the most well-cared for. Judging by the shine, it's regularly cleaned and polished.

Is that a wedding ring? If so, is it from his marriage to Mom, or did he marry someone else and start a new family?

I tear my eyes away, not wanting to know the answer.

Tentatively, Richard gestures toward the empty lawn chair beside me. "Is it alright if I sit with you?"

Unsure what to say, I nod.

He flashes me a quick, cautious smile as he takes a seat. It creaks beneath him when he leans back, catching him off guard.

I know I should probably say something, but I'm at a loss for words. In times like these, I've learned I tend toward taking the offensive approach. It's easier to be angry than to allow myself to hurt. If I open my mouth, I might start berating him. Does he deserve it? Probably, but it's not going to help the situation, so I press my lips tighter.

I'm still furious he left us, but this may be the only chance I'll have to get answers. I have so many questions now that he's here. If I make him angry, he could disappear. The man has already proven he's a flight risk.

We sit together in tense silence, testing the fragile situation, both unsure how to proceed.

Eventually, Richard clears his throat and looks down at his shoes. "I'm guessing you want to know why I'm here."

"Well, that's one of the things I would like to know."

He nods his head patiently. "I understand you're angry. There's a lot to discuss."

"Oh, I'm *so glad* you understand." Anger seeps into my words despite my best efforts to keep it at bay. "I'm so *thrilled* you know *exactly* what it's like to be me in this situation." My arms cross protectively over my chest.

"That's not what I meant," he calmly responds. "I'm sure you have a lot of questions. I'll try to answer as many of them as I can. Where would you like to start?"

My gaze drifts to the ceiling. Obviously, the most important questions are "why are you here?" and "why did you leave?" Neither of those comes out of my mouth, though. Instead, I find myself asking, "Do you have another family somewhere?" Much to my chagrin, traitorous tears roll down my cheeks. I swipe them away.

"No. I certainly do not," Richard answers. His tone speaks of sadness and surprise. "Is that why you think I left?"

"I have no idea why you left. All I know is one day you were here, and the next day you were gone. You never said goodbye. Mom was an absolute mess, and I had to pick up the pieces."

Richard wears a stricken expression. He reaches out to comfort me but stops, uncertain, and withdraws his hand. "I'm sorry. I know you don't understand, but that's how it had to happen. There was no other woman. There never has been, and there never will be. Valerie is the love of my life, and you are my family. I would never have another."

"You're right. It doesn't make sense. None of this makes sense. Who are you, *Richard*?" My words are full of scorn. "Why did you leave? Where did you go? What the hell have you been doing for fifteen years? What makes Mom think that you coming back here would help anyone at all?" I pepper him with questions, one after the other, firing them like vicious little bullets and barely stopping to breathe between them.

Richard flinches when I use his name instead of calling him Dad, but he quickly composes himself. "Obviously, this is complicated, and seeing me is unexpected." He wrings his hands. "But, I am here to help. I know this must be difficult. I can give you some of those answers. Some parts of this story are not mine to tell. For those things, you'll have to talk to your mother."

My knees bounce rapidly, airing my frustration. "Start with where you've been for the last fifteen years."

"Michigan," he says. "I've been in Michigan. I've been living outside of Ann Arbor and working as an instructor for a community college."

"*Michigan?* Why would you go to *Michigan?* We don't know anyone there."

"I know. That's why I chose it. I couldn't be near anyone we knew. I had to leave everything and everyone behind."

"*Michigan...*" I mutter under my breath. I'm not sure where I thought Richard was or what I had expected he was doing with his life, but working as a college instructor in Michigan had certainly not been it. It's just so... normal. Somehow, it makes everything worse. "You left us behind for a change of scenery and a crappy job in a new state? Seriously?"

"No. I left because I had no choice. It wasn't safe to stay."

"I don't even know how to begin to process this."

"Kara, I'm going to tell you things you probably won't

believe," he states directly. Richard places his hands on his knees and squeezes them firmly before continuing, eyes glued to the floor. "I know I didn't believe any of it until it happened to me. I need you to listen to my story and try to suspend your disbelief for a while. If you do, you'll understand why I had to go and why I'm back."

I bury my head in my hands. "Just tell me the truth. I deserve that much."

When I look up again, Richard nods. His eyes grow distant and move back and forth like he's watching a movie only he can see. He takes a deep breath and lets it out slowly.

"Our family, more specifically our ancestors, are different."

"Jesus, I don't need some sort of family history lesson," I interrupt.

"Yes, you do." His tone is firm. "Without it, you'll never understand."

I roll my eyes and adjust myself in my seat.

"Like most of the people in this country, our family came to America as immigrants. They were poor, and they wanted a better life here. In the early 1600s, twelve of our ancestors and many others from their clan boarded a boat, crossed the Atlantic, and docked in Virginia, ready to start their new lives. They could've built homes in the new settlements, but instead, they traveled west on foot until they were deep in the Appalachian Mountains. They constructed their own settlement far away from anyone else, as isolated as they could possibly be.

"My mother grew up in that small, isolated village hidden deep within the mountains of West Virginia. By the time she was born, our ancestors had been living there for hundreds of years. It was the kind of place that wasn't meant to be found. There was no electricity, no running water, and there were no roads to or from the village. No one ever left. It was forbidden."

"It sounds like a cult," I state with disgust.

Richard dips his head slightly in agreement. "In some ways, it was. As I said, no one ever left the village. They provided for themselves by hunting and fishing, fetching their own water from the creeks, and making everything by hand. For the most part, no one outside of our family knew the village existed."

"Why does that matter?"

"What matters is *why* our ancestors chose to live this way. The people in our family are different. We're born with the ability to heal the illnesses of others, even those on the brink of certain death. Our ancestors learned that if they took the blood of the suffering person into themselves, then returned it to the original host, combined with the blood of someone from our family line, the deathly-ill would be cured of all ailments, no matter how serious. They named this process the Sharing. If done correctly, diseases that could maim or mangle a body would fade to nothing. There would be no more symptoms or concerns at all for the Healed. Their life would be spared."

"You know that's ridiculous, right?" I challenge him. "It's scientifically impossible. All that would do is infect both people, and they would die from blood incompatibility..."

Richard ignores me and continues. "Hardly anyone in our family ever fell ill of their own accord. Even injuries healed faster for our ancestors than for others. Broken bones righted themselves in weeks instead of months. Cuts and bruises disappeared overnight. They thought it would be harmless to share some of our family's health with others. So, our family healed people, and for a time, things were fine. Our ancestors were strangely immune to whatever conditions the ill brought to their doorsteps. From the outside, our ability seemed like a gift, but they quickly learned the truth. It's dangerous."

Without thinking, I run my fingers across my perfectly smooth forearms where the cuts from the other day have completely disappeared. My cheek tingles where Jennifer's ring should have marked me.

"Those that our ancestors healed fared very well. Most returned to their homes that same day. They went back to work quickly. It was as if a miracle had been bestowed upon them. The problem came when others in the villages began to fall ill, too.

"At first, the villagers believed the outbreaks were coincidental, but upon closer inspection, it became clear this was not the case. The symptoms of the newly infected mirrored the symptoms of the Healed, but they quickly escalated into something far worse. If the original patient had come in with a fever, those the person had contact with would come down with the same fever. Hours later, their skin would blister. They would hallucinate horrendous visions, and they would find themselves unable to keep any food or water down. Within days, a previously healthy person would end up inexplicably dead."

"Yeah, that's how disease worked in the time before modern medicine."

"No, you don't understand. The Sickness spread like wildfire. Somehow, in healing the first person, our ancestors' blood mutated the illness and made it far more deadly and contagious than it was before. Only we and those we healed were immune. Anywhere the Healed went, the disease would spread, and anyone who came into contact with the Infected would spread the disease to others. Whole villages were brought to ruin in mere weeks.

"Those who had once turned to our ancestors for help began to fear them and their abilities. We were seen as reapers or angels of death. Rumors spread that our ancestors intentionally caused the illnesses. Many claimed they were vying for power, or that they'd made deals with the Devil to kill off our enemies. It didn't matter that our family never had any significant problems with anyone, nor did they practice the Christian faith. Villagers started to refer to our family as the 'Ruin.' Our ancestors were driven away out of hatred and fear."

Richard pauses for a moment and surveys my face, searching for understanding. I shake my head at him in confusion.

"You don't really believe any of this, right?" I ask. "Plenty of people died from untreated illnesses back then, and humans have always been prone to superstition. Look at the witch trials and the crusades."

"I used to think that, too," Richard replies. "My mother, Lily, told me these stories when I was a child. I dismissed them as strange bedtime tales. I was wrong.

"As I said before, when our clan immigrated to this country, they fled from the growing settlements and made their own isolated village in the Appalachian Mountains. They kept their stories to themselves. They didn't tell anyone about their healing abilities or the consequences that came with them. As society advanced around them, our ancestors stayed in hiding. They wanted to be left alone. They feared outsiders, worried they would be captured and tortured for what they could do. More importantly, they worried someone would try to harness their gifts to be used as a weapon against their will. So, they hid. Our family was happy. No one left the village. Everyone was safe. Then, one day in 1832, everything changed.

"A sick young man wandered into our ancestors' village. He told our ancestors he was a traveling tradesman making his way from South Carolina to New York to join his family.

He claimed he had crossed over from England only a few weeks before. Our ancestors offered to let him stay in their village for a few days to rest, certain his illness would pass and he would go on his way. He resisted at first, explaining that he had people waiting for him at his destination, but he eventually agreed to rest. However, instead of getting better, the young man grew progressively worse.

"One of our younger ancestors took pity on the tradesman and told him the truth about our family's abilities. The tradesman didn't believe him, of course, but knowing he was incredibly sick and worried he was going to die, the tradesman agreed to allow the young villager to try to heal him through the Sharing. The young man did this in secret, and after the tradesman miraculously recovered from his illness, our ancestor packed a small bag of supplies for himself and the tradesman, then escorted the tradesman on the long journey to New York. Our ancestor hoped if he kept the tradesman away from others during the journey, one that would take several weeks on foot, he would no longer be contagious and would be allowed to live out his life when he arrived at his destination. Our ancestor was wrong.

"The two men arrived in New York several weeks later and were greeted by the tradesman's family and fiancée. They welcomed our ancestor into their home, thankful he had ensured the tradesman made it safely. Wisely, our ancestor stayed to monitor the impact of the Sharing on the trades-man's family.

"Just as our ancestor was convinced he had defied the odds by helping the tradesman and keeping him isolated for so long, his fiancée became deathly ill. Within hours, the tradesman's mother and father were sick as well. Even the servants in the house became bedridden. Our ancestor did his best to convince the family not to have contact with anyone outside of the home, but they sent for the doctor, who came and went, unable to determine the exact illness that had brought the family down or to help them recover. The fiancée passed first, quickly followed by the mother and father the next day. In the meantime, the doctor infected others around New York as he traveled through busy streets from household to household.

"Our ancestor and the tradesman watched in horror as the consequences of their actions rapidly overcame the great city before them. Our ancestor joined the others who had the means and volunteered to help with trying to stop the ever-spreading sickness. Bodies of the deceased were quarantined and quickly buried or burned. When the deaths began to slow, our ancestor returned home with the tradesman in tow. Only they knew the full extent of what had occurred in New York.

"Almost ten percent of New York's population was lost in the epidemic. Many years later, doctors and scientists declared there had been an outbreak of cholera due to infected goods brought over in a shipment from India. It was the only logical explanation they could grasp."

"Are you seriously trying to take credit for the cholera outbreak? Thousands of people died, Richard. We learned about this in high school history. What's wrong with you?" I ask, stunned. "That's sick."

"It's the truth," Richard answers. "Our ancestor returned home full of shame, and he admitted his deception to our family. He suffered severe consequences for his actions. My mother told me both he and the tradesman were imprisoned for years and forbidden to interact with the rest of the family because of their aberration. But, he taught them a valuable lesson. If they were ever going to agree to the Sharing again, whoever they healed must never leave the village.

"Although he had done his best to maintain our clan's secret, the young ancestor's presence in New York was enough for inklings of our existence to spread through the states. The Ruin became an urban legend to many. Those who were desperate enough to seek us out, those who were too afraid to die, sometimes made the trek into the Appalachian Mountains. When the ill made their way to the village, if they were deemed worthy, they were healed with the expectation that they were never to return to outside society. If they weren't, they were never seen again.

"The village remained small, but it slowly grew. Descendants of the ancestors began to marry the Healed and form families. New members of the Ruin were born and taught the ways of our people, and our secret was kept safe.

"When my mother was a young woman, she felt the village was too small for her. She had learned quite a lot of the world outside from the few who did dare to seek us out. The village would never change, but the world was full of excitement beyond the Ruin's borders. So, not long after her seventeenth birthday, she ran away.

"It was 1971. She knew how to sew and cook, so she took odd jobs, making enough money to travel upstate. By the time she was nineteen, she made her way to Alexandria, and she met your grandfather, Dean. He was in construction and always came into the cafe where your grandmother worked for lunch. They married, and a few years later, I came along. When his job in Alexandria drew to a close, they moved out here to Baltimore where our small family has been ever since."

"Most of our family, you mean. Don't forget, you ran away from here. It seems like abandoning everyone you say you love for your own selfish whims is a running theme in this family if what you've said about your mother is true. Just ask Jennifer."

Richard's face is unreadable as he ignores me and continues his story. "My mother used to tell me tales of the

Ruin when I was young. She talked about their village, their gift, and why it must never be used again. I thought she was an excellent storyteller. They felt so real, but I knew they couldn't be true. Her words went against everything I was taught to believe in school. She told my father the stories, too. I don't think he ever believed her either, but he loved her enough that he let it go.

"Then, when I was fourteen, my father died in a construction accident. He was crushed between two girders. We were left with very little, enough life insurance to pay off the house, but nothing else. My mom took on extra jobs to get me through high school. I took out loans to go to college. Even without a father, my life was very normal.

"Every night before bed, my mother used to make me promise I would never use the gift of the Ruin. I didn't believe it was true, so of course I always agreed. When I moved out and went to college, even when I came home for the holidays, she would make me promise again.

"Valerie actually met your Grandma Lily twice before she died. The days surrounding my mother's death were strange. I received a phone call at work informing me she had passed. No one knew what had happened. The police never suspected foul play. I did. She had never been sick, and she wasn't injured. I pressed the police to investigate further, but I didn't get any answers."

"I'm sorry about your mother. I'm sure that wasn't easy. I don't know what Connor told you before I got here – "

"He told me enough," he replies. His voice is cold.

"You lost your mom when you were young, so you have to understand why I am doing everything I can to keep my mother alive. If you're worried about the experimental treatment – "

"Of course, I'm worried about the treatment," Richard interrupts. "I don't want anything to happen to you or your mom because you've done something illegal, but that's not why I'm here. I'm not finished with my story."

I impatiently tap my foot. None of what he's saying makes any sense, and it has nothing to do with why he left us or helping Mom. He's clearly lost his mind.

"The story of the Ruin should have ended with my mother," Richard says. "I didn't believe any of it was true. I should have listened. Because of me, a sheer act of desperate sadness ripped our family apart. I did something foolish. but I never meant to hurt this family or to disappear."

He takes another deep breath and looks at me. "When you were six, a very close friend of mine got sick. He, much like the tradesman in the original story, had been traveling internationally and came down with a mysterious sickness. Do you remember Evan?"

"Yeah. We used to go down to the National Aquarium and get ice cream in the harbor with him every summer," I answer.

"Evan had been my best friend since I was a child. The houses we grew up in were only a few blocks apart, and when we graduated, we went to the same college. We used to set each other up on blind dates and joke about what terrible taste the other had in women. He's actually the person who introduced me to your mother, albeit by accident. They had an economics class together and were studying for a test when I stopped by his dorm and bumped into Valerie on the way out.

"When he fell ill, I was devastated. The doctors couldn't identify the precise infection, and none of the broad treatments were working. It was a blood infection of sorts, and within a few weeks, he was unconscious and near death. I was terrified of losing him. I remember sitting by his side for days and coming home to you girls at night, trying to pretend like I was fine. It was so confusing for me to see him there in such a state. Evan had never been one to get sick, really. In all of our years together, he had only had a few bouts of the flu and a couple of ear infections. I didn't understand how someone so young and healthy could die so quickly. The doctors were out of options.

"I don't know what possessed me, but one day, in a frenzied state, I found myself shutting and locking the door to his hospital room. I slid my chair under the handle and closed the blinds. He was hooked up to so many tubes that the rest was easy to rig. I made a makeshift transfusion set-up and decided to try the Sharing.

"I knew I must have been out of my mind even as I was doing it. If I had thought it through, I would have been worried about picking up whatever infection Evan had contracted. That was the logical thing to consider. In the moment though, it didn't matter. My best friend was dying, and if I could save him, even through some ridiculous superstition, I had to try.

"I sat on the edge of the bed with Evan, cycling and infusing my own blood into his. Nothing happened for a long while. I was convinced I'd lost it. I had already decided nothing was going to happen when he started to stir. I removed the tubes and reattached them to the IV poles, then unlocked the door, set the chair right, and opened the blinds. I didn't want anyone to see what I had done and have me arrested.

"Slowly, the machines started registering improved vital signs. His heart rate increased, his oxygen levels improved, and he opened his eyes. When his doctors and nurses came in, they were mystified. Before them, the man who had been dying hours before, sat upright in bed, cheeks flushed with healthy color. I couldn't tell them what I had done, so I pretended to be as confused as they were. Maybe I *was* as confused as them. I didn't know what to think either."

"You can't take credit for that! The medications had finally done their job! That had nothing to do with you, just like the cholera epidemic had nothing to do with our ancestors. You were lucky you didn't die! He was lucky to have modern medicine!" I'm fed up with his tall tales, exasperated.

"I would have thought so too if the people around him hadn't started dying."

CHAPTER TWENTY-THREE

oo much anxious energy courses through my body for me to remain seated any longer. With trembling hands, I push myself out of the chair and walk to the window. Sir Meowverick, who has been lounging on the deep sill in a warm patch of sun, arches his back into a stretch, then reaches his paw out to me, purring loudly. I scoop him up and cradle him to my chest. His canine pokes me as he rubs his face against my cheek and meows.

Richard says nothing as I distract myself and watch the crowds of people passing below. A young woman pushes a toddler in a stroller down the cracked sidewalk. Three teenagers stand on the corner, chatting and waiting for the crosswalk sign to change. School must be out. Traffic has picked up, too. Occasionally, a car horn punctuates the silence.

I tell myself I'm not looking for Connor and desperately wishing he would come home, but I know that's a lie. Richard appears to have much more to say. As far as I'm concerned, I've held up my end of the bargain. I've listened to his completely ludicrous stories. They're the raving tales of a madman. There's nothing in them that will help Mom or me. He hasn't explained why he left. This has been a complete waste of time.

Richard's odd conspiracy theories aren't just impossible; they hint toward some sort of sick god complex. I can't comprehend how he's convinced himself our family is responsible for the deaths of so many when experts, backed by science, have already determined the cause.

Has he experienced some sort of break or psychosis? Are there medications he should be on that he isn't taking? And, this Sharing thing, mixing blood and returning it, is ridiculous. It sounds like something straight out of a Stoker novel.

When I glance over my shoulder, he's watching me warily from his seat. I turn back to the window, and in the reflection, I see him run his splayed fingers through his short hair.

"Can I get a glass of water?" he inquires.

"Sure." My reply is curt. "The glasses are in the kitchen."

He moves to the kitchen, opening cupboard doors in search of a clean glass. I take this opportunity to sneak off to the bathroom for a moment of reprieve.

The door clicks shut and I twist the lock. Sir Meowverick leaps gracefully down onto the tile. I use the edge of the sink to hold myself up and fire off a message to Connor.

> Where r u?

He responds almost instantly. He must be keeping a close eye on his phone.

> Killing time @ the pharmacy. Need me 2 come back?

My fingers hover over the screen, torn between two messages: "Yes, hurry" and "No, I'm ok." I type out the first, pause, then delete it. When I don't answer, Connor texts again.

> Need me 2 bring anything back w/ me?

Maybe Tylenol? Some wine? Something harder? Richard's giving me a migraine.

Ur wish is my command.

B here in 30?

Yup. Promise.

I sigh and lock the screen, tucking my phone back into my pocket. There must be something wrong with me. Anyone else would have asked him to come back, but I didn't. *Why?*

Covering for my absence, I flush the toilet and wash my hands. The cat winds around my feet in figure eights. Before leaving the room, I bend down and scratch him behind the ears. He offers an approving nudge, and I wander back to the living room where Richard waits.

He's in his chair, a half-empty glass of water in his hand. His eyes follow me as I settle onto the window ledge. After a moment, he turns to look for a table to set his glass on. There isn't one, so he opts for carefully positioning it on the floor before launching into his story again.

"I was as astounded as the doctors. After the Sharing, Evan was the healthy man I knew again. His recovery made him a medical curiosity. Doctors and nurses from different units stopped by his room to marvel at him. His vitals and all of the labs the doctors ordered were perfectly normal. They insisted he stay a few more days for monitoring, but moved him into a recovery room. Things were fine. You and your mother came to visit, and we played cards. Do you remember that? We were so relieved to see him well again."

I nod. I do remember when Mom brought me to the hospital to see Evan. It's been so long I had almost forgotten.

We stopped at the gift shop on the way up and picked out a stuffed bear and a balloon for him. It was just the two of us that morning. Jennifer was with Mom's parents in Harrisburg for her annual summer visit. We met Richard in Evan's room and spent several hours there.

To my six-year-old self, it was very boring, even though I liked Evan well enough. He noticed when I started to squirm and ordered food from the cafeteria with a little square brownie dessert to make me smile.

Evan was a nice man. I haven't seen him since then.

"It took two days for the early symptoms of the Sickness to show in the staff, the ones who had spent the most time with Evan," Richard continues. "The immunologist was the first to succumb. It happened right in front of us.

"When he entered the room, he was fine. By the end of the conversation, he was flushed and sweating. We watched as he continuously wiped his brow on his coat sleeve while we all talked. He turned to leave the room, and as he did, I noticed he wasn't walking well. He staggered from side to side with each step.

"I stood and approached him as he opened the door. He grabbed onto the metal frame and looked back at us right before he collapsed and began violently convulsing. Your mother called for help, and I turned him onto his side and tried to keep him from hitting his head as he foamed from the mouth. Staff rushed to his aid and immediately lifted him onto a stretcher, wheeling him away to the emergency room. It took a few hours for us to learn he had been dead upon arrival."

"That's awful…"

"It wasn't just him who fell ill, though. Overnight, three nurses who had cared for Evan became incredibly sick as well. They demonstrated similar symptoms to the immunologist, similar symptoms to what Evan himself had suffered.

"Some of them lasted longer than others. Those who survived the longest developed large sores on their skin, hallucinations, and eventually fell into a coma before succumbing to the mutated disease.

"Luckily, it didn't take the hospital long to hypothesize the connection between the sick staff members and Evan's mysterious infection. All of the staff that had interacted with him since the beginning of his care were quarantined in a separate, rarely-used wing. Sadly, several patients and family members who came into contact with those staff members became ill, too. They joined their care providers in isolation, as did Evan and me.

"I should have told them you and your mother had visited Evan too, but I couldn't stand the idea of you locked up in the quarantine rooms, so I begged your mother to stay home and keep you safe.

"The doctors were too cautious to enter the rooms where we were isolated. We were incredibly lucky in that regard because if they had, many, many more would have surely died. Since several of the quarantined were practitioners themselves, the uninfected doctors and nurses provided guidance from behind plexiglass barriers and allowed the infected to care for one another, ordering supplies and having them sent in through a drawer.

"I alone knew what I had done and suspected why this was happening. It horrified me to see nurses and doctors who had only cared for Evan before the Sharing locked away with those of us who came into contact with him after. They didn't need to be there. Yet, there they were, and some of them had even been forced to bring their family members with them due to infectious disease protocols.

"There were children in the isolation unit, Kara. There was nothing I could do. Those people suffered horrific deaths, and I knew they were entirely my fault."

My mouth falls open. I'm speechless. If Richard is making this up, what kind of screwed-up person would involve children? If he's not, how much guilt must he have felt to internalize deaths from natural causes like a mysterious disease? He couldn't have instigated an outbreak of that scale with a single, superstitious act.

"I called you and your mother every day for almost two weeks. Do you remember?"

"I remember." My mouth has gone dry. "You were away for a long time. I could tell Mom was worried about you, but you said you were on a work trip. I thought everything was fine."

Richard bows his head. "I know. We had to lie to you to protect you. That's what parents do."

"Jennifer was gone for a long time, too. She was only supposed to spend a week with Grandma and Grandpa, but you told me they asked her to stay a little longer. She missed her summer camp. She was so upset with both of you."

Again, Richard nods. "It was safer that way. I couldn't keep you from coming into contact with the disease. You had already been to the hospital to see Evan with your mom. But, I could keep her away. It was the only thing I had control over."

The room grows silent again as Richard falls into his memories. His face is pained as he replays the events after the Sharing in his mind. He's quiet for long enough that when he talks again, it surprises me.

"Then your mother got sick," he whispers. There's misery in his voice like he's choking out each word. "It was just you and her at home. I couldn't leave the hospital. You can't imagine the panic I felt when I found out Valerie had it, too. I practically camped by that phone waiting to hear from your mom. I called her, and she called me, and we both waited and waited.

"I don't know how she survived." He trails off, sniffling

and wiping his eyes on the sleeve of his blazer. "But somehow, she did. It took five days for her to pull through."

"She had the flu, Richard," I state. My voice is firm. "I took care of her because you weren't there. That was the first time I took care of her without you, and it wasn't the last. I held her hair when she vomited. I helped her get to and from the bathroom and cleaned up her accidents. I gave her pills to take and kept a cold washcloth on her head. It was bad, but it was only the flu."

"It wasn't the flu, Kara," Richard asserts.

"Yes. It. Was," I manage to grind out through my teeth. "Don't you dare use your god complex to explain away the damage you did to our family. I won't listen to it."

"You will listen to this!" he yells. I flinch, not expecting the outburst. "You *will* listen to this and try to understand. That's all I've asked you to do. I'm still your father, no matter what happened in the past, and you *will* do this. You have to."

My fists bunch at my sides. "Father? You haven't earned that title. You threw it away."

He runs his hand through his hair again, a nervous habit. "Yes, I did, and this is why."

I shake my head, disgusted. "By all means, continue explaining your delusions."

He sighs. "I've had a long time to think about this. The only conclusion I've reached is that Valerie survived because she was married to me. More specifically, I believe she survived because we had children together. A minuscule portion of my DNA must have remained inside of her body, protecting her as it would've protected me, but in a weakened form."

I open my mouth to interject, but he talks over me, continuing his tale.

"That's why you never fell ill, too. You were immune to

the mutated virus because you're my daughter. You're a member of the Ruin."

"That makes absolutely no sense!" I spit, beyond furious. This time it's Richard's turn to be surprised. "How could she have kept any of your DNA? It's not like she could've told her body, 'Hey, I might need this. Let's store it away.' You've gotta be kidding me!"

"There's science behind it," Richard replies. "It's called microchimerism. The child and the mother share cells, and some of them embed themselves into the mother's body. Those cells contain bits of the father's DNA. They can exist there for decades. I've researched this. I'm not insane."

"Oh, yes you are!"

Richard brings his hands up to his temples and rubs them vigorously. "You're missing the point. You have to listen."

I lean back against the sill and stare out at the darkening sky. "What else have I been doing *but* listening, Richard?"

My annoyance doesn't stop him as he plows on.

"I think they would've kept Evan and I locked away forever if they could've, but eventually, the two of us were released. I made sure we carefully avoided coming into contact with anyone else as we exited the building, which wasn't hard to do, as nearly all who worked there were afraid to go near us.

"By that point, I had accepted that my mother's stories weren't fictional, but rather lessons I had failed to heed. I opened Pandora's Box in that hospital room, and part of me feared it wouldn't stop killing. I didn't know what to do. Evan had to be isolated. He couldn't be allowed to come into contact with anyone else. If he did, the Sickness would spread. I knew it with a certainty I had never felt before.

"I tried to tell him the truth, but he wouldn't listen. He dismissed me, as I had dismissed your grandmother Lily, telling me the Ruin and the Sharing were wild fabrications from lack of sleep. I argued with him until I was blue in the face. It took some convincing, but when I dropped Evan off at his house, he agreed to stay away from people, if only for a day or two to let the dust settle and ensure anything left from quarantine had dissipated.

"That night, I came home to you and your mother. I told her the truth too, everything I'm telling you now. She listened and thought about what I said for a long time. We fell asleep together for the first time in weeks, holding each other as tightly as we could.

"I didn't expect Valerie to believe me. In the morning, I wasn't sure she had. She got out of bed with the alarm and went about business as usual, or as close to it as she could after having recovered from a serious and deadly sickness days before. We made you pancakes, sausage, eggs, and fruit salad for breakfast, then we sat at the table and enjoyed our meal together.

"When you went upstairs to play, we talked about the Ruin and the Sharing again. She had so many questions, and I answered them as best as I could. The conversation was painful. It hurt to acknowledge I had taken such a careless risk and put not only our family, but everyone, the human race, at risk. In the end, Valerie decided I was telling her the truth."

"No, she didn't. There's no way."

"She did, and I will *forever* be grateful. I can't imagine the extent of the damage my actions might have caused if she hadn't. Too many people had died already. We couldn't risk the Sickness spreading and killing thousands, if not millions, more.

"So, your mother and I came up with a plan. We packed enough supplies to last the week and called your grandparents. She arranged for you to visit them in Harrisburg with your sister. We gambled that because you didn't get sick, you wouldn't be a carrier. We prayed your health was a sign you were like me, immune.

"It was incredibly risky, but we couldn't leave you home alone, and we couldn't take you with us, either. Thankfully, your grandparents agreed to the visit, so we packed your bags, drove you out, and dropped you off. Do you remember that?"

"I do."

"After we dropped you off, your mother and I went back for our own supplies. We drove to Evan's house to try to convince him to follow along with our plan. We didn't know how, but we had to get him to the village of the Ruin. He had to isolate himself alongside the one group of people he couldn't infect. Of course, we would have to find it first. All I had was my mother's stories. We didn't know how long it would take or if we would even make it, but we had to try.

"The only problem was Evan didn't want to go. As I said, though he had seen the damage I had caused at the hospital with his own eyes, he didn't believe my stories. How could he? We were asking him to give up his entire life for something he thought was a fairytale. He never would have left with us on his own."

"I wouldn't have gone with you, either."

"Your mother planned for that," Richard continues. "We knew how it sounded, so before we told Evan about the plan, she prepared his favorite meal, claiming it was meant to celebrate his recovery. We didn't serve it to him until after we talked. Then, we ate."

"Oh god, you poisoned him, didn't you?" I shift uncomfortably on the sill, feeling the first spark of real fear.

"After nothing but hospital food for weeks, Evan was understandably famished. He had two huge helpings of carbonara and didn't notice when your mother and I ate next to nothing. We pushed our food around on our plates and kept him distracted with conversation."

"Did you kill Evan?" I ask, horrified and afraid to hear the answer. As discreetly as I can, I slip my hand into my pocket, ready to retrieve my phone and dial 9-1-1.

"No! Of course, we didn't kill Evan. Why would we kill him after everything that happened? How could I kill my best friend?" Richard asks, astounded. "No, we drugged him. We knocked him out with sleeping pills." The look on his face begs me to see this as the better option, but I don't know how to feel.

A shiver races up my spine and my bones chill. "What did you do with him, Richard? I don't remember seeing him again after the hospital…"

"We took him to the Ruin."

"What?"

"It took us almost a week to find the village with only my mother's stories to guide us. I felt terrible about what we were doing, but it was necessary. We walked him out to the car before he fell asleep and strapped him into the backseat. Once he dozed off, your mother blindfolded him and monitored him while I drove. We couldn't risk the possibility of him knowing where we were in case he tried to escape and make his way back home.

"Eventually, we had to leave the car and set off on foot. Evan was awake by that point, so we bound him to us and brought him through the mountains. We didn't torture him," Richard says, seeing the alarm on my face. "We took care of him as best as we could. The point of this was never to harm him but to protect other people. You have to understand."

"I don't understand. Are you telling me you and my mother kidnapped your best friend? She wouldn't have helped you do that!"

"She would, and she did." His voice is firm, yet deeply

sad. "We had to. His very presence in the world could have killed thousands of people, maybe even millions. We did what we had to do.

"We found the village in the middle of the mountains, just as my mother's stories said we would. It was bigger than I expected it to be. They wouldn't let us in at first. They saw the three strangers before them, one of them bound and blindfolded, and hesitated for obvious reasons. I couldn't blame them. Nothing about our approach was conventional. But, we were patient and made a small camp by the stream for three days while they made their decision.

"On the third day, they sent a messenger to retrieve Evan and me. Your mother was not allowed entry into the village. I suspected they were worried she would come into contact with one of the other contagions within and carry it out into the world. We left her in the tent, and the messenger led us in.

"The two of us were taken into one of the larger buildings near the front of the village and seated at a small, wooden table. A handful of men and a lone woman sat before us. They asked me to tell our story once more. Their faces were impassive as they listened.

"In the end, they made their decree. Evan was to stay in the village with them. They would care for him, but he would never again be allowed to leave. However, that wasn't their only condition. I was to be sent away and never to return on penalty of death.

"They called it a payment for my aberration. I was told I would not be allowed to return because the knowledge of the Ruin did not belong to me. My mother's abandonment and my actions involving Evan meant I was unfit. I was deemed untrustworthy, so they cast me out, and I was helpless against them.

"I didn't want to leave Evan behind with no possibility of

seeing him again, so I argued with them. I begged to be allowed to return, even once a year. However, they didn't argue with me. Instead, the woman pointed out the window to where we had entered the village. Two men held knives up to your mother's throat. I was informed that if I did not agree to their terms, they would execute your mother as a demonstration of their penalties for disobeying the laws of the Ruin.

"I couldn't let them hurt Valerie and leave you and your sister without a mother, so I reluctantly agreed to leave Evan behind. I told myself he was safe, that he could live out his life without harming others, that I was doing the right thing.

"We were both escorted out of the building. Before I walked through the gate to your mother's side, I looked back at my friend. He shook his head "no" at me so violently I worried he would hurt himself, but I had no choice. When he saw I had made up my mind, hatred stronger than any I had ever seen consumed him.

"I walked away from Evan. I haven't seen him since. As far as I know, he's alive, healthy, and safe, but when I healed him, I completely took his life away. I ruined him."

"No way. If he didn't want to be somewhere, he would've left. You're so full of it."

"Your mother and I made the trek back to the car without speaking and drove to your grandparents' house to bring the two of you home. We never said a word about where we had been. Instead, we asked you about your visit. You thought it was odd that we wanted to know if your grandparents were feeling alright, but everyone was okay. You told us about all of the fun things you did while you were there, and on the way home, we listened to music and laughed.

"We thought everything was fine. Your grandparents never contracted the Sickness. But, it wasn't fine. Back at home, Jennifer did. It was nowhere near as severe as it had been for the others. It must have been a lesser version of what your mother had. Jennifer was only indirectly exposed. She recovered within the week, but it scared us both so much more than I can put into words.

"After a few weeks, strange men started showing up around the house. Evan had been reported missing, and his parents and cousins were searching for him. Since he was last seen with me, I was treated with suspicion. His family had money and connections. They hired a PI, but I knew they'd never find him, not without me.

"That's when your mother and I made our decision. It devastated us to imagine our family separated like this, but we were concerned someone from the village might seek me out and learn of our children, or perhaps even worse, that Evan's family might make the connection and use the two of you against us to find him. We had to do everything we could to keep you both safe.

"We agreed I would leave quickly and we wouldn't tell you or your sister the stories of your ancestors to keep you safe. As painful as it was, we decided to eliminate all contact between the family and me so you wouldn't be tempted to seek me out. Together, we set up a system to contact each other in case there was ever a need — in case one of you found yourself as desperate as I had been and was putting yourself or others in danger.

"My actions destroyed our family, but your mother and I did our best to protect you. That's why I'm here now, Kara. Your actions are endangering not just yourself, but potentially thousands of people, maybe more. You need to stop."

I'm astounded by Richard's accusation. I shake my head in disbelief, trembling with barely contained rage.

"You come back here after all this time, and you tell me our ancestors are responsible for the deaths of thousands of people, that *you* are responsible for the deaths of, I don't even know how many, and you claim *my mother* helped you kidnap your best friend and abandon him with a cult, but you want to turn around and accuse *me* of being the dangerous one for trying to keep my mom alive!" I erupt, unable to control myself.

"I know what you've done!" Richard throws his hands in the air. "I know about the plasma donation. It has to stop. Don't you understand? By trying to save your mother, you're making the same mistake I did. You're risking so much more than you know!"

"What?" Confusion rockets through me. "You came back because of that?"

"I came back to help you."

"Bullshit! How dare you? After everything?"

"My actions are in the past!" Richard bellows back, on his feet now. "You are doing stupid and dangerous things right now! You're breaking the law and trying to bend the rules so you get what you want, but you can't do that, Kara. Don't you understand? You're risking your future and the future of everyone around you!"

I scramble to my feet as well, squaring off against this arrogant, presumptive man who, despite believing in ridiculous legends, has already admitted to committing serious crimes and abandoning our family. My eyes lock on his.

"Compared to you, I've done absolutely nothing wrong! I've begged, borrowed, and stolen. I've bargained my mother's way into an experimental treatment. I've worked my ass off and fought harder than you ever would to give Mom the life she deserves, the life *YOU* took from her when *YOU* selfishly walked out of our home and never looked back. Don't you dare stand there and tell me I'm in the wrong. I would do *anything* for my mother. I would *never* walk away from this and give up on her. That is what *YOU* did. Stop projecting your guilt onto me!"

Richard turns and stalks toward the kitchen, then back

toward me again, pacing. "I've admitted to what I've done, Kara. I have no misunderstandings about my shortcomings and how our family ended up where it is today. But, you need to face the truth. You have to let your mother go. She's ready to die, and as a member of the Ruin — "

"There is no such thing as the Ruin!" I shout. "That's just some bullshit story you came up with to ease your guilt over whatever you did to Evan and abandoning everyone you *claim* you love. Our ancestors are *NOT* responsible for the cholera epidemic. My blood does *NOT* possess some mystical power that could destroy the planet. You're being RIDICULOUS!"

"The Ruin is real!"

"No, it isn't!"

"The signs are already there."

"What signs?"

"Valerie mentioned your arms, the advanced healing."

"I had some cuts and they went away. That's what they do!"

"You have to stop what you're doing. Do *NOT* donate any of your blood, no matter what this company tells you they want it for. What if they figure out what it does? Your blood in the wrong hands could kill millions! Stop this madness and let your mother go. I know it's hard —"

"You don't know anything!" I howl. "You don't know me, or Mom, or Jennifer. You know nothing about us because you haven't been here for *FIFTEEN YEARS*! How dare you try to manipulate me. I don't understand what you stand to gain from all of this, and I don't care. Get out of this apartment. Don't ever contact me again. We're done here."

Richard growls in frustration. "You're just as stubborn as your mother and me. I am *trying* to stop you from making the biggest mistake of your life. You have to listen."

"Get out!" I repeat, hands on my hips and staring at the door.

"You are a member of the Ruin, Kara. You have to stop."

"Oh my god! I am not a member of the fucking Ruin. They aren't real! You're delusional! And, your story is *FULL* of holes. If I was a member of that cult, Jennifer would be, too. She's your daughter! Why would Jennifer get sick if our family's blood is so damn special? Have you considered that? You can't even keep your lies straight."

Richard's face instantly shifts from furious and frustrated to guarded. "That's not my story to tell. You'll have to talk to Valerie."

"Whatever. Get the fuck out of this apartment, Richard Edwards," I demand. "Leave. You're not welcome here."

For a moment, Richard looks as though he's about to say something more, but he doesn't. He backs down. His rigid form slackens and his face falls. He quietly walks to the door but stops when he grabs the handle.

"You're making a mistake."

"Hardly."

"I'm staying in Baltimore," he states. "Connor has my address and my phone number. I sincerely hope you'll change your mind and make the right decision. Stop donating plasma. Stop the experimental treatment. Let your mother go. You can call me if you need to talk. I'll always answer. You may not believe me, but I love you, Kara. I'm trying to help you."

"Leave," I demand once more. "I haven't needed you since I was six, and I don't need you now." I cross the room to stand behind him as he opens the door and steps out into the hallway. Without hesitation, I slam it shut. It rattles in its frame.

Fuming, I press my back to the door and wait to hear him walk away.

"I'm so sorry," he whispers. His footsteps fade as he disappears down the hall.

I run to the window to watch as he leaves, making sure he's actually gone before I collapse and violently sob. I'm still there almost ten minutes later when Connor returns. He scoops me off the floor and holds me as night begins to fall. The bags of dinner he brought with him lay abandoned in the middle of the living room floor.

CHAPTER TWENTY-FOUR

S t. John's cafeteria is crowded at 11:30 in the morning. Ambulatory patients and their loved ones sit around tables or pass through the serving area. Many of the hospital staff mill about with stained and disheveled clothes that match the varying shades of exhaustion visible under their eyes. A low rumble in my stomach reminds me I'm hungry as I pass by. I haven't eaten since early this morning.

It takes me a moment to find a table away from the vast majority of the patrons. For my purposes, I need something quiet with a semblance of privacy. I hadn't counted on the lunch rush when I asked Doctor Mitchell to meet me here. Luckily, there's an empty space, perfect for two people, tucked away in the back near one of the garbage cans. I swipe a few crumbs off of the navy chair before taking a seat and removing my purse and jacket.

I glance around the room, looking for Doctor Mitchell among the crowd. As far as I can tell, he hasn't arrived yet. Something must have held him up. I try not to worry too much about what it might be. If it had anything to do with Mom, he would have called or texted, and it's unlikely he would decide to ghost me and back out of our arrangement now.

When my eyes pass over the hot food line, they land on

Trinity, who notices my attention and offers me a pleasant smile and a wave. I smile back before she turns to speak to the server who's busy ladling out some sort of creamy pasta.

An affectionate warmth settles into my chest at the sight of her. Trinity's honestly my favorite person in this building. Without her, I wouldn't have known about Plasmedics. Through all of this, she's been my guide.

Connor, Ally, and I have made several visits to Plasmedics this week. Between our donation payments and the advance on my check, I've scraped together enough money for the upcoming treatment and stowed away what's left for the ones to follow. I have three more appointments this week, and as long as Plasmedics keeps paying me like this, I'll keep going back. Things are finally heading in the right direction.

A chorus of laughs from a few tables away snags my attention. Fingers drumming impatiently on the table, I turn to look for the source. My hands freeze when my gaze lands on Matthew Collins. The blood drains from my face. Instinct urges me to slip lower in my chair and hide myself behind the potted plant on the stand next to me. There's something unsettling about him beyond his connection to Novemion.

What's he doing here? How had I not seen him when I sat down? Maybe meeting Doctor Mitchell in a public place wasn't such a great idea after all.

Though I've spotted him, he doesn't seem to have noticed me. From this far away, I can't hear a word he's saying, but Matthew's obviously engrossed in a conversation with three older men. From what I can tell, this must be a business negotiation of sorts. Two of the men sitting across from him are dressed in crisp suits. The one farthest away, a neurologist I recognize as Doctor Wong, is wearing his white coat and an expensive sweater-vest over top of a button-down shirt. He looks quite bored, while the man closest to me in a charcoal gray ensemble is nearly rapt, devouring Matthew's words. My guess is Matthew's peddling a new drug, and whichever medication it is, applies best to the closest man's specialty.

I watch Matthew passes a thick stack of papers and a pen to the gentleman in the center. He's tall and balding, and the light from the overhead fluorescents reflects off the top of his head. The ebony skin there shines as though it's been recently polished. I can't be sure why, but my gut tells me this man is on the hospital board.

The middle man flips through the stack while the others wait patiently. My eyes are glued to the exchange. Thankfully, Matthew doesn't look up.

"Sorry I'm late, Ms. Edwards," Doctor Mitchell announces as he places a dark red tray onto the table and slides into the space across from me. His sudden presence startles me, but I quickly regain my composure. "I had an unexpected call from one of my patients. I'm sure you can understand the importance of such a matter."

Tearing myself away from what's happening at Matthew's table, I focus on the man I've come to see. "Of course. I hope everything is okay."

"Me too." Doctor Mitchell removes his jacket and places it over the back of his chair, then pops open the buttons on the cuffs of his sleeves, rolling them up to just below his elbows. He rips open a bag of chips. "She's a very nice woman, not unlike your mother. It's hard to hear things aren't going well for her. Unfortunately, there's not much I can do over the phone." He picks up an item from his tray and peels back the sticker on the wax paper, unwrapping a pre-made sandwich. "Turkey and cheese?" He offers up half. "It's not so bad."

I shake my head. "No, thanks. I ate before I came." The lie slips easily from my lips. I've told the same one too many times before. A turkey and cheese sandwich sounds delightful, but that's not what I'm here for.

Doctor Mitchell takes a bite and dabs at the corner of his mouth with a brown paper napkin where a smidge of mayonnaise has escaped. I glance at Matthew. He still isn't looking this way, but that could change at any moment. I need to get this over with.

"Here," I say, reaching into my purse and retrieving a thick envelope. My hand shakes as I set it down on the table and slide it over to him. I had intended to handle the payment with a little more tact, but my gut tells me this isn't the time to dawdle.

Doctor Mitchell nearly chokes on his food. He drops his used napkin over the envelope, eyes wide in shock. "Now? You want to take care of it right here?"

"Might as well."

He peers around the room conspicuously. "Ms. Edwards, this is highly irregular. I assumed we would talk about your mother's status over lunch, then handle the finances in my office."

"Stop that," I chastise. "People will think something is going on. Look, I don't have time today. I still need to go see Mom and I have a shift in a few hours."

His brow beads with sweat. Reaching down and grabbing one of the clean napkins, I mime wiping my own forehead, then pass it to him. He dabs the dampness away.

"I really think — "

"... For the donation I promised to your fundraiser." I cut him off, speaking a little louder in case anyone is watching. "You didn't forget, did you? I'm sorry it took me so long to get it to you."

Understanding flickers across Doctor Mitchell's face. "Oh, yes. Thank you. I appreciate how much effort you're making for our department."

"Of course. After everything you've done for my family, how could I refuse?"

Reassured by the charade, the nervousness disappears from Doctor Mitchell's face. He lifts the napkin off of the envelope and places the money beneath his tray for safekeeping. "The foundation truly counts on *every dollar* pledged. It makes a huge difference for people like *your Mom*."

Is he asking me if the whole payment is there?

Continuing the ruse, I nod my head in agreement. "I understand. You can count it if you'd like. I wouldn't let the foundation down, not when the cause is so important."

"I would never," he answers. "I trust you have everyone's best interests in mind, Ms. Edwards."

I cast a quick glance back to the other table. Matthew practically radiates satisfaction as the center man signs one of the documents with a flourish. His eyes lift and turn in the direction of our table. Trying to remain inconspicuous, I look away.

An inkling of Doctor Mitchell's usual confidence has returned. "I have an update on Valerie's status for you this morning. So far, it's good news. Her vitals have been fairly stable, and we don't see any excessive bruising or drainage. The incisions are healing well. I'm having some labs drawn this afternoon to check for any signs of infection or changes to her metabolic panel. If those come back clear, then it seems we're doing the best we can for the time being."

"That's good to hear." My legs bounce beneath the table. I need this update, but I desperately want to get out of this room. "What about the treatment? How's that going?"

Doctor Mitchell leans forward, lowering his voice. "It's still early. We won't know whether it will be successful for quite some time. However, with her vitals remaining stable and no outward signs of discomfort, she seems to be tolerating it well. Are you certain you would like to continue pursuing a treatment as *aggressive* as this?"

He's giving me an out, a chance to walk away.

"If it's working, then we keep going," I assert.

"So long as you're certain."

"I am."

"Good. I'll make the necessary arrangements."

One more look at Matthew's table. The men have stood and are gathering their things.

What if he comes over here?

"Thank you for your time, Doctor Mitchell." I extend my hand for a quick shake, ending our own business meeting. "Enjoy what's left of your lunch. I'd like to say hello to Trinity before I go upstairs." It isn't kind to use her as an excuse, but I need an out.

I rise, ready to escape, and sling my purse over my shoulder. Before I can take a step, Doctor Mitchell reaches out and stops me, grabbing my forearm. It catches me off-guard, and I turn back toward him.

"Speaking of Trinity, last night she informed me she gave you the information for a plasma donation clinic nearby called Plasmedics. Have you been there yet?"

Confused, I nod. "I've donated several times now. It's nice to be able to make a difference." What I hope is a convincing false smile plasters itself across my face.

Doctor Mitchell's grip tightens uncomfortably. I pull my arm away.

"Yes, it is. I hear Plasmedics is a lovely facility, state of the art." His eyes are hard as he looks at me. There's something worrisome about his expression. "Just be careful, Ms. Edwards. That donation center has some important affiliations you might not be aware of."

"Affiliations?"

"Yes, the corporation that owns the Plasmedics facility is involved in many different medical ventures. For example, they've recently begun manufacturing a new treatment for lung cancer that has not yet been released to the public. I hear it's called Novemion."

My face blanches. *Plasmedics is connected to Novemion?*

"While Plasmedics and its parent company are doing great things in the world," he continues, "some of the parent company's practices have been questionable in the past. Make sure you're taking the necessary precautions. I wouldn't want you to get involved in anything unseemly."

I clear my throat. Anxiety eats away at the structure of my bones, leaving my legs weak. "Of course. Neither would I."

Doctor Mitchell picks up his sandwich once more. He lifts the bread and layers a handful of chips across the meat and cheese. "Be discreet," he whispers without looking up. "Try not to draw too much attention to yourself. I understand what you're doing, but if anyone finds out what *we're* doing, it could mean serious trouble for all of us."

Swallowing a lump in my throat, I return my gaze to Matthew's table, hoping the two of us have not drawn too much attention to ourselves already, but the four men are gone. I drape my coat across my arm where Doctor Mitchell's hand had been.

"I'll see you around, Ms. Edwards," he adds with a smile, but it doesn't reach his eyes.

"Thank you again."

Doctor Mitchell doesn't look up. Dismissed, I walk quickly toward the exit, aiming for the elevators.

What does this mean for us? Do I have to find another way to pay for Mom's treatments? There's no way I can make enough money without Plasmedics.

I'm so distracted by Doctor Mitchell's revelation that I round the corner without looking, colliding head-on with Matthew Collins.

CHAPTER TWENTY-FIVE

Scalding hot coffee spills down the front of my shirt, soaking through to the skin. I hiss as I lift the fabric away from my chest and stomach, using it to fan the area. Once I realize the burning sensation isn't serious, I look up at Matthew who is doing something similar with his button-down.

"Oh, my god. I'm so sorry." A huge brown splotch stains his front, extending from his stomach to the waist of his slacks. "I wasn't paying attention to where I was going. This is all my fault."

Matthew shakes a few errant drops off of his hand. "It's fine. I never liked this shirt anyway. You're Kara, right? From the parking structure? The girl with the missing ring."

"Uh, yeah." Feigning ignorance, I ask, "You're… Matthew?"

"When it suits me." He flashes me a devilish grin. "Watch where you step. Wouldn't want you to slip."

He offers me his hand. Not wanting to seem skittish, I accept and let him guide me around the puddle marring the otherwise clean tile.

"Visiting your mom again today?"

"Nearly every day," I answer. "I don't like the thought of her being here alone."

"It's funny, isn't it? There are hundreds, if not thousands of people in this building, and yet without the ones we love, we are as alone as we would be in the middle of the mountains."

"I guess that's true."

"Personally, I think life isn't worth living without family. What would we have left?"

I don't want to talk about this with him. I'd rather not talk to him at all. *Why do I have to be so damn clumsy?*

Changing the subject, I gesture toward the spill. "Should we call someone? I feel awful leaving a mess behind."

Matthew lifts his head and scans the room. "No need." He points to the woman behind the greeter's desk. "She's already on the phone. I'm sure it will be taken care of shortly."

"Good."

I step around Matthew, moving toward the elevators. I need to get to Mom's room before I make any more mistakes. "Well, I'm sorry again. I'll see you around."

"Actually, I'm headed that way, too. Walk with me? It's the least you could do after ruining such fine clothes." His expression reads humor, but his words have me trapped. "I'm meeting someone upstairs."

I can't turn back the way I came now. That would be suspicious. Besides, he hasn't offered me any reason to be so uncomfortable around him. He's been nothing but kind since we first met. He helped me find Mom's ring and hasn't berated me for spilling his drink. Whatever's bothering me must be in my head. So, I smile politely and let him walk beside me, keeping my guard up all the while.

"How is your mom? Any improvement?"

"Stable. Not much change."

"I'm sorry to hear that. Not that she's stable, I mean. Just that she isn't going home anytime soon."

I don't have anything to say to that. He might seem kind, but I'm not opening up to Matthew Collins. He's too dangerous, too close to Novemion, and something tells me he's not going away. This hospital is his current stomping ground.

"I'd love to stop by and chat with her sometime."

No, no, no. Stay away from my mom. You can't go near her. You can't know what's happening.

But, those aren't the words that come out of my mouth. Instead, I ask, "Really? Why? You don't know her."

"No, I don't. It seems like a shame if you ask me. Stories like hers are part of the reason my father's company works so hard to develop new medications. I wish we had something ready to help her. We may, in a few months. Time will tell."

Warning bells ring in my ears. *He's talking about Novemion. Change the topic. Steer clear.* I pick up the pace and approach the elevator doors. There's no line, so I jab my finger into the button and wait.

Come on. Come on. Let's go. Unconsciously, I shift back and forth on my feet.

"Cold?" Matthew asks, misreading my anxiety.

"Wet," I offer as an excuse and point to my shirt.

The elevator arrives with a ding. When the doors slide open, an older woman with a walker, two worn tennis balls in the front, and a middle-aged man, likely her son, creep out of the enclosed space. Matthew and I take their places. He presses one button, and I press another. The doors slide closed, sealing us in together. Nowhere to run.

"Don't give up hope yet, Kara. New treatments are coming. Better ones, I can assure you. Our drug, Novemion, could revolutionize the way we treat cancer. Your Mom — "

I cut him off. "I'm not in the mood for a sales pitch right now."

He lets out a breathless chuckle. "Sorry. Novemion is

important to me. I'm leading the trials and the FDA clearance application. I tend to talk about it too often."

The elevator dings and stops at another floor. An older gentleman steps inside. He ignores me and directs a look toward Matthew. The benevolent expression on Matthew's face slips away. He takes three steps back, making room for the newcomer. Something in the air changes.

"Ms. Edwards," Matthew says, shifting to a formal tone. "Allow me to introduce you to my father, Elias Collins, owner and CEO of Coarser Industries."

Elias turns to face me. Unlike his son, who exudes charm, Elias is statuesque. His thick head of salt and pepper hair is precisely cropped. Deep wrinkles carve grooves through his face. A full beard extends down from his temples to his chin, making his jaw appear excessively square, and like the hair atop his head, not one strand is out of place. It gives the impression of someone cold and impassive.

He doesn't say anything but instead turns back to his son.

"Don't you have better things to do than flirt with random women in the elevator?" Disapproval coats his words.

"I was simply talking to Ms. Edwards on the way to meet up with you, Father." Matthew's face is unreadable. His tone is flat.

"So you say." Elias flicks his gaze to me, then directs it back to his son. "If you need to talk so badly, you should be speaking with Xavier Ferndale. I want that deal on my desk by this afternoon."

"It's already been handled."

"It better be."

"It is. I'm capable of doing my job." For a split second, annoyance flashes behind Matthew's eyes.

The anxiety I felt earlier fades. I actually feel bad for him. Elias seems like a real hard ass.

"I was speaking with Ms. Edwards about Novemion. Her mother has cancer."

Elias turns to study me. I freeze as he takes in my worn clothes, stained shirt, and holey shoes. His lips purse, but he says nothing. Instead, he crosses his arms in front of his chest and stares at the elevator door.

"If the FDA approves our treatment soon, we may be able to save her mother's life. Isn't that right, Father?"

"No."

Elias Collins is obviously a jerk, but I hadn't expected that.

"Why is that, Mr. Collins?" I pipe up. My logical side warns me to keep my mouth shut, but as it so often does, my emotional side won't follow directions and speaks of its own accord.

Elias Collins' face morphs into a mask of disgust. "Because, Ms. Edwards. Judging by the way you carry yourself, there's no way you could afford it. Like it or not, medical care in this country is for those with means, of which you have none."

Rage rips through me. My hands ball into fists. This man is the perfect example of why I have to turn to illegal methods to keep my mother alive. His greed and haughty attitude scream indifference. *How dare he?*

"Father — "

"Perhaps you have forgotten, Matthew, that we own and operate one of the largest pharmaceutical companies in the world. How do you suppose that happened? Do you believe I gave valuable products away to anyone with a sad story? You and your ideals. You're as useless as the rest of them. I should have listened to your mother and given this job to your sister. You're nothing more than a child."

Matthew falls silent. He shrinks into himself, defeated.

Based on the way his posture changes, I'd guess they've had this conversation before.

Don't do it. Don't say a word. Let it go. Don't —

"You know, Mr. Collins... Can I call you Elias? I'm surprised you're not a sexist pig. No, you're just a greedy, cold-hearted bastard. Who talks to their son like that?"

Matthew's mouth falls open. Elias starts to speak, but I don't let him, which perturbs him even more. Being a man who gets what he wants, I'm nothing to him. He expects me to back down and act like the good little poor person I am. But, I won't. I'll make him listen. All five foot four inches of me stands to full height. My confidence dwarves him. I make his nearly six-foot stature look small.

"I hope you know what it's like to lose everything someday. I hope you end up in the same position as my mother, but find your bedside empty. I hope you have to stare death in the face and know there's no way out. I hope you have to watch the company you've built off of greed and human sacrifice burn to the ground."

The elevator dings at my floor.

I step in front of Elias Collins and turn to face his son. "Thank you for offering me a bit of hope today, Matthew. That was kind. I think you'll make a great CEO for your *family's*" I emphasize the word, not giving Elias the credit he wants, "company. Again, I'm sorry about your clothes. I'm glad no one was hurt."

He nods, eyes wide.

"As for you, Elias. Have the day you deserve."

I turn on my heel and walk away, still fuming. Elias Collins' eyes burn into my back as I disappear down the hall.

CHAPTER TWENTY-SIX

Mom's face is scrunched in concentration when I enter the room. She's bent over the little tray table, pencil nub in hand, scribbling tiny letters into the empty boxes of a crossword someone must have clipped out of the morning paper. I'd wager Trinity brought it to her before she went to lunch.

"Hey, Mommy," I whisper, leaning down to deposit a kiss on her bandana. I plop my coat and purse onto the floor next to the guest chair and pull her into a gentle hug. She's rail thin, and through the opening in the back of her gown, the ridge of her spine presses against her skin.

"Hey, baby girl." She leans her head against me and smiles.

"How are you feeling?" I ask, taking the seat beside her.

Mom waves the question away like an annoying fly. She hates when I pester her, but how else am I supposed to know what's going on?

"No, really? Is everything okay?"

"The same as usual," she answers. "I feel like a cancer patient. Not much has changed." She drops the pencil onto the tray and leans back against the pillows. "Cooped up and tired of being prodded."

"So, no new pains?"

"Not really. Some of the incision sites itch, but that means they're healing."

"You don't feel sick?"

"No. Why?"

"Your breathing feels alright? Not too strained?"

"I'm fine, Kara. Quit fussing over me." Her brows furrow, but whether it's due to frustration or concern, I can't tell. She looks tired.

"Never. That's my job."

Mom reaches over and takes my hand into her own. She gives it a gentle squeeze. "I know."

I've peppered her with more questions over the last week than usual. Doctor Mitchell swears she's tolerating the Novemion well, but I need to be sure. There's no one else I can turn to for guidance, so I have to rely on Mom's intuition. She knows her body better than anyone.

"Ready for a new bandana?"

"How many days has it been?"

"A few. It's probably replacement time. I can wash your hair…"

"Sure, hon. That would be nice."

Mom loves having her hair washed, what's left of it anyway. I've been doing it since she started her treatments. It's an easy enough task. My hands make quick work of the knot and remove the old bandana. I wad it into a ball and drop it into my purse, and she rubs the newly exposed skin on top of her head while I get things together.

There are empty bowls in the cabinets beneath the small, stainless steel sink. I fill two of them about halfway with warm water, then retrieve a couple of washcloths and Mom's shampoo from the closet by the bed. She scoots forward, making room for me to stand behind her without spilling water onto the pillows, and I dip one of the cloths into the first bowl, soaking it through. When it's wet enough, I wring it out a tad and scrub it gently over her peach fuzz.

The top of the shampoo bottle snaps open with a sharp click. The tiny portion of shampoo that squirts into my hands is cold. I rub them together until it's warm and the soap lathers. Mom sighs when I massage the foam onto her scalp and scrub lightly with my nails.

I use the same rag for the first rinse, wiping as many of the suds off as I can, then dip the clean cloth into the other bowl of water to clear away the rest. When I'm finished, I deposit the bowls and rags into the sink and run a soft-bristled baby brush through the clean strands. She chooses a dark blue bandana with a white paisley print to replace the dirty yellow one, so I slip this over her head and lean her back against the pile of pillows once more.

"You have to work today?" Mom asks.

"Later this afternoon. Jason called out again, so I'm closing Renee's with the night crew, then back again in the morning. Hopefully, they'll let me pull a double."

"You work too much." Her eyes are sad as she studies me. "Do you ever rest? You're always here with me or at Renee's."

Truthfully, I haven't been here as much as I should've been lately. I stop by every day, but my visits have been shorter since Richard showed up and spewed his stories about the family cult. I've been avoiding serious conversations because I know I'll end up telling her Connor called him, and it's easier to dodge the subject when I don't stick around.

I don't want her to worry about me. She would know Connor hadn't called Richard for a silly reason. More importantly, I'm finding it difficult to acknowledge that Mom could have reached out to him any time. No matter how you spin it, it's a betrayal. At the very least, she should have told

Jennifer and me. I can't fathom why she kept things from us. *Was it her pride?*

Guilt over my recent absence warms my cheeks as I tell Mom about other things that have been going on at the apartment. She laughs when I recount how badly Connor burned the scrambled eggs the other day. None of us could scrape them out of the pan. We ended up throwing it out, and Ally had teased Connor mercilessly about his abysmal cooking skills. I tell her Ally has been off with Rob quite often. They seem to be doing well and have a summer vacation planned, just the two of them. I earn another chuckle when she finds out about Sir Meowverick's antics. He jumped in the shower with Connor last night and scared him half to death.

But Mom, ever observant, knows there's something else I'm keeping from her. I can see the gears whirring in her mind.

"That's great, Kara. I'm glad you guys have each other. Want to tell me what else is going on? After twenty-one years, you should know you can't hide things from me. I've got a mother's intuition. Don't keep secrets."

Ironically, secrets are exactly what we need to discuss. The thing is, mine aren't the ones that need to be dealt with.

As I muster up the courage to tell her the truth, my hands busy themselves with other things. I stand and tug the white sheet and knitted blanket up to her waist and tuck her in, carefully folding the edges into a neat line. She waits, watching me work, and doesn't push.

"I saw Richard the other day," I venture, sitting back down. "I went out for a walk, and when I came back, he was talking to Connor. That was a surprise."

Mom folds her hands in her lap, but she doesn't reply.

"Connor called him, I guess. He said you gave him Richard's number."

"I did."

"I didn't know you had it. You told him to call Richard if he was worried about me? Well, that day I had a bit of an angry outburst when I met up with Jennifer. You know how she pushes my buttons. Connor was concerned."

"You saw Jennifer? How is she?"

I hesitate, not wanting to tell Mom the truth. She doesn't need to know how bad my sister's drug problem has gotten. "She's... okay. She wanted to check in on her cat."

"Uh huh," Mom says. She doesn't believe me, but she lets it go anyway.

"That's not the point, though. How long have you had Richard's number, Mom?" I try and fail to keep the accusation out of my voice.

"We've had limited contact since he left."

Her answer confuses me. "Limited contact?"

"He always made sure I had a way to reach him if either of you needed him, just in case."

I can't help myself. Anger rises up inside of me. I fight it down as much as I can, but it seeps into my words. "So, you could have asked him to come back whenever you wanted? He could have helped us after your diagnosis? We could have been a family the entire time?"

She shakes her head. "No, your father couldn't come home. Even knowing how to find him complicated things."

"But, why? I don't understand."

So many things have changed in the last fifteen years, but the same hurt and sadness consume me. The careful wall of numbness I've built during Richard's absence crumbles around me.

Mom looks down and stares at her interlaced fingers. "There was a time when you girls were safer without your father, but I have a sinking feeling things are changing."

Blowing out a heavy breath, I focus on staying calm. "What do you mean?"

"Your father is a complicated man with a complicated past."

"You knew he was crazy then?"

"He's not crazy, Kara, and you know I don't like that word." She raises her eyes to meet mine. "He's just... it was better if he wasn't around."

"He is crazy, Mom. You should have heard the things he was saying!" I fidget with her wedding band, spinning it around and around on my finger.

Her voice drops to a whisper. "What did he tell you?"

I lean forward, propping my elbows on my knees, and drop my head into my hands. "A bunch of delusional babble about a secret family cult, and cholera, and his friend Evan, and this ridiculous thing he called the Sharing. It's some kind of amateur transfusion, I think. I don't know. None of it made any sense."

"He told you about the Sharing? About Evan?"

"He said Evan was really sick and he did some bogus ritual to heal him. I could almost believe that, but then he said you two kidnapped Evan and abandoned him in the mountains with this hidden society. He called them the Ruin."

"Oh, Richard..." Mom says, exasperated. She pinches the bridge of her nose and shakes her head. "Why would you lead with that? It wasn't the right time..."

"What?" I thought she would be shocked, appalled even, but she isn't. Instead, she's frustrated. "That's insane, right?" I prompt, sitting up straight. "Mom, tell me you think he's crazy, too."

She sighs. "I can't do that, Kara. Your father isn't crazy, but he's never been great at thinking before he opens his mouth. That man. I swear, I could smack him upside the head."

I'm dumbfounded. Mom believes Richard's lies? But, why? For the first time, I'm left to wonder if the cancer treatments are affecting her mind.

"Are you serious?"

"Richard's not crazy, Kara, and neither am I. I know it seems that way, but you have to understand. There are many things parents do to love and protect their children. Keeping secrets is one of those things."

"He's delusional, Mom!" It's my turn to be exasperated. "For any of Richard's stories to be true, he would have to possess some sort of supernatural ability. Magic isn't real. It's a fairytale. It's something we use to convince little kids the world has more goodness to it than it does. And, if Richard actually tried the *Sharing*," I emphasize the word with air quotes, "with Evan, he's lucky to be alive. So many things could have gone wrong. He could have picked up whatever Evan had, or if their blood types weren't compatible –"

"It doesn't work that way with the Ruin."

"Okay. Let's pretend that's possible for a second. Even so, how could Richard have created some unknown virus that killed a ton of people? From what I can gather, Evan wasn't contagious. It makes no sense."

"I know it doesn't, but if you'd let me explain..."

Thoughts race through my head, each one tumbling free before I can stop them. "There's no way you would've helped him kidnap someone and abandon him somewhere in the mountains with creepy people you'd never met. That sounds nothing like you."

"I did, Kara. We did..."

"And, there are so many holes in his story. If the mysterious disease was so contagious, why didn't you die? You should have, right? Why did it affect Jennifer? She's his daughter, too. Shouldn't she be a member of that weird cult? I mean, Richard said I didn't get sick because I'm a part of the Ruin. It makes no sense at all."

"Stop, Kara. Stop talking and listen!" Mom's voice is loud and firm as it echoes through the room. The effort of yelling over my fretful questions leaves her out of breath.

Ashamed of myself for losing my composure, I reach over and turn on her oxygen. When I pass Mom the clear mask, she places it over her mouth and nose. Her breath fogs up the inside as she struggles to breathe.

"I'm sorry," I whisper. Tears stream down my cheeks. "It's just, all of this is impossible. I need you to know that. You have to."

Mom pulls the mask away from her face. "Your father," she wheezes, "is not delusional. The things he told you are... true. He... did those things. *I* did those things. Neither of us... is proud of them." She replaces the mask and takes a breath, inhaling the stabilizing gas, and pulls it away again. "I know... it sounds absurd, but your... father is a good man." She breathes in the oxygen before continuing. "I thought he was absurd too, but... after what happened with Evan, I knew he wasn't lying. What he did... was reckless. He made a mistake that cost many people their lives... and cost us our family. That's why he had to leave. I didn't expect him... to tell you all of this, but it's the truth." She leans back against the pillows and closes her eyes.

"Why did you want Connor to call him, Mom?"

She peels open her eyes and looks at me. "Because you're doing dangerous things too, Kara. You keep secrets from me. I'm worried about you. I... don't want you to do something reckless that ruins your life, and I won't be around to protect you forever."

"Don't talk like that." I lift Mom's hand off of the bed and hold it close to my chest. "You're not going anywhere. I won't let that happen. I'll never let that happen."

"I know. That's why you need your father. He's been down this path before."

"Mom…"

"Your father knows the consequences of making rash decisions to keep someone you love alive. He can… give you guidance that I can't."

"He told me to let you die!" I sob, angrily swatting tears away. "I won't do that. I'll never do that."

Mom squeezes my hand tighter. "There's an end to everything, Kara, including life. We've tried so many things already. I know we're out of options. My body knows. I can feel it," she says solemnly. A wet cough punctuates her words.

Letting go of Mom's hand, I pass her a styrofoam cup of ice water from the tray table.

"I'm trying to stop you from going down the same path your father did. You can't throw your life away. I love you too much to see that happen."

"There are always more options. I'll keep looking. You can't give up," I plead. "I'm doing fine. Yeah, things are tough, but we'll get through this. We always do."

Mom shakes her head sadly. "I can see you're struggling. You've lost so much weight. Your eyes constantly have those deep, dark circles under them."

"I'm okay."

"I know about the medical bills. Someone from billing came by the other day. This is so much more than I ever meant for you to endure."

"They're just bills. I'll find a way to pay them."

"I think we have both had about enough. You're so strong, but sometimes it makes you foolish. And, all the secrets…"

"Fine. No more secrets. I'll tell you whatever you want to know. Mom…"

She pauses and sips from her cup. As she swallows, she stirs the ice with the white plastic straw. I wait for her to say something as the moments tick by. When she does, she sounds eerily resigned.

"What has Doctor Mitchell been giving me?"

Her question catches me off guard. "I don't…"

"What has he been putting in my IV bag? It's not saline. Saline is clear. The injections are orange."

Why is she asking me now?

I sit straighter in my chair and do my best to feign nonchalance. "Probably whatever medication they have you on now. Some kind of antibiotic?"

"I'm not on antibiotics."

"Something for the cancer then?"

"I saw my chart. He hasn't prescribed anything."

I freeze. *How did she get her chart?* I thought Doctor Mitchell would have at least listed something to keep people from asking questions. This seems like a glaring oversight. *Why wouldn't he?*

"Doctor Mitchell has been personally changing my bags once a day. Every day. I know he has days off, but even then, he shows up to swap them out. I asked Trinity about it. She says he probably forgot to update the chart, but I don't believe her. So, what's in the IV, Kara? Tell me the truth."

"Mom…"

"You're keeping secrets from me. Tell me the truth!" she demands.

Her breathing strains again. She slips the mask back on, but no matter how weak she feels, she won't back down. I got that trait from her. I'm screwed.

My face flushes with embarrassment at being caught in the lie. "I can't. I'm sorry…"

As if this doesn't surprise her at all, Mom nods her head. "Like I said, sometimes… you do foolish and reckless things. If Trinity… doesn't know what it is, and… you won't tell me, I can only assume… it's something I'm not meant… to have. Can… you tell me I'm wrong?"

I slump back into my chair. "No."

"So… you're keeping secrets, and I… asked Connor to call your father. All you're proving to me is… I was right." She reaches out and squeezes my hand again. "I was right to have Connor call Richard, and I'm… right that you need him now. He will protect you in ways I can't."

"How? What are you trying to protect me from?"

"Yourself."

"Mom, I'm okay. I promise."

"You're not." Her eyes flutter closed. "I can't protect you when I'm gone."

"You're not going to die. We'll get through this." I plead with her, begging her to understand.

"I need you to make me a promise," she mumbles.

"What promise?"

"That you won't try the Sharing."

"Mom, I wouldn't do that."

She shakes her head in stubborn disagreement. "Richard shouldn't have told you. Promise me, Kara. Promise me you won't. It's not a gift. It's a curse. People will die."

I groan, unable to hide my frustration. "I promise. But, I won't stop fighting for you either, even if you have. I'm not giving up."

Mom's breathing slows as we sit together. Our conversation has clearly taken its toll. Her arm gradually lowers to the bed, oxygen mask in hand. I twist the nozzle and turn off the flow before hanging the mask on the hook by the tank. She blinks sleepily at me, struggling to stay awake. Carefully avoiding the tubes and wires, I climb into the bed beside her and curl up under her arm. My head rests on her skeletal shoulder.

"Mom?" I venture nervously, hoping to squeeze in one more question before she drifts off. There's something on my mind I haven't been able to move past.

"Mmm..." she answers.

"Why did Jennifer get sick? If Richard's stories are true, she should have been immune. The Ruin are all immune, right?"

She yawns and nuzzles her head against mine. "Some things are better off left alone," she mumbles into my hair.

"Please, Mom," I beg. "Just tell me. I want to know."

She sighs. Her words are slurred. "Jennifer knows."

"What does she know?"

For a second, I think I've missed my chance, that she's too far gone to answer.

"Jennifer isn't a part of the Ruin. She's not Richard's daughter."

I should be shocked, but I'm not. I think I already knew. "If she isn't Richard's daughter, whose daughter is she?" I ask. "Mom?"

Her answer is barely audible, a mess of jumbled words. I have to tip my head up toward hers and strain to make sense of them, but when they fall into place, my mouth drops open and my body goes numb.

"Evan Knightly, the man we brought to the Ruin."

CHAPTER TWENTY-SEVEN

My clothes stink of stale coffee and grease when my shift ends and I'm able to leave Renee's. After spending the last seven hours working the breakfast and lunch rushes, my hair is tangled and my feet throb. I skipped both meals because I'd been too busy running back and forth between the drive-thru window and the front counter. Christa's daughter is sick, so she had to call in this morning. That left us short-staffed, but it worked out well enough. The neverending list of tasks kept me occupied, and time flew by.

I'm sweaty and running on empty when I step out into the midday sun, stale croissant in hand. It flakes apart as I wander aimlessly in the direction of the harbor. It isn't much, but it's buttery. More importantly, it was free. Since I have a couple of hours to myself for the first time in a while, I savor every bite as I search for a place to sit and relax. I want to be outside in the warm, early spring air and allow myself to breathe.

The last few weeks have kept me busier than usual. With several of the local colleges rotating through their spring breaks, many of my co-workers have been off on vacations to faraway places, tropical resorts and white sandy beaches. I've been picking up the slack. In the last week alone, I've worked nearly sixty hours, and the two weeks before that had been much the same. The overtime pay has been nice, especially without all the extra bills I had before I moved in with Connor and Ally. Add that to the donation money from Plasmedics, and a weight has been lifted off of my shoulders. There's been just enough money to cover Mom's treatments, and I've even bought a few groceries for around the house. Nothing fancy, of course, some bagged cereal, rice, and beans, but at least I'm contributing.

I turn right off of Pratt and onto Pier 3, mingling with the crowd of tourists by the water.

Ally and Rob have been at the apartment for the last couple of days. They're driving Connor crazy, but I don't mind. Rob isn't as bad as Connor makes him out to be. He's kind to Sir Meowverick, and because he nearly always has the munchies, he brings good snacks with him, snacks he's more than willing to share. The skunky smell that wafts behind him can be a bit much, but he doesn't cause problems or make huge messes. He makes Ally happy, too. That's good to see.

Most of the tables and chairs down this way belong to the restaurants lining the path. They're either fenced off or filled with customers, and neither option leaves room for me. My stomach grumbles as I pass Phillips and sidestep a man trying to take a picture of the huge Hard Rock Cafe guitar. I'd love nothing more than to blow a few bucks on a greasy burger or deep-fried crab, but it isn't in the budget. Instead, I plop myself down on the lower steps leading up to Barnes and Noble and dust the last crumbs of the croissant off of my shirt.

One of the best things about chilling in the harbor is unless you're putting on a show, no one pays attention to you. This is one of the places where people are meant to be. At most, strangers passing say, "Excuse me" as they slide by.

The anonymity is soothing, and the warm sun peeking through the clouds is a welcome recharge after a long day. If I lean back and close my eyes, I can be a face in the crowd instead of Kara Edwards, and allow myself a rare moment of peace.

That's what Connor suggested I should do, find a few little things that bring me happiness and stress relief. In between his study sessions and our donations, he's been trying so hard to make me happy. Last week, he brought me a piece of cheesecake and we sat on the trunk of his car together to eat it, watching the sunset. Yesterday, he made me some roses out of book pages from a discarded novel he found at the library. He claims no one can survive a life as stressful as mine without enjoying a handful of moments every day. So, I'm trying. It's hard when I'm constantly being pulled in so many directions, but I want to show him I care.

My stomach growls again when a couple passes by with a paper tray full of fried calamari and red pepper sauce. As nice as it is to sit here and pretend to disappear, I can't stay. If I do, I'll end up splurging on lunch. The temptation is too strong. Forcing myself off of the steps, I make a promise that when Mom's healthy again, I'll bring her down here. I'll let her choose whatever fancy food she wants as her first meal after the hospital. I bet she'll like that. The food in there is atrocious, and I'm sure she's been craving something fried.

Connor won't be able to pick me up for a while. His afternoon class runs until four, and after, he has a study session with Ben. I could catch the bus and go back to the apartment, but Ally and Rob have friends over, too. I don't want to interrupt. Mom's scheduled for an MRI in thirty minutes, which crosses a hospital visit off of my list. So, where should I go?

The crosswalk beeps as I wait with a small crowd. Without thinking, I shove my hands into my pockets. The fingers of my left hand brush up against something hard and ridged. It squishes in my grasp. Confused, I slip it out and hold it up in front of me. It's a balled sheet of yellow legal paper I had stuffed in my jacket the other day. I'd forgotten about it until this moment, but looking at it now, the little wad has me reeling.

Monday, after a particularly frustrating shift, I caught the bus and made my way back to the apartment on my own. I was hungry, tired, and annoyed with Dan after he chewed me out for opening the wrong sleeve of lids when I was restocking, a mistake that literally cost no one anything more than a moment to tie the soft plastic wrapper back up and return it to the shelf. I had planned to take a hot shower and crawl into bed early, but when I looked up, I discovered a note taped to the apartment door. I unfolded it to see that Richard had been there again, and this time he left his contact information, an address here in Baltimore.

I'd been so angry he dared to come back around that I almost threw it away, but as my hand hovered over the trash can, I thought better of it. While I had no intentions of seeking him out, Mom might want to see him again, and it wasn't my place to keep the information from her if she did. I'd been too tired to do anything about it that night, so I stuck the ball in my pocket and stomped off to Connor's room. It's been tucked away in the recesses of my coat ever since.

I pass little shops and tall high-rises as I mill through the streets, opening the paper up. A mixture of curiosity and discomfort floods through me. My legs carry me automatically. I don't plan for it, but when I look up, I realize I've somehow made it all the way to the corner of Hamburg and Wyeth. Richard's apartment isn't far from here.

Why did I go this way?

I should turn around and head back in the direction I came. I could, and no one would ever know I found myself all the way over here. It wouldn't be a big deal at all. Yet, my mind nags at me to search out the address Richard had so hastily scribbled on this piece of paper.

I study the yellow page and consider my options.

I hadn't noticed it before, but I'm surprised to see my father's handwriting looks a lot like mine. His script has the same long loop at the bottom of the 'g' in Hamburg and a similar flourish at the top of the 'h'. The accidental comparison brings with it a strange sense of emptiness, but I can't put my finger on why.

A quick glance confirms I would only have to walk about five minutes farther down the road to find his apartment. I shake my head, torn. On the one hand, today's been going fairly well. I don't want to see Richard and let that go down the drain. On the other hand, a part of me wants to see him again, this time of my own volition and on my terms. Is it the part of me that still feels like a lost little girl? *Maybe,* I admit to myself. Or, it could be the part of me that wants to give him a piece of my mind.

As much as I would like to be, I realized that I wasn't fully done with Richard after I kicked him out of Connor's apartment. I have so many things I need to say to him. It wasn't fair for him to come back into my life and throw it deeper into chaos, and I didn't get the chance to tell him what my life has been like since he abandoned us, about the devastation he left in his wake.

Can these two versions of myself coexist? Can I be angry with him and still want to talk to him?

I should walk away. I shouldn't show him how vulnerable I feel now that he's stirred up so many painful conflicts I thought I'd left behind.

Walk away, Kara. It isn't worth it. He's not worth it.

My feet don't listen. I tell them to turn around, and yet I find myself standing on the concrete slab in front of his apartment. One of the brass numbers is missing from the address plate hanging over the mailbox. I stare at it for a moment instead of knocking, giving myself one last chance to change my mind. No one would blame me if I did.

Against my better judgment, I draw in a deep breath, steeling myself to see the face of my father behind the door, then lift my hand and knock three times.

CHAPTER TWENTY-EIGHT

A series of loud thumps, someone descending a set of stairs, sounds from behind the door. I take a step back onto the sidewalk as the bronze peephole slides open and my father's hazel eye appears. At first, it's narrowed, discerning, but upon seeing me standing there, it grows wider.

There's no going back now.

The peephole slams shut with a thud. The sound of metal scraping against metal fills my ears as Richard pulls back a sliding lock. My heart races when the doorknob twists. Finally, the door opens to reveal him standing there, mouth hanging slightly, dressed in pajamas and a robe.

"Kara?" he asks, surprised.

"Richard." I flash him a tight-lipped smile.

He blinks awkwardly a few times as though he can't believe I'm standing in front of him. "I... I wasn't sure if you'd come."

Twisting, the ball of my foot grinds broken fragments of the concrete against the larger slab. I wrap my arms around myself protectively and grab onto my elbows, something I've done since I was a small child to shield myself from complicated emotions.

"Me either. I went for a walk and... well, here I am. Do

you have a minute? To talk?"

"Absolutely," he answers, regaining his senses. He ties the waist of his robe closed and extends an arm in invitation. "Come in. I'm glad you came."

Unsure of what to say, I enter the apartment, careful to put space between the two of us as I step inside. I glance behind me, thinking for a moment someone might run up and warn me not to go into the strange man's house, but the street outside is remarkably empty for such a decent day. Richard softly shuts the door and passes me, heading down the hall, then pausing.

"Um, the living room is this way." He sounds so uncertain.

The space before me is small and dim, but I hadn't expected anything grand when I knocked on the door. Most of these duplex-style apartments downtown are not very large. They weren't built to be fancy, but rather to house as many people as they could. They're crammed together like neatly organized eggs in a carton, leaving room for little else.

To my right is a set of worn, wooden stairs. These lead to a second-floor space, probably bedrooms. Someone has painted the treads and risers black. The stringers don't match. They've been covered with peeling white paint. The color in the center of each step has faded away from wear, showing dirty natural wood. At the top, a light shines from inside an open room, most likely Richard's. It casts a faint yellow glow down to where I stand.

Beside me, a tiny entry table, bare except for a small pile of mail and a ring of keys, adorns the hall. Only one of the envelopes has a name on it: Michael Wood. The rest of the mail says "current resident" or "neighbor." I pick up the outlier and hold it out to Richard.

"Michael Wood?"

"I needed a new name. It was inconspicuous."

"Ah," I answer, dropping the envelope back down on the table.

My father, the enigma.

The hall extends roughly twenty feet to the back of the building. A sliding glass door is tucked into the far wall. Under the stairs, another door leads into what I assume to be the living room. Richard gestures for me to follow him as he turns and disappears through the frame. My steps are shaky as I do. The thin wooden boards creak under my weight.

The living room reminds me of a frat house. A worn couch with an ugly floral design hugs the wall. An IKEA coffee table stretches before it, and in the corner, there's an ancient television, the kind we used to have before flatscreens became a thing. Next to the couch, a pocket door leads to a pint-sized galley kitchen crowded with take-out containers and dirty dishes.

Richard clears his throat awkwardly when he notices me taking in the mess, then slides the door closed. With a nervous laugh, he adds, "I, uh, haven't been here long. If I knew you were coming, I would have cleaned up a bit. I'm still getting my footing, you know?"

"Yeah."

"Here." He motions toward the couch. "It's hideous, but it's comfortable. Have a seat?"

The last part comes out as a question, not a command, so I drop down onto the far cushion. It deflates under my weight, sinking my bottom deep into the cottony mass. Richard follows suit, taking the seat on the opposite side and leaving room in the middle.

Neither of us speaks. Unpleasant silence fills the room.

How am I supposed to talk to him? Do I jump right in? Blurt out how angry I am that he abandoned us, me? Scream that he ruined my life? That seems less than tactful. Still, it's not as though I can open with "Go Ravens!" or "How about those Orioles, huh?"

Suddenly, I'm self-conscious. I shrink back against the couch.

"Are you hungry? Thirsty?" Richard tries. "I have a few bottles of water in the kitchen. Oh, and those Hot Pockets you used to like. Philly Steak and Cheese?"

I shake my head. My stomach protests, but no part of me wants to accept his food. I'm surprised he would remember something so trivial, though. That doesn't strike me as the kind of thing a father who's willing to abandon his children would recall.

"Please?" he offers.

I sigh. "I guess water would be fine."

Rather enthusiastically, Richard stands and heads into the cramped kitchen. I watch him as he walks away. The pocket door sticks a bit when he tries to pull it. He fumbles with it and resorts to prying it open with his fingers. He's only gone for a moment before he returns with two bottles, one in each hand.

Richard twists the cap on one of the bottles until it cracks, then passes it over to me. "This place was all I could find on short notice. I called in a few favors," he says, opening his own. "One of my colleagues was nice enough to loan it out to me. His son went to college out here. This used to be his apartment."

I take in the dusty spider lamp in the corner. *That makes a lot of sense.*

"No, it's nice." Richard gives me a disbelieving smile, so I add, "I mean, at least you have a place to stay. We lost ours. Connor's been helping me out."

"That's what he said. I'm sorry." Richard takes a drink and sets his bottle down on the coffee table. Twenty or so rings mar the surface. Splash marks surround them. It must have been used for beer pong at some point. "Man, that kid sure has grown. I'm glad he's still around," he says thoughtfully.

"Me too." I take a drink of my water and drop my gaze to the floor. "I don't know what I would do without him."

"So, are you two together now?"

His question surprises me. "Oh, um… Yeah. It's new."

He nods. "Good."

It falls quiet once more.

I should have planned what I was going to say before I came here. Maybe I shouldn't have come at all. This is so confusing. I want to be furious with him, but part of me is either too stunned or too reluctant to hate my father now that he's actually here.

Finally, I screw up the nerve to speak. I can't bring myself to look Richard in the eye. It would be too much. Instead, I talk to the floor.

"I didn't plan to show up here. I need you to know that. I'm still angry with you. You have no idea how much damage you caused, how much went to hell after you left us. I never expected to see you again. I spent years pretending you were dead because it was so much easier than admitting you chose to abandon us. You have no idea what that does to someone. You have no idea what it did to Mom… to me."

"I'm sorry," he starts.

"It's not your turn to speak."

I risk one look into his eyes. Richard closes his mouth.

"You showed up at Connor's apartment out of the blue and turned my entire world upside down. You came back and started spouting off all of these strange things, and I listened to you for as long as I could take it. So, I came here today to say what I need to say. You owe me that much."

Clearly stricken, Richard nods his head in agreement. "I'll listen to whatever you have to say to me, Kara. You're right. I do owe you a chance to share your story."

My eyes drop back to the floor. The traitorous things begin to water as I cast myself back to the night before he left us. My voice is quiet, saturated with pain, when I say, "I remember the last time you tucked me into bed. Do you?"

FIFTEEN YEARS OF HEARTACHE, DISAPPOINTMENT, grief, and anger pour out of me on that stupid floral couch, finally finding their target. As promised, Richard sits there and listens through all of it: the yelling, the cursing, and the tears. Not once does he offer to interrupt me or correct me like I expect him to.

I tell him about how deeply his absence affected Mom and what it was like to wait for him, hoping he would walk through the door. I tell him about everything that's happened with Jennifer and how she abandoned our family, too. I tell him what it was like to hear Mom's diagnosis and how I had to drop out of college to come home and help her. I even tell him about the credit cards and the ever-growing stack of medical bills. It takes hours to catch him up to where I am at this moment. Strangely, opening up to him feels good.

The only thing I don't talk about is Plasmedics. I don't want him leaning back into his fantasies about the Ruin. I just want him to know what happened to our family and our home.

When I run out of words, he lets me sit there and cry. The tears streaming down my face feel different this time. A weight has been lifted off of my shoulders. Some of the rage that's been coiled inside of me has been released. I can breathe. I know this won't fix the suffering his absence left behind, but it feels great to let it go for a little while.

Yet, the same two pieces of me war with themselves. The

little girl who's still waiting for her father to walk back through the door the morning after he left wants him to wrap her in his arms and make everything better again. She wants him to erase those lonely years and replace them with good memories of ice cream sundaes and lazy days at home. But, I can't reach out to him. The adult in me won't allow it. There's too much distance after all this time, a gap that can never be closed. Richard's expression tells me he feels the same way, but like me, he knows there's nothing he can do to turn back the clock. So, we sit there, divided by the past, until I'm able to regain my composure.

My phone screen tells me it's getting late. I hadn't intended to come here at all, and if I stay much longer, I'll end up having to walk to the closest bus stop alone in the dark. While I'm confident I can manage, I'd rather leave while I can still see where I'm going. I've been in this part of town before, but only a handful of times. It would be far too easy to get lost.

Breaking the silence, I announce, "I should really head out."

"Of course," Richard replies. "But before you do, I have to show you something. Can you spare a few minutes? It won't take long."

I hesitate, then agree. Richards looks relieved as he stands and walks out into the hall. His footsteps boom up the stairs while I wait, wiping away the last cold tears. I check the MTA bus schedule to make sure I know where I'm going and when the next one will arrive. Based on the tracker, it looks like I have about twenty minutes before I need to be at the stop. Luckily, it isn't far.

Connor should be home by the time I get there. A single message from him fills the bottom of my screen.

Bringing home Chick-Fil-A. See u soon. XO

I smile and send a message back, telling him I'll catch the bus in a few minutes, and put away my phone.

When Richard returns, he takes up the same seat. In his hands, he holds two things. One is a worn leather wallet and the other is something small made of oxidized copper. He places the second object beside him on the couch and opens the wallet, retrieving a folded and yellowing piece of paper. Almost reverently, he passes it to me.

The corners of the paper are so worn that holes have formed from the pressure of opening and refolding it time and time again. Large, messy handwriting in what looks to be marker says "To Dad" on one side. I unfold it cautiously, trying not to damage it further. Inside is a child's drawing, slightly smeared. A narrow little brick house and four stick figures stare back at me. Each is labeled: Mommy, Daddy, Jennifer, Me. The background is filled with tiny hearts, and a great arching rainbow stretches from one side to the other.

"You drew that for me just before I left," Richard whispers, tears now collecting in the corners of his eyes. "After everything happened with your mother, Evan, and I. You told me you wanted me to have it in case I had to go away for a long time again. At the time, it felt like some part of you knew I was going to leave. I know you didn't, not really, but you couldn't have given me anything better."

I'm lost for words. He kept it with him all this time.

"I know I've caused you more pain than I can imagine," he continues. "I never wanted to hurt you. I don't know if you believe me, but it's true. I love your mother. I love you. I love Jennifer. I wanted to stay with you all so badly. It tore me apart to pack my things and go. There hasn't been a day in the last fifteen years I didn't have this with me. I couldn't have my real family, but I had this. It kept me sane. I looked at it every night before bed. I talked to it when I was lonely or sad. So," he pauses and sniffles, then continues, "I just wanted to show you how much it means to me, Kara. It's my most prized possession. I will carry it with me until the day I die."

I thought I was out of tears, but apparently, I was wrong.

Trying not to ruin the picture, I pass the paper back to him. He holds it for a moment, staring at it intently before folding it and returning it to his wallet. Looking closer, I can see a small, square bulge in the leather where the picture has been.

"I tried to keep up with what was going on in your lives for as long as I could," Richard admits. "It was a lot easier when you girls were still in school. I used to get the newsletters sent to my apartment in Michigan. Your mom sent me copies of your report cards and awards when she could. That's why I kept a P.O. box. After you graduated, it was a lot harder to be a part of your lives from afar. Then, your mom stopped sending things. I was in the dark. I tried to reach out to Valerie, but I never heard back. Part of me thought maybe you guys had moved on with your lives, as you should have. I hoped I was right. I didn't know about any of the recent things until your mom called and Connor texted me. If I had known..." he trails off.

Richard clears his throat and lifts the other small object up, placing it into my palm.

"This was my mother's."

It's a circular locket that dangles on a thin chain. Despite its age, the chain is strong and light. A delicate screw holds both ends together. Engraved on the pendant is a picture of a dainty flower with tiny, bell-shaped blooms cascading off of a single stem.

"What's this flower?" I ask.

"Lily of the Valley," he says with a smile. "I think it's because your grandmother's name was Lily. She never really said."

"It's beautiful," I reply honestly.

"I want you to have it."

Before I can say anything, Richard retrieves the necklace from my hand. He unscrews the clasp and drapes the chain around my neck, securing it before dropping his hands to his lap. I reach down and pinch the little pendant between my fingers.

"I don't know what to say."

He shifts uncomfortably in his seat as I stare at the necklace. "You don't have to keep it if you don't want to. It's just a family heirloom. I was going to give it to you when you turned sixteen, but obviously, I wasn't around. You can sell it if you'd like. I'd understand. But, I thought you should have it."

"I won't sell it," I whisper.

Richard nods, wiping his hands on his pajama pants. "I'm glad you came, Kara. As hard as it was to hear about the damage I caused when I left, I understand why you needed this. I *am* truly sorry. I hope you know that. I'm here now to help however I can. I don't know what I can do, but I'll try."

"Just not with the Novemion?"

Sadness creeps across his face. "No. That's one thing I won't do."

I bow my head in acceptance. "I figured. I had to try, though."

"I haven't been much of a father to you in a long time, but I want to be a good father now. At least, as good of a father as I can be. I'll help you with many things, but things that will put you in danger are off the table. I love your mother. Still, you know where I stand with this. You should let nature run its course."

"I'm going to get her the treatment, with or without your help. I won't give up. "

Richard sighs. "I know."

Standing, I tuck the copper necklace beneath my shirt for safekeeping. "I haven't forgiven you. I don't know if I ever will. But, thank you for listening... and for this."

"I only wish I had more to give." He escorts me to the front door. "Are you sure you don't want a Hot Pocket to go? I could heat one up for you."

"No, thanks. I've got a bus to catch."

I open the door, letting the cooler evening air seep in. Richard watches me as I step out onto the stoop. With a small wave, he moves to close the door behind me, but I stop him.

"Richard?"

"Yeah?" he asks, confused.

"You need to go see Mom. Talk to her. If you really think this is the end," I pause, feeling my chest constrict at the thought, "you might never get another chance."

He leans his forehead against the door frame and shuts his eyes. "Okay. I'll stop by there tomorrow."

I'm halfway down the street before I hear his voice again.

"Kara?" Richard calls. I turn to see him standing in front of his building, barefoot.

"Yeah?"

"Does she want to see me?"

I hesitate. "I don't know."

He says nothing.

"Whether she wants to or not, I expect you to try."

Richard runs his fingers through his unkempt hair. "Okay." Without another word, he heads inside and closes the door.

The tiny copper necklace weighs heavily on my chest as I board the bus. Behind me, the sun sets.

Another record day for the Edwards family, I think as the bus bounces along down the road.

CHAPTER TWENTY-NINE

"I need to get out of this room," Mom tells me as I flip through the channels. "I've been cooped up in here for too long."

It's been over a month since her surgery, and Doctor Mitchell still won't let her go home. She doesn't understand why, but I know it's the Novemion. He wouldn't have the necessary access to administer the treatment outside of these walls, not to mention the added risk of carting experimental drugs all over the city. Keeping Mom here is the smart move.

"Anxious or bored?" I ask, placing the chunky remote on the bed beside her.

"Both. Every day is the same. I eat the same food, stare at the same walls, and watch the same shows. It's one re-run after the next. My life is starting to feel like a re-run. I want to change it up a bit, change the scenery for a while."

"Where do you want to go? They won't let us leave."

"No, I know that. Just out to the garden viewing area. You know, the one where all of those pretty roses bloom in the summer?"

"I think I can do that. Let me clear it with the nurses, okay?"

Mom rolls her eyes. "In all my life, I never thought I'd

have to ask for permission to go for a walk as a grown woman.”

“We need to make sure they don’t have you on any restrictions or have tests planned. You know that.”

“I know,” she grumbles.

“I’ll be right back.”

A few minutes later, I return with a wheelchair.

Mom tosses the blankets off of her legs and slips her feet over the edge of the bed. As we’ve done so many times before, we maneuver from one place to the other. My hands slip under her arms, lifting her to stand. I cringe at how light she is. These days, she’s little more than skin and bone. She adjusts her gown and tucks it beneath her as she sits. I toss one of the heavier blankets over her legs and arrange it so it won’t get caught in the wheels, then drape the other across her shoulders like a makeshift shawl. She eyes the IV bag suspiciously as I slip it onto the chair pole, tucking the tube under her back. The liquid is running low. Orange swirls through the fluid.

“Oh, can we stop at the vending machines?” she asks as I steer her out into the hall.

Laughing, I shake my head. I should have known this was coming. Every time we leave the room, she wants to go to the vending machines. She’s a candy *fiend*.

“Yes, Mom. On the way down. You know, sometimes you’re as bad as a kid.”

“And, proud of it.” She stares up at me with a mischievous smile.

I can’t help but smile back. She reaches out and pats my arm as I push her down the hall.

THE LOWER-LEVEL ATRIUM IS EMPTY, SO I PARK Mom's wheelchair by the windows in between two faux marble benches. She licks the white chocolate and nougat remnants of her Zero bar off of her fingers as I lock the wheels. When I sit down beside her, she hands me the wrapper. I stuff it into my pocket and watch the bustle of pedestrians as they pass by.

"Are you still working all those extra shifts?"

"Whenever I can," I tell her, leaning my head onto her wraithlike shoulder.

"I worry about you working so much." She tips her head onto mine.

"I have to work, Mom. We need the money. Besides, it's just a coffee shop. I'm not breaking my back or anything."

"You don't have to be digging trenches all day to work yourself too hard. Work is work."

"I'm alright."

"It's not worth your health," she counters, swiftly moving into the phase of the conversation in which she lectures me about making better decisions. It doesn't bother me much. I'm used to it by now.

"It's worth it for yours." My answer never changes.

Mom falls quiet, ending today's lecture. Still, she'll try again tomorrow, and the day after that, and the day after that. It's her way of showing she cares.

I lean forward, dig a baby wipe out of my purse, and pass it to her. She wipes her hands and stares pointedly at the copper locket. It's slipped out from under my shirt and rests against my chest.

"Your father came to see me this morning. Did you have something to do with it?"

"Maybe. I stopped by his apartment yesterday to talk to him. I might have suggested he needed to stop by."

"Mmm, suggested," Mom says. "Are you sure that's the right choice of words?"

"Okay, instructed? Is that better?"

She chuckles. "That's a bit more likely."

I pluck the used wipe out of her hand and add it to my small collection of pocket trash. Somewhere in the distance, a baby cries. Mom turns to look for it, momentarily distracted. She's always loved babies. She likes to play with them from across the room, but this one must be down one of the halls.

"Were you surprised to see him?" I ask, drawing her back to our conversation.

"I suppose."

"And?"

"I don't know. I've missed Richard for a long time." Mom sighs. "Seeing him was hard, but I'm glad he came. It would've been nice to talk to him somewhere outside of this place, though. Under better circumstances."

"It seems like the running theme here is wrong place, wrong time."

Mom nods. "Richard's always been like that. I love your father. I'll always love him."

"Why?"

"Because, that's what love is, Kara. It's complicated. I can be angry with him for what happened and also understand why he left. Neither of us had much choice. We had a family to protect. You girls mattered more than anything else."

"How have you forgiven him?"

"I didn't say I have." Mom picks at a loose blanket string by her knees. "I don't know if I ever will, not entirely."

"I don't think I can."

"Forgiveness isn't for him," she says, turning to me. "You don't have to forgive your father. I don't think he expects you to. But if you decide to try, just know forgiveness is for you. It doesn't fix what's broken, and it doesn't mean you have to open yourself up again. What it means is you get to move on and build a life without anger and resentment."

"But, you haven't forgiven him?"

"I've forgiven parts of what happened, and I kept going." Mom reaches out and takes my hand. Purple veins bulge beneath her skin. Every bone in her hand is visibly outlined beneath the surface, and dark bruises from blood draws pepper her arm. "You know, I sent him your school pictures every year. Yours and Jennifer's. I wasn't supposed to, but I did it anyway. We were meant to part ways entirely except for emergency circumstances, but I couldn't leave him in the dark. Richard had a PO box, so I sent him copies of every report card, articles from newspapers, copies of certificates you earned, and letters about what was going on in your lives."

"I know. He told me."

"I'm sorry I couldn't do more for you. I'll always regret that."

"Mom," I interject, "I don't blame you for any of this. Never. Not once."

She sniffles and wipes at her cheeks. "Are you and Connor okay? I hope you're not holding this against him. I asked him to contact your father, but I never meant to put you two in a difficult position."

"We're good."

She lets go of my hand and pats me on the thigh.

The elevator dings and a young family steps out. The mom has a baby strapped to her chest in a soft carrier, and the dad holds the hands of two more children, a girl with a headful of curls and a boy with a buzzcut, as they attempt to skip down the hall without stepping on the white tiles. The little girl giggles loudly when her brother missteps. Her mom shushes her, and the dad scoops the boy up, tossing him onto his shoulders. As they pass, the boy sticks his tongue out at me, and I return the gesture. The girl giggles again, and they leave us behind.

"I remember when you and your sister were that young," Mom reminisces. "You were little balls of energy, too. God, that was so long ago. You've grown so much, and so fast, too. I'm sorry you had to."

"Mom, don't blame yourself. I'm going to be fine, and so are you, by the way. None of this moping. Spring is coming." I point to a vibrant green patch of grass. "The flowers will be back in this garden soon, and I bet you'll be able to walk down here next time without the chair. We have to stay positive."

"If there is one thing I've learned in my time on this Earth, it's that you never know what's going to happen. Life is short, Kara. Too short. Don't waste it on anger and sadness. Find something that makes you feel whole. And, don't hate your father. Richard is a good man. We all face impossible choices and do the best we can with what we have. You'll understand someday. Maybe you already do."

My thoughts drift back to my conversation with Richard. "I don't know what I feel about him, honestly. It's not hate. I'm working through it."

"Good." Her voice is firm. "You and Jennifer aren't close. When I'm gone, he'll be all you have left. I hope you can find some closeness with him."

"Nothing's going to happen to you. I won't let it."

A troubled storm rages behind her eyes.

"Speaking of Jennifer, we need to talk about what you told me the other day."

Mom sits taller in her chair and straightens her blanket. She always does this when the conversation shifts to uncomfortable things. It's like she's slipping on her armor. "What do you want to know?"

"Is it true?"

She worries her hands in her lap. "Jennifer is not Richard's daughter. Not biologically, anyway. I never wanted you two to know. I don't put stock in half-siblings. You two are siblings through and through."

"How can she be Evan's daughter? I don't understand?"

"Richard adopted Jennifer when she was four months old."

Mom had never spoken much about her dating life before my father. I never questioned it. Maybe I should have.

"When I was in college, I dated Evan. We had a couple of classes together, and we were study partners for a while. It just happened. All in all, we were together for a few months. It wasn't anything serious. Then, he introduced me to your father.

"We fell for each other before Evan and I split up. We didn't mean for that to happen either. Evan was your father's best friend. Richard told him that he had feelings for me and he thought I might have feelings for him as well, so Evan and I talked and ended our relationship. It was amicable. I didn't know I was pregnant at the time.

"I found out about Jennifer a month or so after Richard and I started seeing each other. My periods were never very predictable. I only knew because of the nausea. I could barely keep anything down and found myself constantly exhausted. So, I took a test and it came back positive. I told Richard right away. I understood he might have wanted to end things, especially since our relationship was so new.

"He didn't, though. He was thrilled. He told me it was my choice, but if I wanted to stay with him, he would happily raise the baby with me and adopt it after it was born. I was shocked. The only stipulation was I needed to tell Evan what was going on. He didn't want to hurt his friend."

I listen intently as she continues, afraid Mom might

change her mind and stop sharing. I'm tired of the secrets. All they've ever done is wreak havoc on our lives.

"I told Evan, and unlike Richard, he was not thrilled with the idea of becoming a parent at such a young age. Evan had several years of school left since he was going into law. In the end, we all agreed it would be best if Richard was the baby's father.

"There were no hard feelings involved. Their friendship was very strong. They'd been friends for such a long time. It all worked out in the end. Richard adopted Jennifer after she was born. We were happy. You know what happened after that."

"How did Jennifer find out? I mean, you said you wanted to keep it a secret."

"After your father left, Jennifer wanted to know what drove him away. She wouldn't accept my vague answers, so she decided to look for answers on her own. We kept the adoption records in a small fireproof lockbox in the attic, tucked far away where we thought you girls would never find them. Jennifer found the box. She confronted me about it, and I had to tell her the truth then. She told me I stole her life."

"That's why she acts this way?"

"That's why she doesn't come around. She's still angry with me."

"But, why you? Why not Richard?"

"Because," Mom says, "your father wasn't here, and Evan isn't around either, so I took the full force of her pain. She doesn't want to see me because I lied to her for so long. I can't blame her."

"Why does she hate me, though? I didn't lie to her."

"You have to understand. She feels like she doesn't belong. We kept a huge part of her life from her. I may be her mother, but she's been searching for something since she found out. Learning about Evan changed her perception of who she is. When she looks at you, she's jealous and hurt. You don't have to wonder about your life in the same way. You've always known who your parents are. It's complicated, baby. I'm so sorry."

"You didn't do this to hurt her."

"No, but it did anyway. Secrets always do."

My gaze drifts to the IV pole attached to Mom's wheelchair. Only a few drops of the treatment remain. I want to stay here and talk now that she's opening up, but if I don't get her upstairs, I'm afraid I'll tell her what's in the bag. I can't do that. Nothing good will come of it. This is one secret I have to keep.

"Come on. Let's go back."

"Alright." She doesn't argue with me, a sure sign she's tired.

I unlock her wheels and steer her to the elevators.

"Do you think Jennifer will ever forgive me?" she asks when I press the button to call it down.

"I think she will. Just give her time."

"That's the one thing I may not have."

"You have time, Mom. I'll make sure of it."

"You're not a goddess, Kara. Don't make promises you can't keep."

Back in the room, I tuck Mom into bed and hang the empty bag on the bed's IV pole. Her eyes flutter closed, and I step out into the hall, shutting the door behind me.

ALLY, CONNOR, AND ROB LAUGH FROM THE NEXT room as Rob reads off the cards we left in the pile. He brought Cards Against Humanity with him tonight, and even though Connor's exams are tomorrow, we've been playing for two hours. I slipped away a minute ago, excusing myself to the bathroom, but thinking of something else entirely.

I sit on the edge of the tub and stare at the phone in my hand. I've wanted to text Jennifer since I left the hospital. After talking with Mom, everything has changed, yet nothing has changed at the same time. I feel like I owe her an apology for my behavior at the diner, but does it matter? If I tell her what I know, will she care? Will we get along?

My thumbs flash over the screen as I type out a message, delete it, and type a new one. Before I can chicken out, I press send.

> Richard's back.

A notification tells me Jennifer's read it, but she doesn't reply.

> I talked 2 Mom. I know about Evan.

Three dots flash, then disappear.

> I'm sorry about the diner. I didn't understand.

Ok

Her response is short, but at least she's talking to me. I try again.

> Can we plz set this aside for 1 day? I want 2 talk. Mom needs u.

Like before, three dots flash across the screen and disappear, though unlike before, it happens several times. I wait, hoping she'll answer me.

"Come on, Jennifer. Do the right thing for once," I whisper, bouncing my knees to tame my emotions.

I can't.

I blow out a breath.

Plz? Ur still my sister. Can we try?

This last message is left on read for several minutes, so I stick my phone into my back pocket and head for the door. My hand is on the knob when my phone vibrates. I drop the handle and dig it out, wincing as I read the message on the screen.

Don't text me again. We r done.

CHAPTER THIRTY

While the familiar nurse who I now know as Charles isn't looking, I pluck the bandaid off of my arm and toss it into the trash. Each time I donate, he insists on them, citing Plasmedics protocol, but they're pointless. I don't need one for a wound as small as this. The puncture hadn't bled when he removed the needle, and as I search for the site in the crook of my arm, the mark is already gone.

I shrug on another of Connor's hoodies and grab my purse, thankful the warmer weather means I've been able to ditch my coat. It's supposed to be almost sixty degrees this morning, and Connor has plans to take me out for breakfast on our first official date. I've been looking forward to it since he mentioned it over the weekend. I don't care where we're going. It will be great to have this time together, and a restaurant meal means I can escape his well-intentioned, constantly burnt food. My mouth waters as I consider the possibilities. I daydream of eggs benedict and french toast.

"You have a wonderful day, Ms. Edwards," Charles says when we reach the end of the hall. He holds the door open for me. "Don't forget to stop by the desk and collect your payment. Plasmedics thanks you for saving lives." It's the same spiel as always.

"You too, Charles. See you in a couple of days."

He lingers long enough for me to step into the waiting room before letting the door close behind him.

Connor's already outside, so I hop into the payment line and dig out my ID. Behind the desk, a young woman with tightly curled blonde hair, vaguely reminiscent of Marilyn Monroe, smiles up at me when she takes my license. Her hair bounces as she swipes the magnetic strip to bring up my file. Something beeps. She frowns at her computer screen, then glances back at my ID. Seemingly confused, she tries swiping the card again, then enters the information manually.

"Ms. Edwards, it seems there's a freeze in your file. I can't give you your payment just yet. Could you stick around for a moment?"

This has never happened before. "Is there something wrong?"

"No, I don't think so. Let me grab a supervisor." She stands and heads deeper into the administrative area, fading from view as she rounds the corner of a cubicle.

My fingers drum nervously against the glass top of the desk while I wait. A few minutes later, the blonde attendant returns with an older woman in tow. Light glints off of her silver name tag, temporarily obscuring the word "Clarissa." The attendant points to something I can't see on her screen and whispers to the older woman, but Clarissa shakes her head.

"I'm sorry for keeping you waiting, Ms. Edwards. It looks like you have a meeting request from one of our counselors." Clarissa tucks her graying hair behind one of her ears and straightens her tweed blazer, tugging it down. She pushes her red plastic glasses farther up the bridge of her nose.

Now, it's my turn to be confused. "A counselor? Why?"

"With frequent donors, we have a policy in place which requires occasional check-ins to ensure the donor's health and safety. It's part of our philosophy here. We can't save lives if our donors aren't taken care of."

"So, you do this for everyone?"

There's detachment in her smile when she replies. "Yes, it's Plasmedics protocol."

Already, I don't like Clarissa. She's too aloof. I'm reminded of a police officer in an interrogation room.

"Did you meet with my boyfriend? He was here a few minutes ago, and we've donated the same number of times… We come together."

A strange look passes over Clarissa's face. *What was that? Anger? Irritation?*

"What's his last name?" she asks.

"Winters."

She swivels the attendant's keyboard in her direction and searches for Connor in their database. The attendant, whom I wish also had a name tag because I feel a little bad not knowing how to address her, offers me an empathetic shrug.

"No, not yet. It looks like… ah, yes. He'll have a consultation next week. Alphabetical order, you understand."

"Really?"

"Absolutely."

"I don't think I've ever heard of something like that."

"That's how we do things around here," Clarissa snaps.

The attendant fidgets behind her chair as though uncomfortable.

Frustrated, I check the time. "I actually have plans. Can we do this later?"

"Unfortunately, Ms. Edwards, we cannot proceed with payment or further scheduling until this requirement is fulfilled. Surely someone mentioned this procedure before."

"No."

"I'll be happy to credit your account if you can't meet

with our counselor right now," Clarissa offers, crossing her arms over her chest.

I can't be sure, but I get the sense she enjoys the idea of holding something over my head. Now, I really don't like her.

I can't leave without the money, so I let out a frustrated sigh. "No, a meeting will be fine. How long will it take?"

"Not long. Perhaps, ten minutes or so. We have a counselor available if you would like to proceed."

"I don't really have much choice." Impatience colors my response.

"In that case," Clarissa presses the button that opens the door and steps out into the waiting area, "follow me."

"YOU MUST BE MS. EDWARDS. PLEASE, TAKE A SEAT." A curvy woman in a modern gray pencil dress with black panels along the sides stands and offers me her hand. She leans across her large desk. "I'm Nancy Gregory, a medical counselor for Plasmedics, as you know. It's lovely to meet you."

"Yeah, um, likewise," I say, shaking her hand and settling into the chair.

She seats herself across from me and smoothes the fabric over her legs. Not a hair on her head is out of place. Thick black liquid liner spans her eyelids, white lines the bottom, and her bun is so tight it's likely to rip out every hair in her head. Meanwhile, here I am in casual attire.

"You've been coming to Plasmedics for a while now, so I figured it was time we met and discussed a few things. Can I offer you anything? A snack or a drink, perhaps? Clarissa tells me you're fresh off of a donation." Nancy opens her bottom desk drawer and retrieves a few small bags and pouches. "I have juice, chips, cookies... anything strike your fancy?"

"Thank you, but I'm fine. What's this about?"

She drops the food back into the drawer and slides it closed, then arranges several pencils, which were perfectly straight to begin with, on her desk. "It's nothing to worry about. We just need to discuss your donation experiences so far and how you're feeling. As I'm sure you're aware, you're one of our prized donors. We see you more often than most and want to make sure your needs are met."

She studies me with a piercing scrutiny. I try my best to assure her I'm doing fine, hoping we can get this over with and I can get out of here as quickly as possible. She nods along as I share a few details from my visits.

"... Charles has been very kind. He's usually here when I come in to donate. And, I really appreciate the frequency of the donations and payment incentives. I have some extenuating circumstances. The money is very helpful."

"Sure, I understand. Listen, helping people is what we do here. You help *us* by donating, and we help *you* with a little extra cash. It works out well for all involved." She winks and leans back in her chair. The chocolate leather creaks as though it's new. Nancy steeples her fingers and swivels a bit, locking eyes with me. "I'm happy to hear you've had positive experiences with our facility and you're feeling well. However, there is something else. A colleague of mine wishes to speak with you."

Anxiety surges through me. My eyes widen, and I sit up straighter in my chair. "Why? Have I done something wrong?"

"No, dear. Nothing like that. All I've been told is that this is a business matter he would like to handle personally, and it's best not to ask too many questions of the higher-ups.

Please excuse me. I need to let him know we're ready for him."

"I'm sorry. I don't understand…"

Nancy doesn't say anything as she lifts her office phone and holds it to her ear. She presses a single button and waits, smiling at me.

Suddenly, I'm wildly uneasy. My eyes dart around the room, searching for an indication of why I'm really here, but her office doesn't give up its secrets. Aside from a few family photos, a metal filing cabinet, and her hulking white desk, the space is relatively bare.

Her voice cuts through the tense silence. "Mr. Collins, Ms. Edwards and I have concluded our session. The floor is yours."

Panic roots me to the chair. My ears strain to hear the response, but his words are indistinguishable as they drift out of the receiver, nothing but low, quiet tones.

Is it Matthew? Elias? Why would they want to talk to me? Why would they be here?

Doctor Mitchell's warnings about Plasmedics play in my head. Out of necessity, I'd shoved them aside. It hadn't mattered that Coarser Industries owned the facility because I couldn't change my plans. I needed the money for Mom's treatments, no matter the risk. But, if they've figured out who I am and what Doctor Mitchell and I are doing, this could be bad.

Or is this about the elevator? I shouldn't have smarted off to Elias. That was so stupid. The man has more money than I'll see in my entire life. I'm sure he has the power to take his anger out on me if he wants to. *God, why did I have to run my smart mouth?*

"Yes, sir. I will," Nancy tells whichever Mr. Collins before returning the phone to its cradle, ending the call. She rises from her chair and crosses the room. "Wait right there. He'll be in momentarily."

Still processing this potential disaster, I don't protest as she closes the door behind her.

I'M RUNNING THROUGH ALL OF THE POSSIBLE scenarios when the door clicks and opens into the room. Nancy enters first, followed quickly by Matthew.

Well, that was the better option, I tell myself, trying to stay calm.

For the first time, I notice Nancy looks nervous, too. Her professional expression has faded, and she seems out of place.

"I'll take it from here, Mrs. Gregory. Thank you," Matthew states. There's authority in his tone.

"Of course," she answers. "I'll, uh… I'll just go see how things are going up front. When would you like me to return?"

"I'll send for you when I'm ready."

"Understood, Mr. Collins." Nancy moves into the hall. "Will you need anything before I go?"

Matthew adjusts his tie, navy blue and metallic gold stripes, as he closes the door without answering.

That catches me by surprise. I've always had a feeling Matthew was dangerous because of his connection to Novemion, but I hadn't thought of him as cruel. He's shown me kindness on multiple occasions. Shutting the door in her face was downright rude.

He twists the lock and perches himself on the edge of Nancy's desk, a vision of confidence and ease.

Nausea settles into my stomach as I wait for him to speak. I swallow hard.

"How are you today, Ms. Edwards?" He crosses his feet, wrinkling his slacks.

I don't answer his question.

"How's your mom?"

"As well as she has been."

"Mmm," he answers. "That's a shame. I had hoped her new treatment would improve her condition."

I find myself unable to meet Matthew's unerring gaze. "I don't know what you mean."

He huffs. "Of course you do. I stopped in to see Valerie yesterday afternoon. Imagine my surprise when I saw a familiar orange substance swirling in her IV."

Shit.

"Don't try to lie to me."

"What do you want?"

Matthew chuckles. "Want? Nothing. Well, that's not true. What I want is your help."

"I... I don't understand."

"I didn't expect you to. Let's cut to the chase, shall we?"

Matthew pushes himself away from Nancy's desk and stands behind me, his hands on the back of my chair. Not knowing what he's doing back there unnerves me, so I turn to face him.

"I knew Doctor Mitchell was giving someone Novemion. After all, he bought it from me. But, I didn't know it was your mom. After the incident with my father in the elevator, I decided to look into you. You impressed me."

"I only did what needed to be done."

"True, but not many are brave enough to stand up to Elias Collins. No one wants to challenge the billionaire."

I need to take the edge off of my nerves. My skin is practically vibrating. So, I bite my lip until it stings.

"Anyway, imagine my surprise when I learned who you were. I saw your donation schedule here and got curious, so I accessed Doctor Mitchell's files."

"How?" I ask, incredulous. "Medical files are privileged, secure."

"Not if you have enough money. There are very few secrets I can't uncover with the right leverage."

I cringe. He's right. Security will always pale in the face of greed.

"It seems we're both keeping secrets, Kara."

"What?" I push myself out of the chair and back up against the wall. I want him farther away from me.

It doesn't phase him. He simply takes my seat. "My company has not been entirely honest with you, and you've failed to tell me about Valerie's treatment. It's a shame.

"See, Plasmedics is a subsidiary of my father's corporation. We use this facility to research diseases and develop treatments and cures. It costs more money than it earns, but what we learn is quite valuable. In fact, Novemion was created because of a facility much like this."

"What does that have to do with me?"

"We need your blood, Kara."

"Why? It's just plasma. I know my type is rare…"

"Try nonexistent."

I balk. "That's impossible."

"And yet, it is. There's an antibody in your blood we've only ever seen once before. It adapts to diseases faster than the eye can see."

"No…"

"Yes! Imagine what we could do with your blood. Imagine the diseases we could cure, the lives we could save."

"This is absurd." I back quickly toward the exit.

Matthew cuts me off before I can reach the door. "I want to make a deal."

"Huh?"

"You're donating to Plasmedics. Plasmedics gives you money, which you then turn around and give back to me. It's unnecessarily complicated, don't you think?"

"Well, yes but…"

"So, what if we stopped all this unnecessary exchange and came to an agreement. I want you to make daily donations. In exchange, I'll supply your mom's Novemion for free."

My jaw practically hits the floor.

"Think about it. It makes sense."

"You can't be serious."

"I am. *Deadly* serious."

This can't be happening. How did this happen? What is he talking about? I'm nothing. I never have been. Why would Coarser Industries need someone like me? He's mistaken. He has to be.

"What if I say no?" I ask, voice shaking.

Matthew smiles. The usual charm has disappeared, replaced by something sharp and intimidating. "You won't."

"What makes you say that?"

He places his hand on the doorknob. "Because if you don't agree to my terms, the treatments stop. Your mother will die, and I'll turn you in."

My heart nearly stops. "You wouldn't."

"I would and will."

"That's sick."

"No, that's smart business. Help me, and I'll help you. Say no, and I'll cut you off."

"You sound like your father!"

Coldness creeps into his eyes. "So, what's it going to be?"

This is ridiculous, but what choice do I have?

"I need time to think."

Matthew lifts his hand off the knob and straightens his tie again. "You have forty-eight hours. Not a second longer."

I nod. My heart pounds against my ribs. The room spins, threatening to throw me to the floor.

"Two days." He reaches into his jacket and pulls out a business card, passing it to me. "Call me with your answer, Kara. I'll be waiting."

Without another word, Matthew opens the door and leaves me standing alone in Nancy's office, struggling to breathe.

CHAPTER THIRTY-ONE

"Can I get you anything else?" the waitress asks, pen poised over her pad. "We have some decent specials today. My favorite is the Havarti Bagel Sandwich, though I'd suggest trying it with extra cheese." Her vibrant green eyes, a vivid contrast against thick black liner and dark eyeshadow, blink at me as she waits for my response.

"I'm all set," I tell her, wiping my hands on my jeans. I haven't ordered much, a short stack of pancakes with strawberries and whipped cream.

"Are you sure?" Connor asks. "I'll get you anything you'd like."

"I'm sure, thanks. The pancakes will be fine."

"Okay, then. I'll get that started for you." The waitress extends her hand, so I pass her the menu. Connor does the same. She flashes us a quick smile, then leaves between the rows of outdoor tables and vanishes through the patio door.

"Kay, what's wrong? Did I do something?"

Guilt mingles with uncomfortable feelings of panic and dread. I haven't told Connor what happened at Plasmedics. I thought it would taint an otherwise perfectly fine date, but apparently, I'm doing that on my own.

I pause for a moment, weighing my options. My eyes drift

over the old brick exterior of the building and the black wrought-iron fence surrounding the patio area. The sun beats down from overhead, warming the spring air, and the umbrella above our wire table casts a long shadow onto the ground.

Should I tell him what Matthew did? Should I wait? Should I mention it at all? I don't keep secrets from Connor, but the last thing I want to do is worry him or drag him into something even more dangerous than what we're already doing. *Why is everything so hard?*

"Kay?" he prompts. "If I've done something – "

"No," I interrupt. "It's not you. I promise."

Relief eases the tension at the corners of his eyes. "Then, what is it? I can't help if you don't tell me."

"I don't want to mess up our date."

Connor shakes his head and reaches across the table for my hand. I let him take it into his. Gently, he strokes his thumb across the back and squeezes. "You won't. I didn't come here expecting to share a five-course meal with an obnoxiously perfect person. I came here to eat with you, problems and all."

I squeeze back, holding on tighter than I should. "You know my problems are different. They're dangerous."

"And?"

"I don't want to dump them on you again."

"Stop that and listen to me. I'm a grown man. Well, *most* of the time. But, I'm an adult. I'm capable of making my own decisions, and I don't need you to make them for me. Right now, I've decided I *want* to be involved, so you'd better spill or I'll have to march myself down to Plasmedics and find out what happened for myself. You know I will."

He absolutely would.

I sigh and choose the truth. "As I was leaving, someone at the desk told me I had to meet with a *medical counselor*." My fingers bend in air quotes around the title. "They said it was standard protocol."

"So, that's what took so long?"

"Mmm hmm. But, that's not what it really was."

"No?" he asks. Tension creeps back into his features. "What happened?"

"I talked to a woman first. She asked me a bunch of questions about my experiences with Plasmedics, then told me I needed to meet with one of the higher-ups. It was Matthew Collins, the one from the parking structure."

"Shit, really? The one who's connected to Novemion?"

"Yeah."

Connor leans forward and lowers his voice. "Well, what did he say?"

Trying to buy myself some time to think, to put my thoughts in order, I lift my cold glass of water to my lips and swallow several large drinks before setting it down. "He knows about Mom."

His eyes widen. "What? How?"

"I guess he stopped by her room and saw the treatment. He did some digging and put the pieces together."

"Oh, man. What's he gonna do?"

"Honestly, I'm not sure. It depends on what I choose."

Connor tilts his head, confused. "What do you mean?"

"When he found out about Mom, he looked into me. He figured out I was making donations to Plasmedics, too."

"Okay, and?"

"And, he offered me a deal."

Connor nods, urging me on.

"If I start donating to Plasmedics every day instead of on my current schedule, he said he'd supply the Novemion for free. I guess Doctor Mitchell has been buying it from him all along."

"Seriously? That's messed up."

"Uh-huh. The whole thing is so convoluted."

He shakes his head. "Is that even safe? To donate every day?"

"No idea."

"And, if you don't?"

Blood drains from my face and hands as I consider the alternative. "He'll cut Mom off. He said he'll stop the treatment and let her die." I leave out the part where he threatened to turn me in to the police. Connor doesn't need to worry any more than he already will.

"That's evil."

"Yeah, that's what I said."

"He really gave you an ultimatum?" Anger flits across his face.

"Yup."

"You didn't beat him to a pulp?"

I scoff. "No, not this time. There are too many guards at Plasmedics for me to lose my cool."

"What a douche."

"Yeah."

For a time, neither of us speaks. The waitress brings our plates and places them in front of us, perfectly unaware of the disaster unfolding before her. She asks if we need anything, but we assure her we're fine, so she retreats back into the building.

"Alright, Kay. What are you gonna do?"

I'm so tired of dealing with uncaring, manipulative people.

"I don't have a choice. I have to do what he says, right?"

Connor's face falls. His voice is sad and low when he answers. "No."

I immediately recognize what he means. "You know I do."

"I know you *will…*"

"That's the same thing."

"It's not."

"It is to me," I snap.

Connor pushes his food around with his fork. "I know that, too."

He takes a hesitant bite, watching me. I spear my fork into the pancake, staring as the strawberry syrup oozes from the punctures. Several stabs later, I feel a smidge better, having taken some of my frustrations out on the innocent entree.

"Did he say why he wants you to do this?"

"Something about rare antibodies."

Connor perks up. "What?"

"I guess they adapt better than they should. He wants to study them, make new drugs with my cells."

"Okay?"

"Yeah, it's weird. This whole thing is screwed up beyond belief."

The fluffy pancakes are delicious as I shovel the first forkful into my mouth. Talking to Connor must have settled my nerves because my nausea and jitters have calmed, freeing up the energy I had been using to squash my anxiety and allowing me to think. After the first bite, I practically devour the short stack and scrape the plate clean. As I lick the last sweet drops of syrup from the tines, my stomach rumbles, demanding more.

"What now?" Connor asks, finishing his bacon.

Slowly, I spin the fork against the flat white surface of the plate. An idea pops into my head, and I turn it over while the tines leave tiny tracks in the red, sticky residue. I'm no longer frozen in fear but determined.

"That's your troublemaker face," Connor says.

"Maybe," I answer with a slight smile.

"So, what's the plan?"

I push the plate to the edge of the table, leave the fork on my napkin, and lean back against the padded metal chair. "More food."

"Okay, and after that?"

"Can you take me to the campus computer lab? I have some research to do."

THE CAMPUS LAB IS CROWDED WITH STUDENTS finishing exams when I settle into one of the long lines of desks. Connor left me his student ID before running off to class. I dig it out of my pocket and swipe it through the card reader. The computer whirs to life and loads his profile while I tuck my hoodie and purse under my seat.

Scooting my chair closer, I glance around the room to make sure none of the other patrons are staring over my shoulder and open the web browser. My hands hover above the keyboard as I contemplate the blank search bar. I know what I'm looking for, but how do I find it? *Where should I start?*

Matthew and his father may control a powerful company and have enough money to open doors, but Doctor Mitchell's words ring in my ears. Had he meant it when he said the company had been involved in some unseemly things in the past? *If so, what were they? I need to find out.*

"Blackmail works both ways," I mutter.

As I organize my thoughts, a student, likely a freshman by the looks of him, sits down in a nearby chair. He spares me a fleeting look, then stuffs one headphone into his ear and swipes his ID. He doesn't bother with me again as he pulls out a notebook, pen, and two textbooks, depositing them haphazardly by his keyboard. He slips the pen behind his ear and gets to work on a Slides presentation, consulting his notes as he types.

Before, I'd been the only one seated at this bank of computers. I chose my seat purposefully, not wanting to draw anyone else's attention. This newcomer's too close for my liking, so I turn my monitor slightly, hoping it's enough to keep it out of view.

When I'm confident he doesn't care what's going on at my station, I decide to start with a basic search and type out the words "Coarser Industries." Several pages of links populate the screen, everything from the company website to news articles and pages dedicated to their individual drugs.

The company website seems like a decent place to start, so I open the page. The clinical logo for Coarser Industries dominates the top third of the screen. Scrolling down, I find posts about new products, animal trials, and fundraisers for various charities the company sponsors. Half the page is consumed by advertisements. I skim the text, but none of the information is useful, so I change course and hover the pointer over the menu until a drop-down list appears.

The menu is quite extensive, stretching longer than the allotted space on the page. I drag the mouse over the options, and when I reach the bottom, it scrolls, revealing more destinations. It doesn't take long to find what I want: the staff directory. Part of me hopes it might contain useful information on Elias or Matthew, though I'm well aware the company wouldn't advertise its misdeeds.

The screen blinks and shifts to a list of employee pictures, names, company phone numbers, and email addresses that have been neatly organized on the page. At the top, Elias's smug face stares back at me. A few choice words escape my lips, drawing a look from the student beside me. I mouth the word "sorry" as I click on the image and load his bio.

Elias Collins
CEO of Coarser Industries

Elias Collins began his career with Coarser Industries at the age of eighteen. Since then, he has accumulated an impressive thirty-two years within the company.

Mr. Collins has held many different positions at Coarser Industries over the years, starting as a Pharmaceutical Sales Representative under the supervision of his father, previous CEO Jameson Collins, who retired from the position at the age of sixty-eight.

Upon receiving his Bachelor's Degree in Biology and Master's Degrees in Pharmaceutical Manufacturing and Ethics, he went on to fulfill the roles of Biomedical Research Analyst, Hospital Liaison, and Regional Overseer before taking over his father's position.

I nearly snort when I learn Elias has a Master's in ethics. Based on our brief conversation in the elevator, he certainly fooled me.

Since beginning employment with Coarser Industries, Elias has championed the development of over thirty promising new medications, many of which remain in use.

Today, Elias is responsible for thirteen corporate locations, oversees much of Coarser Industries' biological research, and is training his son and heir, Matthew Collins, to step into the role upon his retirement.

Other than learning Elias is quite the educated man, which I had suspected before, this page provides me nothing of use. There's no mention of his marriage or other children, so I can't research them. Disappointed to have found no leads, I return to the staff page and scroll down to the next image. Matthew's photo.

Matthew Collins,

Pharmaceutical Sales Representative and Research Manager

Matthew Collins, son of CEO Elias Collins, has been with Coarser Industries for ten years. Like his father, he joined the family business at the age of eighteen.

Matthew currently holds two positions within Coarser Industries, Pharmaceutical Sales Representative, specifically focused in the north-eastern quadrant of the United States, and Research Manager, assigned oversight of the development of the new cancer drug, Novemion (pending FDA approval for human usage, expected later this year).

Matthew received his Bachelor's Degree in Chemistry and his Master's Degrees in both Business Management and Chemical Engineering.

Matthew currently supports several charitable organizations, including but not limited to Make-A-Wish, the National Multiple Sclerosis Society, and the American Cancer Society.

Interesting, but also irrelevant. It helps to know your enemies, but only if the information provides something useful.

I'm not going to find what I need here.

I hit the back arrow and navigate through the long list of search results, mulling over the other links. They're bland, all press releases and praise. What I want is something scandalous, but where is it? Surely, there must have been some report about the company's misdeeds?

I drag my cursor to the "News" category at the top of the page. If they've been involved in anything controversial, I'm fairly certain I'll find it here.

I click on it and scan the new results, scrolling through

page after page of useless information. The minutes tick by, and an hour later, I'm frustrated and ready to give up. Either Doctor Mitchell had been wrong or was simply trying to offer a warning, or the company has hidden its wrongdoings well. This entire search has been pointless.

Of course, why wouldn't it be? If money can open doors, it can close them, too.

Kicking myself, I click to the next page one last time.

At the bottom of the screen, the very last search result catches my attention. Sitting straighter in the blue and gray padded computer chair, I read the title again, thinking I may have wished the headline into existence. I blink, but the words don't change: COARSER INDUSTRIES STILL SEARCHING FOR MISSING EMPLOYEE.

Intrigued, I load the article.

It's been three weeks since Baltimore resident and Coarser Industries employee, Evan Knightly, vanished from his home.

Shock floods through me as I read the name. Evan Knightly was Richard's best friend, the man he and my mother supposedly kidnapped and left with the Ruin. Jennifer's biological father. Unconsciously, I snatch the copper locket from my chest and hold it up, zipping it back and forth on the chain as I continue to read.

Mr. Knightly, a member of the Coarser Industries legal team, recently suffered a severe illness after completing an international work-related trip which led to his hospitalization. Despite extensive efforts to diagnose and care for Mr. Knightly, medical professionals had been unable to discover the source of the illness or successfully treat the condition. They advised the friends and family of Mr. Knightly to prepare for his imminent demise. However, against all odds, Mr. Knightly miracu-

lously recovered, stumping his care team. He was expected to return to his normal life upon discharge.

Shortly after Mr. Knightly's recovery, sources have confirmed the same unknown illness began afflicting others at the hospital who had come into direct contact with Mr. Knightly. Mr. Knightly, and any others who may have been exposed to the contaminant, were therefore quarantined. Though the medical staff fought to find the source of the mysterious illness and save the lives of those who were exposed, only two patients survived, Mr. Knightly and a friend who visited him when he was ill, Richard Edwards.

My mouth falls open as I take in the words on the screen. At least in part, Richard's unbelievable story had been true. Evan really had been sick and recovered. They had actually been quarantined. People died, and by the sound of it, the death toll had been high.

"No way," I mumble. "No fucking way…"

The student beside me shoots me an intense look. This time, I ignore him and carry on.

When doctors were finally convinced the sickness had been eradicated, Mr. Knightly and Mr. Edwards were released from St. John's hospital. They left the building together, presumably returning home. However, after his release, no one has seen or heard from Mr. Knightly. This drew concerns from his family and employer when he never returned to work. Richard Edwards, the other surviving patient, has also disappeared, mystifying authorities. Whether the two have left together or something more nefarious is at play is as of yet speculation. As of now, there are no leads.

St. John's Hospital, though highly respected in the medical field, has deemed itself incapable of determining the cause of the illness which claimed so many lives and has since partnered with Mr. Knightly's employer, Coarser Industries, in hopes of discovering the lethal conta-minant. As a leading company in the medical and pharmaceutical fields, Coarser Industries hopes to have answers to this unexplained mystery within the next few months. All biological samples from Mr. Knightly and other patients have been transferred to Coarser Indus-tries' possession at this time.

"Oh my god…" I whisper.

"Shut up," my grumpy neighbor grunts. "Some of us are trying to work over here."

I shoot him a nasty look. "So, put your other headphone in."

He groans and turns back to his screen. Annoyed, I continue reading the article.

Elias Collins, Biomedical Research Analyst and Hospital Liaison in charge of this investigation, as well as Mr. Knightly's coworker, has made the following statement:

"Coarser Industries is committed to discovering the source of this volatile disease and preventing further societal contamination. Rest assured, we will find the answers to the questions that have plagued the family members, friends, and coworkers of those who have been lost to this tragedy. Coarser Industries extends its condolences at this time.

We are also taking the search for our missing employee and friend, Evan Knightly, Legal Representative for our Professional Relations division, very seriously. We're working closely with Mr. Knightly's family. It is our sincerest hope that Mr. Knightly will be located and brought home safely."

Mr. Knightly's family has refused to comment on the investigation, as it's ongoing.

If you know anything regarding the whereabouts of Evan Knightly or his friend, Richard Edwards, please contact the local police at 410-555-9672.

"No way…"

With one last disdainful look, the student next to me scoops up his things and logs off of his machine. He curses under his breath as he lugs his backpack further down the computer bank away from me.

"Good riddance."

Agitated, I scan through the article again. Absently, I continue to zip the locket back and forth on its thin chain.

If Evan was actually sick, and he recovered like Richard and the article said, and then other people got sick, and he really went missing, was my father telling the truth? That's impossible…

With more force than I intend to, I tug on the locket. The strain snaps the delicate chain, startling me. It slips from between my fingers and lands with a "tink" on the desk, spinning in circles next to the mouse. The impact must have jostled the clasp because the lid of the locket pops open, sending a dingy object falling to the floor by my feet.

Bending down, I scoop it up and hold it in my hand. It's a folded slip of paper, no bigger than the size of my pinky nail.

Opening it up, I'm surprised to see neat handwriting, faded with age. It must have been written by Richard's mother, Lily. My eyes scan what looks to be a poem.

> We called to Her, and so She came.
> On Solstice night, She heard our pain.
> We asked for help, and She was kind.
> We took Her gift. Our fates were twined.
> Blood was spilled on sacred altar,
> Yet with Her magick, we did falter.
> Our contract broken left Her enraged.

The gift was spoiled and blood curse engaged.
What was rebirth turned fast to death,
Our people shunned, and so we wept.
She waits for us to redeem our clan
Or bring destruction upon the land.

— -*ANCESTRAL PROPHECY*

Scrawled at the bottom is the same familiar symbol from my dream.

CHAPTER THIRTY-TWO

Several flakes of paint fall away from the door as I knock. This time, Richard answers quickly. Unlike before, I called ahead to let him know I was coming. I hadn't given him much time to prepare, thirty minutes at most for the bus ride, but when the barrier swings open into the hall, he's dressed for a visitor. He's ditched the pajama pants and robe in favor of a pair of light jeans and a plain black t-shirt. His hair has been combed away from his face, and the stubble on his cheeks is gone, leaving a neatly trimmed beard and mustache.

"Kara, I'm so glad you decided to stop by." He ushers me inside. A wide smile dominates his features, crinkling the skin at the corner of his eyes. "I was just making sandwiches. It's such a nice day. How would you like to sit out back and eat?"

"Oh, I guess," I answer. I'm not that hungry for once, but sitting outside sounds nice. "I had some questions, actually. I was hoping you could help me with them."

"What about?"

"A few things," I say.

"I'll do what I can."

I follow Richard down the narrow hall and turn into the living room behind him. The pocket door to the kitchen is open, leaving a straight shot to the back of the duplex. Light from the midday sun pours in through the sliding glass doors, illuminating the space.

The apartment isn't quite as depressing as it had been when I was here last. The mess of takeout containers and dirty dishes that had consumed the counters and overflowed from the trash has been cleared. In its place, there's a thin cutting board, a paring knife, a cucumber, half of which is already sliced, and a bowl of cherry tomatoes. A stack of sandwiches towers on top of a paper plate.

"Can you carry some of this out?"

"Sure. Whatever you'd like."

Out back, an old plastic patio set sits in the center of a low concrete slab. I suspect it was once a deep green, but years in the sun have leeched most of the color away. In some spots, it's nearly white. I set the plate of vegetables on it. Richard must have washed it before making lunch to clear away the winter salt and grime. The tabletop is still damp to the touch. The soft plastic bends beneath my weight as I settle into the chair.

Richard takes the seat opposite of me and loads one of the plates with a sandwich and a handful of vegetables, then passes it over. While he makes his own, I pop one of the tomatoes into my mouth. With the slightest bit of pressure, it explodes, coating my tongue in citrusy juice.

"Mmm." I make the noise without thinking, and Richard chuckles.

"You always did like those. Do you remember stealing them straight off of your Mom's plants in the summer? She pretended to be mad, but it made her happy. Any time we could get you girls to eat produce was a win."

I do. "They were delicious."

"Yes, they were." He takes a bite out of his sandwich and licks his lips. "I've grown some on my balcony in Michigan, but they're not the same. I don't have your mother's green thumb." He tosses one of the tomatoes into his mouth, too. "So, what's on your mind?"

Straight to the point. The two of us have that in common. I guess I'll jump right in.

"I've been thinking about the things you told me. The stuff about Evan and the Ruin."

Richard's eyes dart around the yard. It's like he's making sure no one is watching, but we're alone. "What about it?"

"I'm still not sold on the whole supernatural power thing," I tell him. "But, I did some research this morning and found an article about Evan's disappearance. So, I guess that part was true, right?"

He nods, chewing on a cucumber slice.

"The article mentioned Evan worked for Coarser Industries."

Richard frowns. "He did. Why does that matter?"

"Well, they're a pretty powerful company," I answer, dodging the truth. Now is not the time to tell him Coarser Industries owns Plasmedics. If I do, he might shut down. I need information first. "I'm surprised they didn't find him, what with all the money they have." I pop another tomato in my mouth, savoring the taste. Fresh produce hasn't been on the menu for a while.

"They certainly tried." He wipes his hands on his jeans, a gesture strikingly similar to what I'd done at the cafe this morning. The sameness isn't lost on me. "Coarser Industries has far too much influence, more than any one company should have. Their search for Evan was a large part of the reason I had to leave. They knew I was the last one seen with him. I couldn't have them sniffing around and figuring out where we'd taken Evan or dragging my family into it any more than I already had. It was too dangerous."

"But, he worked for them?"

"For several years by that time. Started right after we graduated. He worked with their PR team, keeping the company out of trouble and making sure the media only latched on to the things Coarser Industries wanted them to have."

"That sounds intense."

"It was," he agrees.

Mayonnaise drips out of the sandwich and lands on my shirt. I swipe it away and lick my thumb. "So," I say around my bite of food, "Did he know Elias Collins?"

"Unfortunately." Richard stretches his legs beneath the table, crossing them at the ankles.

"Why do you say that?"

"Neither of us liked him much. His father ran the company, so Elias did whatever he wanted. He talked down to his coworkers and threw them under the bus when things didn't go his way. One of his mistakes cost Evan a huge raise once. They didn't really get along. Elias was an entitled ass."

Not much has changed.

"I've seen him around the hospital," I say, trying to explain my interest. "I don't like him either. I guess I'm surprised he knew Evan, though."

"Evan knew a lot of people. The Knightly family was a big deal fifteen years ago. His father ran his own law firm. Evan was supposed to join the family business after he graduated, but Coarser offered him more money, so he took that job instead. The firm closed after Evan went missing. They spent a lot of money trying to find him."

"His father didn't mind that Evan went to work for Coarser?"

"Oh, he cared. A lot. But, there wasn't anything he could do about it. Evan was a grown man." Richard studies me. "Why are you so curious about him?"

"Just trying to put the pieces together." I dust some of the crumbs off of my hands.

"Fair enough."

"There's so much I don't understand. Like this," I say. My fingers reach into my pocket to retrieve the locket. I place the pendant and chain on the table and slide them across to him. "I was fidgeting with it earlier, and it broke."

Richard picks up the chain and examines the split link. "I'm pretty sure it can be fixed."

"Probably, but that's not the issue."

His forehead furrows, and he cocks his head to the side, confused.

"When it broke, the necklace fell onto the desk and bounced a bit. It popped open, and I found this inside." I fish the slip of paper out of my pocket. "It's a note. I think your mom might have written it."

He reaches out his hand and I drop the dingy message into his palm. Richard studies the neat writing, then passes the paper back to me.

"You're probably right. That looks like her handwriting."

"What is it?"

"I think I have an idea. I've seen something like this before. Hold on." He stacks our empty plates and stands. "I need to grab something from inside."

Richard disappears into the house and returns a few minutes later carrying a lofty pile of folders. Papers spill from the sides and threaten to fall, but he makes it to the table without losing the contents and spreads them out, digging through the stack. I study their labels as he moves them around, searching for something. One reads "Family Lineage." Another says "Norse Mythology." Yet another simply says "The Ruin." Several more are blank. He digs through the second one and pulls a sheet out, laying it on top.

"After everything happened, I started digging into things. I wanted to know where we come from and how we ended up with the Sharing. I was angry at myself for the trouble I'd caused and frustrated with my mother for all the things she kept from me, things that might have stopped this before it started. The Ruin were no help. They wouldn't tell me anything because I was an outsider. So, I had to do my own research. It's taken me years to find this much.

"Bits and pieces of our history have made their way into textbooks and folklore. Like I said, the Ruin became an urban legend over time. That's why I took a job with the college. They had resources I needed. This," he says, waving his hand over the paper, "is a piece I found in a book about Norse mythology and pagan rituals. It looks like that note, doesn't it?"

I lift the page and read through it. He's right. Much of the poem matches what's written on the scrap from the locket. Only a few words differ. I hand the document back to him, and he returns it to the folder.

"Okay, but what is it?"

"I think it tells the story of how we became the Ruin, how we gained the power of the Sharing. Look at this line," Richard says, pointing to the note. "Blood was spilled on sacred altar."

"Yeah?"

"That points to our ancestors performing some sort of ritual. And, see this one?" He points to another line. "This one mentions a solstice. Rituals were often done on solstices. Still are, actually. There are two, one in the summer and one in the winter."

"So, you think our ancestors performed some sort of satanic ritual and made a deal with the devil?"

"No, of course not. Other people thought so, but I know

better. I think they made a deal with a deity. More specifically, I think they made a deal with a goddess."

"A goddess?"

"Yes. I traced our ancestry back as far as I could, all the way to your great-great-great grandparents before I lost the line." He digs a paper out of the first folder labeled "Family Lineage." This time, it's a map. "We originated here, as far as I can tell." He taps a spot in lower Norway. "Then, when things went wrong, our family sailed here." His finger trails across the sea and lands on the edge of Virginia. "But, we didn't settle there. Our ancestors set off through the mountains and built their village somewhere around here." His finger stops moving deep within the Appalachians. "I can't pinpoint it on the map, but that's the general idea. That's where I found them before."

"What does that have to do with them making a deal with a goddess?"

"Because our family was Norse pagan. I have accounts that prove it" he says, holding up the Family Lineage folder. "Our clan was one of the few in the area who practiced a pagan religion then. Their village was small. They clung to the old ways.

"See this?" He snatches the scrap of paper from the locket and points to yet another line. "It says 'we called to Her.' The H is capitalized. That means it's a title, right?"

"Yeah... I guess?"

"And they capitalized 'She,' too."

"Uh huh."

"So logically, that implies they called to a goddess."

"I guess that makes sense."

"Right. So, the only question is, which one?"

I shake my head. It's fuzzy. The buzzing of a thousand bees rings in my ears. *What is this stuff? How long has he been convinced of this?*

Richard reaches back into the Norse mythology folder and retrieves a handwritten page of research. "There are many Norse goddesses associated with healing and rebirth, but if I'm right, the poem refers to this one."

He offers the lined paper to me:

Name: Eir

Meaning: Help or Mercy

Role: Goddess of Healing

Position: Handmaid to Frigg and Odin

Description: Eir, the Norse goddess of healing, is often counted interchangeably as both an Aesir goddess and a Valkyrie, a fierce female warrior known for riding into battle to collect the souls of fallen warriors deemed worthy enough to pass into Valhalla upon their demise.

Notably, Eir has been said to oversee childbirth. On the battlefield, Eir is also known as the one who determines which warriors are allowed to recover from their injuries, and which warriors will succumb to death. Because of this important role, she is often associated with the Norns who were known to spin the threads of fate for humans, determining the length of the human's lifespan.

Little is known about Eir beyond her associa-

tion with healing. Altars constructed in Eir's honor have featured white plants, as the color white is associated with purification. In Eir's case, these flowers, known as "Eirflowers," are thought to represent the cleansing of ailments from the blood. Examples of plants and flowers often left on Eir's altars include peonies, yarrow, garlic blossoms, chamomile, and lilies of all white varieties.

LILIES? AS IN LILY, RICHARD'S MOM? LIKE THE LILY OF THE VALLEY engraved on the locket?

"You actually think this is true?" I ask, tracing the engraving.

Richard nods. "I do."

What am I supposed to say to that?

"You think our family has magic?"

"Yes. I think they made a bargain with a goddess and were given a gift. All of this, it's proof. I suspected as much before, but seeing this," he points to his Mother's note, "confirms it."

"What does?"

"This," he gestures at the poem. His index finger lands on the strange drawing at the bottom. "And, this. That's Eir's sigil. See?" He points to the same symbol in his notes.

"But, that's just a poem, and that's just a weird drawing…"

"They're more than that. You know it. I can see it on your face."

I don't want to believe him. My logical side can't accept his answer. And yet…

What if he's right? What if his stories aren't crazy after all?

Matthew claims my blood has unique qualities, that it can adapt to diseases faster than anything they've seen. He wants my blood badly enough that he's willing to threaten me. He's willing to withhold Mom's treatment and watch her die.

What if this is why?

It's tempting, I'll admit. It would be so easy to abandon scientific reasoning. The odds have been stacked against me for so long.

No. I can't accept this. I won't. Richard's explanations are beyond the scope of reason.

But, if I was so convinced his tales were nothing more than fantasy, why did I come? I wanted answers, true, but I knew the kind he would provide.

"We took Her gift. Our fates were twined," he quotes. His words hang in the air as I stare at him, speechless. "According to this, our ancestors asked for a gift. They were granted the power to heal, but they broke the deal with the goddess, and because of their error, she cursed our family. It makes sense. It's the only thing I've found that explains why the Sharing works the way it does and why everyone around us dies."

I swallow. "It can't be true. All of this defies logic. You get that, right?"

"I do." He straightens up the documents and watches me.

"And you want me to believe in your fucked up fairy tale?"

"It's the truth."

"God!" I groan. "I can't do this. You're asking me to ignore basic reason." I push myself away from the table and pace, feeling the frustration and anger building inside of me. The question is, am I angry at him or am I angry at myself? *This is too much.*

Richard stands and stops me, putting his hands on my shoulders. "Why can't you accept this?"

"Because it's insane!" I snap.

"Then, why are you here?"

That's it. The question pushes me over the edge.

"I don't know!" I shout, shoving his hands away. "I thought you might abandon your ridiculous conspiracy theories and help me, tell me the truth."

"I am trying to help you," he says, wounded.

"No, you're making it worse. You keep spouting off lies. You only pretend to take responsibility for the things you've done. You can't accept all of this is your fault. Instead, you have to blame everything on some stupid curse."

His face falls. "I know what I've done."

"Why can't you just be normal?" I ask. My hands thud against his shoulders as I push him. He lets me, doesn't try to resist. "Why can't you try to fix what you've broken. I don't have time for your delusions. I'm already dealing with so much. After this morning at Plasmedics – " The words slip out before I can stop them.

Tense silence hangs between us.

"I told you not to go back there. That company is dangerous. The things they might do with your blood are – "

My back pocket vibrates, but I ignore it.

"I don't care what they do! They're paying for Mom's treatments. Unlike you, I won't abandon my family," I spit. My words are pure venom. "I won't give up on my mom. I'm not going to run away like a frightened child."

"Kara, no."

My pocket vibrates again. I whip out my phone and jam my finger into the red button, declining the call.

"You have to stop." Richard's words are a command.

My phone vibrates again. My glare lingers on him. *Where does he get off trying to tell me what to do? He lost that right a long time ago. I'm a full-grown woman. I –*

The vibrations continue. Whoever it is has now called me four times.

I lower my gaze to my phone. Instantly, my anger abandons me. Fear floods through me when I recognize the name on the screen.

Hands shaking, I answer the phone. "Hello?" My voice trembles. Every inch of me has gone cold.

"Ms. Edwards, it's Doctor Mitchell. You need to get down here, and you need to do it fast."

"What... what's happening?"

"It's your mother. We don't have much time."

CHAPTER THIRTY-THREE

My shoes screech against the tile as I bolt into the hospital lobby and attempt to skid to a stop at the greeter's station. Unfortunately, the worn soles don't have enough grip to halt my momentum completely. My hip slams into the waist-height desk, jarring the plexiglass divider and knocking several piles of papers and pamphlets to the floor. I clutch my side where the painful impact registers and draw in a shallow, frantic breath.

The sleepy attendant's eyes widen with confusion as she takes me in.

"Oh my god, hon. Are you okay?" she asks, rising from her seat. She takes several steps toward me and reaches out a steadying hand, but I wave her away.

Every muscle I possess is engulfed in flame, burning from my unexpected race through the packed city streets. My lungs refuse to properly inflate. I gulp, forcing air down into the deepest corners of my chest. Bile rises in my throat. I barely manage to squash it. My body doubles as I reach for the stability of my quaking knees.

"Valerie... Edwards..." I grunt. My voice is strained. Every syllable is painful. "Where... is my... Mom?"

Understanding dawns on the attendant's face. She moves

quickly, fingers flying across her keyboard as she types in Mom's name. "She's in the ICU. Room 317."

My body moves of its own accord, digging deep into my last reserves of strength and leaving the entryway behind. The woman yells after me, but her words are lost beneath the sound of blood rushing through my ears. I opt for the stairs, slamming through the doors and bounding up the steps, struggling to suck in the thinnest stream of air. I'm wheezing and ready to collapse as I clear the landing. One more set of heavy steel doors separates me from the ward. I brace for impact, preparing to drive my shoulders into the metal, but a concerned stranger sees me coming and holds the doors to the intensive care unit wide.

Doctor Mitchell emerges through an open curtain not far down the hall, clipboard and empty IV bag in hand. I must be a wild sight because he dumps both onto the floor and streaks toward me, reaching out his arms. Only feet away, my legs give out, dropping me hard onto my knees. Black speckles crowd the edges of my vision, threatening to pull me into the void. Faintly, my ears register his worried voice as he calls for a nurse. My eyes slip closed as he and whichever staff member comes to his aid worry over me.

Mom. I have to get to Mom. He said we don't have time. He said…

"Kara? Can you hear me?" Doctor Mitchell asks. His fingers peel open my eyelids. A bright light flashes, momentarily blinding me. Weakly, I turn my head away. "Kara? It's Doctor Mitchell. You're in the intensive care unit at St. John's Hospital. You've collapsed outside of your mother's room. If you can understand me, I need you to nod."

My head is too heavy. I strain to lift it, but gravity pulls it back down.

"Good. Take slow, steady breaths," he instructs. "I'm

going to lift your arms above your head to open your airway. Focus on my voice."

For once, I do as I'm told. I lay completely still, letting him maneuver me, limp like a rag doll. A chill seeps in where my skin touches the cool linoleum. My clothes stick to me. He presses a stethoscope to my chest and listens to my whistling inhales.

"You're going to be okay. Did you run all the way here? We need to slow your pulse. Your body needs to rest."

"Kara, baby?" a woman's voice cuts in. It's Trinity. She must be the one who came to his aid. "Your mom needs you to breathe. Come back to us. We're right here."

Something icy and wet touches my forehead. My eyes blink open at the sensation. Doctor Mitchell holds my wrist between his fingers. He stares at his watch, counting.

"It's coming down," he tells Trinity. "She's going to be alright."

"Yes, she is." Her soft fingertips push stray strands of hair away from my sweaty forehead. "Kara's a strong woman. She just needs a minute, isn't that right?"

Somehow, I nod. She rewards me with a dazzling white smile.

Trinity helps me into the chair beside Mom's bed, then passes me a styrofoam cup of ice water. It wobbles in my hand. She catches it, raising it to my lips. I take a drink. It dribbles out of the corner of my mouth, but I manage to swallow the freezing liquid. It shocks me. Suddenly, I'm thirsty. I chug half the cup before coming up for air.

"Good. How are you feeling?"

"I... I don't know."

Doctor Mitchell slides the curtain closed, plunging us into near darkness. He says nothing but watches me closely.

My pulse and breathing may be back under control, but panic distances me from reality. Doctor Mitchell leans against the wall by the curtain, but is he really there? Trinity's saying something, but I can't make out the words. Mom's cramped room is fuzzy around the edges. Nothing stays in focus. It's hard to form coherent thoughts.

The rhythmic sucking and whooshing of a ventilator grates against my ears. I blink and drag my eyes to the head of the bed, searching for the machine. There it is. The thing I've feared most. Numbers flash on the screen. Two tubes run from the ventilator to the hospital bed where they merge. Air pumps into Mom's lungs. Her chest rises and falls robotically.

"Mom?"

My hand reaches out to the tubes. I'm half-convinced all of this is nothing more than a vivid dream. My fingers brush up against hard plastic. It's not a mirage. I wince and withdraw my hand. My blood runs cold.

"What happened?" I ask, not caring who answers. I can't tear my eyes away from her face. It's too peaceful. Too serene. "She was fine."

"Oh, hon." There's sadness in Trinity's voice. "Things around here change in an instant. We never know how the day is gonna go."

"Valerie's lung collapsed early this afternoon," Doctor Mitchell adds. "We did our best to resolve the complication, but I fear it will not be restored."

"Her lung?"

"The healthier of the two."

"But, the treatment – "

He flashes me a warning look. Trinity doesn't know. "As

you're aware, we've run out of treatment options. The unfortunate reality is we have reached the end of the road."

I'm numb. The room is too small. Mom is too still. The machine is too loud.

"Nurse Trinity, I need to ask you to clear the room."

Trinity's eyes bounce between Doctor Mitchell and me. She's waiting for my permission, but I can't form words.

"Nurse Trinity?" he repeats. His words are a question, but his voice is a command. "Would you excuse us, please?"

My lips move. "It's fine."

"Are you sure?"

"Yes." I blink back stinging tears.

"I'll be right out here." Trinity stands and places a gentle hand on my shoulder. She squeezes once, then pulls back the edge of the curtain. I can't meet her eyes, can't look away from Mom. If I blink, she might disappear. I feel nothing as Trinity's footsteps recede down the hall.

"Ms. Edwards, we've exhausted our options," he starts as soon as she's out of earshot. "With this new development, our current course is no longer viable. Novemion can't repair this. I'm sorry. There's nothing to be done. We need to discuss end-of-life care."

"But, she's my mom..." I lift her hand off of the knitted white blanket and twine her fingers with mine. "She's my mom."

"It's time to let her go."

DOCTOR MITCHELL AND TRINITY HAVE LONG abandoned the room. The clear bag of saline, no longer swirling with Novemion, drips into the chamber and down Mom's IV tube. The clock above the bed ticks, ticks, ticks,

ticks away the hours. Night has fallen. I haven't moved from the chair. I don't know how.

I should call someone, text someone, but who? Jennifer? She wouldn't care. Connor? Ally? They'd want to be here, but they can't. Not in the ICU. Richard? Would Mom want him here? I should tell someone what's going on.

I can't take my hand out of hers. What if I let go for a moment to send a message, but when I reach back to take it into my own again, her fingers have gone rigid and cold?

No. No. No. No No No No No.

The saline drips, drips, drips.

The ventilator whooshes, whooshes.

My heart thrums a steady rhythm. Ba-doom. Ba-doom. Ba-doom. Ba-doom.

I'm so tired.

DOCTOR MITCHELL IS HERE. HE'S TRYING desperately to tell me something, but no sound comes out of his mouth. I blink, and he's gone.

Suddenly, I'm someplace new. It's distant, strange. I'm in a clearing, I think? Long grass tickles my strangely bare toes. Trees surround the edges of the space. Stars blink in and out in the dark sky above.

I'm not alone. Fingers thread through mine, and whoever it is grips my hand. But, who is it? *Who would be all the way out here? Why am I out here? Why is the air so warm?* Humidity clings to my skin.

I turn my head to the left and find Trinity. Her piercing eyes, unnaturally blue, linger on me. She bends down until her face is so close to mine I can feel the heat of her skin. She brushes a lock of hair away from my ear and whispers. Though there is no other noise, her words are hard to hear. She pulls away and lets go of my head, repeating her message and pointing to the trees. This time, the sound is clear: "Follow."

I run, letting my feet glide over the dew-soaked ground. Dirt squelches between my toes. I fly under low branches and over jutting roots. The canopy blots out what little light there was from the full moon. A stick cracks to my right, warning me of another's presence. I press my back against a thick tree trunk, disappearing into the shadows.

People in strange clothes traipse through the gnarled forest, carrying cloth bundles. Intermittent moonbeams cast them in an ethereal glow. Trinity's command rings in my ears. As quietly as I can, I sneak along behind them until they break out of the trees and into a perfectly circular clearing. In the center is an artfully arranged pile of stones.

They speak words I can't understand as they lay their bundles upon the plinth. Each unwraps their fabric, baring their cargo in the silver light. White flowers spill out amongst masses of fragrant herbs and shining gems. They tumble over the front of the altar – yes, that has to be what it is. White petals drift through the air and flit across the ground. The barren dirt of the clearing is hidden beneath the silky gifts.

A double-edged knife is lifted to the palm of one of the strangers. They draw it across the delicate skin with a soft hiss and pass the blade along. Everyone does the same. The last discards the blade. They surrounded their altar full of offerings, letting the blood drip down onto the flowers.

Heat floods through the small clearing. A violent breeze whips the strangers' cloaks around their feet. A figure... so familiar, yet indistinguishable, appears. Shadow surrounds the female form.

I know her. My mind struggles to grab onto the memory of this person. *Why do I know her? Who is she?*

Someone speaks yet more words I can't understand. They step forward, falling to their knees before the woman. The strangers bend their heads to the dirt in supplication. The crowd begins to chant. "Eir. Eir. Eir. Eir. Eir."

The shadow figure leans down, lifting the closest beggar to their feet. A gasp echoes through the crowd. They reach for their neighbors, weeping and holding each other in their arms.

"Just the one," the shadow woman commands, this time in a tongue I understand. "One, and no more. Do not steal from Death. Do not break your vow."

The strangers assent, and I could swear the woman turns to face me before a swirl of silver light and shadow encompasses her. With a flash, she fades into the trees, leaving the strangers alone once more.

I WAKE WITH A START, NEARLY JUMPING OUT OF MY chair. I'd been slumped over Mom's legs. My back aches. My head throbs.

How long was I asleep?

My eyes flick to the clock. 2:17 am. Last time I checked the clock, it was almost midnight.

The ventilator whooshes. Mom's chest rises and falls.

The saline drips, drips, drips.

The clock ticks, ticks, ticks.

My dream swirls through my head.

What was that?

But, I know what it was. It was the origin of the Ruin. It was the deal Richard told me about.

Was that real? How could it be real?
I run the tubing of Mom's IV through my fingers.
The saline drips.
My pulse thrums.
If it was real, can I save my mom?

CHAPTER THIRTY-FOUR

I should feel foolish for considering Richard's stories about the Ruin, but I don't. Standing at the edge of Mom's bed, the part of me that demands I make logical decisions has abandoned me. In its place, I'm left with the suffocating presence of fear. It coils itself around me like a fully-grown python, constricting. The dark is approaching, but I'm running on empty. I'm pure emotion, raw.

The bed creaks when I sit down beside her, but she doesn't stir. Her eyelids flutter as though she's lost in a dream. Doctor Mitchell said something about sedation, though I didn't hear his exact words. Wetness streams down my cheeks as I press my forehead to hers.

"Mommy?" My voice is childish as I choke out the word.

I wasn't here when her lung collapsed. I was supposed to be, but I went to Richard's instead. My head was full of stupid questions I thought I needed him to answer.

I should have been by her side. I should have washed her hair. I should have picked up a tiny bottle of nail polish at the gift shop and painted her nails like she wanted. I should have been here. But, when she needed me most, she was alone.

"I'm so sorry," I sob.

Does she know I'm here now?

"Mommy, I'm here," I tell her between sniffles. "I should

have been here before. I wasn't, and that's my fault, but I won't leave you. I'm right beside you. I'm not going anywhere this time. I promise."

Leaning back, I straighten her blankets. She doesn't stir.

My mother is dying. There are no more treatments. No more options. There's nowhere to turn. Despite everything, cancer won. This is it, her last few days, maybe hours. Then, I'll be alone. I'm losing the only parent I've ever had. The one who rocked me when I was sick. The one who went to every parent-teacher conference. The one who told me bedtime stories. The only one who would never leave me. But, she is. She's letting go. There's nothing I can do.

Nothing.

What if there is?

We tried all of the traditional treatments. Mom had multiple rounds of chemotherapy and radiation. She underwent surgery after surgery. None of it helped. The tumor grew. New ones formed.

Doctor Mitchell gave us another chance with Novemion. I thought it was working. He thought so, too. We were both wrong.

So, what do I have left? Everyone is telling me to let her go. I can't do that. I can't. Maybe it's selfish. Maybe holding onto her so tightly is the worst thing I've ever done. I don't care. There is no world without her in it. Not yet. She's so young. *I'm* so young. I need my mom.

All that's left is Richard's fairytale, and even I know that's a leap. He came back after fifteen years spouting nonsense about family curses and Norse goddesses like it's normal, just something people do. I wrote him off. I dismissed it completely.

Then, Matthew threatened me. He told me my blood was anomalous. He has a background in science. If Richard's wrong, his claim makes no sense. Why would my blood be different than anyone else's?

And, there's the newspaper article about Evan's disappearance. Richard hadn't made that up. The reporter said Evan was supposed to die. The doctors and nurses had run out of options. He didn't die, though. He healed. He walked out of this hospital as healthy as he had been before.

Plus, I had that dream about the strangers in the clearing. The altar and offerings. The goddess wrapped in shadow and moonlight.

What if it's true? What if I was wrong? What if I don't try? What if I refuse to believe in the impossible and let Mom die because of my stubbornness?

The smooth IV tubing slides between my fingers as I trace it up to the dripping saline bag.

Everything I would need is right here. Right in front of me. There are needles in the cabinet. I've seen the nurses use them. I wouldn't have to leave the room.

My legs move of their own accord, taking a few short steps across the cramped space until I'm standing in front of the cabinet. My hand trembles, hovering over the handle.

I could use Richard's story about the Sharing as a guide. He said it didn't take long. I could give Mom my blood, then before anyone notices things have changed, we could slip out the back door. We wouldn't come into contact with anyone. No one would have to know. No one else would have to die. I wouldn't have to be alone.

My fingers wrap around the cool metal. With barely a pull, the door pops open.

A voice in the back of my mind screams at me, begging me to stop now before it's too late, but I lift one of the packaged butterfly needles.

It's so light. So simple. It wouldn't even hurt. The needles the nurse at Plasmedics uses for my donations are far larger than this. One little poke.

The scissors the nurses use to cut gauze lay in the compartment beside the bandages and tape.

I could snip the tube, attach the butterfly, and seal the gap with tape. It wouldn't be hard. I could do that...

Ba-doom. Ba-doom. Ba-doom. Time slows. The Sharing calls to me. The hairs on my arm rise. I'm lifting the scissors out of the drawer. The clock ticks, ticks, ticks, ticks. My hands shake as I see it play out in my mind. I raise the scissors to the tubing, ready to clamp down and sever the line from the bag.

Mom stirs.

Before I have time to think about the strange compulsion, I shove everything back into the cabinet and slam it shut. In no time, I'm back at her side.

"Mommy?" I beg. "Mommy, can you hear me? Mom?"

It was nothing more than a tremor, a twitch of consciousness. She's already lost to the sedation.

I jump as several hearty knocks sound from behind me. My eyes fly to the curtain and find Matthew Collins standing there.

"I'm sorry. Have I interrupted something?"

His face is smooth, projecting indifference, but I can tell by the slightest upturn of his lips he enjoyed startling me. I press my hand against my chest, willing my pulse to slow.

What is he doing here?

"I was so sorry to hear of your mother's worsened condition. Doctor Mitchell contacted me a few hours ago. I thought it best to make a personal visit, given her..." he hesitates, "situation."

"Get out," I snarl. "You can't be here."

"Oh, but I can." Matthew pushes himself away from the wall and steps into the room, sliding the curtain closed behind him. He straightens his suit and slips his hands into his pockets before walking around to the other side of the bed. "I can be anywhere I want."

"You're not welcome here."

"I never said I was."

My hands ball into fists at my side. His arrogance sets my teeth on edge. It takes everything I have not to jump across this bed and hit him. I want to feel his nose crack beneath my fist. That would bring him down a peg. But, I can't. I need to keep calm and avoid drawing the staff's attention.

If I attack Matthew, I'll be thrown out of this hospital, no questions asked. He's an important man, and I'm no one. I promised Mom I wouldn't leave her. I won't. I can't. She'll die alone.

Matthew offers me his signature grin. His eyes travel over my body, taking in my stance. I'm certain he knows exactly what I'm thinking, and he's reveling in it, which only serves to increase my anger. "Kara, I thought we were friends, or partners at the very least. And yet, you look as though you'd like nothing more than to maul me. I've only ever tried to help, haven't I?"

"Help?" I scoff. "Help? The last time I saw you, you cornered me in an office and threatened me. What kind of help is that?"

"Now, I'll admit. I could have handled our situation with more tact. For that, I apologize."

"I don't need your apology," I spit. "I *need* you to *leave*."

He sits on the foot of Mom's bed as though he belongs there. "You have no idea what you need. Have you even considered my offer?"

Seeing his expression of mock concern sends me deeper into a rage. My breaths grow shallow and ragged. "Oh, screw your offer," I hiss. "And, get away from my mother!"

Matthew sucks air through his teeth. "Such a shame. So quick to abandon your allies. What a waste. I thought you were smarter."

"Fuck... you. Leave!" I growl.

"Alright." Matthew throws his hands up in defeat. "I can

see when I'm not wanted." Rather obediently, he heads for the exit.

It's all an act. He's waving his influence in my face. He wants me to feel pathetic and ashamed.

Matthew's hand is on the curtain, ready to pull it back, but instead, he turns to me. "It's a pity your mom has to die because *you* won't listen to reason."

"What reason?" My words are no longer quiet, but I don't care. "Novemion won't fix this!"

"No, it won't, but I may have something that will."

Quicker than I thought possible, I cross the space to stand at his side. He's inches away, towering over me as I glare up at him. "What the hell is that supposed to mean?"

Matthew sighs. "What? Do you think Novemion is the only powerful medication I have access to, Kara? Don't be obtuse." He shakes his head, clearly disappointed. "I told you our company uses plasma donations to formulate new drugs. I told you that *your* blood is special, different. You've been donating with us for months. We've had time to analyze certain patterns and test several theories."

"And?"

"And, I think we have exactly what you need."

"There's no way. Doctor Mitchell said – "

"Doctor Mitchell is limited in his field of study. He doesn't know what I do. He doesn't have a team of respected scientists at his disposal. In essence, he's useless."

"You're not?"

Matthew chuckles. "Hardly. See, this new medication we've developed has been tested on several breeds of animals. It doesn't stop the spread of cancer, Kara. It consumes it entirely. Within hours, the tumors riddling the bodies of the little critters are gone. Poof. Like they never existed."

"How?" I ask. "That's not possible." Slowly, I back away.

"Science… magic… call it what you like. All you need to know is it works. I can save your mom. If you're willing to try, that is."

I collapse into the discarded chair, struggling to breathe. "Nothing you do is free."

Matthew sighs. His interest in the conversation wanes with my continued resistance. "No, it isn't. What kind of businessman would I be if I gave our products away? You heard my father."

"What do you want?"

"Not much. An agreement."

"An agreement?"

"Yes, as such. Sign your mother over into my private care. I can have her transported from here to my facility in less than an hour. Once there, my medics can administer the new treatment to her. What do you have to lose?"

"You tell me," I snap. My cold fingers wrap around the arms of the chair in a feeble attempt to steady myself.

"Very little. You'll stay in the facility for the duration of your mother's care. Whenever we need you to do so, you'll donate your blood to the cause. After all, at this stage, we can't make more medication without source material."

"You want to keep me on tap like an ale?"

That earns me a full-chested laugh. "So to speak."

"And, when it's done?"

"It's done." His tone is cheerful, detached. "You'll be free to leave at your discretion. We won't bother you again. You have my word."

"What's the word of a psychopath worth?"

"More than you'll ever earn, I can assure you."

I glance back to Mom, lying still and helpless on the bed. Only the ventilator forces her to breathe. Matthew follows my gaze, looking for all the world like he couldn't care less which decision I make. Maybe he doesn't. After all, Coarser Industries has plenty of time to find more people like me.

But, he's won. He knows it, too. There are no more options except his. Either I take his deal or let my mother die. I'm Alice falling down the rabbit hole, tumbling end over end into chaos without anything tethering me to reality. Mom is my only anchor. I need her to live. I'll do anything. I've never felt desperation like this.

"So, what's it going to be, Kara?" he finally asks, checking the time on his watch. "You're running out of options, and I have a business to run. Tick tock."

I gulp. "I'm not some lab rat you can use and toss out."

"Of course not," he croons. "You either agree to this arrangement of your own free will, or I walk away from this room right now. So, I'll ask you again. What are you going to do?"

Cornered and defeated, I bow my head. Once more, I reach out and take Mom's still hand into mine.

"I'll do it," I answer, "but you have to promise to leave everyone else alone. Doctor Mitchell won't go to prison. My friends and family will be safe. This is between you and me."

"Deal," he says with a cocky grin. "Now, excuse me. I have an important call to make."

CHAPTER THIRTY-FIVE

The early morning sky opens up, releasing a torrent of rain less than an hour later as two paramedics lift Mom's bed into the back of an ambulance. In a matter of seconds, I'm drenched. My thin t-shirt sticks awkwardly to my skin. They fiddle with wires and battery packs, ensuring the ventilator runs as it should while I wrap my arms around myself in a pathetic attempt to ward off the chill. It's no use. Goosebumps ripple down my legs and my teeth chatter.

Doctor Mitchell stands beside me in the cool, spring rain. His sodden white coat hangs heavily off his shoulders. Water runs in rivulets down his fingers. He's eerily still. I've never seen him so haunted.

"You're certain this is what you want?" he asks, meeting my gaze. "These people are, well, not what they seem. I'm coming to understand them more and more each day."

A droplet slides down the back of my neck, making me shiver. "I don't have a choice."

He turns his eyes to my mother. "There's always a choice. I fear you and I have already made several incorrect ones by this point."

"Me too." Water beads on my eyelashes. I try to blink it away, but it quickly returns. "What's done is done."

Monitoring equipment sparks to life in the back of the ambulance. Doctor Mitchell studies it, still treating Mom like his patient. I can't tell what he's thinking, but his face falls when he speaks again. "Valerie is a good woman. So are you. Don't let them…" he trails off as one medic steps out of the back, gesturing for me to climb in. I wait for Doctor Mitchell to finish his thought, but he doesn't. Instead, he mutters, "Good luck, Kara. I wish you both the best."

He reaches for my hand, but I pull him into an embrace. Doctor Mitchell and I have had our share of contentious moments, and yet, he's always been kind. I know he meant well while Mom was in his care despite his sometimes cold bedside manner. He risked his career for us. He risked prison. I can't thank him enough.

"You too," I tell him as I pull away. I offer him a sad smile. "Be safe."

"I'll try. However, I'm afraid that's not up to me." His brow creases. "I would advise you to do the same. No matter the outcome, I believe you have a difficult road ahead."

One of the medics wraps his hand around my elbow, impatiently pulling me into the back. "We'll take it from here, sir," he instructs, his voice stern. "This rain isn't getting any weaker. I'd suggest you go back inside."

And just like that, I'm sitting on the hard metal bench across from Mom as he pulls the doors closed and the ambulance lurches into drive.

"Why are we here?" I ask as the medic pushes the doors of the ambulance open, revealing the Plasmedics parking lot. "I thought we were going to a private facility."

"I go where I'm told," he answers. "Step outside."

The man hadn't spoken a word to me as we drove through the heavy traffic. In fact, he seemed to avoid looking in my direction entirely. Was it something I'd said or done? Or, more likely, did he not care who he was transporting as long as he was paid?

I try to convince myself this is the case as I step around his wide shoulders and climb down the slippery step. My shoes land in a puddle at the sidewalk's edge, making me grimace. Hurriedly, I back away from the vehicle, giving him and the other EMT the space they need to unload. My water-logged socks make uncomfortable squishing sounds with each step. The fabric of my shoes suctions to my toes.

The two of them unclip several straps and release the wheel locks before lifting Mom's bed and dropping the metal legs down with a heavy click. Though they're gentle enough, the ventilator tubes bounce when the wheels come into contact with the hard ground.

I move to follow them, but the sound of a sleek black sedan pulling into the lot draws my attention. Water sprays from my hair as I whip my head to the side. The expensive car splashes across the asphalt and parks beside the ambulance. Matthew's face peers out from behind the windshield. His umbrella emerges first, then his long legs and perfectly coiffed head. He holds the fabric high above himself as he dodges puddles and meets me on the sidewalk. Without a word, he extends his arm to encompass me beneath the umbrella's protective shield, though it's pointless. No part of me is dry.

The men have already wheeled Mom inside. Matthew ushers me toward the entrance to Plasmedics, eager to get out of the rain. This time, no guard sits in the atrium when the doors slide open. As far as I can tell, the building is empty. Plasmedics isn't open yet. It won't be for hours.

"You're treating her here? At the donation center?" I ask, ringing out my hair.

Matthew chuckles as he shakes the water off his shoes. "Don't be daft. Plasmedics encompasses the first floor of this building, but we own the entire thing. The facility has many uses, only one of which involves plasma donation."

I hadn't considered the rest of the floors. My trips here have been confined to the first. There had been no need to wander.

He leans his umbrella against the wall, point down. It steadily drips, saturating the space. Clearly, he doesn't care because he walks to the elevators and presses the button. Machinery whirs to life as the cabin lowers to the first floor. He glances at his watch, checking the time.

"Somewhere you need to be?" I ask, annoyed.

"Always," comes his smart reply. "I'm a busy man."

"Of course you are."

He raises an eyebrow at me, not missing the sarcasm in my tone. My lips press into a thin line.

The elevator doors slide open with a ding. Matthew wraps one arm around my shoulders and pushes me forward. The unwelcome touch sends anger surging through me. I shrug him off and move to the far corner. He says nothing, instead pressing another button and leaning against the opposite wall.

"When we reach our destination, I have more papers for you to sign. Legal formalities. Authorizations. That kind of thing."

I nod. I had expected as much. It's never just one document. Before leaving the hospital, I had to sign seven.

The buttons blink as we ascend, illuminating one floor at a time. We approach the sixth and the elevator slows. Matthew steps to the front, blocking my view. He emerges into a brightly lit hall when the doors peel back. The overpowering scents of bleach and disinfectant slam into me as I follow him, making me gag.

Once more, my reaction amuses him. "We keep things sterile here. I'm sure you understand. We can't have contamination corrupting our research data."

I swallow the excess saliva filling my mouth. He turns and marches down the long hall, not waiting for me. I struggle to keep up, shoes squeaking on the tile.

Sterile is the perfect word to describe this facility. There's nothing remotely inviting about it. From the shining floor beneath me to the spotless ceiling above, everything is white or muted gray. I trail behind Matthew, taking in the strange space.

If I had been Alice falling down the rabbit hole back at St. John's, the sensation is amplified here. This building is so symmetrical. It's like walking through a funhouse. Steel-gray doors are spaced roughly every fifteen feet. Each is closed. No sounds emanate from inside. Adjacent to every door is a wide, horizontal window. These give no view into the spaces behind them. They've been screened with an opaque white film. The only indications we're not passing the same rooms over and over are large, square signs that read "Ward C" and display the room number. These hang above each entrance.

Absolute silence penetrates my ears. This space is cold and lifeless. It makes my skin crawl.

How can anyone recover here?

"Where did they take Mom?" I ask. My words are too loud as they echo off the walls. I cringe.

"To her room. She's perfectly safe, I assure you," Matthew answers without turning back.

A woman, maybe ten years older than me, rounds the corner at the end of the hall. Her dark gray scrubs and smooth olive skin contrast with our bright surroundings and her spotless lab coat. I notice her clothes first. They're pristine, not a wrinkle in sight. My eyes travel up to her face. As she takes us in, her cherry-red lips thin, giving her a cold and grim expression. She pats the top of her head where a slick bun sits. I search for a nametag on her shirt, but there isn't one. She stops about a foot in front of us and tilts her head.

"Ms. Edwards, I presume. If you would please follow me. I'll escort you to your room."

My eyebrows knit together in question. "My room? No, I'm here with my mom, Valerie Edwards."

Matthew takes two steps back, putting distance between us. His reaction doesn't go unnoticed. I turn to face him, looking for answers, but instead of explaining, he flashes me a mischievous smile.

"Not anymore," the woman replies. "You'll be coming with me." She reaches for my arm and wraps her thin fingers around my bicep. Long, pointed nails dig into my skin.

"No, I need to make sure she's safe," I assert. I rip my arm away from her grasp. "I'll come with you after I know she's okay."

"You'll come with me now," she commands. There's a sharp edge to her words. The hand that had held me reaches into her pocket. "Your mother is fine. There's no need to fret."

"I have to see her. I have to know where she is. I can't go with you."

Matthew laughs as panic consumes me.

"Ms. Edwards, we can either do this the easy way," she says calmly, "or the hard way."

She withdraws a shining syringe filled with a cloudy white liquid. A drop glistens at the needle's tip. As she does, two large men step out of the closest room and flank her. "I was assured you knew better than to resist before your arrival, but I've prepared the necessary precautions, just in case."

"I'm not going anywhere until I know where you've taken my mom!" I bellow, rapidly backing away.

The woman doesn't flinch, but her expression sours. "Pity," she says. "I was looking forward to a pleasant afternoon."

The two men surge forward and seize me, gripping me so tightly their touch burns my skin. I kick and struggle as they drag me down the hall. Matthew observes the scene with amusement as I call to him. Victory twinkles in his eyes.

They shove me through one of the doors with more force than necessary. Without warning, the men release me. I hurtle toward the bed in the center of the room, colliding roughly with the starchy sheets. Instinct takes hold. I whirl around, lashing out. I kick at the knees of the man closest to me, but he easily avoids the impact, pushing me back against the mattress and disabling my right arm. The other comes too close, and I smash my head into his, sending stars swirling behind my eyelids. He grunts and mutters, "bitch," but pins my other arm down. My feet skid uselessly beneath me as I try to stand.

The woman enters the room and flicks the syringe. A few drops land on my face. I scream as the men push me farther down, confining me. She plunges the tip into my shoulder, sending pain zinging through the joint. Within seconds, my body falls limp.

The guards release my arms, letting me slide down to the floor. The woman narrows her eyes at me as though I've been a terribly inconvenient part of her day. She gestures wordlessly for them to lift me onto the bed, and they do. They drop me harshly before she dismisses them from the room.

I can't turn my head, but I can see the door slowly close behind them. There's no knob on the inside, only a round, plastic pad meant for a key card. Paralyzed, I'm helpless as the woman arranges me on the bed and straps my wrists and ankles into thick velcro restraints. She fastens them so tightly they bite into my skin and restrict blood flow. As she works, my fingers and toes grow cold.

The woman covers me with a blanket and busies herself turning on multiple machines. Some I recognize, and some I don't. She places a needle in the crook of my arm and hums, hooking a clear tube to one I identify as an apheresis machine. In my opposite arm, she places another needle and tube, this time trailing it up to a pole at the corner of the bed. There, she hangs a bag of the same cloudy liquid. She flicks the chamber, forcing it to drip down, before stepping back and observing the room.

She must be satisfied with what she sees because the woman turns her attention to me. "Until you learn to behave yourself, you'll be administered a paralytic." She points to the bag of medication on the pole. "We can't have you trying to escape. You might hurt yourself or others, and that won't do. This is merely a precaution, you understand.

I most certainly do not understand.

Just wait until I can move.

"It looks like we are all set here," the woman says cheerily. "I'll be in shortly to check your vitals and make sure the medication isn't too strong. We wouldn't want you to suddenly stop breathing on us, would we?"

I wish you would stop breathing. If I could strangle you, I would.

"Here, let me get this set up for you," she sings, reaching for a remote. She points it at the wall across from me where a flatscreen television flares to life. "Do you see that little camera on top, there? It ensures we can see you at all times. Don't do anything rash. If you do, we'll have to come in and… take care of the problem, so to speak. And this," she flips through channels until she lands on a view of another room, "is your view of your mother. See, dear? She's perfectly safe, so long as you behave."

What does that mean? So long as I behave?

"We have more than one way to handle unruly patients here, Ms. Edwards." She hangs the remote on the wall behind me. "Don't forget that."

Hatred radiates from me as she rounds the bed. She retrieves a card from her pocket and taps her ID badge on the reader by the door. It swishes closed behind her and clicks as she leaves me bound to the bed, terrified and powerless. My eyes water as I see Mom, limp and out of reach, in another room much like this one. The medic from before sits in a chair by her side. He fusses with his phone, ignoring her completely.

What have I gotten us into?

CHAPTER THIRTY-SIX

There are no visible clocks in my prison, and the windowless space gives little insight as to the passage of time. No matter how hard I strain to listen, no sounds drift in from the hall. This room is its own bubble, isolated from the rest of the world.

The apheresis machine churns, but its sounds are muted. A steady stream of blood rushes through the tube into the machine. The crimson line dangling over the edge of the bed is the only shock of color in the space.

Concentrating, I try to wriggle my fingers, to pinch the tube and stop the flow, but they lay limp beside me, courtesy of the rhythmic dripping of the cloudy fluid. Until it wears off, I'm at the mercy of the icy paralytic coursing through my veins.

Not that I could move if I managed to fight off the drug. The velcro restraints leaving deep impressions on the skin of my wrists and ankles would make sure of that.

Mom doesn't stir either. The only movement on the screen is the fidgeting guard. He's abandoned his phone in favor of watching television. His soundless visage laughs before rising and pacing to the door. The man is gone for a while before resuming his station in the chair. He doesn't even glance at Mom.

I need to think of a plan, a way to get the two of us out of this mess, but my mind is as paralyzed as my limbs. Try as I might, I can't wrap my head around a solution.

No one knows where we are. Doctor Mitchell is aware I had Mom transferred, but the paperwork hadn't listed an address. If it had, I wouldn't have been surprised to see that the ambulance brought us to Plasmedics.

I should have called Connor and Ally to tell them what was going on. Why hadn't I? They couldn't have come to see us in the ICU or accompanied us here, but they would have known how desperate I was, how hurt. They might have put the pieces together once they realized the two of us were gone. Connor knows about Matthew's threat.

Richard. I should have called my father. I hadn't, if only because I didn't want to start another argument or hear him demand that I let her go. Maybe he could have talked some sense into me? No, I doubt it. The decision had been made as soon as Matthew extended his offer. I was never going to back down.

There's more to this drive to save her than I've been willing to admit to myself. It's not only that I don't want to lose the woman who loved me when no one else would, or that I'm afraid, or because I'm selfish and weak. It's a tug deep inside me that screams this is what I have to do. I have to save Mom at any cost.

I've considered the options before. I know the ways this could play out. But, logic doesn't win over instinct and emotion. I'd die to save her. I know that now.

My thoughts are consumed with my failures as I flick my eyes between the silent screen and the slowly draining pouch.

My fault. Worthless. Coward. Disappointment. Useless.

The last drop exits the IV chamber and slides down into my arm.

I expect the woman to know as soon as the medication is gone. I imagine she has another bag waiting to replace the empty one. Most likely, they'll keep me paralyzed for as long as they need me, then dump the two of us into a medical waste bin and cut their losses.

She doesn't rush into the room and change out the drug, though. Things stay as they've been.

Slowly, painfully, the paralytic wears off.

It's been quiet for so long that when a shrill beep sounds outside, I start. The lock releases with a deafening click, letting the door swing into the room. Matthew, as cocky as ever, saunters in with a paper coffee cup in hand. The logo on the side, aimed intentionally in my direction, tells me he went to Renee's. It's a taunt, a reminder he can go wherever he pleases while I'm trapped here at his will.

An impish grin breaks out on his face before he raises the cup to his lips and takes a drink. He makes a show of savoring the taste before setting it down on the empty counter.

"It looks like you've settled in well."

"You're a sick bastard, you know that?"

"So they say." He takes a seat by my knees and leans in close. "I truly wish you had followed Doctor Wolff's directions earlier. Kidnapping is not my typical MO. Yet, here we are."

I scoff. "Why are you here, Matthew? Don't you have better things to do? You're such a *busy* man."

"And you, Kara Edwards, are now my top priority. I've canceled the rest of my plans. Thought you could use some company."

My eyes narrow into slits. "I'd rather live in the sewers with the rats."

"Be careful. That can be arranged."

Matthew leans across me and plucks the remote from its position on the wall. He toys with it for a moment as though considering an idea.

"Your mother has such a lovely room, doesn't she?" he asks. His eyes travel over the screen before returning to me. Without waiting for an answer, he continues. "She has everything she needs. It would be such a shame if things were to go wrong, wouldn't it?"

"Don't you dare," I growl. "If you touch her – "

"What will you do? Hmm?" His eyebrow raises. "Glare at me? Call me names? Please. You're nothing but an insolent child."

He's right. With the paralytic gone, I can move my fingers and toes, turn my head, and squirm, but I can't escape. I can't attack him. All I have are empty threats. They won't get me far.

"Let me explain how this is going to work. You cooperate with me, and your mother keeps her ventilator. Fail to cooperate, and my friend," he gestures at the screen, "will provide you with some… motivation. Shall I demonstrate?"

Matthew presses one of the buttons on the remote and speaks. It must be an intercom. The man on the screen snaps to attention and approaches the camera.

"How's our guest doing?"

"Mr. Collins," the guard grunts. "There's been no change. Things are as expected."

"Good, good. Our other guest finds herself in need of encouragement." He turns to me, holding the remote near my face. "What do you think? Fifteen seconds?"

I struggle against my bonds, but it's no use. They hold fast. The edges of the restraints cut into my limbs.

Matthew simply chuckles. "Yes, let's start with that. Fifteen seconds will do."

Panic surges through me as the guard moves toward Mom's bedside. He reaches for the ventilator tubing, holding it tightly in his fist.

"No!" I scream, thrashing. "Stop this! Stop!"

The guard doesn't comply with my demands. He looks to the camera and squeezes the tubing, crushing it in his grasp, cutting off Mom's air supply.

Her unconscious form is still at first, but as soon as her body registers the absence of air, it jerks, seizing on the bed. Matthew taps out the seconds with his foot, uncaring and cold.

"Matthew! Leave her alone! Stop! Stop!"

He takes in the scene with a look of mild curiosity but doesn't respond. When the fifteen seconds have elapsed, he raises the intercom. "That will do."

The guard releases the tube. Mom's body relaxes. It's done.

"Anything else, sir?" the guard asks as he approaches the camera again.

"No, that will be all. Resume your duties."

"Yes, sir."

Matthew leans back across me and hangs the remote on the wall. When he rights himself, there's a look of smug satisfaction on his face.

"Do you understand, Kara?"

I bite down on my tongue. The pain keeps my wicked mouth in check.

"Well, just in case you don't, let me spell it out for you. Right now, you and your mother are locked in soundproof rooms. My staff is well-paid to do as they're told and look the other way when I need them to. You could scream through the day and night. No one will help you, and no one outside will hear you. If you choose to fight the staff, the paralytic will be administered again, and again, and again."

He waits for me to answer, but I say nothing. I don't know if it's out of spite or self-preservation, but for once, I fight the urge to spit venom.

"Even if you were able to break free of your restraints, which I highly doubt, there's nowhere for you to go. There's no doorknob in this room. There's no window for you to break out and escape through. But, these things are not your biggest motivation to behave, now are they?"

Traitorous tears fill my eyes as I look at the screen. Matthew reaches out and swipes away the few that run down my cheek. I recoil at his touch. The sensation makes my stomach curdle.

"You know, it's your fault you're in this situation. I extended a perfectly reasonable offer when I asked you to make daily donations. You chose to ignore me. I had every intention of working alongside you peacefully. "

"This is not going to end well for you. I'll make sure of it."

"Empty promises from a stupid little girl," he chides. "I would like to see you try."

"Why is my blood so damn important to you? What the hell are you doing?"

For a moment, Matthew studies me. Thoughts churn behind his eyes. "Do you really want to know?"

"What do you think?" I spit.

"I suppose I don't see the harm," he muses. "You won't be leaving this facility alive."

His words are meant to shock me, but I hadn't expected I would. Why would he let me go when I know so much?

He sighs when he doesn't get the reaction he wants. I've ruined his dramatic reveal.

"Fine," he says with a pout. "We're manufacturing bioweapons."

"Excuse me? Bioweapons?" I'm dumbfounded. My head lifts off of the thin pillow as I stare at him. "You've got to be kidding me."

Matthew straightens, satisfaction and pride strengthening his posture. "Not in the slightest. I told you your blood is unique."

"*You* said my antibodies would allow you to make new medications and cure diseases. You never said shit about creating new ones. How did you go from saving thousands of lives to biowarfare? That's sick."

Matthew eyes me with contempt. "Trust me, it wasn't a long leap. Coarser Industries has had its hands in such things for decades. Fifteen years, to be precise."

"Fifteen years?"

"Oh, yes."

I gulp. *Fifteen years since Richard left. Fifteen years since Coarser Industries investigated Evan's disappearance. Fifteen years since the outbreak.*

Matthew narrows his eyes as he leans closer. "What do you know of Evan Knightly?"

CHAPTER THIRTY-SEVEN

Matthew appraises me, searching for a reaction, but I won't give him one. I can't. He's set the board and dropped me in the middle of an incredibly dangerous game.

With only the sounds of the apheresis machine and the dripping paralytic to keep me company as I spent countless hours trapped in this room, I've had more than enough time to consider Richard's stories. They defy all logic and fly in the face of every ounce of science I've ever learned, but whatever lingering doubts remained when I stood by Mom's bedside at St. John's have long since faded.

"Evan who?" I ask, feigning ignorance.

"Kara, your deceit wounds me. After all, Evan was your father's best friend."

"My father left us when I was a kid. I barely remember him, let alone the people he spent time with."

"So he did. Such a sad story, is it not? Poor Kara Edwards, six years old, abandoned by her father. But, you had your mother. Then came terminal cancer. What will you do when she's gone?"

Fury threatens to crack my composure. His targeted words have struck home. I narrow my eyes and bite my tongue, fighting the urge to thrash against my restraints.

"You'll practically be an orphan. It's a downright shame. The truth is, I don't care what happens to your mother. Now, your father… Well, that's a different story. I'd love to get my hands on him. The two of you could fuel our research for decades, maybe more. Your blood alone could sustain this company for years."

So, he knows about Richard. Great. I had hoped he didn't. *How much does he know? Does he know Richard's back in town? Does he know where to find him?*

I need to test the waters. "If you see him, tell him his daughter says hello. Not that he'd care. He's never coming back."

"I'll be certain to do so," Matthew answers. His response is flippant, giving nothing away. "Do you know why he left or has your mother kept you in the dark?"

"We never knew, and I don't care. I'm glad he's gone."

He shakes his head. "Coarser Industries was assigned to the biohazard containment investigation that took place after Evan Knightly fell ill. St. John's was wildly unequipped to handle such a case, but we had renowned scientists at our disposal, equipment St. John's could only dream of. It fell to us to identify the cause of the outbreak. We analyzed every sample, every ounce of biomaterial. Do you know what we found?"

"I have no idea what you're talking about."

"Liar. There wasn't much, just a splash inside an old IV we collected from Evan's room. We thought it was his blood at first, that it might have washed into the tube when a nurse improperly flushed the line. It was exactly like yours, full of strange antibodies and proteins. When we realized what the blood could do, we looked into Evan's entire family. The funny thing was, no one else had the same anomalies.

"Then, we learned about Jennifer. Did you know she was adopted?" He pauses, eyeing me. "Your mother refused to allow us to speak with her, let alone draw a blood sample. Such an inconvenience. But eventually, your sister went looking for Evan. We learned of her probing and offered to help in exchange for a simple test. She agreed to our terms without hesitation. Imagine our surprise when her blood gave us nothing, either. We were thoroughly stumped.

"Valerie was our only lead. Father was convinced she knew what happened to Evan, but no matter how hard we tried to break her, she never budged. She's quite a strong woman, your mom. Annoyingly so. You know, we didn't even consider you because you had no biological relation to Evan. That was our biggest mistake. How fortuitous Valerie developed cancer and you came running home."

I can't help but breathe out a sigh of disbelief. "Yeah, I'm sure she thought so, too."

"Finally, we had something we could work with. We offered that imbecile, Doctor Mitchell, the Novemion, a serum which we developed using trace components of the sample we thought was Evan's blood, by the way."

I gulp. *They used Richard's blood? That can't be good.*

"It was my idea. I told my father she would call for help if she thought we were the only ones who could save her. But, Doctor Mitchell didn't offer the treatment to Valerie. He proposed the deal to you. That was a miscalculation on my part. I hadn't considered you would make the decision as her caregiver."

"You look positively heartbroken about it."

Matthew nods his head. "Destroyed, can't you tell?"

Sadistic bastard. "Why don't you let me out of these restraints so I can hug you? Make you feel better?"

"Nice try." He purses his lips. "When you started donating with Plasmedics, I put two and two together."

"So good at math!"

He scowls. "I knew Evan wasn't the original source, then.

It had been Richard, the sole uninfected survivor. My discovery was a breakthrough. Father was thrilled."

Keep him talking, I tell myself. *Find out what else he knows.*

I roll my eyes. "Glad to help you with your daddy issues."

"You're one to talk," Matthew retorts.

Keep pressing the father button. It's working.

"Is that why you're so obsessed with me? You have to show off? Convince him you're worthy? It'll never be enough. I saw the way he looked at you. I heard what he said in the elevator."

Matthew growls, clenching his fists and refusing to look me in the eye. "Without a living donor, our potential is limited. The sample we had was dried, contaminated. We managed to replicate components of the blood, but not all of it. We've used our findings to synthesize countless drugs in the last fifteen years with just a few drops. Our medications have outperformed anyone else in the field. But, with your blood? With fresh samples provided daily? There's no limit to what we can do."

"You just said you created medications that helped people with," I refuse to say Richard's name, "the blood you had. You were saving lives! What the hell, Matthew? How did you jump to bioweapons?"

This is it. I need to know. What have you done?

"The strangest thing happens when we inject your blood into our test subjects. The sick ones recover from their diseases, but then all the other animals in the room die."

No... no, no, no. This is not good.

"Actually, any living creature, animal or human, involved in the treatment process dies. Our policy for biohazardous containment is strict, of course. We immediately quarantined all involved out of fear of accidental exposure. The deaths stopped with those who had direct contact. That's when we knew how valuable your blood could be.

"We took samples from those who died and interestingly enough, found mutated forms of whatever disease our scientists had been trying to treat. These mutations are new. There are no existing treatments. Even if we had known what was happening, there was no way we would have been able to save a single person who had been in those rooms."

"You're killing people…"

"True. Quite a few people in this company have given their lives in the process of understanding the absolute oddity of your blood, but that's a price we're willing to pay."

"Human lives are not expendable!" I bellow. "These are people with families and friends. You have to stop this."

"What we've found in your blood will be worth unfathomable amounts of money. We intend to refine it. Harness it. My father and I will be the wealthiest people on this planet."

"You would rather condemn humanity to death and destruction to line your pockets?"

"There's no money in eradicating disease. We're a pharmaceutical company. Treating things is what we do, and we'll be the only ones who know how."

"You're sick!" I shriek.

Matthew sneers and leans into my ear. "The best part is," he whispers. His hot breath burns against my skin. *It's all because of you.*"

Practically buzzing with rage, I slam my head hard enough into his face that my ears ring. Waves of pain shoot through my skull and nausea roils my stomach, but I manage to grunt, "I would rather die than help you."

Matthew brings his hand up to his eye, steadying himself as he pulls away. "You little…" he shouts, but before he can finish his sentence and withdraw far enough out of range, I spit on him. "Arrrgh!" he bellows, standing above me. "You'll pay for that!"

His arm flies at me, slamming into my cheek. My teeth

rattle. Strapped to the bed with Matthew out of range, I'm defenseless. He swings again, and again. My eyes swell shut and my lip splits. When he stops, I barely have the strength to groan.

"I won't…" I start, feeling blood drip from my mouth and nose, "give you another drop… of my blood. I won't be a part… of your sadistic… scheme!"

"Kara," Matthew says in his trademark patronizing tone. "Do you really think you have a choice?"

The last thing I hear before I black out is a sickening crack as he brings his fist down on my nose.

CHAPTER THIRTY-EIGHT

Beep. Click.

My eyes fly open as the lock disengages. Adrenaline courses through me. My hands and feet tingle, but I don't bother fighting the restraints. They won't give. They never do. I'm as helpless now as the day they hauled me into this room.

How long has it been? A week? Two? There are no lengthening shadows to tell me when night is coming. The fluorescent light never goes out. It's just me, the machine siphoning my blood, and occasional visits from Matthew or Doctor Wolff.

When were they here last? The swelling has gone down. I can see out of my right eye and breathe through my nose. I couldn't do that when Matthew last stopped by to torture Mom. It must have been a while ago.

Muffled voices sound from the hall.

My brain is heavy and foggy. Rather than paralyzing me, Doctor Wolff has taken to sedation. The last dregs of the drugs are only now wearing off. I will my eyes to remain open, glaring at the crack that leads into the darkness.

Night. It must be night. They wouldn't have turned off the hall lights otherwise. There's no need to illuminate the space if everyone has gone home.

I brace myself for Matthew to walk through the door. *What sadistic plan has he prepared for me this time?*

"Are you sure this is the right room?" a man whispers. The words are barely audible.

"No, are you?" a second man answers.

"How would I know?"

Is that Matthew? It doesn't sound like him. He wouldn't whisper. Neither would his sycophantic guards. They'd burst in without hesitation, perverse grins on their faces, thrilled to know I'm at their mercy. These visitors are quiet, too indecisive.

The owners of the voices shuffle, staying out of sight as the crack widens. A hand appears between the door and the frame. Still, no one steps inside. I lean my head closer, straining to listen.

"The key worked, didn't it? It has to be this one," the first voice comes again.

"It's a master key. Of course it worked," the second answers. There's mild irritation in his tone.

"I'm just saying…"

"Sshh!"

"We have to get inside and shut the door. Someone will see the light if they come this way."

The hall falls silent as if the men are weighing their options.

I try to speak, but my voice has gone hoarse. "H-hello?" The sound is gritty like sandpaper. I clear my throat and try again. "Hello? Who's out there?"

Two familiar eyes peer through the gap. In less than a second, the door flies open.

"Kay?" Connor dashes to my side. He stops short when he takes in my injuries and the cuffs on my limbs. "Oh my god, what has that sick fuck done to you?"

My heart swells at the sight of him, and I can't hold back

my sobs. He's here. Connor came. He's standing by my side. His hands move quickly, working to unfasten the restraints.

"You're not real," I tell him. "You can't be. I'm imagining you again."

"I'm real," he assures me. He presses a too-light kiss to my cheek, careful to avoid the lingering bruises. "We're getting you out of here."

"How did you find me?"

"I called the hospital when you never came home. Doctor Mitchell told me you signed Valerie over into Matthew's care, and I knew something was wrong. After he threatened you, I figured there was no way you would do that unless you had no other choice. I called and called, and you never called back. So, I picked up your dad and he helped me figure out what the hell was going on."

I want to thank him. I need to tell him I'm sorry for disappearing like this. I have to explain. I open my mouth to say those things, but even as I try to form cohesive sentences, the words fade on my tongue. What actually passes my lips is a different truth. "I thought I was going to die alone."

I was certain I would never see anyone I loved again. The only contact I would get was the video of Mom lying comatose in that godforsaken bed. Matthew would do as he promised, drain me dry and leave my body somewhere it would never be found.

I stopped feeling. I stopped fighting. I was hours away from giving up entirely.

My hands slip free from their bonds. Blood surges back into my veins, burning a path to my fingers as I flex them. I wince as Connor frees my feet next, then pulls me into his arms.

He's shaking. His grip is too tight, but I don't care. He can suffocate me in his embrace if he wants as long as he doesn't leave me.

Connor came. Connor's holding me. It's over.

The door slides into place with a soft whoosh, drawing my gaze. Richard, the owner of the second voice, stands with his back against the wall.

"Richard?"

"I'm sorry it took so long." His expression is pained as he moves toward me. "They had this place locked down like Fort Knox. We found you days ago. Getting in took time."

I nod. Matthew wouldn't have made it easy for them. The movement makes my head throb.

Connor peppers my face with feathery kisses and wipes away my tears while Richard busies himself with the tubes and wires. He gently removes the needles from my arms. A few drops of my blood patter to the floor.

"I'm sorry if I hurt you," he says, squeezing my hand.

"Thank you," I whisper.

"I left you once. I'll never do it again." Richard rubs my back, just like he used to do when I was a little girl, while Connor holds me and rocks me.

Gradually, I regain control of myself. Connor loosens his hold as I pull away.

My arms are leaden when I lift them to my face to assess the damage Matthew has done. Even with my enhanced healing, the swelled patches squish beneath my fingertips. It's not as bad as I thought, but his attack had been more than brutal. Thankfully, nothing was broken.

I reach down and rub my ankles. The skin is tender where the restraints have bitten into them. Deep indentations circle the fleshy place above my ankle bones.

I hadn't noticed what my rescuers were wearing until Richard moved away from the bed. Both he and Connor have dressed in crisp, sage-colored scrubs. They must have planned their disguise before breaking in. An ID card pokes out from Richard's chest pocket. The key.

He moves purposefully through the room, collecting anything that's come into contact with my blood and placing it into one of the pillowcases. There's a small steel sink in the corner nestled into the counter where Matthew usually leaves his coffee. He hauls the bags from the machine up to the sink and rips into them, dumping the contents down the drain, and wiping up whatever remnants stick to the surfaces. When he's finished, there's not a trace of my blood to be found.

"We have to go," Richard announces when he glances down at his watch. "The guard will come this way soon."

"Can you stand?" Connor asks me.

"I can try."

"Here," he lifts my legs over the edge of the bed and wraps my arm around his shoulder.

With his help, I manage to stand, but only just. The ground is a thousand feet below me. I sway. He catches me, holding me closer.

"We have to find Mom. They took her to another room. I don't know where it is. We have to get her to Doctor Mitchell. He can help."

Richard's eyes zip to Connor's. His expression falls. "We can't."

"We're not leaving her here," I assert. "She needs us."

"We'll find Valerie," Connor states, leaning his head against mine. "That was always the plan. Doctor Mitchell is the problem."

"What?" I'm confused. *Is Doctor Mitchell in on this? He couldn't be. He had been so kind, and the way Matthew talks about him...*

"We went to Doctor Mitchell's office as soon as we learned where you were being held. I thought he might be able to help," Connor says. "That's when we found him."

"Found him?" Dread seizes me.

Richard tosses the pillowcase over his shoulder like a sack. "He was dead on the floor."

I gape in awe. "Dead? Are you sure?"

"He was already cold by the time we arrived," Richard answers.

No, not Doctor Mitchell. He was so young. He was a good person. A wave of grief slams into me. Matthew did it. I know he did. Not personally. He sent one of his thugs. My fault. I'm the reason he's dead.

Connor takes a step forward, and I follow his lead. "It wouldn't have mattered if he wasn't. He'd lost too much blood. His office was like a scene from one of those mafia movies. It scared the hell out of both of us."

"I searched through his records as quickly as I could before we called for help," Richard adds. "It turns out Doctor Mitchell went digging for information himself. He had a lot of material on Coarser Industries in a folder hidden behind a file cabinet. We found the floor plans for this building there. The hardest part was getting one of these." He pats his pocket and lifts out the keycard. "The staff are pretty tight-fisted. It took quite a few drinks and some rather... *unseemly* maneuvers to get my hands on this one."

I take a step forward but stumble.

"Don't try to walk on your own. Not yet," Richard instructs. "We'll help you until you can manage. By the looks of things, you've been restrained for a while. Your muscles will need time to adjust."

"We have to find Mom!" I repeat, louder this time. "It's my fault she's in here. If Matthew was willing to have Doctor Mitchell killed, I know what he'll do to her."

"We'll find her, Kay," Connor answers soothingly. "I promise."

"All I've seen of her since we got here is what they showed me on that stupid screen."

"Then, we'll start around the corner," Richard states with assurance. "We'll open every door if we have to. We'll get you and your mother out of here safely, no matter what it takes."

Despite everything, I believe him.

"And the blood," he adds. "We have to get that back, too. I know you think I'm crazy," he begins.

"Not anymore," I answer. "Matthew told me what they're going to do." My voice is heavy with shame.

"What, Kay?"

I swallow hard and look away. "They're making bioweapons."

Richard's face pales. For a moment, I worry he's angry with me, but he doesn't chastise me or yell.

A look of fierce resolve settles over him. "We need to move. Now." He presses the stolen ID badge to the circle on the wall and we plunge out into the darkness.

CHAPTER THIRTY-NINE

"How many more are there?" I whisper as Richard presses his stolen key against yet another sensor. The lock disengages with a jarringly loud click, and the door swings into the shadowy space. Another empty room. Another dead end.

"I don't know," Connor answers. He squints into the shadows, counting. "Four? Five? It's too dark. I can barely see a few inches in front of my face."

This is taking too long. Any minute, a guard could come our way and find us searching the facility. While I've regained some stamina, I'm in no shape to run. As it is, I'm relying on Connor to hold half my weight. My joints wobble with every step, and my muscles burn. If it weren't for his arm wrapped tightly around my waist, I'd be a crumpled heap on the floor.

We need to find Mom. We have to get her out of here before it's too late.

Richard releases another lock. Empty. And, another. Nothing. One more. He presses his palm flat to the door's surface.

A feeling of dread overcomes me as he gives it a light push. I open my mouth to warn him, but before I can speak, it gives way. Blinding light spills into the corridor, slicing through the darkness. Disoriented, I bring my hand to my eyes and squint. Sparkling white specks populate my vision.

"Well, it seems we have visitors, Valerie." Matthew's sarcasm floats out of the room. "Richard Edwards, is that you? What a wonderful surprise. Oh, and Connor. If I had known you two would be joining us this evening, I would have prepared a welcome party. Please, forgive my lack of hospitality. Come in."

Connor tenses beside me. His fingers dig into my ribs. Slowly, my sight returns, revealing a scene that sends ice through my veins.

Matthew sits casually on the side of Mom's bed, one leg crossed over the other. Despite the late hour, he's immaculately dressed. His perfectly coiffed blonde hair shines beneath the fluorescents. As I gape, he uses his free hand to adjust his necktie. The other, to my horror, drapes possessively around my mother's shoulders. He presses her close to his body and gives her a squeeze. Without the ventilator, Mom gasps for air. Her lips have taken on a faint blue tinge. Her glassy eyes flutter open and closed.

She's so weak.

The hand Matthew used to adjust his necktie drops into his lap, wrapping around the black grip on the hilt of a shiny silver gun. "Your mother has missed you, Kara. She's been asking about you. Honestly, where have you been? These two let you out of your room half an hour ago."

"Get away from her," I growl. I pull away from Connor, taking several shaky steps forward. He reaches for me, but I swat his hand away. "Get your filthy hands off of my mom."

"Aw," Matthew pouts. "That was rude. You hurt my feelings." He lifts the gun from his lap and presses it to Mom's temple. "After I've been such a generous host. Do you really think that's the best idea?"

"Kara," Richard warns. "Don't."

"I agree," Matthew croons. "Don't do anything foolish. It won't end well for Valerie. We wouldn't want that, would we?" Casually, he waves the gun, the gesture encompassing the three of us. "I know you don't care what happens to you, but what about them? Everyone you love is in this building."

"You wouldn't," I challenge, stepping into the room. Connor and Richard flank me defensively. "You're too much of a coward. You're a pretty little rich boy who's never had to get his hands dirty for anything."

"See, I told you she thinks I'm attractive," he confesses, leaning his head against the top of Mom's and staring back at me maliciously.

"Where are your lackeys, huh? Do you even know what to do with that thing?"

"Don't push him," Connor whispers. "Doctor Mitchell…"

Matthew cocks his head to the side. "I most certainly *do*. If you insist, I'd be happy to provide a demonstration." His hand flexes, finger tightening over the trigger as he points the gun straight at me.

"What do you want?"

"What I've always wanted. Your cooperation. Nothing has changed."

Mom grunts and tries to pull away, but Matthew pulls her closer still.

"You're a kidnapping, murderous psychopath!" I roar. Violence radiates through me. "You expect me to cooperate?"

"Those things are irrelevant. Stay with me willingly. Stop fighting, and I'll let them leave. All of them." His eyes flick to Richard and Connor, then he tilts his face to Mom. "Even you. You're a pathetic little thing."

"Your words are meaningless," I spit.

"Hardly." Matthew's eyes harden to solid steel. The muscles in his jaw tense as he glares at me.

"Even if I agreed to your stupid deal, you'd go after

Richard as soon as you had me locked up in my room. You as much as told me so before."

"You're not listening!" He groans in frustration. "It doesn't have to be that way. Things have changed. What I said is I want you to stay *willingly*. No more fighting means no more restraints. No more sedation. I could set you up with a nice space here. You would have everything you need. If you agree to my terms, you'll live a long, happy life in my facility. I won't need your father."

"Sure, the happy life of a rat in a cage. Screw your deal."

Matthew's eyes narrow into slits. He presses his lips into a thin line. "I'd reconsider if I were you. If you don't take the deal I'll kill them all, here and now. Right in front of you."

My heart lurches as I study Mom's helpless figure trapped in Matthew's arms. He nudges her temple with his gun, and she winces. Her shoulders barely rise and fall as she pulls in short gasps of air.

"You would never let anyone leave. They know too much.

"Too much? About what, may I ask? About me? About the company? Well, if that's the thread you're trying to pull, it seems we all know more than we should, don't we? For example, I know exactly where your father and boyfriend live. Isn't that useful information? It would certainly come in handy if I had to, say, send someone to their homes in the middle of the night to suffocate them in their sleep, wouldn't it? I also happen to know both of them were aware of your involvement with your mother's illicit cancer treatment. A pity. I'm sure if the right person were to learn such information, there would be serious consequences. Mmm, and I also know… well, let's save that little surprise for later. You know how I love surprises."

I swallow the hard lump rising in my throat. "You'll have them killed no matter what I do, just like you did Doctor Mitchell!"

"I don't know what you are insinuating," Matthew coos. "I had no involvement in that unseemly matter. All evidence indicates Doctor Mitchell was killed by a disgruntled family member of one of his patients. A woman, actually. The police are searching for possible suspects as we speak."

My eyes widen as shock blasts through me.

"Do you know of anyone who may have been unhappy with his treatment plans? Anyone who suddenly vanished around the time of his death?"

"You… you pinned it on me?"

"Call it reassurance," Matthew responds. "Motivation? Incentive? Whatever makes you happy."

"Bastard." I draw my eyes level with his.

"You don't have a life to go back to. No apartment. I saw to that before I knew how important you were. No job. Renee's already filled your position. You're utterly dispensable to everyone else. Everyone but me. Add to that an extensive search by local law enforcement… Well, you're better off here, aren't you? So, stay. Do the right thing."

"You're despicable, a monster. You've taken everything."

"Not yet, but I will."

Without warning, Mom's head snaps violently to the side, slamming hard into Matthew's face. He tumbles backward and releases his grip on her frail body, leaving her to slip from the bed.

Startled by her sudden attack, I jump. Richard rushes forward to catch her, snatching her into his arms a second before her limp body would have collided with the tile.

This is it — the distraction we needed. Mom knew. She's saving us!

Matthew clutches the side of his head and swears heavily under his breath. A thin line of blood trickles from his bottom lip. He licks it away with the tip of his tongue.

Richard hauls Mom up and wraps her arms around his

neck, sliding one of his arms under her knees and cradling her back.

She's so small.

Connor reaches for me, ready to grab my hand and tug me out into the darkness, but I can't let him. We won't make it. Matthew's already raising his gun. He swings it wide, aiming the barrel straight at Mom.

"No!" I shriek. My eyes race through the room, searching for anything I can use as a weapon. They land on a metal bedpan. Without thinking, I pluck it off the counter by the sink and raise it over my head, darting to Matthew's side, and bring it down on his arm. He fires but misses.

Mom and Richard have nearly cleared the room when Matthew fires again. This time, the shot hits its mark. Richard cries out, and I turn my head without thinking. A bright red patch of blood blossoms across my father's calf.

Instinct has me desperately rushing to his aid, but Matthew grabs me by the wrist and pulls me back. The brutal jerk threatens to dislocate the joint as he reaches for my throat.

"Kara!" Connor screams, running toward me, but I swing the bedpan again, clocking Matthew above his ear with a devastating blow. He grunts as he collapses at my feet, blood dripping from a gash on the top of his head.

I bring the bedpan down on his arm again. This time, the gun drops from his hand and zips across the floor.

Matthew grunts and tries to shove me away, but I'm no longer in control of my body. Again, and again, and again the bedpan crashes into him. A sick crunch of shattered cartilage follows a particularly violent impact. Another lands on his forehead. Another to his jaw. Another to his cheek.

Connor rips me away from Matthew as he buckles. The bedpan slips from my blood-soaked, trembling fingers and clatters to the tile. I sob as I recognize the severity of what I've just done.

"Is… is he dead?" I choke out.

Connor glances at Matthew but doesn't answer. "Are you alright?" he asks Richard instead.

My eyes travel over to him. My father leans heavily against the door frame. A slick puddle of crimson has gathered at his feet.

"I will be," Richard answers. He groans as Connor leans down to inspect the wound.

"It's just a graze." Quickly, Connor scrambles to the cabinet above the counter and retrieves a rubber tourniquet. His deft fingers make fast work of the band, tying it above Richard's wound. "Here," he says, checking his handiwork. "That should be enough to stem the bleeding for now. Can you stand?"

Richard shifts Mom's weight in his arms. She doesn't respond. He lifts himself away from the entry and grits his teeth but takes several steps into the hall.

"Get Kara," he calls as he limps away. "I've got Valerie."

I catch a glimpse of my reflection in the bedpan. My face is stark white and my whole body shakes. I nearly collapse, but Connor swoops his arm beneath mine and steadies me on my feet.

"Hey, it's going to be okay," he says, pushing my hair out of my face and tugging me into the hall after Richard. "We're getting out of here."

"Not yet," Richard interjects.

"What?" Connor asks, incredulous.

"We have to find the blood. We can't let them have it. You know what they were going to do."

"We don't have time!" Connor insists. "We have to get them out of here."

Mom peers over Richard's shoulder at me with a determination she shouldn't possess. She speaks in wheezing gasps. "We... will... make time."

I watch her in awe. For the first time, I realize how strong my mother truly is, how strong she's always been. Shame and guilt rush through me for ever thinking Mom was losing her mind or doubting her strength.

Slowly, I nod. "We're not leaving a single drop behind."

Mom's pallid face fills with pride as she takes me in, and in this moment, no matter what happens next, I know I have finally decided to do the right thing.

CHAPTER FORTY

I can't focus as Connor guides me back the way we came, an after-effect of my adrenaline-fueled rage. It's wearing off more and more with each step, leaving exhaustion and numbness in its wake. I should be helping them come up with a plan, but instead, my thoughts linger on the sticky spray that clings to my hands.

There's more blood than I realized.

I left the bedpan behind with Matthew's body, but I can still feel the weight of it in my grip. My bones vibrate with continued phantom impacts. In the darkness, I can't see Mom and Richard or the many empty rooms. All I can envision is his crumpled form at my feet.

The gravity of what I've done sinks in.

Shivering, I pull away from Connor and force myself to stand on my own. I use the wall for support until I trust my legs to follow my commands. It takes less time than before to find my balance. When I pull my palm away from the white paint, a crimson handprint remains. I can't tear my eyes away.

Frantically, I scrub at the blood on my skin. It stains my filthy jeans and shirt but refuses to wipe away. Panic bubbles in my chest.

What have I done?

"We've already checked this floor," Connor reminds Richard. As always, he's right by my side, ready to catch me if I fall. "There's nothing here. It's all supply closets and empty rooms."

Richard grunts and adjusts his grasp on Mom's legs. "They must be storing it on another level."

Did I kill him? Connor didn't answer me. I can't remember if he was breathing. What if I didn't? Which is worse? I need to warn them.

My lips part and my hollow words echo in my ears. "We don't have time to check every floor. If Matthew isn't..." I can't bring myself to say the word, "he could wake up."

"I know." Richard's tone is grim.

"So, what are we going to do?" Connor asks, grabbing my hand.

I cringe, knowing Matthew's blood is rubbing off on him. I don't want that. I never wanted him involved in any of this. He deserves so much better. He's a good person, and I'm... well, after what happened back there, I don't know what I am.

The elevator looms in the distance. We're almost there.

"We need to get your mother out of here," Richard says, picking up his pace. "I'll take her down to the car where she can rest. The two of you can check the next floor. If we hurry..."

But, I don't hear the rest of what he says. My eyes have latched on to a serious problem, one I hadn't considered in my state of shock. The strain of carrying Mom through the halls has loosened the tourniquet Connor tied around Richard's leg. The wound may only be a graze, but that hasn't stopped it from leaving a thin trail of blood in his wake. I stop and reach for Connor, horrified.

"What, Kay? What's wrong?"

"Richard?" I call. "We have another problem. Your leg – "

"My leg is fine." He turns to face me. The moment he realizes what I mean, his face falls. "Shit."

"We can't clean this up," I tell him. "And, back in the room when he shot you, you bled there, too."

"I have to set you down," he tells Mom. There's a tenderness in his voice reserved specifically for her. I haven't heard it in years. "It might be uncomfortable. I'm sorry, Val."

"It's… okay," she breathes.

Richard plants a soft kiss on her forehead, then he bends at the knees. As gently as he can, he lowers her to the floor and props her against the wall. She offers him a faint smile when he murmurs indistinguishably into her ear.

"Connor," Richard says, "I need your help. Is there anyone else in this building?"

"I don't think so," Connor answers. "I haven't seen them bring anyone in. As far as I know, it's just Matthew and a few guards."

Richard hesitates. Judging by the expression on his face, he's torn. He turns to Mom, wordlessly communicating in a way only lovers can. Despite their years apart, she nods.

Richard blows out an uneven breath. When he looks back at me, his mouth is set in a hard line. "We can't worry about them."

"I… what do you mean?"

Connor studies Richard. Like Mom, he must understand, but I'm completely lost. He squeezes my hand. Sadness weighs on his shoulders. "Plan B?" he asks.

"Plan B," Richard confirms.

"What does that mean?"

I'm surprised when it's Mom who answers me. "We…" she wheezes, "burn it… down. All of it."

"Go through the cabinets in the rooms and the supply closets," Connor instructs. Facilities like these are full of flammable chemicals. Grab anything you can find — rubbing alcohol, acetone, floor cleaners, even bleach. Dump it all. We'll make a trail through the hall."

"But, how are we supposed to set the fire?"

"I've got that covered." Richard stands and digs a gold Zippo out of his pocket. When he flicks the lid, a blue and orange flame sparks to life. It shimmers against the shadows. "Never leave home without it."

"We need fabric, too," Connor adds. "It takes longer to burn. We should soak the beds. If our goal is to bring down the entire building, we can't rely on a quick blaze to do the job. Oh, and open up the oxygen tanks."

I blink, surprised. "What did you do, research arson?"

"Maybe."

"Always have a backup plan," Richard says. "Now, come on. Let's get to work."

By the time Connor emerges from the last room, arms laden with bottles, chemical fumes saturate the air. I choke on the stench as I twist the knob on the oxygen tank and meet him in the hall. He tosses the empty containers aside and passes me a heavy bottle of bleach.

"This won't burn on its own, but it will explode when we light the ammonia. Be careful. Don't get it on you."

I glance over at Mom, worried about her breathing. Richard, crouching by her side, holds a torn piece of blanket across her mouth and nose, shielding her from the worst of the vapors. It's helping, but it won't for long.

Sputtering, I splash the walls and leave a trail that leads from the corner to the steel elevator doors.

"We can't take that," Connor tells me as I reach him. "It's too dangerous. If the blaze catches as quickly as I think it will, we could be trapped inside, or an explosion might blow it straight off the pulley and we could end up crashing to the bottom. We'd be crushed."

"How are we gonna get Mom down the stairs? Richard's leg…"

"I'll carry her," he tells me. "She's light enough. Do you think you can make it down?"

"I've got Kara," Richard answers. "We can manage, right?"

I nod. "Right. Just get her out of here safely, okay?"

"I promise, Kay. Trust me?"

"Always." I toss the empty jug to the side and cough. My throat is raw, and prolonged exposure to so many noxious smells has my head throbbing.

"Is that it?" Richard asks. "The last bottle?"

"I think so," Connor answers. "I've raided every place I could think of. Did you open the tanks?"

"Every last one of them," I tell him.

Richard drops the strip of blanket and pulls himself up to stand. "Connor, help me get Valerie up. She won't be able to breathe with this stuff in the air. We have to get her out of here. Now."

Mom's eyes barely flutter as they lift her off the floor. Connor cradles her in his arms like a toddler.

Before I can open the passage to the stairwell, staggering footsteps sound from around the corner.

"Matthew," I whisper.

Connor's arms tense around Mom.

Matthew's gun emerges first as he guides himself into the corridor. His gait is unsteady. As he squints through the shadows, he waves the weapon clumsily, unsure where to aim. His other hand clutches the side of his head where I landed my final blow. Either his sight has been affected by my attack, or his head wound has rendered him confused. He's drenched in blood. It's dried on his clean-shaven jaw and runs down his shirt, staining the fabric nearly black.

Matthew slips in a puddle of the flammable liquid, but he quickly regains his balance. His eyes land on the four of us, and his face contorts with rage. As he aims his gun in our direction, his unsteady arm shakes.

"You couldn't just take the deal, could you?" he screams. There's no hint of the self-assured man Matthew was as he hobbles toward us, kicking aside empty containers. "Look at what you've done!"

"What I've done?" I ask incredulously.

"You couldn't do what you were told!" he bellows back. "You've ruined everything! Do you have any idea of the damage you've caused?"

"Oh," I scoff. "Yes, I do. And, I'm about to cause a lot more."

Matthew shakes his head. "What the *hell* are you talking about?"

"Give me the lighter," I command. Without hesitation, Richard drops it into my hand. "Connor, get her out of here."

"Not without you," he replies. I turn to argue, but his expression is one of immovable determination. "I'm not going anywhere, Kay."

"Richard," I prompt. "Do it. I'll meet you outside."

My father's expression fills with pride and pain. "Sorry, kid," he tells Connor.

Before Connor can reply, Richard shoves him into the stairwell.

"You," Matthew spits as he sloshes through the mess, "are not going anywhere. "I'll kill all of you, and I'm going to enjoy every last second of it."

"Oh, yeah?" I taunt, my thumb hovering over the lid. "Do you hear that, Matthew? What do you think that is?"

He stops and cocks his head to the side, listening. When

he realizes what's happening, his eyes widen in fear. He whips his head around, registering the labels of the empty bottles and connecting the dots.

"You wouldn't dare," Matthew growls. "You'll kill us both, you stupid little bitch!"

"What do I have to lose?" I hold the lighter high, savoring the shock and despair on his face. "Goodbye, Matthew." I poise my thumb. "Burn in hell."

As fast as I can, I back up to the stairwell doors and kick them open. With one last look at the monster racing toward me, I ignite the Zippo and throw it, aiming for the trail I left behind. The flame flickers as it sails through the air and lands in the middle of the combustible fluid. Fire bursts down the hall like a living being, consuming everything in its path.

Matthew dives out of the way, and I launch myself down the stairs, taking two and three at a time. I stumble but use the railing to regain my footing. Small explosions sound from the upper floors as I crash through the heavy set of steel doors at the bottom.

Richard holds the exit open, and the two of us make a break for it, rushing into the empty parking lot. For the first time in weeks, fresh air wafts over my skin. I inhale deeply, clearing my lungs.

Connor waits by his car at the back corner of the lot, Mom held safely in his arms. Moving faster than should be possible on an injured leg, Richard tugs me across the asphalt. Before I know it, he's ushering me into the backseat. Hastily, Connor lays Mom across my lap and slides into the front passenger seat. Richard clambers into the driver's side and shoves the key into the ignition. The tires screech as he slams his foot down on the gas.

As Richard maneuvers the car onto the road, I stare back at Plasmedics, watching as the windows glow orange and red against the dark sky. A deafening "boom" sounds as flames burn through the lobby, devouring the building.

I turn my gaze to Mom. She reaches up and holds my cheek lightly in her hand.

"We made it out," I tell her as her eyes flutter closed and her arm falls into her lap. "Hold on. We'll get you help. You're gonna be okay."

She doesn't respond. Tears stream down my cheeks as I watch her shallow breaths.

"Don't give up now. Don't you dare. I'm gonna fix this. Please, Mom. Hang on."

Richard presses the gas pedal to the floor, accelerating to top speeds as he merges onto the expressway.

"Why are we leaving the city?" I demand. "We need the hospital. We have to get Mom to someone who can help!" My eyes search the rearview mirror as I try to read my father's face.

Richard quickly looks at me, then back to the road. "We're saving your mother's life. I just have to get us there in time."

"Get her where?" Connor asks.

"To the Ruin."

CHAPTER FORTY-ONE

The world wakes around us as Richard barrels down I-70 West. I barely notice as the sky shifts from obsidian to a shade of rich purple, then lightens to a vibrant pink. The edges of my vision cloud with exhaustion as I take in the familiar towns and cities. I may have been repeatedly sedated at Plasmedics, but I can't remember the last time I actually rested. Every moment in the facility had been tinged with fear and despair. I long for the release of sleep but can't allow myself to give in. Not yet. We may have escaped Matthew's reach, but our journey is far from over.

Richard knows where we're headed, but I certainly don't. To be honest, I'm not entirely convinced this is a good idea. *Hasn't he been warning me away from the Ruin this entire time? What if we don't make it there? What if they follow through with their threats and kill us all rather than offer Mom sanctuary in the village?* I have more questions than answers. I want to ask Richard, but the words don't come.

Instead, I focus on Mom sleeping fitfully in my lap. In the time it's taken us to escape Matthew's claws, her skin has gone translucent. Her lips have darkened to deeper shades of blue, and her breaths have become more and more ragged. There's fluid in her lungs. It gurgles with each shallow inhale. There's nothing I can do except hold her and whisper to her, assure her everything will be okay.

Memories of our years together creep into my thoughts as we pass places Mom and I have been. I'd spent the day in Arbutus with her and Ally when I was a freshman in high school. I'd been struggling with a bully, so Mom insisted we play hooky and try something new. We went to a Hawaiian Poke restaurant. I remember chewing on the raw, marinated tuna, then spitting it out into a napkin. The texture of the fish wasn't great, but the flavors were delicious. Mom and Ally laughed when they caught me.

We zoom past Catonsville, and another memory of Mom helping me write to my pen pal at Hillcrest cuts through the haze.

The longer I resist my body's commands to rest, the more my muscles ache and my head pounds. A wire cage wraps itself around my skull and drills into my teeth. Impossible hands tighten the screws binding it to my molars. I lean my head against the glass of the window, but the cold pane only provides temporary relief.

A sign for Frederick fades into the distance, and though I've fought hard to remain conscious, my eyelids slam closed and refuse to open again.

THE CAR SLOWS TO A STOP AS RICHARD PULLS OFF the interstate and turns onto an unfamiliar highway, waking me from a dreamless state. My heart slams into my ribs. Connor's soft snores drift from the front seat. Mom's unconscious form is still. Her chest rises and falls sporadically. The vein in her temple, all too visible, thrums with her thready pulse.

Beyond my window, scraggly mountains covered in budding trees loom against the horizon. Pines mix with oak, maple, and yellow birch. Outcroppings of shattered slate surround the road. Mist gathers around the rim of the forest, lending an ominous feel to the otherwise scenic route.

Richard's face in the rearview mirror is impassive as he concentrates on the road before him. His hands are steady on the wheel as we snake through the ridge. We pass a dented metal sign for WV-29 South.

West Virginia, I think. *I must have been out for a while.*

"Are you sure you know where you're going?" I whisper.

Richard briefly turns his gaze to me, breaking his silent focus. "Unfortunately, yes. I wish I didn't."

I nod, rubbing the sleep out of the corners of my eyes. "How much longer?"

"It's not far to the turn-off. We should be there in about twenty-five minutes."

"What then?"

Richard shifts in his seat. "Then, things are going to be more difficult. We'll have to carry your mother through the woods."

My gaze travels down to Mom's frail frame, and a sinking feeling settles in my stomach. I frown. "How far?"

"If we were all relatively healthy, I'd say, maybe three hours. With Valerie..." he hesitates, "I don't know."

Just weeks ago, I had balked at Richard's stories. I would have denied the existence of the Ruin with my dying breath. Now, I'm following him into the unknown and leaving Mom's survival in his hands.

Life is strange.

"Are you sure this is a good idea? You said they're dangerous."

Richard doesn't answer. He adjusts his grip on the wheel. The skin over his knuckles tightens, whitening.

My thumb slides along the back of Mom's hand. Her cold, thin skin is covered with blue and purple bruises. They continue up her arms and disappear into her sleeve. A man's handprint wraps around her bicep. Hatred for Matthew surges through me, but I shove it down. It doesn't matter anymore. He can't hurt her now.

"Will they help her?" My voice is strained.

Richard lowers his head and sighs. "I hope so. They've helped others before. All we can do is try."

"And, if they don't?"

He reaches one hand into the backseat and squeezes my knee. "If they don't, we'll say our goodbyes."

I stifle a sob and lay my hand across the top of his. Unlike Mom's, his is muscular and full. His eyes widen.

"Thank you," I mutter. "For coming back. For telling me the truth even though I refused to believe it. For getting us out of Plasmedics. I'm sorry I was so cruel. You didn't deserve that."

Richard shakes his head. "Don't apologize to me, Kara. I deserved everything you said to me and more."

"No…"

"I did. And, I'm sorry. I hope you know that. For all of this." He wraps my hand in his, and I don't pull away.

As I return my eyes to the scenery flashing by, my defenses shatter. The walls I've built in his absence crumble. I blink away tears and allow myself to be vulnerable. "I do," I tell him. "And, I forgive you. For all of it. I understand. You made an impossible choice, and I never realized it hurt you, too. But, I see that now, and I forgive you… Dad."

GRAVEL CRUNCHES UNDER THE TIRES AS DAD PULLS off of WV-29 South onto a narrow back road. The new path leads us onto a rickety covered bridge too tight for more than one car at a time. Luckily, we have the road to ourselves. The wooden slats rumble as we cross a wide swath of running water.

Connor stirs and stretches. When he realizes he fell asleep, he casts a guilty look in my direction. His eyes rove over Mom, and he offers me a sad smile. "I didn't mean to pass out."

"It's okay," I assure him. "You didn't miss anything. I fell asleep, too. It's been a long drive."

"How is she?"

I shake my head. "Not great." I can't bring myself to say anything else.

The road forks and Dad steers the car to the left. The forest around us thickens. The gravel disappears, leaving only a two-track through the trees. Mom coughs, spitting flecks of blood onto her lips. I cradle her head and plant a kiss on her brow, but she doesn't wake.

We pass a handful of dilapidated farmhouses and half-rotten, collapsed barns on the two-track, but soon, all signs of civilization disappear. About a mile up the road, Dad slows as we approach a bright yellow sign: "Dead End, No Exit." An almost imperceptible path leads deeper into the woods through the trees to the right. He maneuvers Connor's car through the gap. Shrill screeches fill the interior as thin, low-hanging branches scrape across the roof. Mom squirms in my lap, irritated by the sound.

The movement is reassuring. She's still aware enough to respond. I cover her ears.

"We're here." Dad throws the car into park and switches off the ignition.

Surrounded by the shadows of the wild forest, the marrow in my bones chills.

My trepidation must be plain as day because Connor unbuckles his seatbelt and turns to face me. He reaches across the back of his seat and gently places his hands on my shoulders. "We don't have to go in there, Kay. It's your choice. We can turn back if this isn't sitting right."

I swallow and stare into the depths of the trees. Goose-bumps break out along my arms.

"What do you want to do?" Dad asks. "You know our options."

"We've come so far," I whisper into Mom's ear. "Through chemo, and radiation, and surgery, and everything at Plasmedics." My forehead presses against hers. Her eyes flutter. "We can't give up now. We have to try."

"You're sure?" Connor asks.

"No," I answer. "But, we're going to do it anyway.

"The supplies are in the trunk," Dad instructs Connor. "Grab a pack. We're losing daylight."

CHAPTER FORTY-TWO

Our heavy packs make circling through the mountains a difficult feat. Even after resting, my body protests such strenuous activity. There's no clearly marked path through the trees. It doesn't help that branches and thorny bushes continuously snag on the fabric of my grimy jeans and whip into my cheeks. Climbing over fallen trunks and avoiding hidden patches of scree near cliff edges slows our pace. We can't afford to lose our footing, not this high up. One wrong move and we'll be sliding into a ravine.

The landscape isn't the only thing we need to worry about. Before we left the car behind and ventured into the woods, Dad warned us about the wildlife that makes its home in places such as these. "We're not in the city anymore," he reminded us. "You'll need to be careful. The animals in this forest *will* defend themselves. Tread lightly."

Trying not to trip and staring into the shadows in search of dangerous creatures has my senses on high alert. My eyes dart between the trees, and my ears prick at every unexpected sound. Black bears, coyotes, bobcats, cougars, and panthers lurk in the Appalachian Mountains, and those are just the predators we would be able to see. Others are too small to spot, like brown recluses and black widows. High in the treetops, wasps buzz. Worse yet, rattlesnakes like to hide in crevices and beneath the leaves.

"We should stop here to hydrate and eat," Dad announces when we reach an outcropping in the mountainside. He snaps off a tree limb and pokes around before deciding the area is safe.

"No," I argue. "We have to keep going. Mom needs – "

"Valerie needs us alive and healthy so we *can* keep going." He tosses the stick aside and holds out his arms, assisting Connor as he settles Mom's limp body on the ground. "We can't help her if we pass out in the woods, Kara."

"He's right," Connor pants. His pack lands with a thud beside a boulder. "I need a break. She's light, but she's dead weight." I scowl at him, and he holds up his hands. "Sorry, bad phrase. You know what I mean."

Dad retrieves a water bottle from his pack and cracks open the lid, drinking deeply. Connor does the same, then gestures for me to follow. Reluctantly, I do as I'm told. It's a relief to lift the hefty bag off my shoulders and set it down, if only for a few minutes.

Several water bottles and granola bars later, we stuff our trash back into our packs and resume the trek, leaving no trace of our presence behind.

"STAY IN THE SHADOWS," DAD COMMANDS. HIS weak leg trembles as he dodges a puddle of mud. "The village is just over the crest of the hill, but we don't know what we're walking into."

"Shadows. Got it." Connor grunts and shifts Mom's weight. Unable to see the ground beneath him, he plods straight through the sludge. His foot slips, and I cringe.

Tension knots his forearms and biceps as he regains his balance.

We've been hiking through the forest for more than five hours, and though both Dad and I have tried to help carry Mom across the treacherous terrain, Connor has shouldered most of the burden. I don't know how he did it, but whatever inner well of strength he's been drawing from is running dry.

My arm flings out to steady him as he slips again. "Are you alright?"

"Just tired," he answers, but that's an understatement. He's practically dead on his feet.

"I can help," I offer. "You don't have to push yourself so hard."

"I'm fine. Don't worry about me."

"I'll always worry about you." My fingertips gently trail down the back of his arm before I let my hand drop to my side. He's dripping with sweat.

"I promise, Kay." He's determined. "Your mom and I will be okay. We can rest at the top of the hill. Why don't you go see what Richard needs?"

I watch him warily for a moment as he shakes off his shoe, flinging mud onto the moss. His grip on Mom's knees and his arm around her torso never waver. As long as Connor has her, she's safe. There's no question about that.

"Meet me at the top?" I ask, though it's not really a question. *Where else would he go?*

Connor raises his eyes to the summit and sucks in a deep breath. He blows it out slowly, preparing for the steep incline. "Give me five minutes. We'll be there."

"Okay." I plant a kiss on his cheek, then turn to climb.

Dad waits near the edge of the trees, cloaked in the shadow of a towering Oak. As silently as I can, I pick my way through the sparse brush and join him. As I reach the tree-line, the harsh light of day momentarily blinds me. My eyes have become accustomed to the depths of the woods.

Rapidly blinking, I realize we're standing at the border of a shallow valley. A ragged mountain looms over a cluster of wooden, cabin-like buildings beyond a sturdy log wall and heavy-looking gate. Time has smoothed the once-rough structures. A fast-moving stream burbles through the center of the clearing, wrapping around the left side of the barricade and disappearing into a different patch of trees. Two people guard the entrance, but the area is otherwise clear.

"Is that..." I start to ask, but my words trail off.

"The village of the Ruin," Dad answers. "We made it."

"It's real," I mutter in astonishment. "I mean, I knew it was. Well, I wanted to *believe* it was. But, now that we're here, it's *surreal*."

"I know the feeling."

"I kinda thought it would be smaller?"

A sharp crack sounds from less than a foot away. I turn, expecting to see Connor disentangling himself from a patch of burrs or kicking aside a fallen limb. Instead, I find a squat, balding man with distrustful brown eyes staring back at me. He presses the barrel of a rifle against my sternum. Frantically, I search for Connor and Mom. Two more guards, a woman with a messy gray bun and a boy no older than twelve, flank them as they ascend the remainder of the hill.

"Easy," Dad says, throwing his hands up in surrender. Another man, taller and thinner than the one threatening me, presses a shotgun to his back. "We're not here to cause trouble."

"Then why *are* you here?" the taller guard snaps. He nudges Dad with the barrel of his gun. "You didn't wind up here by accident."

"No, we didn't," I answer. "We need your help."

"Help?" The squat guard studies me. "You wandered into

the middle of the mountains looking for help? What kind of stupid are you?"

I shoot the man a disdainful look. "I'm not stupid." I point to Connor. "The woman he's carrying is my mother."

"And?" the gray-haired woman asks.

"And, she's dying." The truth is bitter on my tongue.

The young boy rakes his eyes over Connor and Mom. "She doesn't look so good."

"Shut up, Aspen," the woman barks. "That doesn't concern us."

Connor shifts uncomfortably as the woman raises her gun higher, aiming it at his face.

"You don't understand," Dad starts, but I interrupt before he has time to finish his sentence.

"I know about the Ruin."

"Don't call us that!" she shrieks. The furious woman takes several steps toward me, backing me into the trunk of the Oak. "We do NOT answer to that name."

"Calm down, Bella," the squat man instructs. "I'm sure she meant no harm."

"He's right. I'm sorry. I only meant I know about your people and what you can do. My mom needs your help. She needs the Sharing. That's why we're here."

"How do you know about that?" Bella growls, her face inches from mine.

"It doesn't matter. We don't help strangers anymore," the thin guard answers. "We haven't for a long time."

"We aren't strangers," Dad tells him. "We're part of the clan, or at least, my mother was. My name is Richard Edwards, and Kara is my daughter. This is her mother, my wife, Valerie. The man carrying her is Kara's boyfriend, Connor."

"Edwards?" the man guarding me repeats. "I've heard that name."

"You're the traitor's son," Bella chimes in. She shifts her hateful gaze from me to my father and takes several steps back. "Lilliana, the one who broke the laws and left."

"I am."

"You thought you could come here and demand something of us because of your blood?" The taller guard scoffs. "That's not how it works. Your mother made her choice. You're not welcome here. Neither is your daughter. You don't belong."

"Please," I add. "How can you hold my grandmother's mistakes against us? I had nothing to do with her decision to leave, and neither did my dad. He wasn't even born."

Bella opens her mouth to speak, but the squat guard cuts her off.

"Bring the sick one closer," he instructs Connor. "Now."

The young boy shoves Connor forward. Connor casts him a look of contempt look but follows instructions. He stops in front of my guard, and the balding man lowers the rifle from my chest. An audible sigh of relief escapes me.

He watches Mom draw several ragged breaths before raising his eyes to mine. "How much time does she have?"

My voice cracks. "We don't know. Not long."

Tense silence fills the forest as the man considers my words.

"Bram, we can't," Dad's guard insists. "You know what she said."

"Let her decide," Bram tells the thin guard. "Take them to the gate. Not this one. He stays. We can't have him exposed." Bram brings his eyes to Connor's. "Hand over the mother. Wait here in the forest. Do you understand?"

Connor swallows and looks to me for guidance. When I nod, he answers, "I do."

The thin guard rolls his eyes and swings his shotgun over his shoulder. "This is a bad idea," he grumbles as he reaches for Mom. As gently as he can, Connor passes my mother into the guard's arms.

"You think everything is a bad idea, Orrin," Bram retorts.

"I happen to agree," Bella adds.

"Then, I guess it's a good thing I'm in charge of the watch today. Shut your mouth and get to the gate. No more arguing."

THE LATE AFTERNOON SUN SINKS CLOSER TO THE horizon as Dad, Bram, Orrin, and I wait outside of the village gate. As soon as we arrived, Bella and Aspen abandoned us, returning to their posts in the forest. No doubt, they're keeping a close eye on Connor from somewhere in the trees.

At the guards' insistence, we left our packs with Connor before they escorted us into the valley. One of them contained a small, red tent, which he's busy assembling under the canopy of the massive oak. Every few seconds, his head turns in our direction. I know he'd be down here in an instant if I needed him, but it wouldn't be safe. I don't know how close he could come to one of the Healed without being infected. I'm not willing to take that risk.

The creaking of hinges draws my attention back to the village as the gate swings open. A woman with waist-length snow-white hair steps through the narrow opening and approaches us. Her expression is stern, but there's kindness in her features. Dark gray eyes take in the scene before her.

Orrin steps forward, bringing Mom to the woman. She stops and examines Mom's frail frame. In her presence, the entire valley stills.

"What is this about?" she asks Bram. There's no hint of emotion in her words.

"I found them in the woods," he answers. "That one is sick."

The white-haired woman tilts her head to the side. "I can see that."

"The man says he's Richard Edwards. He claims they're part of the clan."

"So they are. Though, he was warned not to return when I saw him last."

Bram's eyes shoot to Dad. Annoyance seeps into his words. "You've been here before?"

"Fifteen years ago," Dad answers. "I brought another here. He needed shelter, and Calla took him in."

Calla? Does Dad know her?

"I told you what would happen if you came back."

"This is different."

"Calla?" I ask, putting my thoughts into words. "You know each other?"

"We do," Calla confirms. She steps closer to Dad and lowers her head. "Richard is my nephew. At least, he would have been if my sister hadn't broken the laws and escaped."

My jaw drops. "So, that makes you…"

"Your great-aunt. Sort of."

I'm speechless.

"Valerie needs your help," Dad tells her. "Don't turn her away."

"We don't heal strangers anymore. It's too dangerous."

"Calla," Dad pleads. "I brought her to you. I could have done it myself. You know that."

"I do."

"Or I could have," I add, finding my voice.

Calla turns to address me. "You have the gift?"

"She does," Dad answers for me.

"How do you know?"

"When we brought Evan here, Kara had been exposed. She didn't get sick."

Calla pinches the bridge of her nose. "You never told us you had a child."

"I never intended for you to know."

"Why?" she spits. Her eyes narrow as she asks, "What did you think we would do?"

"I didn't know *what* you would do. I only knew I wanted to keep her out of this. Safe."

"Despite what you may *think*, Richard," she retorts. "We aren't in the practice of killing people. That job falls to you. How many have died at your hands?"

The blood drains from my father's face. "Too many. No more."

"And, you?" she asks me. "Have you learned from your father's mistakes, or are you just like him, too selfish to consider the consequences of your actions?"

"I had an opportunity to heal my mother, but I chose not to if that's what you're asking."

Calla doesn't speak as she approaches me. "Why not?"

"I don't want anyone to die for me. She wouldn't either."

"Bram," Calla instructs. "Take Valerie's pulse."

"Yes, Priestess."

"Priestess?" I ask, confused.

"I lead the clan," she answers. Her eyes follow Bram as he takes Mom's wrist into his hand.

"It's weak. Too weak. I don't know, Priestess. It would be close."

"What? What would be close?"

"We're determining if your mother would survive the Sharing."

My heart drops into my stomach.

"What ails her?"

"Cancer," Dad supplies. "Stage four. Terminal. We've tried everything."

Calla returns to Mom, running her hand along the top of Mom's head. A look of concern settles over Calla's face. Her eyes narrow. "This is the woman who came with you before?"

"Yes. This is my wife."

"Strange," Calla whispers. "She survived the Sickness, too. Did she not?"

"She did."

"Yet, she wasn't Healed? She's never had the Sharing performed for her?"

"Never."

"Her sickness is not natural," Calla asserts. "She's been exposed."

"I don't understand," I whisper.

"Cancer is a disease of mutation." Calla's words are certain. "Richard, have you never considered that, as the one person who has ever survived exposure to the Sickness, her cancer may have been caused by it?"

"I..." Dad struggles to find words. "It crossed my mind, but..."

When Calla's eyes turn back to me, they're full of sympathy and sadness. "This woman can't be helped."

"No..." I feel myself speaking but hear no sounds. In an instant, the last shreds of hope I've been clinging to are obliterated. The ground drops out from beneath me. "You have to. We brought her all this way. You're her last chance."

Dad is speechless.

"How she survived the initial exposure is beyond my scope of knowledge. Should she be exposed to our blood again after such an occurrence, the results would be unpredictable at best. There's nothing we can do except provide her with a place to rest. We can offer you shelter and comfort for whatever time remains. I'm sorry, child."

"But, she's my Mom…" I repeat the phrase I've said so many times. "I can't lose her."

"Children are meant to lose their mothers and fathers," Calla says as she wraps an arm around me. "Come. I'll find her a soft bed and have Orrin start a fire to warm her. You and your father can remain by her side. She would want that, yes?"

I nod, unable to speak.

"Then it's settled. Richard, go tell your friend on the hill and return. Bram will wait for you at the gate. One of the kids will bring him some food in a while. He should be safe there for the time being, but warn him to go no farther than the creek. I'll station an extra guard in the woods tonight."

Orrin ambles through the small opening in the gate, turning sideways to escort Mom inside.

"We'll honor your mother," Calla whispers into my ear. "She was brave and strong. I've only known you for a few short minutes, but I can tell by the daughter she raised. You'll have a chance to say your goodbyes."

Numbly, I let her lead me into the village.

"Everything will be alright in time," Calla assures me. "I promise."

I disagree. Nothing will be right again.

CHAPTER FORTY-THREE

"I tried." Dad's haunted voice drifts over to me.

The logs stacked beside the hearth fill the room with the scent of pine. It's difficult to tear my eyes away from the flickering flames. They're mesmerizing. The cabin had been cold when Calla and Orrin brought us in, but it's not anymore. Despite this, I can't seem to get warm. I hold my hands out and flex my fingers, trying to absorb the heat. It doesn't do any good. The freezing sensation is coming from a deep, hollow place inside of me. Part of me, my last inkling of hope, is still waiting at the village gate. Without it, I'm lost.

Calla's words play over and over in my mind. *"Her sickness is not natural… She's been exposed… This woman can't be helped… say your goodbyes."*

I should be wracked with sorrow and grief, but I can't feel anything. I'm numb. My eyes close.

This isn't how it should have been. None of it. We should have all come to a place like this together on a family vacation. Mom should be resting comfortably, cancer free. Dad should be getting dinner ready for the family. Jennifer should be healthy and sober. I should be curled up by the fire with a book.

I want to be in that reality, but when I open my eyes

again, the dream shatters. We're not on vacation. We'll never be that family. We're too broken. Mom's dying in a tiny cabin in the middle of the Appalachian Mountains, hours away from home and the only life she's ever known.

Turning my back to the fireplace, I cast a long shadow over the space. It stretches across the planked floor and up the far wall. My eyes linger on a bed roughly half the size of a twin that's been shoved into the corner. They travel down the length of Mom's still form to the foot where a tiny pedestal holds a pitcher and wash basin. A Lily of the Valley has been painstakingly painted on the porcelain.

Always lilies. Why?

A creak from the corner snags my attention. I drag my eyes away from the pitcher. Four small coat pegs hang near the cabin door. A simple chest of blankets, now half-empty, sits underneath them. The rest of the contents have been layered on the bed to keep Mom comfortable. Two rough-hewn chairs and a round table are pressed against the outer wall. Dad occupies one of the chairs. He shifts uncomfortably and stares down at his muddy shoes.

"She doesn't deserve this. *You* don't deserve this." His voice cracks.

My footsteps echo as I move to sit beside Mom and take her hand into mine. "No, we don't. No one deserves this, but that doesn't make it your fault."

Despite the multitude of covers, her skin is clammy and cold. I stroke my thumb across the back and marvel at how much she's changed since her diagnosis.

I've asked too much of her. Mom wouldn't want this. The woman lying in this bed is little more than a shell of Valerie Edwards. She was ready to let go before we left St. John's. She kept fighting for me. It wasn't for her. I know that now.

Dad drops his head into his palms. "What if it is? You

heard Calla at the gate. She said the cancer could have come
— ”

His words are cut short by a gentle knock on the cabin
door.

“Dinner,” Calla calls as she pushes it open and steps
inside, not waiting for us to let her in. Her heavy dress
swooshes as she carries a tray in one hand and crosses the
room. Chilly night air follows in her wake. She lifts the wash
basin and pitcher from their pedestal and sets them gently on
the floor, balancing her tray in the space where they had
been.

Orrin follows behind her with two more. He deposits his
trays on the table by Dad before reaching into his pocket and
producing spoons and woven napkins.

“Sit,” Calla instructs, pointing to the empty chair.
“You need to eat. You and your father have had a long
journey.”

I don’t want to leave Mom, but I take up the chair beside
Dad. He slides one of the trays over to me and dips his spoon
into his food.

Calla offers me a kind smile before turning to Orrin.
“That’s all for now. I’d like a few moments alone with our
guests.”

“Yes, Priestess,” he answers. Without another word, he
steps outside, closing the cabin door and shutting out the
unwelcome cold.

“Dinner is venison, sweet potatoes, corn, and stewed
apples. We’re still finishing last year’s harvest, but the meat
is fresh.”

“What about – ?” I start to ask.

“Your friend has been fed as well. He’s resting comfortably in his tent. We gave him a few extra supplies and
showed him how to start a fire. It gets cold in the mountains
at night. We won’t let him freeze.”

"Thank you." I should say more, but those are the only words I have.

"You're welcome." She sits in my abandoned place on the bed and interlaces her fingers, dropping them into her lap. "He seems like a kind young man."

"He is," I answer, pushing my meal around with the spoon. It smells delicious, but I can't bring it to my lips. Instead, I stare at the tray meant for Mom.

She won't eat it. She doesn't have enough strength. They're well aware of that. Yet, they prepared the meal anyway. The act was kind, but it hurts.

"You've changed," Dad says as he takes a bite. "Last time I was here, you threatened to have us killed. Now, you're offering shelter and food. Why?"

"When I last saw you, I was angry. There's so much of Lilliana in your face, Richard. It hurt to look at you and see her. Lily betrayed us all when she left, but her abandonment affected me the most. When you came back, it reopened the wound, and when I learned what you had done... You must understand. Knowing a member of my family brought about such death and destruction was a dishonor. I was ashamed."

"So was I. I always will be."

"I know."

Calla's eyes flick to Mom before returning to us. "It's been fifteen years since you brought Evan and your wife to our gates. That's a long time. I grow tired of anger and causing pain. We all have."

"I can relate," Dad adds. "Wherever I go, pain follows."

"Such is the curse that plagues us. Our ancestors were once known as a clan of great healers. People would travel vast distances to seek our family's expertise. They were respected, helpful members of society. It's a shame they brought destruction upon us. What remains of our people have chosen to do so no longer."

"Mom would be ashamed of me," I say, not realizing I've spoken my thoughts aloud until Dad reaches across the table and grabs my hand.

"No," he interjects. "You did what you thought was right. She'd be proud of you."

"No, I didn't. I did what I thought was best, but I knew it wasn't right. I wanted to save her no matter the cost. I've been selfish and stubborn."

Calla smiles, a hint of sad humor glinting in her eyes. "I see you've inherited the family traits."

"What if her last thoughts of me are of all the ways I've let her down? I've failed."

"They won't be, child. They never are," Calla promises.

"I couldn't let her go."

"No one wants to let their loved ones die. Holding onto every second you have makes you human," Dad replies, squeezing my hand lightly.

"Is that why our ancestors made the deal with Eir?" I ask, bringing my tearful eyes to Calla.

"I think you know the answer."

"Why was she so cruel, then? If all we wanted was to save the people we love, why would she curse us?"

"The goddess Eir didn't curse us. We brought the curse upon ourselves. Our ancestors were given the gift of life and told to use it once, and once only. When they did not heed her warning, they threw the universe off balance. Death does not take kindly to humans plucking souls from her grasp. So, to restore balance, she claimed more. The curse of the Ruin is entirely due to human fallacy. You mustn't blame the gods."

"What about the prophecy?"

"The prophecy?"

"The one my mother kept in her locket," Dad answers. He must have memorized the poem because he repeats it back to her flawlessly.

"Another example of human fallacy. Our people refused to accept responsibility for their actions. They needed someone to blame. Assigning the guilt to a divine figure assuaged the guilt. Still, Eir did no wrong."

No one ever takes responsibility, myself included. When will we learn?

"I am truly sorry we cannot help your mother, Kara." Calla's mouth turns down at the corners and her eyelids close. "There's more to our history than you know. To perform the Sharing now would bring about far worse than the Sickness that follows. We cannot risk repeating the past."

"What do you mean?" I ask.

"Eat and I will tell you," she asserts. "This is something even the people in this village do not know."

I lift the spoon to my lips and taste the salty gravy first, followed by the tender, wild meat. As I chew, my stomach growls. Calla tucks the blankets tighter around Mom.

"There was a time when we tried to heal someone twice," she begins. "Though the Healed tend to fare well, they are not impervious to disease. Many years ago, one of the Healed in our village became ill a second time. A well-meaning member of our clan unwittingly performed the Sharing, seeing no harm in healing someone already secluded from the world. They were wrong."

"What happened?" I ask, digging into the stewed apples.

"The basis of sharing is a mutation, a biological change. Having been exposed to our magic twice, their mortal form couldn't endure. The poor woman became monstrous. Her limbs elongated. The skin on them hung from her bones. It was a horrific sight, or so I'm told. She tore through the village, leaving carnage and destruction in her wake. Our guards barely managed to put her down before she broke free to release her terror on the world."

I swallow. Calla's description sounds eerily familiar. "I dreamt of a creature like that. Twice, actually."

Calla nods her head. "Then, you have experienced Eir's warnings. As I've said, Eir is not to blame for the curse. She wants us to make amends for what we've done. The goddess isn't cruel. She must have sent you prophetic dreams to save you from that fate."

"If I had healed Mom, that's what she would have become?"

"It is certainly so."

"I nearly did it at the hospital," I admit. "Doctor Mitchell told me there was nothing else we could do. It was like I went into a trance. I knew I shouldn't, but I wanted to. I needed to."

"I remember the feeling." Dad's words are distant. From the way his expression has changed, it's clear he's lost in his memories. "I couldn't resist."

"That's the compulsion," Calla says. "It's a consequence of our gift. Where there is power and life, there is a need to use it. The magic is stronger than us. It takes hold. But, you resisted."

"I was interrupted."

"Divine intervention at work," Calla states. "You have Eir's favor. I believe she intends for you to lift our curse."

"What?" Her words shake me. "I can't break a curse. That's ridiculous."

"It's not," Calla insists. "You may be the only one who can."

"But, how?" Dad asks, as confused as I am.

"We owe the universe a debt," Calla answers. "A large one. We have taken things that don't belong to us, and to break the curse, we have to offer a sacrifice large enough to fill the void."

"Sacrifice?" I ask.

"Death," she replies. "When our ancestors asked for the power to save a life, they did so to save someone they loved. The universe exists on a principle of balance, give and take. To fulfill the debt, we have to sacrifice the life of one we hold dear."

"As in murder?" I blurt. "I wouldn't kill anyone." Even as I say the words, my thoughts drift to Matthew. *I was willing to kill him, wasn't I?*

"Not murder, Kara. Acceptance. The sacrifice requires us to set our gift aside and let someone go."

Understanding dawns. "Mom?"

"Yes," Calla acknowledges with a sigh.

"But, why? What did we do?"

"You've done nothing to deserve it. The truth is simple: our debt is one none of us could hope to repay. We saved someone from sickness, so a sickness must be what takes them, but members of our clan do not fall ill. Even if they did, the debt must be repaid by someone innocent of our crimes, someone who has never performed the Sharing. We have none here who can fulfill both conditions."

"No one? None at all?" Dad's words are tinged with disbelief.

"None," Calla responds.

"But, there are people here, right? People who aren't from our clan?"

"There are, but the only other humans we interact with are those who have been Healed. They are tainted by our blood. I've come to understand this must be why Lilliana was called to leave the village. Eir had a hand in her departure."

"Why would Eir want my mother to leave?" Dad asks.

"She left the clan and formed a new life. She created you, Richard, and you created Kara. You had children with a woman outside of the clan, a woman who had never been Healed. Your interactions changed her, and she survived. You gave us a way to repay our debt, and now, as painful as it is, we have a chance to remove this abomination from the world."

My eyes are glued to Mom as she continues.

"You must let her die, but her death will mean so much more than human loss. It will mean the end of a centuries-long plague upon this Earth. It will mean salvation for all who might have been destroyed. It will right wrongs that have already happened and prevent countless more."

I want to argue with her, but I can't. There are no more treatments. She can't be helped by the Sharing. I won't destroy her and let her become a fiend. In a matter of hours, Mom will be gone.

"What do I need to do?" I manage between sobs.

"Give her to Eir," Calla answers. "Let her live her last moments in love and comfort, then dedicate her funeral pyre. That's all. No complicated magic, no deals, simply an honorable goodbye."

I scoff as I wipe away the tears streaking my cheeks. "Just do the hardest thing anyone could ever do?"

Calla sighs again. "Yes. Let her go."

Silence fills the cramped space as Dad and I exchange a glance of love, loss, grief, and finally understanding. He squeezes my hand again.

I close my eyes and shut out the world, hating myself for admitting defeat, even though I know she's right. "Will Mom make it through the night?"

Calla considers her. "I believe so, but not much longer."

"Okay."

Dad squeezes my hand again. I blow out a breath, steeling myself. Emotion threatens to overtake me, but I can't let it. I have to stay strong for Mom for as long as I can.

"In the morning, I need your help," I tell Calla, slipping my protective mask back on.

"What can we do?" she asks. Her voice is empathetic and kind.

"I need her carried out to the clearing by the creek."

"We can see to that," she says. "But, may I ask why?"

I move to the bed and lift Mom's hand into mine once more. "It's peaceful there. One last time, we're going to see the sunrise."

CHAPTER FORTY-FOUR

Though it shouldn't take this many people, Dad and three members of the Ruin carry Mom through the sturdy gate and into the clearing. I think it's a sign of respect. The makeshift stretcher barely sags beneath her frail frame as they set out across the grass. It can't be heavy. She's even smaller than she was when we arrived yesterday. She's withered away more than I thought possible overnight.

I move to follow them into the open, but Calla reaches for my arm. Her grip on my bicep is soft yet assertive. I raise my face to hers, and she lifts her other hand to tuck a stray strand of my ratted hair behind my ear. I haven't bothered to change or bathe since we arrived. To her credit, Calla pretends not to notice.

"Your friend is waiting for you by the creek where the clearing meets the mountainside. He'll be safe there. No Healed are permitted to leave the village, so there's no chance for infection. Do not let him cross the stream. I cannot assure his safety then."

"I won't."

Connor will be there. My Connor. Dad and I won't have to sit with Mom alone as she fades into the darkness. He'll keep me whole.

"We do not wish for any additional losses."

"Neither do I."

"I'm sure. Though I'm certain your mother's sacrifice will not be in vain, I have no control over the magic which has already been worked before she leaves this world. That is up to Eir." She lowers her arm and looks out into the clearing at the stretcher. "When the moment has passed, I've given Richard instructions to find me. Your friend must remain outside the village, even after her departure."

"You're not coming?" I ask.

"This is a time best spent with those who loved your mother most. While I respect her and her sacrifice, it is not my place to be by her side. I will remain with my people until the time is right."

"I understand," I tell her. And, I do. She's offering us privacy to grieve. I'm thankful.

"When you're ready, our clan will follow the four of you up the mountain." Calla's gaze drifts to the looming peak. "We will honor your mother's life, but we cannot carry the burden. It must fall to the three of you."

"Why?"

"It is an act of dedication, of devotion. You must carry the weight of loss to Eir's altar and lay it before her."

I follow her gaze to the tip of the towering slate. "It's steep."

"It is," she agrees, "but we've spent many years wearing a footpath to the altar. The ascent should be less treacherous than your time in the forest."

"Okay."

"We'll be right behind you, Kara Edwards. You do not make this journey alone."

"Thank you, Calla. For everything," I tell her.

"I only wish I could do more."

I nod because there's nothing left to say.

This time, she doesn't stop me when I step through the

gate. I don't look back. There's no point. Nothing waits for me with the Ruin anymore.

I cradle Mom's head in my lap beneath the early morning sky. Only feet away, the rapidly moving stream burbles. Connor sits beside me, his arm wrapped around my hips. Dad tucks heavy blankets around Mom's legs and feet, keeping her warm.

"Remember when I was little and I wanted to be a pirate?" I ask her, though she doesn't stir. "You made me a swashbuckler costume for Halloween. That was maybe two years after Dad left? I can't remember. I wanted to run away and go on great adventures. Things at home were hard, and I thought sailing the seas would be better. You laughed and told me I'd get scurvy without my vitamins, but you still stuffed one of your old purses with those gold chocolate coins.

"Jennifer made fun of me for pretending to sword fight with an empty paper towel roll, but you took me over to the swing set in the park and showed me how to step across each one like it was a booby-trapped path to the treasure. You told me you and I would go on adventures one day. I guess you were right. Look where we are, Mom. We're in the middle of the Appalachian Mountains. It's beautiful."

Connor wraps his arm tighter around my hips while I break down. "I remember that," he tells me. "When I came over, you drew a curly mustache under my nose with a Sharpie. My mom was pissed."

A tiny laugh slips out of me. "It came off."

"Yeah, four days later." He plants a soft kiss on my cheek.

"I thought it made you look handsome."

"When you were maybe three," Dad cuts in, "you used to drag this fuzzy blanket your mom made you through the house. It would get filthy, but you absolutely refused to let us wash it. Do you remember that?"

"No," I answer. "I was too little."

"We had tacos for dinner one night, and you got grease all over the blanket. You used it to wipe your face like a napkin. I tried to pry it away from you, but you fought me tooth and nail. Your mom saved the day when she ran you a bath and washed you and the blanket. She was clever like that."

"I don't think I told you what she said to me when I graduated from high school," Connor adds. "Ally and my parents were still up in the bleachers, but she came down and wrapped me in the tightest hug. She was so proud, even though I wasn't one of her own. Valerie told me I'd be a hero. Not like a superhero, but someone who changed the world."

"You're my hero," I say as I lean my head onto his shoulder. He smiles.

We tell stories about Mom as we watch the sky shift from a flat gray to shades of red, pink, orange, and yellow. Dad recounts how Mom got into a bar fight once before I was born because someone insulted him when they were playing pool. Connor talks about how Mom used to sneak him cookies and candies before he went home after his visits. I remember things I'd long since forgotten, like the time I hid a tiny painted turtle in the closet for two weeks before she found it, the time I got into her makeup and tried to put it on but ended up looking like a clown, and how she used to let me sleep in her t-shirts when I was small. Before I know it, the sun crests over the top of the forest. It fills the clearing with sparking yellow light. The refraction of the ripples in the creek sends rainbows onto the slate. It's a sight to behold.

"Look, Mom," I beg. "The sun is coming up. Just one last

time, open your eyes. I won't ask you to fight. This is all I want. Open your eyes and watch it with me. Please."

A light breeze ripples the tops of the trees.

"Please…"

Mom doesn't stir. She's too far gone. Her body is ready to rest. Her breath slows as I stroke the soft patch of hair on her scalp.

I press my forehead to hers and lower my voice so only she and I can hear. "I love you, Mommy. I'm so sorry for everything I've done. I wanted to keep you with me. I wasn't ready, and that wasn't fair. I'll never be ready, but it's time to let go. Stop fighting. Let go of the pain. I'm here. Dad's here. Connor's here. You're not alone."

Mom's eyelids flutter as my tears fall. They open, ever so slightly, as I kiss her forehead and struggle to breathe.

"K…ar…a," she mumbles, and the faintest smile appears on her face. Her eyes drift to the sky above before they close.

Her chest stops rising and falling. Her shoulders still. I press my fingers to her wrist, and her heartbeat slows.

"I love you," I whisper again, barely able to speak.

The thrumming beneath my fingers ceases.

Pain drags me down into a bottomless abyss. I can't feel Connor's touch anymore. All I know is the limp body in my arms.

She's gone.

Mom's gone.

I don't remember collapsing onto the dew-soaked ground, but I must have because the next thing I know, Connor is lifting me into his lap. He holds me in a tight embrace, rocking me as he did so many weeks ago on his blood-soaked bathroom floor. I cling to him as though he is the only person who can keep me tethered to this Earth.

Dad crawls across the grass and joins us, taking both of us into his arms. We're broken, the three of us, shattered by the impact of Mom's loss. We hold onto each other like we never have before.

Everything has changed.

It feels like we sit together for hours in agonizing grief. Time is deceiving in the wake of death. The sun barely skirts across the horizon, though every moment with Mom gone is an eternity. Eventually, I run out of tears and my throat is raw. I look to my father, and he reads my thoughts without having to utter a single word.

Go to Calla.

And, he does.

CALLA KEEPS HER PROMISE. WHEN DAD RETURNS, the whole host of the Ruin trails in his wake. Calla leads them. A black, hooded robe has been pulled over her white hair. Symbols, drawn from what looks to be charcoal or ash, adorn her face. I look at the rows of clan members behind her, and all have some variation of the markings on their foreheads, cheeks, and noses. Every one of them is silent, carrying something small in their hands.

"We are sorry for your loss," she says as she lifts me to my feet. "It is far greater than anyone should endure. Our people have brought offerings for your mother and Eir to ensure she is honored properly as her spirit leaves this plane. The smoke from the pyre will carry her to the afterlife. Eir will certainly welcome her into her warm embrace."

I can't speak, so I nod.

Numbly, I watch as Bram and Orrin instruct Dad and Connor regarding how to prepare Mom's body for the pyre. Dad dips a rag into the creek and cleans the dirt from her face, hands, and feet. Bram and Orrin help Connor discreetly replace her worn clothing with clean, black fabric. They return her to the stretcher and cover her with a translucent shroud. Then, it's time for me to take the lead. They've done all they can.

Dad takes his place beside me at Mom's feet. Connor holds the two posts by her covered face. We count down from three so our movements are coordinated. It takes more detachment than I realized I could summon, but my trembling legs propel me to stand. I lift one of the corners of the stretcher.

"Face the mountain," Dad instructs. He's doing his best to be strong for me. I see it in the set of his jaw. "Don't look back. You don't want to fall. That won't do anyone any good."

Carefully, I turn and put Mom's body behind me.

I don't want to do this. I don't want to do this. I don't want to do this.

With one final deep breath, we start the climb.

"OUR PEOPLE GATHER AT THE PYRE TO HONOR THE life of Valerie Edwards," Calla booms from the base of the altar where Mom's body has been ensconced in layer upon layer of kindling. "Though she was not of the people," she continues, "she belongs to the people. Wife of Richard, daughter-in-law of Lilliana, and mother of Kara, we give her the greatest of respect upon this, her passing. May her brave spirit be claimed by the goddess Eir, and may she be ushered into a peaceful afterlife. Though she is gone, her influence will always remain."

In unison, Calla and the clan utter words I don't understand.

"Valerie Edwards was a warrior. Though she saw no battlefields, her valiant spirit allowed her to raise her daughter into the young woman who stands before us today. Through her daughter, we have witnessed her strength. May she be found worthy of the hall."

Again, the Ruin chant a reply in a different language.

"Kara, daughter of Valerie, will speak over her mother's body before we send up the smoke to the gods and goddesses. She will dedicate this pyre. Kara, please step forward."

With my eyes fixed on the pyre, I amble closer to Calla. She extends her arms to me, and I take her hands into mine.

"What... what do I do?" I ask. "I don't know the language."

"You don't need to," she answers. "Speak to Eir. Tell her of your pain and your loss. Ask her to accept your mother's soul. Say your final goodbyes."

"I don't want to mess this up."

"You won't. Not if you speak from the heart."

She leaves me standing by the pyre as I stare down at the offerings - pots of food, sachets of pungent herbs, and ornately stitched cloths - that surround the base of the altar and have been draped over the kindling. Behind me, Orrin passes Dad a torch. It sparks to life, sending the sickeningly sweet scent of accelerant up my nose.

"Eir," I whisper, feeling foolish standing before so many people. "You may not know me. No, that's wrong. You certainly do." I shake my head. "I don't know what to say. I've never prayed to you before. I'm sure there are fancy words or something, but I've never been taught anything about deities or funerals. So, I'll do what Calla suggested and speak from the heart, I guess."

My voice thickens as I choke back the emotions overwhelming me.

"The woman on this altar is my mother, Valerie Edwards. She's the best person I've ever known. She wasn't perfect, but she loved me with everything she had. And, I loved her. I always will. She had cancer, and I fought to keep her here. I did everything I could, even dangerous things. Some of them I shouldn't have done. I know that now. Still, my actions led us here to your altar and the Ruin.

"You warned me what would happen if I gave in to the temptation of our secret. I didn't understand what it meant then, but I do now. I had the opportunity to try the Sharing, but I never followed through. Calla says it was divine intervention, and for that, I thank you. I couldn't have lived with myself if something like what she described had happened to my mom."

I pause, focusing on my breathing.

"I stopped fighting this morning. I let her stop fighting. And now, she's on her way to you. In just a minute, Dad and I will light this kindling and send up the smoke Calla claims will ferry her soul to the afterlife. Please Eir, take her soul to a wonderful place. She deserves it."

My chest constricts, and I tip my head to the sky. "Lift the curse from these people. I dedicate this pyre to you, goddess. Keep my mother safe in the afterlife, and spare the people behind me from their horrendous fates. They're sorry. I'm sorry. Let this be done."

Dad approaches me when I fall silent. He halts beside me, staring down at the offerings, too. Neither of us speaks. Everything that needed to be said was spoken in the clearing. There's no blame or anger between us as he extends his shaking hand and passes me the torch. I look to Calla for guidance, but she only nods. Dad bows his head as I slowly lower the flame to the kindling and plunge it into the depths.

In a second, the pyre ignites. The flames stretch from end to end, racing through the twigs and cloth. Fresh leaves mixed in with the kindling begin to smoke. Dad and I back away and rejoin Connor among the crowd. A tower of gray haze pours from the pyre, stretching into the sky and shutting out the morning sun.

The wood crackles and snaps as the altar is consumed. All eyes watch as the fire grows taller. Sparks flash and land on the scree at our feet. A sudden silence falls over the mountaintop. Birds that had been chirping their early morning songs fade away. The insects cease their incessant buzzing. Even the sounds of our feet on the loose stones muffle.

"She's coming." Calla's words cut through the void as the sky above darkens. The smoke from the pyre blots out the sun. It swirls around our feet, snaking through our ankles and curling around our waists. When it finds its way to my chest, I'm unable to breathe.

Only Connor is unaffected. Panic consumes him as the entire crowd, myself and Dad included, drops to its knees.

"Kara?" His lips form my name, but no sound reaches my ears. "Kara!"

An all-consuming void slams into me. Black spots spiral behind my eyes until they block my vision entirely. A sucking sensation pulls at my organs. My heart ceases beating. My ribs constrict as though they will implode. Connor's hands grip my shoulders and shake me. I focus on his presence, counting the seconds.

As suddenly as it came, the pain disappears.

My vision clears, and I cast my eyes to the sky. The darkness is gone. The soaring smoke is all that remains.

Calla gasps, lifting herself off the ground and stumbling toward the altar. The offerings, kindling, and fire have disappeared. A pile of ash sits upon the table of slate. There's no body, not even a fragment of bone. In its place, nestled among the ashes, is a single white plant.

I rise and join Calla. She sifts her fingers through the ash and lifts the plant up by its roots.

"Is that?"

"A Lily of the Valley," Calla answers.

"What does it mean?"

"There are two sides to the plant, as with anything," Calla states as she marvels at the perfect little bells hanging from rich green stems. "On the one hand, Lily of the Valley represents pain, loss, and death. On the other, a return to happiness and brighter days. Eir has accepted your offering, child. Your mother has found her place in the hall of heroes, and we are finally free."

EPILOGUE

The motel quilt scratches at my jeans as I perch on the edge of the bed. It's old, like everything else in the room, and small cigarette burns dot across the top layer of the fabric. I pick at one of them as Connor flips through the channels on the ancient television, searching for any news about the chaos we caused in Baltimore a few days ago.

Earlier this morning, he had tried using his phone to search for articles, but the burner we picked up at a back-woods gas station in a small town three hours back doesn't get much signal in the middle of the mountains. He hadn't been able to convince the search engine to load, let alone find anything useful.

Click. Click. Click.

Dad's arms are laden with convenience foods when he limps through the motel room door. At this point, I suspect most of it is psychosomatic. The wound itself has long since healed. I'd bet it was gone before we ever stepped foot in the village of the Ruin.

I'm glad Dad was able to talk to Evan after the curse lifted. Calla led us to his cabin when we returned to the village. The mood had changed drastically among the people, both of the Ruin and Healed alike. Dad had been worried

Evan wouldn't speak to him after what he had done, but fifteen years changes a lot of things. Rather than lash out at his childhood best friend, he introduced us to his wife and two children. They were thrilled to meet Dad because, without his mistake, Evan never would have come to the Ruin.

Funyuns, Doritos, and powdered donuts drop onto the matching quilt covering the second bed, and after removing the keycard from the lock, he places a greasy brown bag from the local diner beside the snacks. The scent of meat and fries has my stomach growling. I reach over and snag the bag, digging through its contents without a hint of shame.

"The bottom one is mine," Dad announces. "You two can fight over the others."

"Yeah, thanks," I answer absently, passing the bag to Connor. He retrieves his meal and sets it down beside him without bothering to unwrap it. I hold out the bag to Dad who places it on his nightstand and disappears into the tiny bathroom.

I too had the opportunity to speak with Evan before Calla loaded us down with supplies for our trip back to the car. I told him about Jennifer's situation and how much she had struggled with learning she was adopted. As a final request, I asked him to find her when he and his family left the village behind. His wife was less than enthusiastic, but it seemed like he was going to follow through.

Mom would have been happy to know our journey to the Ruin did more than break the curse. It gave us a chance to reunite part of our broken family.

Every day without her hurts. It's strange, but somehow it feels like she's still here. Dad tells me it will get easier over time. I'm not sure that's true. Some things are too hard to let go of, but I'll try to keep going. That's what she would have wanted.

Eagerly, my finger slides under the sticker on the aluminum foil. The wrapper falls away, revealing one of the best-looking cheeseburgers I've ever laid eyes on. Ketchup and mayonnaise ooze from beneath the top bun when I give it a light squeeze. The scent of garlic replaces the faint smell of mildew and bleach, and the sight of the gooey cheddar has my mouth watering before I lift it to my lips and take a huge bite.

Click. Click. Click.

Connor finally lands on the local news.

"... to stop by the post office to drop off your donations by six pm tomorrow. In other news, the city of Baltimore is still reeling from a mysterious fire that left a local plasma donation center in ruins..."

He hastily drops the remote to the bed beside him and picks up his sandwich, a monstrosity of ham and provolone. With his eyes glued to the screen, he unwraps it and stuffs the end into his mouth.

Dad steps out of the bathroom, listening intently.

"Plasmedics, a local plasma donation center owned by world-renowned Coarser Industries, burned to the ground early Monday morning, taking the lives of several guards and thousands of life-saving plasma donations with it," the reporter begins. "Police have determined the fire was an act of arson, as flammable chemicals had been distributed throughout one of the building's floors before the fire was set.

"Matthew Collins, son of CEO Elias Collins, personally responded to the fire alarms and barely managed to escape from the blaze. He was badly injured, suffering several significant burns and multiple fractures and breaks due to falling debris.

"Coarser Industries faces setbacks with their new revolutionary cancer treatment, Novemion, in the wake of the fire, as much of the testing for the drug was taking place in the upper floors of the facility. Earlier today, father and son made a statement to the public about this tragedy. Let's watch."

I nearly choke on my food as the images on the screen shift from the reporter to Elias and Matthew Collins standing behind a solid wood podium. Both are dressed immaculately, as stoic as ever. Only Matthew seems worse for wear. A dark, fading bruise covers half of his face.

"He's alive," I whisper, horrified. "How?"

Elias Collins speaks.

"As CEO of Coarser Industries, it is with a heavy heart that I share news of a profound tragedy which has befallen our subsidiary company, Plasmedics. Due to an act of violence against our organization, three of our employees lost their lives in a horrific fire Monday morning. This unfathomable act of violence not only left several families grieving the losses of their loved ones but also resulted in the destruction of invaluable materials used to further scientific advancements which could cure some of the deadliest diseases today.

"The plasma donation efforts of hundreds of citizens were rendered moot due to this heinous act. Our newest, most impressive cancer treatment drug, Novemion, shown to not only decrease cancer cell growth but to aid in reversing damage caused by cancerous cells, has been all but lost at this time.

"I myself almost lost one of the most important people in my life, my son Matthew, to this senseless act of destruction. I count myself incredibly lucky to be standing by his side today."

"He sounds like a robot," Connor mumbles around his mouthful of food, still staring at the television.

The image on the screen flashes back to the reporter, who continues her teleprompted speech.

"Coarser Industries was preparing Novemion, the company's newest cancer treatment, for submission to the FDA with anticipated acceptance for use in human patients as early as this June. Approval of this drug has been highly anticipated within the scientific community; however, this setback could delay manufacturing by months or even years."

The video feed returns to Elias and Matthew. This time, Matthew speaks to the camera. His glittering eyes, sunk deep into his face behind an obviously broken nose and a possible fractured eye socket, stare through the screen and straight into the room.

"We at Coarser Industries have a profound respect and value for human life, and that is why these events have impacted us all so greatly. Plasmedics, alongside our parent organization, seeks to explore new medications and provide cures for the incurable so all humans, not just those with wealth and power, can lead longer, happier lives."

"Yeah, right." I snap at the screen, chewing my food. *Every word coming out of his mouth is a lie.*

A reporter from the crowd asks Matthew how he felt when he was trapped inside the burning building and how he managed to escape. Smoothly, he replies, "Of course, being inside Plasmedics as it burned to the ground was terrifying. I tried my hardest to help those trapped alongside me to get out of the building in time, but when the beams began to collapse on top of us, there was nothing I could do. I'm incredibly lucky and grateful to have escaped from the facility, and only wish I had been able to save the others, my friends and co-workers, too."

"What's Coarser Industry's plan going forward?" another man in the crowd asks.

"We believe everything happens for a reason," Elias chimes in. His son takes a step back from the podium. "As tragic as these events have been, we have learned a great deal about fire suppression technology and important safety protocols which we will now implement in all Coarser Industry buildings worldwide. Furthermore, we plan to reopen our Plasmedics facility as soon as possible. We will rebuild the facility with the new safety measures in place and install a monument to our brave employees who perished in the fire at the site. We will not allow their deaths to be in vain."

Many in the crowd bob their heads, seeming to approve of Elias's empty words.

"We would like to thank Baltimore Emergency Services, the local Police, and Fire and Rescue for their tireless efforts battling the blaze so it did not reach the surrounding buildings. These public servants were the real heroes in this tragedy."

The man who asked the question nods enthusiastically, holding his microphone high.

The local reporter once again dominates the screen.

"The location for the new Plasmedics facility has not yet been announced, though there is speculation the company may contract with St. John's hospital to rent out several offices where donors would be able to make their donations until the new facility is completed. Matthew Collins had one more thing to say on the matter."

Once again, the image flashes to Matthew.

"There is important work to be done in the Plasmedics facility. Mark my words, this work *will* happen, one way or another. It will take more than one arsonist, or a few arsonists as the police suspect, to destroy *everything*," he says, emphasizing the word, "that we have worked for. Our company will never give up. To the terrorists who set our building on fire, know Coarser Industries will find you. We will ensure you are brought to justice for your crimes. That," he says with a charming smile, "is a *promise*." This last word is laced with venom.

My pulse thumps like a drum, causing my ears to ring violently as the news program returns to the local reporter once more. Heat crawls its way across my skin, flushing my cheeks. Sweat beads my brow as she wraps up her segment on the Baltimore fire, then turns her attention to a new dog adoption program at a local shelter. The burger, which only moments ago had been so appealing, turns to ash in my mouth. I swallow it with a dry gulp and turn to Dad, who looks just as anxious as me. He's gone pale, and his grip on the frame of the bathroom door is so tight the trim creaks, threatening to split.

Connor squeezes my knee reassuringly, but when I tilt my face up to his, he's no less worried than Dad or I. Fear and doubt linger behind his eyes.

"We have to tell Ally." Connor's voice is cold.

"No," Dad commands. "You can't contact her. The safest thing you can do is leave her alone."

"What about us?" I ask, petrified.

"We aren't safe here," Dad says under his breath.

"What do we do now?"

With one last lingering glance at Connor and me, Dad's face hardens into deep resolve. "Run."

Thank you for reading *The Ruin*. I hope you have enjoyed this work.

Do you have questions for the author? If so, reach out to me at smoran@obsidianinkwell.com and you might have them answered!

Please feel free to leave an honest review on Amazon or Goodreads. I look forward to writing for you again soon!

Want more from Samantha Moran? Keep reading for an excerpt from *Dealings in the Dark,* and be sure to check out her list of published works!

Find The Ruin *on Amazon*

Find The Ruin *on Goodreads*

Q) Why did it take you so long to write *The Ruin*?

Believe it or not, *The Ruin* is actually the first book I ever finished. The process of writing *The Ruin* took more than five years. I started drafting this book in late 2017, months after my first child was born, and finished my first draft in late 2022.

When I started this journey, I didn't believe in myself as a writer. I told my husband that becoming an author was one of my lifelong goals, and he believed in me, but imposter syndrome held me back time and time again. I would go for weeks, months, and once close to a year between writing new chapters because of my own mental limitations.

It took me a very long time to overcome my self-doubt. Eventually, I decided I wasn't going to hold myself back anymore. I finished the remaining components of the first draft (over half of the manuscript) within six months. I just had to get out of my head.

Of course, real life often intervened, too. I live with Multiple Sclerosis, have worked as a teacher for seven years, and have a family of my own. These things take time.

Q) Why did you set *The Ruin* in Baltimore, Maryland?

After I graduated from Western Michigan University, my husband and I moved to the suburbs of Baltimore, Maryland for a year. As Michiganders, born and raised, we wanted to get away from our home and see what else the world had to offer.

While we lived there, I fell in love with the city. There was something new around every corner. While Baltimore had its ups and downs, just as any location would, the art and culture of the area made it feel like the city was truly alive. That's why I wanted to set *The Ruin* in Baltimore, as both a nod to the amazing experiences I had there and to the contrast between life and death, good and bad.

Additionally, Baltimore has a long history of oncology treatments and advancements. While some of it stems from awful circumstances, John's Hopkins - Baltimore is still considered one of the leading cancer treatment centers in the United States, and according to a Newsweek article published in 2021, is ranked number eight in the world. Given Valerie's situation, it was absolutely the right choice for her care.

Q) Is this how plasma donation works in real life?

I tried to stay as true to the actual plasma donation process as I could. Through my own experiences donating plasma in college and research, I constructed the narrative of Kara's, Connor's, and Ally's experiences with Plasmedics.

Do I believe a plasma donation center could somehow weaponize donation material? No. That part came entirely from my creative mind.

Please don't let *The Ruin* discourage you from donating. Plasma donation saves lives! For more information, visit RedCrossBlood.org.

Q) Why did you choose to focus on the Norse goddess Eir?

Early on, I knew I wanted the curse of the Ruin to be based on a deal with a deity gone wrong. I didn't want to focus on the well-known deities for this tale, but rather on an impressive and lesser known figure. So, through research into the Norse pantheon, I landed on Eir.

As Richard's notes suggest, Eir was a powerful figure, sometimes seen interchangeably as a Norn (fate), Valkyrie, and goddess. She was known to oversee childbirth, to choose who lived and died on battlefields, and to support medical professionals. She was perfect for the task. Thus, the reimagining of a deal made with Eir was born.

Q) Why did you choose to end *The Ruin* in the manner you did?

I know, I know. Kara wanted so badly to save her mother. However, this all goes back to the concept of balance.

In the original deal made with Eir, the members of the Ruin asked for magic in order to save someone they loved. Therefore, in order to break the blood curse engaged when they misbehaved, a similar sacrifice had to be made.

Kara and her mother fought for so long and so hard that the woman they brought to the village wasn't truly her mother anymore. It was a necessary sacrifice, and in doing it, Kara saved more lives than she could ever know.

In the original manuscript, I allowed Valerie to live. She was taken into the village of the Ruin and never allowed to leave again. It simply wasn't enough balance, and the universe demands a properly weighted scale.

Q) How do you feel about those who struggle with mental health and addiction?

Mental health is equally as important as physical health. Much like the universe, the body requires balance. A happy mind and a well-tended body lead to a happy life. Therefore, I respect any and all individuals who struggle with mental illness just as much as I would respect someone like Valerie who is struggling with cancer.

A struggle is a struggle, and all deserve support and love.

As far as addiction, I view addiction as a serious mental health issue. Whether it be food, alcohol, drugs, or something else, I love and support those who struggle with this condition. I hope those who live with addiction can reach a place where they are willing, able, and ready to accept help.

There is an additional page of resources for those who are struggling with their mental health and/or addiction following this Q&A. If that includes you or someone you love, please feel free to use this as a place to start when searching for useful resources. Remember, I am not a medical professional and have only provided this list as a place to begin. I wish you and those you love well.

Q) Are any of the components in *The Ruin* inspired by real-life people or events?

If you've read any of my other works, you've probably noticed that loss is a prominent motif. That's because I've lost a great number of people I love in my thirty years of life, from family members to friends and students.

My grandmother died of cancer when I was only seventeen-years-old. A family friend died of cancer when I was in college. My husband's grandmother died of cancer less than two years ago. From these amazing individuals, I created Valerie (though her tragic flaws did not stem from true stories).

Q) Is there going to be a sequel to *The Ruin?*

If I have to give you an answer to this question right now, I'm going to have to say no. I struggled with this book for a very long time. It has become my pride and my nemesis. The amount of power it took for me to draft and publish this book is unfathomable. I don't feel comfortable saying I will continue the story of *The Ruin* in any long format.

However, I will consider either a short story or a novella which throws back to the original deal made by members of the Ruin clan and Eir. And, who knows? Maybe someday the story of *The Ruin* will inspire me again. The ending of this book does leave the door open just a crack in case I should change my mind. :)

RESOURCES FOR ADDICTION AND MENTAL HEALTH

Kara and Jennifer Edwards are fictional characters who struggle with the realities of addiction and mental health detriments in *The Ruin*, but they're only imaginary representations of the struggles many people face every day.

Addiction and mental health crises are serious matters. If you or someone you know struggle with either of these conditions, know that you don't have to suffer alone. There are many resources available to help individuals through these difficult situations. As a place to start, I have provided a few of those resources here.

Remember, I am not a medical professional, and what I have provided here does not constitute a complete list of places you can turn to for help. I highly recommend you engage in your own research outside of this text to find further resources and determine the care and assistance you or someone you love may need. I advise you to seek help from a certified professional for any serious issue.

If ever you feel like harming yourself or others, or if a loved one expresses these feelings, please contact a certified professional immediately.

In the meantime, I wish you nothing but health, happiness, and daily improvement with any addiction and/or mental health struggles you may have.

Stay strong. The world is better with you in it. You are not alone.

ADDICTION ASSISTANCE

- Substance Abuse and Mental Health Services Administration (samhsa.gov)
- Shatterproof.org
- Mental Health and Substance Abuse (USA.gov)
- AddictionHelp.com
- AmericanAddictionCenters.org

MENTAL HEALTH ASSISTANCE

- NAMI.org
- MentalHealthFirstAid.org
- CDC.org
- MentalHealth.gov
- MHANational.org

BONUS CONTENT: DEALINGS IN THE DARK

As a bonus, please enjoy this excerpt from *Dealings in the Dark,* the first book in the Cursed Souls series.

(This title is unrelated to *The Ruin.*)

Dealings in the Dark

Book One Of
The Cursed Souls Series

Samantha Moran

CHAPTER ONE

The box in my hand rattles as I quickly walk down my old road beneath the light of an early autumn moon. The stars in the sky tonight are absolutely stunning. The air is still warm and humid, and the leaves have just begun to change. There is a refreshing breeze that causes the branches of the old willows to sway back and forth, almost as if they are dancing. The bits of gravel under my feet crunch against the soles of my worn Chucks, announcing my presence to anyone and anything that cares enough to listen.

Were I out here for any other reason, I might find my stroll enjoyable, leisurely even. I might listen to the frogs and crickets in the swampy underbrush tell their stories of the day. I might sit underneath one of the willows and drink a hot cider. I've done those things many times before.

But tonight, nothing about this walk is enjoyable. Every movement in the shadows makes me jump. Every crunch in the woods steals my breath and makes my whole body buzz with anxiety. I need to get this done, fast. The night is not safe anymore.

I hear a strangled whisper in the distance as the creature

calls out my name. I'm not stupid enough to turn around and look, not this time. It almost had me before. I won't acknowledge it again. If I do, it will mean the end for me. The creature has caught my scent and has been stalking me for weeks. If it knows I can hear it, that I can see it, it will only make the hunt that much more thrilling. There will be no help for me.

I'm not ready to die.

The sounds of running water fill my ears as I approach the creek and the road veers sharply off to the left. I follow the path, staying as close to the water and as far away from the trees on the other side as the road allows.

For whatever reason, the creature is afraid of the water. Whenever I approach the creek, it always backs away. The sounds of its strangled cries grow softer as the creek burbles. I allow myself one deep breath to calm my nerves as I hug the water's edge. I relish the sense of momentary safety. It won't last long.

Before me, the road splits into a fork. To the left, it hugs the bank of the creek and promises continued safety, but that is not the path that I need to follow.

I hold the cigar box tightly to my chest as I test the wood of an old rickety bridge that leads off the right. I haven't crossed this bridge in years, not since I was young. The boards squeak in protest as I step forward, but to my relief, they bear my weight.

I move slowly, tip-toeing from one board to the next and stepping over the places where planks have fallen into the water below. The bridge isn't long or terribly high, and the creek isn't deep, but it is fast-moving right now, and if I were to fall in here, I would be in serious trouble. There's no one who would find me here, at least until the morning.

I'm running out of time. I don't know how long the water will keep the beast at bay. Not indefinitely, I'm sure. I can't do this with the creature on my heels.

As I reach the end of the bridge and step onto the clay path on the other side, I desperately want to turn around to see if the beast has abandoned its hunt. My whole body fights to do so as I continue to force it forward toward my destination against every instinct of self-preservation. Out here, alone in the dark, I am easy prey, and leaving my back unguarded feels so very wrong.

I pick up speed, ducking underneath wild overgrowth and dodging debris from the last thunderstorm. The scents of decayed leaves and wet soil overwhelm my senses. I'm almost there. Almost.

Ahead, I can see my destination. Like a guardian, the old one-room schoolhouse looms over a four-way split in the path, the structure long since abandoned. In the light of the moon, it casts a shadow so long that the path is almost consumed. The school's double doors swing on their rusty hinges, grinding and groaning with the light breeze.

No one has cared for or claimed this space in years. It's perfect for what I must do now. There will be no interruptions or distractions.

Eager to reach my destination, I break into a run, and the rattling of the box intensifies as its contents bounce against the thin cedar sides. Thirty feet, twenty feet, ten. I skid to a halt at the center of the crossroads and fall to my knees, out of breath. Stones planted deep within the clay dig into my shins painfully, but I don't care. I made it to the crossing. The first part of my task is complete. I tentatively let out a sigh of relief.

I shift on my knees, twisting to retrieve an old spade and a lighter from my back pocket. I drop the lighter on the ground beside me. I use my hands to clear away the rocks and sticks in front of me before retrieving the spade and piercing it into the clay repeatedly, loosening the soil until I can dig up the earth and pile it by the side of the hole.

Once the hole is deep enough, I drop the spade beside the lighter and open the cigar box. I scan the contents again, just to make sure that nothing was lost on my journey. It's all there: dandelion leaves, wormwood, mandrake root, smoky quartz, a lock of my hair, a large black candle, and a small vial of my blood. I pull the candle out of the box and close it up, then place the box into the hole, burying it and patting the clay down firmly on top.

My hands shake as I place the candle atop the freshly turned earth. I close my eyes and feel for the lighter, lifting it up and squeezing it firmly in my hand. I pray to whoever might be listening that this will work. It has to. I don't know what else to do.

"I summon thee," I whisper my command. "Cross over into this plane. Hear me." I follow this with the difficult Latin words from my grandmother's near ancient grimoire, repeating them five times, then once more uttering my command. "I summon thee. Cross over into this plane."

I flick open the lid of the Zippo, springing to life a bright blue flame. Hesitantly, I tip the flame against the wick of the candle until it catches. Smoke curls up from the flame, gray and thick. It sparks, and the flame shoots high up into the air. Black wax drips down the side and puddles onto the clay below, spreading out from the candle and spilling toward me like a winding snake. I pull myself up from my knees to stand and watch as the wax drips farther and farther away from the source until it connects with my shoe. The ritual is working.

I take a step back, then skirt the candle and approach the old building. Cautiously, I scan the inside before entering. Old wood and metal tablet desks are tipped onto their sides. The place smells of mildew and rot. A large slate board, still bearing the marks of my childhood drawings, lines the farthest wall. Moonlight streams in through holes in the ceiling and the breeze whistles through spaces between the boards.

It's empty.

I close the doors firmly behind me as I step inside, shoving an old, busted table in front of them to keep them from opening of their own accord. It isn't much, but I hope that it will at least slow the creature down when it finds me. I just need it to buy me time.

It's quiet in the one-room schoolhouse. Only the sounds of my breathing and the creaking beneath my shoes echo in the large, abandoned space. I squeeze my black tourmaline and obsidian necklace for protection, a gift from my grandmother, as I pick my way through the remains of the once-loved classroom until I reach the slate board, as far away from the doors as I can be, and I wait. I close my eyes, breathing as quietly as I can, and listen.

Moments later, a deep chuckle behind me tells me I am not alone.

ACKNOWLEDGMENTS

I want to offer a special thank you to those individuals who have made this novel possible.

Thank you to my friend Marissa who beta-read each chapter of the final manuscript as it was completed. You helped me more than you know!

Thank you to my friend Maura who answered my panicked phone call and was willing to share her valuable insight into such an important matter. I love that we're always there for each other, no matter how much time has passed. You'll always be my sis!

Thank you to my mom for believing in my ability to write and trying to get me out of my own head. She's been on me to finish this book since the year I started. Well, here it is! Now, you have to read it. *Wink*

Thank you to my husband John for reading each of the chapters as they were completed, even at one (or three) in the morning.

Thank you to my friend Heather for standing at the bus stop with me and listening to me rant about this book whenever I was frustrated.

Thank you to MJ Pankey and Charlie Nottingham for helping me with genre and keyword selection. Your input has been so incredibly valuable. I was lost without you!

Thank you to my college professor, Dr. Adrienne Redding, for meeting with me during your office hours to discuss my early chapters, even though this novel has nothing to do with your courses. The tea and treats were delicious, too.

Thank you to my first ever team of ARC readers. I wasn't sure what to expect, but you blew my mind. #BookTok <3

Thank you to my readers for picking up this book and seeing it through to the end. I appreciate each of you more than you know.

ABOUT THE AUTHOR

Photo Credit: Ashley Klaasen Photography

Samantha Moran is a proud Magna Cum Laude graduate of Western Michigan University with a Bachelor's in English Education and experience teaching English and Language Arts courses to secondary and college students in urban and suburban settings. She is a loving mother of two amazing children and has been happily married to her husband since 2015. She and her family reside in southwest Michigan. Samantha lives with Multiple Sclerosis which sometimes severely impacts her daily life. In her free time, she loves playing Dungeons and Dragons, reading, writing, and spending time with her family and pets, Sugar (a lab mix) and Caleigh (a calico cat).

For more information about Samantha Moran, visit her website at www.samanthamoran.net.

ALSO BY SAMANTHA MORAN

Short Works:

"Stages of Grief: A Short Story," 2022

Without You: A Novelette, 2023

Tales of Grief and Healing: A Complete Duology, 2023*

"Death's Nell," Releasing 2023

The Cursed Souls Series

Dealings in the Dark (Book One), 2022

Bound and Betrayed (Book Two), 2022

Legacy of Lies (Book Three), Releasing 2023

Tales of Grief and Healing: A Complete Duology is a compilation of "Stages of Grief: A Short Story" and Without You: A Novelette.